KT-520-987

29111

WITHDRAWN

WITHDRAWN

Silvercairns

'For a moment they stood where they were in silence. Fergus felt suddenly awkward in the presence of an emotion which embarrassed him. When he had seen the girl recklessly running on to the quarry path he had been enraged . . . but when she had looked at him with those tear-filled eyes, something had happened to his anger, and to his heart.'

For years Fergus Adam has thought only of granite – the famous granite of Silvercairns which has made his tyrannical father rich. But now, seeing the beautiful tear-streaked face of Mhairi Diack, come running to fetch her father from the quarry to their tenement home where her mother is dying, he suspects that his life will never be the same again.

Nor is it. For, poor though the Diacks are, they become inextricably entangled with the wealthy Adams. Mhairi's father, brother and lover Alex all work in the quarry. Her impulsive brother Tom has almost come to blows with Fergus's brother Hugo, who has caught the eye of her wayward friend Lizzie Lennox. And Fergus's bored and pretty sister, Lettice, finds herself fascinated by Tom's strength and arrogance as he works on a wall in the gardens of Silvercairns House. Between and within the families, tensions arise, tragedies loom. And Fergus has no idea how to deal with them, or with his unexpected feelings for Mhairi . . .

Agnes Short's new historical romance is a tender story of love and loyalty. Set in nineteenth-century Aberdeen, it expertly weaves together the worlds of pampered rich and struggling poor, linked by the jagged bowl of living rock that is the granite quarry of Silvercairns.

Also by Agnes Short

The Heritors (1977)
Clatter Vengeance (1979)
The Crescent and the Cross (1980)
Miss Jenny (1981)
Gabrielle (1983)
The first fair wind (1984)
The running tide (1986)
The dragon seas (1988)

under the name of 'Rose Shipley'

Wychwood (1989)

under the name of 'Agnes Russell'

A red rose for Annabel (1973)
A flame in the heather (1974)
Hill of the wildcat (1975)
Target Capricorn (1976)
Larksong at dawn (1977)

Agnes Short

Silvercairns

Constable · London

First published in Great Britain 1990
by Constable and Company Ltd
10 Orange Street London WC2H 7EG
Copyright © by Agnes Short 1990
ISBN 0 09 469820 1
Set in Linotron Ehrhardt 11pt by
CentraCet, Cambridge
Printed in Great Britain by
St Edmundsbury Press Ltd
Bury St Edmunds, Suffolk

A CIP catalogue record for this book
is available from the British Library

0094 698 201 2215

Part 1

It had begun like any other October day in the tenement in Mitchell's Court and Mhairi Diack, shivering in the half-darkness with the other girls as she waited her turn at the pump, had no inkling of what was to come.

There was still a nip of night frost in the air, the cassies of the Kirkgate struck chill under her bare feet and where the water splashed from brimming pails it was instantly crusted with ice. Her father and her brother Tom had wrapped their hands in an extra layer of cloth this morning: the haft of a mason's pick could freeze to a man's hand, though as Tom had said, with Ma's porridge inside them they'd soon be heated through by the time they'd walked the two miles to the quarry. Tom was an optimistic lad.

Mhairi pulled her plaid closer about her shoulders and stamped her feet to keep the circulation going. One day, she reminded herself, she would leave all this behind her. She had done well at school. She had won the class prize for handwriting and had come second in arithmetic and reading. Her ma and da had been real pleased. She would have liked to learn more, but Ma had needed her at home, and anyway the schooling money was required for her brothers. But she could bake and sew, she was handy about the house, and soon, when the little ones were older and Ma didn't need her so much, she would find a job in one of the big houses, like Lizzie's cousin. But she would not stay a housemaid for long. Like Cinderella in the fairy-tale she would meet a prince . . . Well, perhaps not a real prince because they lived in palaces hundreds of miles away, but someone rich and handsome who would whisk her away into a new life . . .

She was lost in the usual dream when Lizzie Lennox pushed in front of her and jolted her rudely back to reality. As usual, Mhairi told her to mind her manners and wait her turn. As usual Lizzie gave her an earful of filthy language and stuck out her tongue, but it was a ritual exchange, without malice. The

Diacks and the Lennoxes had lived on the same stair for as long as Mhairi could remember, which made Lizzie almost family. If she had been real family, of course, it would have been different – Mhairi would never let wee Annys use words like that – but Lizzie was not real family and Mhairi took no notice. If Mhairi was to grow up a lady, as she fully meant to do, she must learn to ignore such insults with proper disdain. Her ma had told her ladies never lost their tempers or put out their tongues or swore and her ma knew. She had been a kitchenmaid in a big house in the West End until 'Cassie' Diack met and married her.

Ladies had maids to brush their hair every day, her ma said, and they kept their hands white with lemons and cucumbers. They sang songs at the piano while gentlemen in elegant dark suits with jewelled pins in their cravats turned the pages. Not the sort of songs the lads sang after a night at Ma Gibbs' either, but romantic songs, with pretty tunes. Her ma knew some of the songs and, if she was in a good mood – say the stocking mannie had paid her extra or her da had come home with all his pay instead of wasting it in Ma Gibbs' or the Lemon Tree – then sometimes she would sing to them, when the kale pot was emptied, and the last scrap of bread eaten, and Tom and her da, as working men, had a mug of ale each in their hands. Lorn and Willy, her little brothers, would crouch on their creepie stools by the fire, wee Annys would climb on to Mhairi's knee, stick her thumb in her mouth and let her eyelids droop, then her ma would take up one of the interminable stockings she knitted for the stocking mannie and sing.

Agnes Diack had an attractive voice, clear and true, and a wide repertoire of songs, not all of them from the drawing-room. But there was one song that was Mhairi's favourite. It was called 'The Land o' the Leal' and was so sad and beautiful it made her want to cry. *There's nae sorrow there, John, there's neither cold nor care, John, the day's aye prayer in the land o' the leal . . .* The mere thought of it brought a faraway look to her face and now, inside her head, she began to hum it quietly to herself. She hardly heard the grumbling voices around her at the pump.

'Stuck up, stuck up, Mhairi Diack's stuck up!' Lizzie Lennox chanted, out of boredom as much as anything, but, like the rest of them, she was too cold in the dawn frost to put any energy into it. Her dress was even skimpier than Mhairi's, her plaid more threadbare and both items as grubby as her blue-bare legs and chilblained feet. Besides, if she didn't get back home sharpish, her da would have the switch waiting. 'Bible' Lennox was a man of cruel rectitude and no patience. Everyone in the Court was a little afraid of him.

To the east, beyond the Castlegate, the sky was lightening. The fishing boats from Footdee would already be launched and there would be a path of deep gold on the sea. Thinking still of her ma's singing, Mhairi wondered whether the land o' the leal was as beautiful as the sea with the dawn sun upon it. Or as Silvercairns against a sunset sky? Her ma said the land o' the leal was the same as heaven, but Mhairi didn't believe it. Heaven was for preachers and people like Bible Lennox who thought a smile on Sunday was wicked. The land o' the leal was somewhere calm and beautiful where there was no cold or poverty or hunger, no ugliness or pain; a lovely, shimmering place of slanting sunlight and rainbow dreams, a place where everyone was at peace.

'Why doesn't she get a move on, the selfish cow!' grumbled Lizzie and someone jostled Mhairi in the back. There was quite a crowd waiting now, from knee-high children scarcely bigger than the pails they held to hump-backed, shuffling old women with no teeth and hands like hens' claws.

Lizzie was right. That Maggie Henderson from Galen's Court was taking an age, giggling and whispering with the Pirie girl who everyone knew was a bad lot, and neither of them looking what they were doing so that the water splashed outside the pail more often than in it, but at that moment two figures turned the corner from the direction of the Guestrow and the girls burst into a gleeful, squealing duet.

'What you got under your apron for us this morning, Lackie Grant?' 'Got yer wee hammer at the ready, have ye, Lackie?' 'Not so wee, neither, is it Maggie?' This with a dig of the elbow and a knowing leer. Then, both together, on a shriek of laughter, 'Show us yer scabblin' pick, Lackie, and give us a treat!'

Mhairi looked round to see Alex Grant and his brother Donal coming down the cobbled incline towards them, Alex tall, broad-shouldered against the dawn sky, his hair glinting red in the strengthening light, his brother slighter, darker-haired, with an anxious, watchful expression, as if he expected attack at any moment. Both wore thick serge trousers and woollen shirts, high-buttoned waistcoats, cloth caps and heavy nailed boots, but only Alex carried a leather bundle of tools.

As they drew nearer, Mhairi, looking from under discreetly lowered lashes, saw that Alex was swaggering a little and grinning. Then he saw her looking at him and winked. Blushing, she looked quickly away, while all around her the girls squealed their delighted taunts, which grew more daring as the boys passed them and went on down the slope towards St Nicholas kirk. Alex's whistle came clear and joyous as birdsong on the crisp air. He did not look round.

Suddenly the chant changed and a cruel note entered the girls' voices. 'Deaf and dumb, cat got your tongue . . .'

'Shut up, you stupid bitches!' cried Mhairi before she could stop herself and was instantly appalled. Maggie Henderson stared at her in astonishment before breaking into delighted laughter. Then, quick as lightning, she scooped up a handful of water from her pail and threw it in Mhairi's face. 'Wash yer mouth out, Mhairi Diack. I'm black ashamed o' ye, that I am. *Language*,' she said to Beth Pirie in a parody of shocked gentility. 'I never thought to hear the like! I could blush with shame, that I could!'

'Some chance,' said Lizzie at Mhairi's elbow. 'She wouldna' blush if you stripped her naked at the Market Cross and painted "harlot" on her bum! Whores!' she shouted after the departing pair. 'Watch ye dinna get the clap!'

This time Mhairi was too mortified to reprimand her, but it was her turn at the pump and she hid her burning cheeks by bending over the handle and pumping twice as fast as was necessary. Lizzie's allegiance could be as embarrassing as Lizzie's antagonism, but she should have known that Lizzie would side with her: the loyalty of the tenement was strong and Maggie Henderson and that dreadful Pirie girl were not Mitchell's Court. Cheeks still flushed, Mhairi straightened under the weight of her brimming buckets and shouldered her way through the other women to the open street. The buckets were heavy, but she did not falter, walking straight-backed and proud in spite of the hand-me-down shabbiness of her skirts and the dragging weight on her too-thin arms. The public humiliation of Maggie's actions was bad enough, but her own self-humiliation was worse. How could she have shouted such words?

Then, as she remembered the reason, Mhairi's heart twisted with a different pain. Why were people so cruel? Turning like a pack of wild beasts to savage anything weaker than or different from themselves? Poor Donal, who did no one any harm, enduring, uncomplaining, in his silence. Except, she thought, with new anxiety, no one would know if he did complain! Suppose, even now, he is weeping inside, on and on, with hopeless despair? The thought was dreadful . . . She must ask Alex as soon as she saw him. Alex would know.

Alex Grant and her brother Tom had been friends for as long as Mhairi could remember. They had attended school together in the Gallowgate, played truant, stolen apples, gathered driftwood together, played bools and pennystones, stolen rides on Willy Guyan's cab-horse, thrown stones at cats and, sometimes, windows. Once they had stolen raisins from Abercrombie's shop for a dare, been caught by the old man and thrashed together. On one notorious occasion they had sampled the delights of Ma Gibbs and had staggered home supporting each other with spectacular ineptitude, finally finishing up on the steps of Marischal College where they had sung bawdy songs till removed to the tolbooth by a passing constable. Afterwards, Cassie Diack, mild man though he was, had taken off his belt and given his son 'a taste o' the tawse' while Mhairi and her mother had covered their ears with their hands and closed their eyes, tight . . .

On all these occasions, except the last, Alex's brother Donal had been a faithful acolyte, close as Alex's shadow.

Five years ago, when they were both fourteen, Tom Diack and Alex Grant had become apprenticed to the granite trade, though Tom's ambition was to blast out granite chunks from a quarry of his own, and Alex's to own a mason's yard, 'Where Donal can make us statues and balustrades, trace designs on headstones and do all that fancy lettering.' For Donal, for all his limitations, had a skill with a pencil that no one could better. With the certainty of dreams, Mhairi knew the boys would both be rich one day, rich as 'Headstane' Wyness who made tombs for royalty, rich as Old Man Adam at Silvercairns.

Meanwhile Tom and Alex worked at the quarry face, with Cassie Diack and half a hundred other men, learning how to bore blasting holes in solid rock, to dress blocks of stone for the building trade, to wield a scabbling pick and hammer till a few deft strokes could fashion a sett to the regulation size for the streets of Edinburgh or London. And when the opportunity arose, Alex found Donal a job in the quarry too, with the horses. He showed Donal what was required of him, kept a watchful eye open for trouble, and was never far away if Donal needed him. And in all the years Mhairi had known them, she had never seen Alex anything but gentle with his brother.

So, if a strong, fine-looking, honest man like Alex Grant could be kind to the helpless, why should a pack of women turn and savage poor Donal? Mhairi was ashamed of her sex.

But as she felt the crisp morning air on her cheeks, smelt the salt on the wind and saw the pink blush spread across the eastern sky she forgot the girls' cruelty and remembered only her mother's haunting song. *But sorrows sair are past, John, and joys are coming fast, John . . .*

She was singing as she reached the foot of the stone steps that led up, outside the crumbling building, to the first-floor entrance of the tenement in Mitchell's Court where the Diack family lived in two damp-walled rooms. They were lucky, her mother said, to have two rooms. Many families had to make do with one, and families larger than the Diack's too. At least there were no Diack grandparents to need house-room.

But as Mhairi mounted the worn stone steps, which in spite of her mother's constant scrubbing were filthy yet again, she wrinkled her nose against the sour smell of night-soil and open drains, and vowed, as she vowed every day of her life, that one day she would live in a sweet-smelling house, with a front door of her own and a little flower garden, where she and her 'prince' would sit together on a summer's evening and sip tea. There would be clean curtains at the windows and a water-closet and no neighbours on the common stair to tip their filth on to the steps and swear. Daringly, for the second time that day, she opened the door to her secret dream and peeped in. She would marry her 'prince' and they would . . . Swiftly she slammed tight the door. It was tempting fate even to form the words in her innermost thoughts.

Afterwards, she wondered if perhaps that was it? She had tempted fate and fate had punished her? But at the time she felt only the familiar comfort which her secret dream always gave her, with its simple certainly that one day everything would be gloriously different.

Mhairi was smiling as she leant her shoulder against the door and pushed it open. In the inner room she could see four-year-old Annys, still in her night shift, bouncing up and down on the bed the three boys shared. Annys's and Mhairi's own bed had been folded away when she rose and pushed out of sight under the other. The younger boys were nowhere to be seen and Mhairi remembered she had packed them off to the shore already, to search for driftwood for the day's fire before it was time for them to go to school.

In the room which was both living-room and her parents' bedroom, were a deal table and benches, a kist for clothes, a box bed on one wall, shelves for pots and pans, a much-washed and faded curtain at the window and a rag rug in front of the grate. It was dark after the dawn brightness of the open street and it took Mhairi's eyes a moment to adjust to the gloom. Then she saw her mother sitting in her customary chair.

But it was not customary to see her in it so early in the day, with the floor not swept, the pots not scoured, the fire not tended and the bed as dishevelled as when Cassie and she had left it at five that morning. Mrs Diack was as house-proud as circumstances allowed, and the stockings she knitted for the stocking mannie in the Kirkgate were always spotlessly clean and the stitches so fine 'you could pull them through a wedding ring,' as she herself would boast, but only to her daughter when she was teaching Mhairi to do the same. The sooner Mhairi learned to knit stockings as neatly as her mother, the better off they would be. The stocking mannie paid more for fine work than for coarse and, as Mrs Diack said, it took the same amount of knitting for both. But what Mhairi really wanted was a job like Eppie Guyan had, a job in a big house where she could watch and work and learn so that when her prince came to claim her, she would not disgrace him, but would know exactly how a real lady should conduct herself. Maybe next year her mother would let her go to the hiring fair? Annys, twelve years younger than Mhairi, would be five then and old enough to help with the baby.

At the thought of that baby Mhairi's hope faltered, but only for a moment. If her mother could not spare her next year, then she must wait till the year after. Surely Annys would be old enough by then? And at least her mother was not like some women in the tenements. She didn't let herself go as her girth increased. Though her clothes might be threadbare and faded, with gussets of a different colour, or let-out seams, they were always clean, and though her dark hair had premature strands of grey, it was well brushed and coiled into a neat bun at the back. Ladies, she told her daughter, took a pride in their appearance and just because you lived in a tenement instead of a big house and hadn't the dress allowance to buy a button let alone a ball gown, that didn't mean you couldn't do the same. Agnes Diack had been a handsome girl and was handsome still, despite incessant child-bearing and the weariness of fighting from one day to the next to keep a toe-hold on respectability. Mhairi was proud of her and, knowing that she resembled her mother, secretly hoped to be as handsome herself one day.

And one day, when Mhairi had that fairy-tale house of her own, her mother would come to live with her and do nothing all day but sit in the drawing-room with her embroidery, like the ladies at Silvercairns.

'I hope I wasna too long, Ma,' she said cheerfully. 'There was that many folk at the pump I could hardly . . . Is anything the matter, Ma?' Her mother was doubled up in her chair, hands clasped across her stomach, groaning. She looked up as her daughter spoke and Mhairi was shocked by the fear in the faded blue eyes, the grey despair on her face. 'Mhairi, lass . . . thank God you're back.' Then she gasped and the low, half-stifled scream frightened Mhairi more than any words.

'Mammy gie us a penny doon, here's a mannie comin' roon' . . .' chanted Annys, unconcerned, still jumping up and down on the bed.

'Be quiet, Annys! Ma's not well. Is it something you ate, Ma? The herring, maybe? It wasna just . . .'

'No, Mhairi, it's not the herring. It's . . .' She stopped on a gasp and the blood left her face. When she could speak again, she said, 'I was only lifting the kettle to fill it . . .' and added, with a sort of desperation, 'Don't ever marry, lass . . . it isna worth it.'

Mhairi was shocked. Her ma never talked like that. Her ma and her da were happy together, not like some in the tenement. 'Would you like a drop of brandy, Ma?' she asked anxiously. 'To make you feel better?'

'No, lass, ye don't understand. It's too soon. Three months too soon. I reckon you'd . . .' She stopped, clenched her teeth, and went on again, through dry lips. 'See to the lads, Mhairi, and wee Annys. Then you'd best fetch Ma Mackenzie.'

Ma Mackenzie, midwife, sick-nurse and, some whispered, abortionist, had assisted all the Diack children, living and dead, into the world, as she had most of the children in the teeming tenements that backed the Guestrow and the Gallowgate. A kindly woman, not without skill, she did her best. Besides, she was cheaper than any doctor and more sensible. She knew family circumstances. She would not recommend calf's foot jelly and complete rest to a woman with ten children and barely enough to live on. Instead, she would pass the word around and neighbours would drop in with a cake or a wee bottle of stout, a new-baked loaf or a cheese. Those who had, shared. So Mhairi knew that Ma Mackenzie, unless she was actually assisting a woman in labour, would come at once and her rooms in the Gallowgate were not five minutes away.

Mhairi felt a wave of relief. Her mother was not ill, merely having the baby. She knew her ma didn't need another baby, but there didn't seem to be any choice in such matters. Women had babies whether they wanted them or not. It hurt them, sometimes a great deal, but afterwards they were well again. The main thing was that her ma was not poisoned or suffering from some dreadful disease. There was really nothing to worry about.

Swiftly, Mhairi dressed Annys and left her, protesting, with the Lennoxes. She headed off Lorn and Willy on the stairs, relieved them of their driftwood bundles, thrust three halfpence each and a jammy 'piece' into their hands and packed them off early to school. 'And see ye give the dominie his money,' she called after them. 'And dinna play hooky!' Then she made up the fire, set a pan of water to boil, put the brandy bottle ready, with a glass beside it (for Ma Mackenzie), and snatched up her plaid.

'See she comes right away,' managed her mother, grey-faced, the knuckles of her hands white where she gripped the arms of her chair. 'And . . . oh, dear God . . . hurry . . .'

'I'll not be long, Ma. Don't worry. Everything'll be all right.' But Mhairi's heart was pounding now with her mother's fear. She jumped the steps two at a time, sped out of Mitchell's Court into the Guestrow, turned north towards Ma Mackenzie's tenement and ran.

'Must you take such an age?' snapped Lettice Adam, glaring at her maid in the gilt-edged dressing-table mirror. 'I should have thought you knew how to arrange my hair by now. You have practised long enough.'

'Yes, Miss Lettice,' said Eppie Guyan, her face expressionless. 'I'm sorry, Miss Lettice.' She secured the last blond ringlet with the last hairpin and said, 'There, Miss Lettice. You look real lovely this morning.'

Mollified, Lettice Adam looked at herself in the glass, turned her head to one side then the other, held up the tortoiseshell-backed hand mirror to enable her to see the effect from the back and said, 'Well, I suppose it will have to do.'

In fact, she was more than satisfied. Eppie Guyan, for all her dour expression, was adept at dressing hair and had only to see a drawing, or another woman's hair-style, to be able to copy it to perfection. Of course, thought Lettice smugly, not everyone had such a slender neck, such a classic profile, such an abundance of gleaming yellow hair as she. She stood up, smoothed the front of her corset and admired herself sideways on in the pier glass between the two deep, many-paned windows.

The Adam town house, in the Guestrow, had been built two hundred years before, and built to last. With massive walls, stone spiral stairs, dark panelled rooms with window embrasures four or five feet deep, it was not in the height of modern taste, but it was large, comfortable, well furnished, and, most important for Lettice Adam's purposes, it was in the centre of town. Though Lettice continually complained about the warrens of disgusting tenements that crowded the side alleys and courts all around them, the house itself stood like a castle, proud, turreted, impregnable, safely cushioned by the Adam wealth against all contact with the tenements' unpleasantness or poverty.

The room had been her mother's until that lady died two years previously. Panelled and floored in oak, with a greak oak four-poster bed and oak shutters at the windows, it might have been a sombre room except for the scarlet and blue bed hangings laced with gold thread, the gold rope tassels and fringes, the white bedcovers and the brilliant Indian carpets on the floor. There were brass candlesticks on dressing-table and writing desk, more on the overmantel, a gilt-framed oil painting of Mrs Adam in her youth – a pale, blonde lady with a timid expression – and the fire was lit every morning at five so that the room might be warm before Miss Lettice ventured out of bed some three hours later. Lettice did not particularly like the room, finding it old-fashioned and dull, but she knew better than to say so. She much preferred her rooms at Silvercairns, but one could not possibly live in the middle of nowhere once the autumn season had begun. It would take her an age to drive the two miles into town whenever she wished to attend the Assembly rooms or the theatre or to visit friends, and the roads in winter could be treacherous.

'Everyone lives in town in winter,' she had protested daringly when, at the end of summer, her father had suggested that this year they remain at Silvercairns.

'Do they indeed,' growled Mungo Adam. A frowning, grey-whiskered and grey-bearded gentleman of intimidating mien, he was known to all the world, though prudently behind his back, as Old Man Adam. In spite of the slight stoop, due as much to the necessity to come down to other people's levels as to advancing years, he still stood over six feet tall in his stockings, and in full morning regalia of white wing collar and dark suit, heavy gold chain across heavy worsted waistcoat, he was an imposing, not to say intimidating figure. His three children certainly found him so, especially since the death of their mother had removed the gentle, diplomatic filter which had deflected or diluted the worst of his disapproval before it could reach them. Now, the filter gone, there was nothing, except Aunt Blackwell, who was worse than useless, to stand between them and the full force of paternal authority.

Lettice, as daughter, ought to have fared best, and in many respects did. But too often lately she had been required to act as hostess to her father's 'boring old fools' as she disrespectfully described his many business acquaintances. Also, since the departure of her governess, she had found that instead of the unbridled round of frivolity which she had anticipated would take the place of French lessons and the interminable piano, she was forbidden any but the most heavily chaperoned entertainments, and then only of her father's choosing. Fortunately she had been able, with the example of Fanny Wyness and Amelia Macdonald, to persuade him that dancing lessons were an essential ingredient in a young lady's upbringing and, as the class was exclusively female, she had had equal success in disposing of Aunt Blackwell who was happy to sit dozing over her embroidery by the fire until her young charge returned. Lettice fully intended to add drawing and painting lessons to the list of essential female occupations. They said the drawing master in the Castlegate was a dream. All the girls were in love with him, though of course her father must get no inkling of that.

Lettice Adam was sixteen, precocious and bored. She had been smugly aware since an early age that she was destined to be a beauty and already several of the 'old fools' had expressed their appreciation in sundry surreptitious and unorthodox squeezes and pattings, under cover of the dinner table-cloth or a convenient sofa. Her father, she suspected, would have horse-whipped the culprit, had she reported the fact: she chose not to tell. She enjoyed her power over the 'old fools' and was rapidly learning to extend that power to younger victims, though here she kept more than one wary eye on her father. His plans for her had not yet been openly declared, but she was shrewd enough to know that were he to suspect her of 'carrying on', she would be married off post-haste to the first available old fool of his acquaintance. As these included several widowers, all more or less repugnant to her, Lettice remained outwardly as demure, obedient and innocent as even the sternest father could have wished while inwardly she grew more scheming and ingenious.

It was with what Hugo called her 'saintly innocence' look that she had replied to her father on that occasion.

'But, Father, Hugo will be at the college before the month is out and it will be so much more convenient for him to live in town.'

'He can do that anyway, without our help. There are lodgings enough.'

'Of course, Father dear, but one hears such tales of students in lodgings . . .' She paused fractionally before adding, 'Away from the supervision of home.' Hugo would not thank her for that. In fact, she knew he had already asked around for lodgings in the expectation that the Old Man would be safely out of the way at Silvercairns and the town house let, or shut. But that was Hugo's problem. 'Please, Father? It would be so much more sensible.'

'And Fergus?' Old Man Adam had growled, knowing he would give in. He was rich enough to own two houses so why not live in them?

'Fergus can stay on at Silvercairns if he wishes,' Lettice had said, with a pretty wave of her hand. 'Or, as I suppose we should really close the house and put everything under dust covers, he could move into the lodge with the MacLemans. Or,' she had finished flippantly, kissing her father lightly on the top of his bald patch, 'if he cannot bear to be so far away, he could put up a hut in that beloved quarry of his and sleep with the granite.'

'That beloved quarry, young lady, is our livelihood and don't you forget it.' But Old Man Adam had agreed. Silvercairns was shut up for the winter months, except for a couple of rooms for the use of Adam himself, and his eldest son Fergus, should the need arise. The MacLemans kept an eye on things and Lettice was right about the roads: it was all right for himself and his son to travel on horseback to Silvercairns, but under snow or ice it was no track for a wheeled carriage. Besides, his daughter was sixteen. It was time she went out into company and found a husband. Briefly, Adam regretted his wife's death. But there were plenty of suitable women among his acquaintances to keep the girl on the right track, and he had one or two private ideas of his own, for his sons as well as his daughter. An alliance with the Macdonald family, for instance, or the Fyfes, could bring them nothing but good, as far as business went. The Macdonald yard handled contracts as far afield as Liverpool, London and Wales and, though the Silvercairns granite was justly renowned, there was increasing competition. Only last week they had lost an order for an important London monument to a quarry at Peterhead, where the granite was of a pinker hue than Silvercairns', though he was prepared to swear it would take no better polish.

So the Adam household had moved back into town and while Fergus and his father spent their days in quarry work, Lettice sampled the frivolities of the autumn season, and her brother Hugo joined her, until such time as the new session opened and he was required to attend the Marischal College. On this particular morning, however, the entertainment was of an educational kind.

'It's past nine o'clock already, Miss Lettice,' said Eppie when she considered the girl had admired herself in her small clothes for long enough.

'I am perfectly aware of the time, thank you very much. And stop speaking to me as if I was a child. I thought I told you to address me as "Ma'am".'

'Yes, ma'am, I'm sorry, ma'am. Will you be wearing the lemon silk this morning or the rose taffeta, ma'am?'

'Let me see, which did I wear last time? Was it the yellow?'

'No, it was . . .'

'Hold your tongue, girl. I was not speaking to you and when I want your opinion I'll ask for it! Well, what are you standing there with your mouth open for? Fetch me both of them, and my blue.' The yellow suited her well enough, the rose did wonders for her complexion, and the blue deepened the colour of her eyes in a most flattering way . . . but which to choose? For there was no saying who she might meet this morning, if she timed it right. Excitement sweetened her temper and, to show she bore her no ill will, Lettice gave Eppie a ribbon she had finished with (it was not quite the right shade of pink) and a lace collar with a pulled thread.

The dancing class in Mr Corbyn's academy in Belmont Street was late starting. Mr Corbyn had taken out his hunter, checked the time, tapped his fingers impatiently on the piano lid and replaced the watch in his waistcoat pocket a dozen times before the last young lady arrived. He could have started without her, of course, but as the missing damsel was Lettice Adam it was more than his teaching contract was worth. Old Man Adam expected service, and that meant not starting the class without his daughter. Knowing Old Man Adam's insistence on punctuality in his own staff, Mr Corbyn had been tempted more than once to complain about his daugher's shortcomings, but had always thought better of it. He had an uncomfortable suspicion that criticism of an Adam might be regarded by Old Man Adam as high treason and was not prepared to put it to the test.

Mr Corbyn was a neat, twinkle-toed gentleman of a vaguely Continental appearance which he encouraged by an unorthodox taste in neck-cravats and mulberry velvet trousers. He was a musician as well as a dancing master and had published two books of songs, with pianoforte accompaniment, at his own expense. But it was his skills in teaching the cotillion, the allemande and other necessary social dances 'as newly studied with the first masters of the art in Paris' that had brought him most fame – and profit. But he was a punctilious man and when his 9.30 a.m. class for young ladies had still not commenced at a quarter to ten, he was understandably irritated, no less so because the young ladies concerned seemed no whit disturbed. If anything, the opposite. Consequently he was less than obsequious when the offending latecomer at last arrived.

'Ah, Miss Adam. I was beginning to think you had mistaken the day. Perhaps you will be so good as to put on your dancing pumps with all speed so that we need lose no further time?'

Lettice Adam ignored him. Instead she took off her wrap with infuriating slowness, all the time calling greetings to the dozen or so young ladies who had been chattering happily together at one end of the long, uncarpeted room while Mr Corbyn paced up and down at the other and the pianist rubbed and blew upon her mittened hands to combat the chill in the unheated air. They seemed in no hurry to begin. Not for the first time, Mr Corbyn suspected there was method in Miss Adam's lateness and that the rest of the girls were in collusion with her. It might not be altogether irrelevant that the young gentlemen's class was due to commence at twelve noon and that if the girls were late, a meeting was inevitable.

'Miss Adam, are you ready?' he called with ill-concealed annoyance.

'Oh, yes, Mr Corbyn,' smiled Lettice sweetly, and executed a perfect and remarkably graceful curtsey. She wore a pale blue gown of a flattering cut, with flounces and ribbons in all the right places, and a matching blue ribbon in her ringleted gold hair. She appeared to be all girlish innocence and demure obedience, but Mr Corbyn was not deceived. Perhaps his greatest asset as a teacher of young ladies was his complete indifference to the female sex. Smiles and dimples left him unmoved, but even he conceded that Lettice Adam was, as he had overheard one of the young gentlemen say, 'a damned fine girl'. She was also, he suspected, a damned spoilt one, but that was none of his business.

'Then perhaps, at last, we might begin?'

'You see that one wi' the pointed nose and the ringlets?' said Lizzie Lennox, heaving Annys Diack up in her arms so that she might see into the lighted window. 'In the blue dress wi' the beads. That's the Adam girl. Stuck-up bitch.' She spoke without rancour, as she would comment on a side-show at a fair. Which it was. That was the advantage of the darker, autumn days when rich folk lit lamps before they closed the shutters and poor folk could see inside, for nothing. It was as good as the panorama or the circus, if you chose right, and Lizzie Lennox was good at choosing.

Small for her fourteen years, with a shock of fiery hair and surprisingly lustrous brown eyes, she had had the minimum of schooling. For three halfpence a week she had attended the Frederick Street school and learned to read and write and sew a plain seam, but little else. Then the three halfpence had been needed for the next child and Lizzie had left school, to the relief of all concerned.

She had been up for employment last hiring fair, but no one would take her, whether because of her stunted appearance, or because her father demanded of any prospective employer that he repeat the shorter catechism on the spot, or merely because she put her tongue out at any and everyone behind her father's back was not known. There was talk of her going to the factory but any vacancies always went to bigger, stronger-looking girls. Lizzie didn't care. Her cousin Eppie was keeping an ear open on her account and when she heard of something suitable, Lizzie boasted, she would get Lizzie a job in a fine house in town. Eppie said the grand folk gave you their old clothes, if you were lucky, and even if you weren't, you got a uniform and plenty to eat. That would suit Lizzie fine, till she found something better. Meanwhile, she helped her mother with the washing and took the older of the neighbours' children off her hands. Ma Lennox ran a sort of crèche for the women who worked at the factory or elsewhere and for a halfpenny, Lizzie would take the walking infants out. She took them to the Castlegate to see the fine business gentlemen strolling on the Plainstanes. Peered into the windows of the Reading Room till the doorman sent them packing. Teased the cab-horses and exchanged banter with their drivers. Or they trailed up Union Street, mimicking the fine ladies behind their backs, and pressing their noses to the windows of the Fur Shop or Abercrombie's Emporium.

Or, if it was market day, Lizzie showed them how to pinch apples or oranges without getting caught. Or rather, if she saw that they had been spotted, she would say loudly, 'Put that down this instant or I'll skelp yer backside,' and to the wifie, with an apologetic smile, 'I'm that sorry, so I am. He's an awfu' wee devil, that one.'

Sometimes she took them to play in the kirkyard of St Nicholas, frightening them with tales of bogles and ghosties, or of the 'Burkers' who stole dead bodies, till the beadle chased them out. Or, if it was term time, they hung around the Marischal College, jeering at the students. But best of all was if there was a party in one of the grand houses in Upperkirkgate or the Guestrow. Then they watched the guests arriving in their phaetons and horse-drawn cabs, made loud comments and giggled insults, till the chandeliers and the liveried servants overawed them and they stared open-mouthed at what little they could see of the rich dresses and the jewels, the sparkling glasses of unknown liquids, the heaped ashets of strangely decorated food.

'I wouldna eat birds wi' their feathers on if ye paid me,' breathed one child when a servant bore aloft a platter on which reposed a brace of pheasant decorated with their own tail feathers.

'You would if you was a real gent,' said another. 'You'd have to.'

'Then I'm glad I'm nae a gent.' But it was empty vaunting. All of them knew that inside those lighted rooms was a different world from theirs and that however they might jeer, it was a better one. Like a fairy-tale. Or heaven. Just as the dancing class in Mr Corbyn's rooms was a different world from theirs, a world where girls paid money to prance about half-naked, in shoes that were so thin they were worse than useless, while a woman in a lace cap and mittens played the same tune on the piano, over and over, and a man in silly clothes danced.

It was a different world, and it fascinated them.

This morning, they were lucky. Lettice Adam had early complained about the light in the dancing room and Mr Corbyn, although it was a wicked waste, had ordered the lamps to be lit. As a result the scene was illuminated like a magic lantern for the clutch of children in the street.

'And that one in red, wi' the big bum,' continued Lizzie, shifting the weight of the child in her arms, 'that's Fanny Wyness whose da makes the headstones to keep dead folk in their graves.'

'Where? Where? I canna see,' wailed Jessie Bruce, an undergrown child of five, with a squint. She tried to haul herself up on the railings and ripped a new tear in her skirt. Lizzie dumped the Diack child on the ground and clouted Jessie, almost in the same movement.

'What you want to do that for, you daft quine? Your ma'll kill me.'

'I want to see,' sobbed Jessie, wiping her nose on her hand, and Lizzie, relenting, hauled her up by the waist and held her precariously against the railings.

'Go on, then, look. But hurry, 'cos you're killing me.'

'It's not her bum, it's her petticoats,' said Jessie, disappointed. 'And what's she jigging about like that for?'

'Maybe she's got fleas,' suggested a small boy with freckles and a pair of trousers several sizes too big for him. The ragged clutch of children squealed with delight. 'And lice!' 'And bed bugs!' 'And forky tails!' 'And clegs!' They jeered and hooted with derision, all envy forgotten.

'See this!' Gleefully Lizzie Lennox dumped Jessie on the cassies, spread her tattered skirts in a parody of Lettice Adam's own and made an elaborate, mocking curtsey. She executed a few steps of an imaginary, stately dance, then in frenzied pantomime, began to scratch her head, her armpits, her knees, her crotch, while her gaggle of small charges shrieked their delight. In final insult, Lizzie flicked up her skirts and scratched her bare bottom just as Lettice Adam glanced out of the window – and the first of Mr Corbyn's young gentlemen turned the corner into Belmont Street.

'Be off with you!' shouted Niall Burnett, brandishing his cane with all the arrogance of nineteen years and a long-established family estate. Other young men joined him and, faced with such odds, the children prudently scattered, but not before Lizzie had derisively flicked her skirts, and an immodest amount of flesh, in Niall's direction. To establish beyond doubt who was victor in this particular field, she gave him a two-fingered gesture and, for good measure, put out her tongue. Then, taking Annys Diack's hand, she strolled impudently through the middle of the group, saying to no one in particular, 'Some folk have nothing better to do than make fools o' themselves, jigging about like puppets at a fair. I'm real sorry for them and that's a fact.'

'Ought to be horse-whipped,' muttered Niall angrily, his cheeks flushed. 'Or transported. I don't know what the magistrates are thinking of, letting scum like that pollute the public streets.'

From the doorway where, with perfect timing, the ladies' class was even now emerging, Lettice Adam looked over the group of young men clustering at the steps, saw the usual crowd, felt the usual disappointment, and vented her annoyance on the nearest. 'Which everyone knows should be left clear for superior scum like you?'

Behind her, someone giggled. In the entrance hall there was now a cheerful mêlée of chattering and laughter as the girls noticed the boys, but Lettice's face remained solemn, her blue eyes large with pretended innocence as she barred Niall Burnett's way.

'Good morning, Miss Adam,' he said and bowed, though the clipped nod of the head was more insult than courtesy. 'Your wit, I see, is nimble as ever, if predictable.'

'As predictable, Mr Burnett, as your delusions of grandeur,' countered Lettice sweetly. 'Though why you should think yourself superior to anyone quite escapes me.' Behind her Fanny Wyness giggled again and Amelia Macdonald smothered a smile before saying quickly, 'Don't take any notice of her, Niall. Can't you see she is only trying to aggravate you?'

'Now whyever should I do that, Amelia, when it is plain to see that the poor boy has had quite enough aggravation as it is? He looks quite faint and pale. Insulted and set upon by that dreadful harpy and her band of fierce villains? He deserves all our sympathy and support.'

'Instead of which,' drawled Niall, 'it seems I am to be set upon afresh by a different, equally dreadful harridan. I almost prefer the other.'

'You may be right,' said his nearest companion, looking over his shoulder to where Lizzie's disreputable band had retreated to a safe distance on the corner of Union Street. 'She's not a bad-looking wench. A fine head of hair.'

'And a fine head of lice to go with it, no doubt.'

But before his companion could dispute the point, or Lettice Adam protest, Mr Corbyn's ominous voice was heard from the depth of the hallway. 'Gentlemen! I am waiting.'

With sundry whispers, giggles, coy looks and a surreptitious wink or two, males and females hastily dispersed, the former into the dance hall, the latter into the street. But not before at least one of the young gentlemen, less than outraged by Lizzie Lennox's behaviour, had cast a last, admiring glance in her direction.

He couldn't help thinking that in a year or two, in one of his sister's dresses and with her hair properly brushed, that lass could be as handsome as half the girls in Mr Corbyn's dancing school. No, dammit. A darned sight more handsome, or his name wasn't Hugo Arbuthnot Adam.

* * *

Fergus Adam reined in his horse at the lodge gates of Silvercairns and looked with troubled eyes at his family home. The grand house of Silvercairns was falling. The fact was obvious, he thought with futile anger, to anyone with a practised, quarryman's eyes, but his father, who had been a quarryman all his life, refused to see it. Silvercairns would stand, the old man said, as long as the quarry gave up its granite. The fact that the quarry crept ever closer to the lawn below the terrace, that the rhododendrons were grey with granite dust, and that every windowpane in the house rattled whenever a new seam was blasted open left Mungo Adam unmoved. More than once, Fergus had suggested they acquire the neighbouring land in order to extend the quarry away from the house rather than towards it, but his father would not hear of it.

'Why waste money on land we don't need? There's enough rock in the quarry we've got to build Aberdeen twice over,' he would say, his grey eyebrows meeting in a belligerent frown. 'What's more, you'll not find a better granite anywhere. Quartz, felspar and mica in practically equal proportions and as finely grained as you could wish. Takes a good polish, too. What more could anyone ask?' When Fergus attempted to draw his father's attention to the cracks in the east wall of the house, Old Man Adam brushed his fears impatiently aside. 'Imagination. You always did have too much of it. I blame your mother for that, with her novels and her fairy-tales, but the quality of our granite is no fairy-tale and Silvercairns is built of the best of it. I tell you, Fergus, that house will outlive the pair of us, and generations more. But we owe it to those generations to exploit our quarry. To extract our granite for houses, bridges, public buildings, roads. It is our duty, Fergus, our God-given duty, to work that quarry to the last speck of granite dust, and by God I intend to do it!'

As he urged his horse on past the gates of Silvercairns towards the quarry Fergus could not help wondering whether his father's sense of duty would have been so strong had the quarry been less lucrative. As it was, Silvercairns was the richest quarry in the neighbourhood and Old Man Adam one of the richest men in Aberdeen.

Fergus Adam both loved and feared the quarry. Ever since his first visit to the face at the age of five, when he had been taken to see his father's workmen, dressing a granite block for one of the balustrades of a bridge in London, he had been fascinated and increasingly awed by the jagged bowl of living rock which, it seemed to him even then, was ever-changing, ever-different: brooding in shadow, glinting in sunlight, shimmering rainbow-bright after rain; silent in moonlight, thundering in pain and anger under the fire man's blast, catching men's voices and echoing them, over and over into vibrating silence, or holding birdsong, perfect and sweet as in a cupped hand. In his child's imagination he saw the quarry as a huge primeval animal, faceless and formless, its moods unpredictable and awesome, which chose, for reasons of its own, to crouch in obedience at the doors of Silvercairns. But should anything anger it, that creature would be quite capable of rising up and destroying the Adams, their house and all their lands in a thunderclap of doom. For the rest of his childhood Fergus could not hear the distant rumble of a quarry blast or the rattle of windows in their frames without the momentary fear that the beast had risen.

But that first visit had been more than fifteen years ago and the quarry had been only seventy feet deep then. Now it was nearer a hundred and twenty and when the present layer of granite was exhausted, they would blast deeper still. Mackinnon, the quarry manager, had explained to Fergus how granite was made, centuries ago, by molten matter solidifying into igneous rock. A man called James Hutton had seen it all in a vision, while walking in Glen Tilt. Great streams of bubbling lava spreading underground, with no way to get out, and being squashed and pressed for aeons till they cooled into crystalline rock. Aberdeenshire was full of granite, Mackinnnon said, though you couldn't always find it. Quarrying was long, hard work and often there were concealing layers of sandstone or the inferior rock the men called 'barr' but if you persevered, Mackinnon said, you could find granite wherever you looked. Mind you, some granite was better than others. Things like colour, texture and crushing strength made all the difference between a poor granite and a better. At Silvercairns they were lucky. When Mungo Adam leased the quarry, two years before Fergus was born, it had been nothing but a scratch on the surface, Mackinnon said, and a miserable, discouraging scratch at that. But Old Man Adam had persevered and now look at it.

Fergus reined in his horse at the stables, dismounted, handed the reins to the lad who hurried forward to meet him and made his way towards the quarry office across the loading yard. Here there were stacks of paving setts, or cassies, waiting to be transported to the harbour, piles of ashlar blocks, dressed by the men on the quarry floor and awaiting similar shipment, smaller heaps of the rubble which Old Man Adam hoped to dispose of for road surfacing (he was in Aberdeen chasing up the contract even now), cranes and barrows and loading platforms, the usual paraphernalia of the stone yard. Fergus remembered when it was no more than a bare strip and a tin hut.

But that was years back. Mackinnon was an old man now and retired. Six months ago, Fergus had taken over the quarry management himself and since then had had no thought or time for anything else. He knew his father was watching his every action, judging his every decision, measuring quality and quantity of every new blasting Fergus ordered, and keeping his own tally-sheet.

A new foreman had been appointed when Fergus took over, though Mackinnon was often to be seen in the office or the loading bay, even on the quarry floor, making sure, as he explained, that he'd left everything shipshape for the young master. Fergus was glad of his reassuring presence. There was not a man in Scotland who knew more about boring and blasting and Mackinnon had a feel for the lie of the granite 'posts' which no amount of book-learning could supply. Unerringly, he would select the exact place to drill, one man would sit on the rock and hold the drill upright, while two more would take turns to wallop it with an eight-pound hammer. Every twenty minutes, they would change round, again and again, until the hole was eighteen or twenty feet deep. Then it would be filled with powder, tamped with a wooden ramrod, and the fuse inserted.

That was the point which still thrilled Fergus, as it had done when he was a child. The messenger would go round warning the men and sending all the horses and carts to the surface, the final warning bell would ring, the quarry would empty of men, until only the fire man at the fuse was left. Then, at the signal, the fuse would be lit and that man, too, would race for safety while the fuse sputtered and danced across the quarry floor towards the powder charge. In the waiting silence every birdcall, every distant dog, every falling pebble could be heard – until the explosion blasted open the rock-face in a thunder-clap of fire and billowing smoke, flying stones and the long, slow rumble as the granite mass broke apart and fell ... and afterwards, with the smell of powder choking in the air, the intermittent patter of smaller stones until the last splinter settled into silence. However many times he saw it, Fergus still felt the fear and excitement and the unparalleled thrill of pitting man's puny strength against the very bed-rock of the earth . . . and the sense of mingled triumph and anticlimax as the men streamed back into the quarry to separate the blocks into workable sizes, these for paving stones, those for building masonry, that for the plinth of a special statue, that other for the foundation of a bridge . . . And Fergus would pick up the nearest piece of new-blasted stone and examine it afresh, with undiminished wonder, for the silver specks of quartz, the particular combination of white mica and black mica, felspar and hornblende which gave the granite of Silvercairns its fame.

Famous it might be, Mackinnon had told him, but it could kill as easily as any other rock and safety, he had impressed upon the boy right from the start, was of prime importance. 'Approach the granite in a proper spirit of respect and deference,' he had said, 'and the granite will reward you. Treat it carelessly and it will kill. Besides, you owe it to the men. They're good lads and willing, but they can be feckless sometimes and it's up to you to keep them right. A good workforce deserves, and rewards, good care. Just remember, Master Fergus,' Mackinnon had finished, with unusual solemnity, 'every man killed in your quarry leaves a widow and children on *your* conscience.'

Fergus had been preoccupied with safety all week. Those hair-line cracks in the wall of Silvercairns were only part of it, and a part that could wait. More immediately, they had an order for a fourteen-ton block of granite to be fashioned at Macdonald's yard and, the block successfully blasted from the rock and trimmed to shape on the quarry floor, the question of raising it to the surface had presented problems. Then the carpenters had come up with a special carriage and rigged it up for a team of eight horses. With a crane and levers the block had been safely loaded on to the carriage, wedged in place and was even now on its slow way to the surface, up the long spiralling path from the foot of the quarry.

Fergus, still thinking of safety, was discussing with his foreman where should be the next point to start blasting when there was a sudden whinnying from the stables, a shout, the sound of panting close at hand and someone ran stumbling past the window and on across the yard.

'Hey, you!' George Bruce, the foreman, had the door open and was in the yard in a flash, Fergus close behind him. 'Come back!' Instead the intruder ran straight for the quarry path where even now the pack-horses were labouring upwards with that great granite monolith.

'Good God!' said both men together, then, 'After her!' cried Fergus, 'before it's too late.'

Mhairi Diack, breathless and exhausted after her two-mile run, caught a glimpse through a gap in the rowans of the house which had been her dream castle for as long as she could remember, and found new strength to run on. Below her, to the east, lay Aberdeen, with the sea beyond, and the long road she had travelled from the tenement in the Gallowgate, past the kirk of St Nicholas, up Schoolhill, on to Carden Place, then west until she reached the smithy at Hirpletillam and turned off the main road on to the quarry track. Her father walked the distance twice a day and thought nothing of it. Or if he did, he never said so, though the road must try his poor chest something wicked.

The track to the quarry was well trodden, by the feet of the quarrymen and by the hoofs of the horses who dragged the carts of ashlar, paving setts, and the smaller stones known as 'junks' and 'litters', and, today, the huge, fourteen-ton block of granite that was to go to Macdonald's yard to be dressed and polished, then all the way to London for a plinth for a statue, so Alex said. A special team of horses had been re-shod for the purpose and Donal was one of the lads in charge.

The smithy at Hirpletillam shod all the quarry horses, and was a warm and friendly place to spend an hour or so, especially towards the tail end of the year when the quarry stone struck cold as Greenland ice and the hammer shaft stuck to the hands. But today, instead of lingering with the other idlers to watch the furnace turn the black metal to spitting scarlet fire, Mhairi had sped past without a glance, merely feeling the heat wrap round her and slip free again as she ran on. Now, if she looked back, she could just make out the tiny spark of the blacksmith's forge in the distance and, if she listened, hear the sharp ring of hammer on metal. Above her, from the west, where the track met the quarry, came the different, distant sound of metal on stone.

Ahead of her, further up the track, Silvercairns stood in its pool of green silk above the grey-white pit which was the quarry. Her brother Tom said the green strip was shrinking and that if he were Old Man Adam he would blast from the other side, or take a lease on a neighbouring hill, but Tom was not Old Man Adam and they said the granite from the Adam quarry could pay for a hundred mansions like Silvercairns, twice over.

Mhairi slowed briefly to a walk, gathered strength, and drove herself once more into a run: a plodding, chest-rasping run now, feet dragging and muscles aching for rest, but still a run. The rowans grew thinner, gave way to bracken, scrubland and brambles and she could see the house clearly now, bobbing up and down on the horizon with each stumbling step. Desperately, she pushed back the dread and tried to find the usual wonder and bewitchment in the sparkling grey stone of Silvercairns. Unlike Fergus Adam, she saw no flaws in its elegance: only a silver castle on an eminence, with green lawns and flowers. Not for her the tell-tale cracks and the subsidence, but tall, white-framed windows, a hint of heavy velvet hangings, of polished furniture and glinting chandelier. Alex and Tom trudged past here every day on their way to the quarry; Donal passed and repassed several times a day, leading horses to the forge, or into town; but to them Silvercairns was just the boss's house; to her it was her mother's land o' the leal.

There was no smoke from the chimneys now, because the family had removed to town for the winter, so Lizzie's cousin Eppie said, but in the spring tranquil smoke would rise again in a dozen feathered columns from the corbie-stepped and battlemented roof and there would be warm bedrooms, busy kitchens and the mouth-watering welcome of a breakfast room with a clutch of steaming chafing dishes on a laden sideboard. Under silver lids, so Eppie said, and half of it sent back to the kitchen uneaten, like as not. Mhairi thought of their own breakfasts – thin porridge in the chill damp of dawn in an overcrowded tenement, and then only after Da had taken his fill. Though he ate little enough these days, with the cough wracking his chest till he doubled up with the pain.

Pain. Mhairi's mind filled again with the memory of her mother's anguished cries as the dark stain spread over the sodden cloth . . . 'Run,' Ma Mackenzie had said. Desperately, driven faster by fear, her lodestar that granite symbol of aristocratic assurance clean-cut against the sky, she ran. Faster, faster, as the path levelled on the last stretch to the quarry entrance, and her breath came loud and harsh in her throat. Faster . . .

She dreaded her arrival at the quarry face, dreaded her father's shock, dreaded the long trek home again, and most of all she dreaded what they would find when they reached the tenement which had been home for all her sixteen years. But still she ran, panting now, stumbling, until she rounded the last bend and was suddenly in the yard, with the stables and outbuildings and piles of stone, and, beyond the office, the flat sweep of path which skirted the quarry's edge.

Beyond the scatter of scrubland and bushes at its rim she could see, in the pit of the quarry, tiny men chipping at the rock-face, others dressing broken blocks of granite, still more men squatting on the ground, hammering at smaller blocks of stone. Those were the setts or cassies her father made, to go to pave the streets of London. She saw a group of horses and carts, small as beetles, waiting patiently to be loaded in the pale dust-bowl of the quarry, and the long, winding thread of the path which led round the sides of the bowl and up from the quarry floor a hundred and twenty feet beneath. Half-way up the path was a double team of horses, plodding slowly under the weight of their granite burden, with men at the leading reins and more following. Donal would be one of them. But Cassie Diack would be with that group of men on the quarry floor.

Pausing, she waved, once, in hope that he might see her, then, remembering the message she had to give, clenched her teeth quickly over a silent prayer and set off again, faster now that she was almost there, towards the path into the quarry itself.

'Hey! You! Where do you think you're going, ye daft quine?' The door of the quarry office was flung open and a burly man in a mason's leather apron, rope tied at the waist, shook a threatening fist. Behind him, a young gentleman shouted. She should have called at the office, asked the foreman to take her message, but Mhairi was beyond thought. 'Run,' Ma Mackenzie had said. 'Run and fetch yer da,' and now that she could see that tiny figure, squatting in his moleskin trousers and dust-encrusted apron beside the pile of granite setts, the doors of her mind burst open and she realized what had been the last words Ma Mackenzie had called after her. Ignoring the shouts behind her, she sped across the yard and on to the quarry path.

'Stop! Come back here!' Both men were shouting now, coming after her. She turned her head, saw them, ran faster, over the quarry rim and down on to the spiral path which led to the quarry floor. The ground was hard under her feet, slippery with granite dust and sand, on one side the quarry wall, on the other, nothing . . . The ground shook under her feet, she heard their feet pounding closer, turned her head in terror, and fell.

Stabbing pain in her hand . . . the rip of cloth as her blue drugget skirt snagged on a stone . . . stars danced in her eyes, then a strange, bright darkness . . . Ma will be angry, was her first thought. It was good cloth. Then she remembered. But she would mend the skirt, patch it somehow, make it up to Ma. If . . . Fear washed through her and she clenched her teeth to shut out the unthinkable. She realized her left knee was burning with pain and her hand was throbbing. There would be blood . . . She closed her eyes briefly against the thought, then jerked them open in alarm as a hand touched her arm, a voice said, 'Are you all right, lass?' George Bruce, the foreman. But on the path, on a level with her face, she saw a pair of leather boots, gentleman's boots of excellent quality though they were at the moment layered with dust. And above the boots, trousers . . . not workman's moleskin or serge but gentleman's best worsted. She scrambled to her feet, forgetting the stinging pain in her knee and hand, smoothed down her skirts, pushed back her tumbled hair, and found two angry faces glaring into hers.

'You little fool. You could have been killed.' 'The horses . . .' 'Could have startled them . . .' 'Sent them over the edge into the pit.'

Desperately she looked from one to the other – George Bruce, the foreman, dark-browed and stern, and the younger man, paler, tight-lipped, but equally angry – while their words swirled round her like a cloud of unheeded flies and she heard only that voice inside her head saying over and over *Run and find your father, lass*. Suddenly, taking them unawares, she dipped under Bruce's arm and took to her heels again – only to be brought up short within yards when the foreman lunged after her, seized her by the arm and jerked her back.

'Please!' she cried, before he could speak. 'I must find my father before . . .' Fear welled up to choke the words in her throat and tears blurred her eyes. That other man took a step towards her and she cried in desperation, 'Please, Mr Bruce. I am to fetch him home. Before it is too late!'

'Don't you know you could have been killed?' demanded George Bruce. A burly man with a stonemason's strength and stamina, he had overtaken the girl with no trouble, and though she had dodged him once he had her now by the arm and she would not do so again.

Fergus Adam, standing a little apart and higher up the path, saw the team of horses below still labouring their slow way upwards, like so many beetles crawling up the quarry wall, and when he thought of what might have happened, he shuddered with imagined dread. Only last week a horse had reared in Market Street, the chain of the breechin had broken, and the ton weight of stones had run out of control. The runaway cart had gone clean over one man and only Providence had saved him from fatal injury by steering the wheels safely on either side of him. But here, if the leading horses had been startled on the narrow quarry path, there was no saying what might have happened – cart running backwards out of control, with fourteen tons of granite for impetus, or the whole thing, horses and all, over the edge on to the quarry floor. He had a brief mental picture, in slow motion, of the cart falling, horses and men falling with it, of that granite block separating from the rest, thundering down on to the quarry floor, splitting open, showering boulders and debris – and crushing all in its path. And of his father's face when he heard of the disaster. Like his own foreman, he gave vent to his relief in anger.

'How dare you force your way in here, young woman! You could have killed my men, lost a month's work, done untold damage.' Then he saw the tears standing in her eyes – eyes as blue and clear as the Scottish sky – and, his anger cooling as a different emotion took its place, he turned to Bruce and said irritably, 'What is she doing here anyway? Surely she knows women are not allowed?'

'You'd best tell me, lass,' said the foreman with rough kindness, though he still held her prudently by the arm. When she hesitated, looking nervously from one man to the other, young Mr Adam turned his back, arms folded, impatient foot tapping on the hard-packed earth and, after a moment's uncertainty, in low, hurried tones Mhairi did.

'And Mrs Mackenzie said Da's to come at once, afore it's . . .' She choked briefly on the terrible words then, as Fergus Adam half turned his head, fear gave her new courage. 'My father is to come home at once,' she finished, with a kind of despairing dignity, 'before it is too late.'

George Bruce read the poverty and hopelessness behind the words, the human tragedy he saw daily in the city tenements where he had lived himself until a year ago. Poor lass. She'd be left, like as not, to fill her mother's place, until she was old enough for some man to take her and add to her burdens. He had a daughter himself, much the same age as this girl. George Bruce had not risen to authority without a certain streak of ruthlessness and a necessary pandering to the boss's humour, but if ever it was a case of us and them, he knew where his innermost loyalties lay.

'Right, lass,' he said, suddenly brisk. 'Your da's Cassie Diack, yes? And young Tom'll be your brother? Leave everything to me.' Then he turned to Fergus Adam. 'If you take the lass to the office, Mr Adam, I'll send her father and brother to you. Oh, and you might tell the stable lad to harness up the spare cart. There's tools to be collected from the smithy and he can give the Diacks a lift. The extra run'll do no harm. That's what Mackinnon would do,' he added quickly before young Mr Adam could protest. Then he loosed Mhairi's arm and strode off down the quarry path leaving the girl in young Adam's charge.

For a moment they stood where they were, in silence. Fergus saw that she was fighting back tears and looked quickly away. He felt suddenly awkward in the presence of an emotion which both embarrassed him and made him ashamed. When he had seen the girl recklessly running on to the quarry path he had been as angry as George Bruce. When she fell, he had felt only relief that she had been stopped in time. But when he had spoken to her and she had looked at him with those tear-filled eyes – like morning dew on harebells – something had happened to his anger, and to his heart.

For months, even years, he had thought only of granite, until his heart had taken on something of the same stonelike quality, but now, seeing the naked fear and anguish in the girl's face, he was touched with unexpected compassion. He wanted to shield her somehow from whatever threatened her, to bring the light back into those soft blue eyes. At the same time he was aware of the insuperable gulf between them – the favoured son of a rich father, he had never known hunger, as he suspected this girl had often known it; had never felt unprotected or threatened. Even when his own mother died two years ago there had been none of the intensity of emotion which emanated from this girl in frightening waves of love and fear. Only lowered voices, soft-treading servants, solicitous doctors, and, finally, silence. Fergus had loved his mother, but she had always somehow stood aside from daily living: her death had not torn apart the fabric of his life. But, looking at the tear-streaked, wild-eyed girl on the path in front of him, he suspected her life would never be the same again.

'Come with me,' he said, with awkward authority, and added, more gently, 'It is warmer inside.'

When he had ushered her into the office and indicated a chair, sent the office boy to instruct the stable lad and to fetch brandy and hot tea, he retreated behind the safety barrier of his desk and made a play of consulting his ledgers while he studied her. Poorly dressed, as was to be expected, but clean, apart from the obvious dust of her recent journey. Her hair gleamed dark as jet under its dishevelment, and her eyes, when he inadvertently caught her looking at him, were of a shade of blue as deep as hyacinth. She looked weary, frightened, forlorn, yet there was a strange waifish beauty in her face and a dignity in her bearing which surprised and vaguely unsettled him. His father's workers had always been mere workers to him: Mackinnon had told him often enough to guard their welfare and he did, insofar as checking safety regulations and making sure the men were paid on time. As for their families – he remembered Mackinnon saying something about every quarryman killed in the Adam quarry leaving a widow and children on the Adam conscience, but he had never thought of those widows and children as *people*. And now here was one of them, admittedly not orphaned yet, but not anonymous either. In fact, disturbingly real – more real in some ways than his sister Lettice – and at the same time appealing, with a vibrancy of emotion which seemed to fill the room with its intensity. He could think of nothing appropriate to say.

On his desk was the tender he was supposed to be preparing for the supply of granite for a row of elegant new houses in Victoria Street, but as he tried to concentrate on the figures, he found himself wondering instead what sort of house the Diack girl lived in. One of those disgusting tenements his sister Lettice was always complaining about behind the Guestrow, perhaps? For a fleeting moment he had a picture of the Diack girl on the steps of an elegant granite house, with lawns and trees . . . then shook his head impatiently and took up his pen. She had come to call one of his workmen home, that was all. And he could ill afford to lose anyone, even for a day, with the frost gripping harder at night and the days shortening and that London contract to fulfil. Deliberately he closed his mind to compassion and thought only of his father's anger should the quarry fall behind with its orders.

In the extending silence, Mhairi watched him from under lowered lashes and, in spite of the fear which thudded, regular as a heartbeat, through her shivering body, studied his face with meticulous care. This was young Mr Adam, she thought with awe. Fergus Adam of Silvercairns. He had been born and brought up there, eaten his breakfast in that great polished dining-room of silver-lidded dishes, and one day, when his father died, he would be the laird of Silvercairns himself. Looking at him surreptitiously, Mhairi felt a twinge of disappointment. He was well dressed, to be sure, with spotless linen and a suit of the best quality woollen cloth. He had a gold chain across his waistcoat and a gold ring. All the same, when you looked closely, he really did not look much different from her brother Tom, or Alex Grant. His hair was longer perhaps, and silkier, his complexion not so weathered, but her brother Tom was handsomer and Alex Grant was better built. The comparison made him seem less august. She had expected from her mother's stories that a gentleman like Mr Adam would be somehow different from other men – more princely, though she could not define how that princeliness would show.

But her knee was stinging against the rough cloth of her skirts, and her hand burnt and throbbed. One eye on Mr Adam, still apparently absorbed in his ledger, she half turned in her chair, inched up the material and surreptitiously inspected her knee where a mesh of tiny cuts welled beads of blood. She hadn't fallen since she was Annys's age and she realized that she was still trembling with the unexpected shock. Quickly she inspected the damage. It was nothing. Merely a graze. Her hand was the worst. She was searching her knee for any pieces of embedded grit which would have to be removed lest they fester, when something made her glance up and she saw Mr Adam looking at her. As if through his eyes she saw her raised skirt, her white, bare leg, and embarrassment flooded through her, with a deep and burning shame. She scrambled to her feet, pretending unconcern, but she could not control the blush which stained her cheeks a deep, incriminating red.

'You are hurt,' he said, pushing back his chair. 'Why did you not say? You need warm water and a bandage.'

'No. It is nothing. A graze, that is all.'

When he did not speak, but continued to look at her with an expression she could not read, she twisted her hands nervously together and winced with unexpected pain. She glanced down at her cut hand and bit her lips as she saw the freshly oozing blood.

He stood up, crossed the room. 'Show me,' he ordered.

'No!' She backed away, her hands on her thighs, as if to keep her skirts in place, and saw shock flicker briefly across his face, then amusement.

'I meant your *hand*, Miss . . . Diack, is it? I thought I saw blood.'

Ashamed of her involuntary reaction, and mortified on his behalf as much as on her own, Mhairi, trembling, held out her hand. On the ball of her thumb a three-cornered wedge of skin had been torn back, like a flap, and there were gritty pieces of stone embedded in the flesh from which new blood oozed rich and red. It was too much. She had run and run till her chest rasped with the breathing and her knees were like jelly and now . . . Her eyes filled with tears of weakness. The sight of blood always made her head swim and her stomach fall apart. And at home her mother was lying in that dreadful, spreading pool. As she watched her own blood well up and spread slowly across her hand, darkness blurred her eyes and swirled through into her brain till she felt strangely weightless and free.

'Dear God!' She did not hear the words, or feel the arms which caught her as she fell. She had slipped into a calm dreamland where she lay on a river bank, in peace and sunlight, with the sound of lapping water and birdsong and a dear, loving face bending over her.

Then the water was a basin at her head, a damp cloth on her brow, and the face that of Mr Adam, grave with concern. Before she could gather words to speak, he was holding a glass to her lips and urging her to drink. Obediently, she did so, and the fiery liquid galvanized her into embarrassed consciousness. She was in his chair, at his desk. A basin of water and a cloth lay among his papers. There was a smear of blood on the open page of the ledger and more on the cloth. Her cheeks burnt with shame.

'I am sorry,' she said, attempting to rise to her feet. 'I did not mean . . .'

'Stay where you are,' ordered Mr Adam. 'I have bound up your hand, but when you get home you had best bathe it properly.'

She looked down to see a rag tied around her left hand. No, not a rag. A spotless linen handkerchief with a hemmed border and embroidered monogram. Mr Adam's own. She looked at him, appalled. 'But . . .'

'Say nothing,' he ordered. 'Drink this.' Again the glass, again the fire. He was standing beside her now, looking down at her with an expression of relief and she saw that his face was not as plain as she had thought. It was fine-boned and delicate, with dark eyes in which she read kindness and compassion and . . . hastily she looked away. What would her mother say if she knew that her daughter was alone with a young man, a gentleman, who had . . . who had what? Caught her when she fell? Carried her in his arms across the room? She blushed afresh at the thought.

'Ah, you have colour again in your cheeks. That is good.'

'I am sorry,' she managed. 'I have been a trouble to you.'

'I will not deny that you alarmed me,' admitted Fergus. She watched him pour whisky into a second glass and drink before he continued. 'But the sight of blood can be unnerving and you had run a long way, on a painful errand.'

His words brought all her fears rushing back and without thinking she cried her anguish aloud. 'I wish they would come!'

So do I, echoed Fergus, inside his head, for he found the girl's presence strangely disquieting. She was young, sixteen at most, but with a womanly grace and vulnerability which went straight to his heart. When she had slipped, unconscious, to the ground, he had felt momentary panic, then when he realized she had merely fainted, that panic had changed to a kind of exultation. He had scooped her up and held her longer than was strictly necessary, while her dark hair rippled thick and silky over his arm and her sleeping eyelashes lay thick on her waxen cheeks. Her young breasts rose and fell gently under the cotton material of her bodice and her arm where the sleeve fell back was white and firm. He had felt a moment of extraordinary communion with her before common sense returned and he had placed her gently in his own chair. When the office boy arrived with tea and whisky, he had sent him back again for water at the double, had washed the girl's torn hand, doused the cut with whisky for good measure, and bound it with his own handkerchief. But that moment when he had held her, senseless, in their circle of private silence, still stayed with him. Now he said only, 'They will come.'

As if in answer, there was the sound of hurrying steps in

the yard, a clamorous knock at the door, and the circle was broken.

Cassie Diack held out his raw and splitting hands to the brief warmth of the brazier and winced as the blood began to circulate again. One of the apprentice laddies had lit the brazier first thing, but its steady heat made little difference to the stone-fed chill of the quarry floor. There had been a hard frost the previous night and the stars of the Plough had been bright as lamplight. The sky was clear again today, but it needed a hot sun to penetrate the depth of the quarry at Silvercairns. Not like Corrennie where the quarry was gouged out of the hillside, or Tom's Forest or Craiglash. When the sun was low in the sky, as it was in the winter months, then large parts of Silvercairns quarry remained in shadow.

But, looking upwards, he saw the shadowed face of granite was topped by a rim of bleached grass and autumn bracken, sunlit gold against the midday sky. High above in the quivering light a hawk hovered. Inland, to the west, reflected Cassie with a twinge of the homesickness which had not left him in spite of the twenty-five years he had spent in Aberdeen, the stags would be bellowing their challenge to the echoing hills. In the croft where he had spent the first fourteen years of his life, whoever lived there now would keep a wary eye for predatory foxes, set snares, lift the year's potato crop, dig, while his wife would milk their cow, make butter and cheese, count the hens and their dwindling eggs, and work at the big house too, like as not, to make ends meet. He had done right to come to the city when his parents died. Done right to marry, father children. Done right to seek the mason's trade. He could measure and trace and trim, knew a good stone from a bad by the touch of it, could even identify the particular quarry a block of granite came from and, once, had been able to dress and shape the perfect baluster with nothing but a scabbling pick and hammer. Then the dust had caught him and he no longer had the breath. Some of the older men, when they began to lose their skills, were put to stone-breaking for the roads. When his time came, Cassie doubted he would have the strength for that. But by then, Tom would have served his apprenticeship, God willing, and Lorn and Willy would be following. Meanwhile, he could still trim and shape a causeway sett faster than any man, and dress a granite block smoother than most. He had a steady job, and money. But never enough money, and sometimes it seemed to him, in memory anyway, that the simple poverty of his childhood croft was preferable to the teeming squalor of the tenements which crowded them on all sides at Mitchell's Court. Another child would not help, either, though he loved his children, as he loved his wife, with simple, uncritical pride and devotion.

Tom, his eldest boy, was a good lad and already showed real talent for the mason's calling. His years in the quarry had firmed his muscles, steadied him, given him a confidence he had not had when he first came among the older men as a raw apprentice, gullible and unsuspecting. But he had taken their teasing in good spirit, as had his friend Alex Grant, and had been quick to learn. He would go far – as long as the dust didn't get his lungs as it had insinuated its way into Cassie's. There was a time when Cassie could have wielded an eight-pound hammer as effortlessly as any man, have taken his turn at the rock-boring and thought nothing of it. Now, he spent his days seated, like as not, or squatting on haunches, chipping away at the endless piles of granite setts which went to surface the roads of Aberdeen, Edinburgh or London. He had done so many now that he had no need to measure, but could tap the three-inch wide, brick-shaped block with the minimum of strokes and know that it was accurate.

But it was tedious work and not what he wanted for his son. Tom would build bridges, royal monuments, palaces . . . as he himself had once dreamed of doing.

Cassie looked across the quarry to the far side where Tom was one of a three-man team marking out the boring holes for the next section of rock to be blasted. Tom stood, legs braced apart, both hands gripping the heavy hammer which he swung back and down, in perfect double rhythm with his partner, striking the steel rod which the third man steadied on the rock. Cassie saw the sparks fly as hammer struck steel and hoped to God the foreman knew what he was doing. With old Mackinnon there was never need to fear: he knew his job, he knew his men, and he knew his granite. He wouldna risk a stray spark like yon lighting where it had no business to light and maybe igniting a powder keg o' trouble. The new man, George Bruce, knew his job right enough, but maybe he knew it a mite too well and over-confidence could lead to trouble. Besides, everyone knew that Old Man Adam had put his son Fergus in charge for a trial period while the Old Man busied himself travelling up and down the country trying for contracts with all this new building work the railways were bringing. They said there was to be a line from Forfar to Aberdeen one day and when it came, that would mean building enough, what with bridges and viaducts and no doubt a railway hotel. But Fergus Adam was on trial and that meant he was driving them all at full gallop to prove to his da that he could make the quarry spit out twice as much as any man. Only yesterday he had ridden into town himself to order six more barrels of blasting powder from Cruickshanks. Looking at that regular, darting spark of fire, Cassie hoped the young master, too, knew what he was doing.

Cassie was turning his hands over in the heat of the brazier, for a last lingering minute, and watching his son's confident strength with a different warmth, deep in his heart, when he became aware of some sort of a disturbance on the quarry path. The foreman was signalling. A man shouted, then another, passing on the message. And suddenly Cassie Diack realized the name they were shouting was his. He was to go above, to the quarry office, at once.

Oh, God. They had seen him idling, wasting company time warming his hands at the fire. Who would feed his children if . . . His heart pounded painfully and his breath failed him. Mackinnon knew a man's hands worked faster when they were warm, but did the new man know it? Oh, God . . .

Then he realized that Tom had downed his hammer, that Alex was crossing the quarry floor to take Tom's place, his face concerned. Then Tom was at his side.

'Leave your tools, Da. Alex will bring them later. We'd best hurry. It's Ma,' he added, as his father looked uncomprehending, then, as the last of the colour drained from his father's face, 'It'll be all right, Da, you'll see. But we'd best go, all the same. Mhairi's come for us. You know how she fusses, Da, and likely it's nought to worry about, but we'd best go. Ma'll likely be expectin' us. Then we can come back and finish here later. And if maybe it's getting dark, then we'll bide at home wi' a hot toddy or some o' Ma's fine soup and take a fly holiday. Ma'd like that. Nay, dinna look so downcast, Da, it'll all be fine once we're home, you'll see.' But Tom's determined optimism was sorely strained as, grey-faced and labouring painfully for breath, his father stumbled up the long path beside him, leaning ever more heavily on Tom's arm. They caught up with and overtook the eight-horse team drawing the granite monolith to the surface and Tom wondered briefly if it might be better to put his father on the cart with the stone, but decided the slow inactivity would be even worse to bear.

'It's all right, Da, dinna worry so,' said Tom, over and over, but by the time they surfaced into the quarry yard even Tom's optimism was flagging. 'Go straight to the office,' they had told him, 'and see the boss.' He led his father across the yard, threading quickly between the heaps of kerbstones, rubble and setts towards the plain stone building with its two plain windows and its plain wooden door. Then he raised his hand and knocked.

'Come in.'

They doffed their caps in unison, and stepped inside.

Before anyone could speak, Mhairi shot to her feet and flung herself across the room.

'Oh, Da,' she cried, burying her face in his chest. 'Thank God you've come. I ran as fast as I could to fetch you, but we must hurry. Ma's ill and Mrs Mackenzie said . . .'

'Hush, lass, hush.' Cassie put his arms protectively around his daughter, and looked over her head at Fergus Adam, who gave the briefest of nods.

'You may go, Diack, and the lad. There's a cart waiting in the yard. But we'll expect you back tomorrow, mind.'

They were out in the yard before Mhairi remembered. She stopped, turned, saw Fergus Adam still standing in the office doorway, took a step towards him. 'I am sorry, Mr Adam. Your handkerchief . . .' She fumbled at the knot, but he said, 'Nonsense. Keep it,' and did not need to add, 'I have plenty.' Then he smiled and she forgot that she had ever thought him plain. 'I hope your hand heals quickly, Miss Diack.' Blushing, she gave him a quick smile, a shy 'Thank you,' and a moment later was scrambling up into the waiting dray cart. The stable lad took up the reins, smacked the horse into motion and they drove out of the yard and on to the track for Hirpletillam and Aberdeen.

Afterwards, it was the light that Mhairi remembered. The pale shaft of sunlight picking out the squares of faded colour on the bed – like tiny patches of stubble or distant winter fields – and her mother's hand lying limp and pale as any lady's hand on the rough surface of the blanket.

Her mother's eyes were closed, her face like wax, and Mhairi did not need Ma Mackenzie's whispered apologies to know there was nothing now that anyone could do.

'I'm sorry, Cassie,' the woman was saying, 'I did my best.' But Cassie had dropped to his knees beside the bed, taken his wife's hand in his and was kissing her eyes, her cheeks, her hand while the tears coursed down his face. Agnes Diack stirred, opened her eyes, said, 'I'm sorry, love . . .'

They were all there, Annys whimpering and clutching at Mhairi's skirts, Lorn and Willy, large-eyed and frightened, fetched hastily from school, Tom biting back the tears. Ma Mackenzie had withdrawn discreetly into the background and was doing something with a small paper bundle. For the first time Mhairi thought of the baby and knew, with a rush of relief, that it was dead. Afterwards, she was to torture herself with remorse for that thought, but at the time she could think only of her mother, slipping away from them in spite of their entreaties, leaving them to fend as best they could for themselves . . .

But her mother was murmuring something and Cassie motioned Mhairi to come closer. 'Your ma wants to speak to you, lass.' He moved to let Mhairi nearer though he still held tight to his wife's hand. She reached out the other to Mhairi and Mhairi took it, trembling at the lightness and frailty of her mother's once firm grip.

'I'm sorry, Mhairi love, but I reckon you'll have to manage without me. Look after your da. His chest's nae awfu' good and he'll likely be lonely. Promise you'll care for him? And the wee ones?'

'I promise, Ma,' gulped Mhairi.

'Nay, dinna cry, lass. Remember the land o' the leal. *I'm*

wearying awa . . .' Her mother's valiant attempt at a song broke the last of Mhairi's control and she gave up all attempt to stay her tears. 'Listen, Mhairi,' said her mother with urgency, 'this is important. Are ye listening?'

Dumbly, Mhairi nodded.

'*Never lose hope.* Hope makes everything bearable. Remember that and ye'll survive. And remember all I taught you about being a lady? I know how much you wanted that job in a big house, and I'm sorry, but you will see wee Annys grows up right for me, won't you, lass? I wouldna want her to stray . . . And you'll see none o' them go to the poorhouse?'

'I promise, Ma,' managed Mhairi through her streaming tears.

'You're my good, dear daughter, Mhairi, and I love you . . .' Mhairi flung herself on her mother's breast and hugged her, sobbing, till Cassie drew her gently away.

'Nay, lass, your ma's wearying and it's Tom's turn now.'

Obediently Mhairi straightened, kissed her mother's cheek, and made way for Tom. Then it was the turn of the little boys, and finally her father lifted wee Annys to the bed for her mother to hold and kiss. Then Agnes Diack, worn out with the effort of seeing to her family's needs for the last time, turned her head against her husband's shoulder and closed her eyes. No one knew at exactly which moment she died, only that the silence stretched and stretched until gradually they realized that it was a different silence, and that the room was a different, lonelier place.

Ma Mackenzie busied herself discreetly with necessary arrangements. Mrs Lennox was sent for to help. The minister called and went again. Lizzie Lennox arrived, for once solemn-faced, and removed the three youngest upstairs. Tom went out to find someone from the Masons' Lodge to make arrangements for a coffin. Mhairi watched as the women laid out her mother and dressed her in clean linen. She looked calm and beautiful and, with her hands folded across her breast, as ladylike as even she could have wished. And all the time Cassie Diack sat motionless on the wooden chair, leaning slightly forward, forearms on thighs and hands hanging loose between his knees, staring unseeing at the floor. Occasionally he coughed and Mhairi would go to him with ale or a glass of the linctus her mother made him take, but he merely shook his head and she retreated again, baffled as to how to help him, while her mother's words rang over and over in her head. 'Look after your da . . . keep wee Annys right . . . see none o' them go to the poorhouse . . . you're a good daughter, Mhairi . . .' And she would see. She *would* . . . but while her heart wept for her mother, she wept also for the hopes which had gone with her mother to the grave.

Neighbours came to pay their respects and to commiserate. Even Maggie Henderson and Beth Pirie. Cassie welcomed them all with quiet dignity but after that left any conversation to Mhairi and Tom while he resumed his chair beside the bed, keeping his own silent vigil until the funeral should remove his wife from him for ever. Alex came, with Donal. Said he would explain to the foreman at the quarry. Cassie seemed not to hear, or if he did, to be unaffected. But Mhairi worried on his behalf. Hadn't young Mr Adam said, 'We'll expect you back tomorrow'?

'It'll be all right, Mhairi,' said Alex kindly. 'They canna sack a man for his wife's funeral. The Lodge wouldna' let them.' He took her hand and squeezed it in reassurance, but she did not believe him. 'They' could do anything. Hadn't those factory girls who had left before working out their notice been ordered back again under threat of three months in jail? It didn't matter that the wages were minimal and the work intolerable. The masters had the law behind them and could do what they liked with their workmen, and though Mr Fergus had been kind to her, he was still her father's boss and one of Them. But if Tom and her da lost their jobs at the quarry, how would she keep the family out of the poorhouse, as she had promised her ma?

When Tom came back, the arrangements made, she took him aside and whispered, 'What will we do, Tom, if you and Da lose your jobs?'

'We won't,' said Tom and Mhairi noticed a new firmness in his voice. It was not the light-hearted optimism of the old Tom, but a new note of resolution. 'Or if we do, we'll find another.' He stopped, looked at his father who still sat motionless, staring at the floor, his only movement the coughing which gripped him all too often with a breathless, rasping pain.

'I tell you one thing, Mhairi,' he said quietly and she heard anger in his voice now. 'I'll not slave in the dust all my life to fill another man's pocket. To see my wife die in poverty and my children in danger of the poorhouse through no fault of my own. Look at Da. Broken by grief right enough and death can come to the highest, but it wasna grief that broke his health. It was a lifetime's dogged work. No man could have worked longer or harder – and for what? It's nae fair, Mhairi.'

Mhairi knew Tom was grieving for his ma, and for his da's pain too, and that maybe the anger helped him bear it, but the words he spoke were dangerous and they frightened her.

'It's the way things are, Tom,' she said anxiously. 'Ye canna change them.'

'Why not? Are the poor always to be poor and the rich rich? How rich do you think Old Man Adam would be if we masons refused to work for him? What would he do then?'

'You musn't say such things, Tom. It's not right. What would . . .' She almost said, 'What would Ma say?' but checked herself in time. Ma had yearned after things ladylike, had wanted her daughters to be ladies in behaviour if not in status, but there had been no resentment in her ambitions, no envy. Only the gentle acceptance with which, Mhairi realized, her mother had greeted everything life sent her, including death.

'I know what you were going to say,' said Tom fiercely. 'But Ma accepted too much and look what it brought her!' He choked angrily on his tears, brushed an impatient hand across his eyes and went on, 'Alex and I have been talking. One day, when we've skill and money enough, we intend to set up on our own. Mackinnon says a good craftsman with just a little financial backing could get hold of a patch of ground somewhere and build up his own business in no time and when we've worked out our apprenticeships . . .'

Mhairi ceased to listen. 'Just a little financial backing,' he said. How could he be so naïve? So baselessly optimistic? If it was that easy, why didn't everyone do it? Mackinnon himself, for instance? If her da had worked all his life in the granite with nothing to show for it but a pair of ruined lungs and the clothes on his back, what hope was there for Tom? Even if he was the best mason in Silvercairns quarry, he'd still be paid the same. Pittance wages for pittance living. The only ones who made money were those who had it already, like the Adams.

She looked down at her hand where the cut was healing over

well enough. She had laundered the handkerchief already and pressed it with care, folded it and hidden it away in the kist, with her mother's best linen and her Sunday dress. 'Keep it,' he had said, and she knew he would not miss it. A fine lawn handkerchief was nothing to him, whereas to her . . . For the first time, doubt entered Mhairi's dreams. Perhaps Tom was right? Perhaps there was something wrong somewhere. Like her ma, she had never grudged the Adams their beautiful house. She still didn't. It was the way things were, that was all. Nobody chose to be born rich or poor, into this family or that, because there could be no choice. God made the world as he saw fit to make it and it was good. All the same . . .

But when Tom finished speaking, she voiced no doubts. Tom deserved his dreams and she would not shatter them as fate had shattered hers. For Mhairi had crossed from childhood to adulthood in the space of an afternoon and had put childhood dreams behind her for ever.

After the funeral all the neighbours came in for the customary demonstration of solidarity and support. Early in the day Mrs Lennox had come down the stair to take over arrangements, but Mhairi insisted on doing everything herself. 'I promised Ma!' she said fiercely when the older woman tried to insist and with an understanding shrug, Mrs Lennox retreated. 'Poor wee lass,' she reported to her husband, 'and her father not long for this world neither, by the looks o' him.' She set to and baked shortbread and oatcakes to go with the whisky, and sent them down later, via Lizzie, with strict instructions to 'Mind ye keep your thieving fingers oot o' yon basket or I'll skelp yer backside!' Mhairi accepted the offering as she did the many others that arrived with their donors from up and down the neighbouring tenements. She made tea for the womenfolk, while Tom poured whisky and ale for the men, Lorn and Willy offered plates of this and that, and Cassie himself sat silent in the fireside chair where Mhairi had put him, the glass of whisky untouched in his hand.

'It's the shock, like as not,' said Mackinnon kindly. 'Dinna worry, lass. He'll be better by tomorrow.'

'I'm that sorry for ye, Mhairi lass,' said Ma Mackenzie. 'Your ma was a good woman, God rest her soul. But you're doing a fine job. She'd be right proud o' you.'

Annys followed Mhairi round the room, tugging at her skirts and wailing over and over, 'Where's Ma? When's Ma coming back?' until Mhairi gave up all pretence and said fiercely, 'She's not coming back, Annys. Not ever.' But when the child howled in fresh anguish, Mhairi snatched her up and cuddled her close, saying over and over, 'Don't cry, love, I'm your ma now. And your da's still here, see? And Tom and Willy and Lorn. Hush, Annys, hush. It's all right.'

But it was not all right. Looking at her father, desolate at the fireside, at her brother Tom, determinedly brave, at her younger brothers, wandering lost and forlorn in the unfamiliar company, at her little sister, still sobbing on Mhairi's breast, she knew that it would never be all right again.

'Don't despair, Mhairi,' said a quiet voice at her side and she looked up to see Alex Grant standing beside her, his face full of sorrow and concern. 'Be brave, as you always are. And true. You'll win through one day.' Then he bent his head and kissed her on the cheek and the first light shone in the darkness of her misery.

Part 2

Lettice Adam was restless. This winter season was proving as disappointing as the last to the point where she almost wished she had followed her father's wishes and stayed at Silvercairns. What had seemed fun last year seemed merely tedious now. Her dressmaker, hairdresser, furrier and milliner bored her. Aunt Blackwell drove her to distraction, with her incessant talk of our dear Queen and whether or not she would visit Scotland again, as if it mattered one way or the other, for if she did she would hardly be likely to come as far north as Aberdeen. As for Lettice's silly, twittering friends, with their endless chatter about the latest fashions and whether they would line their new season's cloaks with velvet or with satin, she was beginning to find their company equally irritating. But most of all the young men of her social circle bored her to the point where she could almost have looked upon one of her father's 'old fools' with tolerance. At least they talked about something solid. Investments, contracts, profits. Those were tedious, too, of course, but in a different way. Like porridge. It was difficult to say what Hugo's circle talked about: except horses, drink and girls. Lettice admired her younger brother. He was light-hearted and handsome, popular with everybody (except perhaps his father) but his relentless frivolity could be tedious. Should it ever come to a straight choice, which God forbid, it might be better to spend one's life eating porridge than to exist on endless raspberry sorbet.

Perhaps the weather had something to do with it? Short, dark days and long, blustery nights when the wind howled in the chimneys of the Adam town house, rattled shutters at windows, stirred bed-curtains and lifted mats on draughty floors. Days when the fires sulked and refused to burn, when rain pelted the windows in relentless sheets, or when the sea haar crept over the city and blanketed everything in clinging mist. But she was just as restless and dissatisfied when the sun shone from a cloudless sky and a hard frost crusted everything with white.

She almost envied Fergus his work at the quarry and she certainly envied Hugo his college life. Though when she had rashly said as much one dinner-time, and a Marischal College professor who was one of the guests had arranged for her to attend a public lecture, she had lost interest after the first five minutes. The truth was she was hungry for something, but she did not know for what.

She tried her hand at housekeeping, but finding it comparatively easy her interest palled. Besides, what was Aunt Blackwell for but to keep house? Aunt Blackwell bore the brunt of Miss Adam's dissatisfaction but, as a poor relation who knew when she was well off, she prudently kept her comments to herself and by so doing unwittingly increased her niece's irritation.

So when Hugo arrived home one blustery Saturday afternoon in early November with a handful of companions, all in the liveliest of spirits, and announced that they were *en route* for a Temperance meeting at which the uncle of one of them was speaking, Lettice welcomed the opportunity as godsent and insisted that he take her too.

'Father cannot possibly mind,' she told Aunt Blackwell virtuously, 'especially if you come too.' She paused long enough for her aunt to think she meant it and to regret the loss of her afternoon nap, then said with mischievous solicitude, 'But of course, Aunt Blackwell dear, if you do not feel strong enough to venture out this afternoon, and it certainly is a little blustery, then to set your mind at rest, Fanny and Amelia shall come with me instead.' Notes were immediately dispatched to the Wyness and Macdonald houses and half an hour later, the ladies suitably clad in fur-trimmed cloaks and bonnets, their hands concealed in ribboned muffs, and the gentlemen in overcoats and tall silk hats, the party set off down the Kirkgate and into George Street.

The meeting had already started when they arrived and the hall was almost full, mostly of virtuous ladies of a charitable mien, though with a sprinkling of gentlemen, there either as escorts to the ladies or because of their own ecclesiastical or reforming zeal. A pair of gas lamps hissed their yellow light over the platform which had been tastefully adorned with evergreens and a small fire struggled, unsuccessfully, to combat the autumn chill. The audience was, as was to be expected, sober.

Thus the somewhat noisy entrance of Hugo's party provided the opportunity for several pointed reminders of the evils of drink, the way it impaired the senses, squandered the talents, damaged good manners and generally destroyed the fabric of civilized living. Hugo and his friends took it in good part, interposing only the most genial of remarks and the occasional slurred 'Tally-ho'. When the reverend uncle stood up to speak, Hugo loudly ordered absolute silence and two minutes later was fast asleep. So were three of his four companions, while the fourth, the nephew, stared in glassy-eyed concentration at the speaker and, whenever he paused for breath or effect, mumbled, 'Hear, hear.'

Fanny Wyness fidgeted in her chair and was soon whispering behind her muff to Amelia Macdonald, but for once Lettice listened to the speaker with close attention. She had noticed one or two familiar faces in the audience, including her father's bank manager, Duncan Forbes, and, to her surprise, the one-time foreman of her father's quarry. Mackinnon, was it? When she had insisted that Hugo bring her too, it had been purely for the diversion. She had had no interest in the social aspects of the meeting, or in the insidious damage that alcohol could do to society and most particularly to the poor and ignorant. Nothing in her life had yet stirred or jolted her enough to make her see anything beyond the rim of her own comfortable nest. But as she looked about her she was intrigued by the social mix of the audience and by the possibility that Temperance might be some sort of new vogue. She was also intrigued by the speaker. On the platform of reverend gentlemen, mostly elderly, bewhiskered and stern, Hamish Dunn stood out like a sunflower in a gravel pit. He was younger than Lettice had expected, being no more than thirty: more like a cousin than an uncle. He was tall and broad with a build more suited to the smithy or the mason's yard, or to striding kilted through the Highland heather, than to the constrictions of the pulpit, and his hair was a distinctly unclerical red. When he spoke it was with the soft cadences of the native Gaelic speaker and Lettice remembered that Hugo's friend Andrew was from somewhere in the West. Certainly Hamish Dunn's speech was far more interesting than that lecture at Marischal College and, remembering her father's extensive wine cellar and his penchant for good brandy, she resolved, with mischief, to repeat some of the more trenchant points at her father's next dinner party, after the claret had circulated freely. But apparently it was whisky that was the greatest enemy.

'Do you know,' declared the speaker, after half an hour of exhortation, 'that if all the grain which this country converts into intoxicating drink were baked into quartern loaves they would form a road twenty-five feet broad which would stretch from London to New York?'

But Hugo had woken up. 'I dispute that, sir!'

'I assure you, Mr Adam, it is Mr Adam, is it not?' and the speaker leaned forward to verify the point, thus neatly ensuring, as Hugo realized afterwards and too late, that the entire hall would do the same, 'I assure you, sir, that my mathematical calculations are correct.'

'Correct they may be, sir,' conceded Hugo, enjoying himself. 'In fact, I will go further. Correct they *ought* to be or our Scottish education system is much at fault. But correct or not, they are patently ridiculous. A road of *bread*, on the *sea*? The loaves would bob about on the waves, for one thing, and for another they would go soggy and disintegrate long before they reached New York, and the fish or the seagulls would gobble up every crumb.'

The few appreciative giggles were quickly drowned in a chorus of 'Sh!' and 'Sit down' from all around them and several of those in front turned round to glare their disapproval.

Hamish Dunn smiled with what seemed genuine amusement, then said kindly, 'Mr Adam, I will make allowances for your youth and inexperience and also, dare I say it, for your condition which does far more than any words of mine could do to prove the rightness of our cause.' Murmurs of approval from the audience. 'And as you find my first analogy inappropriate, or perhaps are merely unable to see beyond the analogy to the substance, let me try to illustrate the magnitude of the problem in a simpler way, more suited to your understanding.'

Clever, thought Lettice with approval. One in the eye for Hugo. She was beginning to enjoy herself.

'Suppose those same loaves were laid end to end,' continued Dunn,' they would *three times* encircle the globe!'

'Not the same loaves, sir,' argued Hugo, unabashed and

warming to his theme, 'because, as I said, they would be soggy, if not already disintegrated. Now had you said an *equivalent number* of loaves . . .'

But two burly officials were making their way along the row towards Hugo and before he could elaborate his argument further, he had been lifted bodily and ejected from the hall. A sudden draught and a swirl of autumn leaves accompanied the slamming of the door. In the momentary silence which followed, his voice came cheerfully clear from the street outside, 'Cast your bread upon the waters!'

Blushing with fury and mortification, Lettice collected the rest of the party, except the speaker's dutiful nephew, and followed.

Out in the street the thin sunlight struck bright, the air fresh after the constrictions of the hall. Leaves swirled in golden drifts across the cassies and from somewhere overhead and to the north came the urgent clamour of geese on the wing. They found Hugo leaning happily against a wall and apparently unrepentant.

'Look,' he pointed upward to the long arrow-head of trailing birds. 'Geese. They're frightfully clever. Know where they're going and go there. Can see for miles. Your uncle's bread road wouldn't last five minutes once they spotted it.' He looked round for Andrew Dunn and not finding him, said, 'Oh dear. I hope old Andrew doesn't get court-martialled for bringing in riff-raff.'

'Hugo, you are an ass,' said Lettice angrily. She realized she did not want to be classed with Hugo's riff-raff, not by Hamish Dunn anyway. 'I was just beginning to enjoy the afternoon and you had to go and spoil it.'

'Apologies, old girl. No need for temper-tantrums. Tell you what. I'll write Andrew's uncle a fulsome apology, putting it all down to the demon drink! Then all will be forgiven.'

'I doubt it,' she snapped. 'Did you see who was in there? Father will hear from half a dozen different people by tea-time what a spectacle you made of yourself. And of me.'

'But, Lettice, you have always said you don't care tuppence what anyone says.'

'Hugo, shut up!' Nevertheless, he was right. She had boasted often of her indifference to public opinion. But now she found she wanted Hamish Dunn to think well of her. It was silly, of course. He was only a preacher with a bee in his bonnet about drink and probably had not even noticed she was there. She was angry with herself as much as with her brother when she said irritably, 'For goodness sake, Hugo, pull yourself together. You are in enough trouble already. And you will be in even more if you arrive home in this state. You would be well advised to walk about in the fresh air until your head is cleared. In fact, let us all walk to Split-the-Winds and back.'

'Do you really think we ought?' asked Fanny Wyness, consulting her fob-watch. 'Mama will be expecting me.'

'No, she won't. Not yet. We are all at a Temperance meeting, remember, and it cannot possibly finish for another hour.'

'But suppose one of those women saw us leave and tells Mama? I am sure I saw Mrs Burgess there and Mrs Farquharson.'

'For goodness sake, Fanny, the whole town will know by tonight anyway! You left because you were feeling faint, or ill or bored. What does it matter? Anyway,' she finished, losing patience, 'Hugo and I are going for a walk. You can come or not as you please. It is all the same to me.' With that, she turned her back and set off up the road, dragging Hugo unwillingly behind her. She did not bother to turn round. If she had, perhaps the rest would have followed. As it was they looked at each other, hesitated, then with one accord turned the other way and went dutifully home. Fanny Wyness was right: there had been too many familiar faces in that Temperance audience and Hugo Adam had got them into enough trouble for one day. As for Fanny, she had remembered just in time that if they walked to Split-the-Winds they would eventually pass her father's granite yard and possibly even her father himself.

The Wyness granite yard had been in business for over twenty years and was both well established and prosperous. Macdonalds in Constitution Street had been the first yard to introduce a granite polishing machine, but George Wyness had quickly followed suit and work that had once taken many months of arduous manual labour with sea-sand and polishing blocks could now be executed in a matter of days. Granite to be polished was laid flat on bogies and passed mechanically to and fro under cast-iron rings which scoured the surface with sand and water so that only the smallest and most intricate work was still done entirely by hand.

Legend had it that Macdonald had got the idea on a visit to the British Museum in London where he had seen polished granite from the land of the Pharaohs. He had gone home, experimented, noted the success of steam power in a neighbouring factory, and adapted it for his own purposes. Whatever the truth of the story, the result was beyond dispute and the first polished granite tombstone sent to London had caused widespread interest. That was over ten years ago, but recently Macdonalds had scored another triumph. They had revived the art of portrait statuary in granite – 'an art forgotten since the Ptolemies,' as they proudly claimed – and the fifth Duke of Gordon now stood immortalized in a fourteen-ton monument of Dancing Cairns granite, on a pedestal which two apprentices had dressed and polished in a mere three weeks. It was a triumph which the rival granite yards found hard to bear and more than one of Macdonald's workers had been approached with offers of higher wages to tempt them away, or with money to part with the templates for the more intricate monumental work.

George Wyness would dearly have liked the publicity of that Duke of Gordon statue for his own yard, but his workmen had neither the skill nor the knowledge to attempt such a thing. Yet. His yard made hearthstones, mantelpieces and headstones, plinths and ornamental cornices, even balustrades, but the transfer of a plaster statue into granite was something he had never dreamed of. Now that the breakthrough had been made, however, there was no reason why not. There were dukes enough and princes. And no reason why what had previously been executed in marble should not be rendered equally well in granite. Granite was strong and durable, sufficiently varied in colour and shade to suit all tastes, and when polished was virtually unaffected by weather as the rain glanced off and ran away before it could lodge its destructive acids in the surface. In fact, granite was the ideal medium for public monuments to past heroes and kings. All that was needed was skill and capital and Wyness knew from long experience that the latter could usually buy the former.

It was the latter, however, that was in short supply. With the inexorable advance of the railway northward, he had invested heavily, as other businessmen were doing, in the various railway companies which seemed to spring up almost overnight. The railways would bring both building work and profit. As an investor and a granite merchant he would reap the benefit twice over. But the railway had so far reached little north of Perth and dividends had been small and few. In time they would come in plenty, but meanwhile he could well do with extra capital to develop his yard.

That was where his daughter Fanny came into the picture. It had long been George Wyness's aim that his daughter should marry Fergus Adam. An alliance between the two families would consolidate what had for years been a reasonably good working arrangement. But lately Old Man Adam had become too fond of negotiating contracts direct with the customer instead of channelling business through Wyness's yard and twice recently, when Wyness had required a particularly fine-grained granite block for a double tomb, Adam had kept him waiting more than a month. When Wyness had protested, Adam had told him, quite curtly, that he had a big order to fulfil and if Wyness couldn't wait his turn then he'd best go elsewhere.

It was the idea of the big order which had unsettled Wyness as much as anything. His life was as comfortable as he could wish it, his house in Skene Square commodious and elegant, his garden productive, his larder well stocked and his cellar more so. His wife was contented and his daughter well provided for. Moreover he was a figure of some standing in Aberdeen circles, with a seat on the council, and his wife had her charitable committees. He even kept a phaeton, a smart double-seater with hood and German shutters, though mostly he preferred to go on foot. Yet the idea of Adam making all that fortune had irritated him, and, to tell the truth, made him envious.

Monuments were all very well as a good, steady source of income, but there was no doubt that the big fortunes were to be made in the building trade. With Aberdeen expanding daily, with roads, houses, bridges, and goodness knows what else springing up wherever you looked, there was an endless market for good building granite on their own doorstep, but when that market extended far outside the town and south as far as London, even beyond the seas, the opportunities were limitless. There was a big harbour development planned, too, and when the railway arrived . . . Wyness had started his yard from scratch, little more than twenty years ago. Now he had two rows of sheds, with a polishing lathe and a cutting saw, with bogies and even a small crane, and a workforce of two dozen skilled men as well as apprentices and saw-boys and labouring lads to clean up the yard. He had done well. With a bigger yard he could do better. But it was the yards with their own quarries that did best of all, and it had long been Wyness's aim to unite with the powerful Adam family. What better way to do it than by a union of their children?

Fanny, he knew, was willing. Already, with his full approval, she spent a gratifying amount of time with Lettice Adam, not merely at dancing classes and suchlike, but socially too now and then. Friendship with the sister was the first step along the desired road and Fanny was a good-hearted and obedient girl. She would be content to be guided by her father, especially when that guiding steered her in the direction of Fergus Adam who had always been a good-looking lad and, with manhood and increased responsibility, had become positively handsome. Unfortunately, he had shown little interest in marriage and none at all in Fanny. Perhaps it was time to begin the campaign?

So, when Wyness saw Fergus's brother Hugo and their sister approaching down the lane on that autumn afternoon, he hurried from his inner office and out into the yard to greet them.

'Ah, Mr Hugo, glad to see you taking the air. So bracing at this time o' year. And Miss Lettice, looking charming, as always. What like's your father?'

'He is well,' said Lettice, with slight surprise. She knew for a fact that Wyness and her father had met over some business deal only yesterday. 'And yourself?'

'Well enough, well enough. I canna complain. But come away in. I'll send a lad for tea for Miss Lettice while you and I, Mr Hugo, take a wee look around. Then you can tell your father how that last block of Silvercairns granite has taken the polish. Like a mirror it is, though I say it myself.'

'I'd love to, Mr Wyness,' said Hugo solemnly, 'but I am afraid we cannot stay. We are expecting guests.'

'Come on now, laddie, one wee minute will make no difference, surely? Step inside, step inside,' and he held open the gate for them with such insistence that there was no escape. Lettice lifted her skirts distastefully as she stepped into the yard which was littered with dust and gravel, broken bits of stone and slabs of granite of various sizes and in various stages of preparation. From the open doorway of the sawing shed leaked a small river of mud though the comparative silence indicated that sawing had mercifully stopped for the day. It was growing late on a Saturday afternoon, but men were still working in various parts of the yard, chipping away with mall and puncheon, or tracing lettering on to headstones by means of a template. In one part of the yard was a stack of rough blocks, awaiting their turn at the saw, but there were also many examples of work in progress.

Having refused tea, Lettice glanced idly over the various inscriptions, while her small foot tapped in growing impatience as Hugo dutifully inspected piece after piece of his father's now-polished granite. Some pieces were covered with cloths from prying eyes, others protected by straw or wood shavings in wooden packing cases, awaiting dispatch. Hugo moved solemnly after Mr Wyness, nodding approval, and playing the dutiful son. No doubt, thought Lettice sourly, he thinks that present rectitude will somehow cancel out his earlier misdemeanour.

Sacred to the memory of . . . To the dear memory of . . . Hic requiescit . . . Lettice's eyes moved restlessly over the monuments, seeking something other than the endless *In memory of* and saw a small pink granite slab with a curved top, the picture of a dove with an olive branch in its beak roughly traced on the stone and underneath, *In the hope of everlasting joy*. The stone caught her attention by its modest simplicity, its clear faith, and its lack of all pomposity or pretension. She was looking for a name when 'Headstane' Wyness and her brother came up behind her.

'I see you are admiring our handiwork, Miss Lettice. Yon's a special order . . . Not that they're not all special to the relatives of the deceased. Dinna misunderstand me, but the customer supplied his own pattern for that one. Our pattern book wouldna do, seemingly. And I have to admit it's a bonny design. Pretty, isn't it? Fine for a young lady.'

'Yes,' agreed Lettice and was careful to avoid Hugo's eye as she added, 'I will bear it in mind.'

'Not that the deceased was young, now I think of it. A mother who died in childbirth. Tragic, tragic.' Briefly he adopted his professional face, then went on, 'But I expect you know the party. Wife of one of your workmen, Mr Hugo. Name of Diack?' Hugo shook his head and Lettice raised a questioning eyebrow. 'Ah, well, maybe I'm wrong. But you'll know the artist – he's one o' yours right enough. That lad over there wi' the Adam delivery cart. Which reminds me. You can thank your father, Mr Hugo, for sending round the block I wanted wi' such speed. I said I needed it sharpish like, but I hadna expected it afore Monday, and . . .'

'Artist, did you say?' interrupted Hugo and looked with surprise at the youth who was holding the horses' heads to steady them while workmen manoeuvred the crane to unload the stone. 'But he's just a stable lad.'

'Maybe, but yon design's been greatly admired. I've had several inquiries already for similar and I can see we're going to have to include it in our book.'

'Then you'd best speak to my father about the copying rights,' joked Hugo and slapped Mr Wyness playfully on the back. 'It being an Adam design.' Then he took his sister's arm, said a cheerful goodbye and escorted her out of the yard.

'That should give the devious rascal a sleepless night or two,' he said cheerfully when they had left the Wyness yard far enough behind them.

'But does that boy really work for us? I've never noticed him.'

'Neither have I – but it would not do to let on. And he was with the Adam delivery cart right enough. Come to think of it, I might have seen him around the place. Surly sort of fellow. Never speaks.'

'At least no one could ever lay that charge at your door,' said Lettice. But the remark reminded her of the Temperance meeting and Hamish Dunn and yet again she hoped he did not think too badly of her.

'You must write that letter at once,' she said when they reached home. 'Before Father has a chance to hear of the matter. At least then you will appear to be contrite, even if you are not.'

'How well you know me, sister.' But, contrite or not, he went straight to his room and was engaged in writing the necessary letter when he heard the front door crash open and his father's ominous voice.

'Hugo! Come here this instant. I want a word with you!'

'Oh-oh. Too late,' said Hugo, but there was no escape. He screwed up the half-written letter, tossed it into a corner and stood up. He might as well get it over with.

From across the yard, Donal Grant watched them studying the gravestone and willed them with all his being to go away. The dove was for Mhairi and her poor dead mother, not for all the world to stare at and copy for themselves.

He had done the drawing as a love-offering, to cheer Mhairi in her grief, and because he knew it would look perfect on Mrs Diack's grave. It had taken him weeks before he was satisfied. He had even written the inscription, in the sort of lettering which he knew would look right. He had watched the masons working and knew how such things were done so that when Mr Diack gave the drawing to Mr Wyness, it was easy for the carpenter to make a pattern and a template copy so that the mason could prick it out on to the stone. He had drawn the shape of the headstone, too, and the gentle curves of its top. He had taken Alex one Sunday to the Wyness yard and pointed out the colour of the stone he wanted – a pink Corrennie – and Alex had explained it all to Mhairi and her father. He had explained to Mackinnon too, who told the Lodge, and somehow arrangements were made and the money found. It had taken a good while, one way and another, but now, a year after Mrs Diack's death, the stone was almost ready. The earth would be well settled on the grave and soon the stone would be set in place.

The nearest Clydesdale lifted a heavy fetlocked foot and let it fall with the ring of metal on stone. The animal was growing restless and Donal laid a soothing hand on the powerful neck to quieten him. He felt the muscles under the thick velvet skin, the warmth and sweat and power, the obedient acceptance of indignity, and willed all his loving understanding to flow through his fingers and into the animal's being. But the last rope had been secured and the crane was already raising the granite block to swing it out of the cart and on to one of the Wyness trolleys, which would convey it into the cutting shed to await the saw's attention first thing Monday morning. Thence the slab would pass on to the polishing lathe before being returned to the yard to be ornamented and lettered and given the finishing touches. It was a process Donal knew by heart now, spending so much time, as he did, motionless at his horse's head, and watching everything that went on. He had grown used to keeping his eyes alert and watchful, to seeing behind as well as in front of him, to looking to left and right, above and below, like a wary, threatened bird. To see was to know and sight was the only means he had of contact with that silent, mouthing, violent world. Sight and touch. But touch could take many forms and Donal was acquainted with the rough as well as the gentle.

But his horses were never rough, great, heavy-shouldered beasts though they were. They understood and loved him and he had only to lay a hand on a flank, to twitch a rein, and they obeyed. Donal was happy with the horses, except when one of the men who did not know him came into the stable yard and shouted – and shouted again, and struck him if Donal did not do what was required. Afterwards, Alex always knew, and would brood with an anger that frightened Donal. He did not want Alex to shoulder his burdens. He wanted no retaliatory violence on his account. But most of all he did not want Alex to be hurt, as he surely would be if he fought Donal's battles for him. So Donal tried to conceal from his brother any hurt he might have suffered, deliberate or unwitting, and while Alex might suspect that someone had tormented Donal, or struck him, Donal himself would never tell. The bruises were nothing. He had fallen, that was all. Baffled, Alex would give in, but he would watch his brother with particular care in the days that followed, though at the quarry there were long hours when it was not possible. Donal would lead his team of horses down the long spiral path to the quarry floor, collect his load, lead them up again, while Alex worked at the quarry face, or on shaping the blocks of fallen rock. But sometimes Donal was given a written order and sent into Aberdeen and then Alex had no means of telling who, if anyone, had tormented him. But as Donal grew taller and stronger, Alex's worry eased. Donal might have abhorred violence, but at least he had strength and muscle enough to resist should the need arise. And one day, when Alex owned his own yard as he fully intended to do, then Donal would work with him and be safe.

But until that glorious day arrived, they both continued to work for the Adams in the quarry at Silvercairns, with Tom Diack and his father and half a hundred other men.

For Alex had been right in one thing: the funeral over, the Diacks, father and son, returned to the quarry and found their jobs awaiting them. Though for how long in the father's case became an increasing worry. Remembering Mhairi's anxious face as her father coughed and fought for breath, or stared silent into the fire with an expression of grey despair, Donal clenched his fists and willed the Adams to keep Mr Diack on, to give him lighter work, to pay him more. After all, Cassie Diack had worked at Silvercairns quarry since before Mr Fergus was born.

Remembering Mr Fergus, Donal shifted uncomfortably from one foot to the other and looked yet again to see if the load was safely stowed away in the Wyness sheds. Mr Fergus had been stern and left Donal in no doubt that he was to hurry into town and hurry back again. Besides, it would soon be dark and though the horses knew their way well enough, the darkness made Donal nervous.

But the last rope had been loosed, the tailboard snapped back into position, and Wyness's men gave both the horses and their keeper a friendly slap to indicate the work was done. 'Aye, aye,' said one, 'That's you away,' and 'Right enough,' said the other. 'Mind how you go, lad.' Then they raised their hands in friendly farewell and Donal did the same. He got on well with Wyness's men. They treated him right, gave him tea, let him warm his hands at the fire if he'd long to wait, and accepted him as one of them. They knew not to tell him things when his back was turned, but to indicate by gestures, or to draw. Most important of all, they knew he was not stupid, and never treated him as if he were. Unlike some people. Remembering, Donal led his horses smartly out into the side lane and thence to the street. Here he leapt neatly up on to the empty cart and touched the horses into a steady walk towards St Andrew Street and the Upper Denburn road. Mr Fergus would be waiting.

He was skirting the back of Gordon's Hospital when a dray cart emerged from a side entrance and he pulled up his own horses to allow the dray cart right of way. He did not hear the sound of approaching hoofs from behind him, nor the voice bellowing in fury, 'You again! You should have been back at the quarry an hour ago! We don't pay you to moon about town in company time. What have you got to say for yourself, eh?'

The dray cart had moved off safely and Donal, unsuspecting, gathered the reins to follow. He looked briefly to right and left, then over his shoulder, and just had time to see the arrogant young face, the twisted mouth and raised, gloved hand, before the horseman lashed his whip down hard across Donal's shoulders. 'That will teach you to answer when you are spoken to, you idle fellow! Now get back to Silvercairns at the double!'

Lizzie Lennox saw the exchange from the corner of Blackfriars Street and whistled softly to herself. 'I wonder what's put young Mr Hugo into such a temper? Had another row with his father, like as not.' Lizzie's cousin Eppie, though inclined to act superior because of her position, was not above gossip, and the whole of Mitchell's Court and Galen's too knew that young Mr Hugo and his father did not get on. Mr Hugo was by way of being one o' they student laddies but seemingly he spent more time in the taverns than in his lectures. Not that Lizzie blamed him. She couldna see the pleasure in all that book learning. She'd had enough o' yon reading and writing at school to last her a lifetime and if she were that Hugo's father she'd put him to the quarry wi' the rest o' them and make him do an honest day's work. He'd be the boss one day anyway, like as not, wi' yon Fergus a sickly-looking sort of a lad to her way o' thinking, and a boss couldna be a good one unless he knew the work himself.

'Why did that man hit Lackie's Donal?' asked Annys, tugging at Lizzie's skirt. 'Was he being bad?'

'Don't be daft, Annys, you know fine Donal's never bad. He doesna know how.'

'Then why did the man hit him, Lizzie? Why?'

'For pity's sake, Annys, how would I know why?' snapped Lizzie. 'I'm fair sick to death o' your questions. Why this, why that, all day long. It's enough to drive a body out o' her wits.' Lizzie Lennox had had a frustrating day, one way and another, what with Squinty Jessie Bruce being caught stealing an apple in the market and Lizzie having to pay for it cos the wretched child had bitten it and the wifie refused to believe it was in all innocence. 'I've seen you afore,' she had shouted over and over, 'wi' your gang o' thieving bairns. Wicked it is, downright wicked! They should be in the poorhouse, the lot o' them, and as for you, lass, the penitentiary's too good for you, leading bairns astray. You need transporting!' and much else besides till she'd collected quite a crowd. Then the wifie'd demanded her money, over and over, threatening Lizzie with the watchman and goodness knows what else, till she'd had to hand over the tuppence she was saving to buy muffins. And when she'd fetched Squinty a slap round the ear, with a heartfelt 'Now see what you've done, ye daft quine!' yon stupid Henderson boy had kept whining, 'But it's nay Jessie's fault, Lizzie. You told her to do it.' She'd be right glad when Eppie got her that kitchen job she'd promised. Anything would be better than trailing this lot around town.

'Why are you cross, today, Lizzie?' asked Annys, tears welling up into her solemn eyes. 'I don't like it when you're cross.'

Lizzie glared and the Henderson boy, trying to make amends, said quickly, 'Let's go to the theatre! We'll maybe see the folk arriving for the evening show.' All the children, except Annys, jumped up and down and squealed, 'Please! Please!'

'If you all promise to shut up and behave,' said Lizzie, relenting, 'I might, just might mind, take you to smell the coffee roasting at Angus Fraser's. Then you can watch the folk going in and out of the glassblowing exhibition next door. They say yon mannie does a rare likeness of wee dogs in glass and we'll maybe see one if we're lucky. Would you like that?'

But Annys would not be pacified. 'I don't want to see a glass doggie,' she gulped, 'I want Mhairi. I want to go home!'

'Well, ye canna, so shut your mou'. Mhairi telt ye to come

wi' me and you know fine you've to do as Mhairi says. Mhairi's at yon Working Society place and she'll nay be back till late, so ye'll come wi' me and like it.'

But she picked Annys up and carried her till the child's sobs ceased, and when Lizzie's arms got tired and she put her down again, she still held the child's hand. It wasn't Annys's fault she had no mother, poor wee mite, and Mhairi'd be home soon enough.

The object of the Aberdeen Ladies' Working Society was to employ poor, unsupported women of ascertained respectability to make clothing that the rich might buy, to give away in charity, and the poor might buy for themselves at the lowest possible cost. Mhairi had been lucky to find employment with them, being not strictly 'unsupported', but she was an excellent needlewoman and her stockings in particular had impressed the committee. Mrs Wyness had been full of praises and the more so when she heard of Mhairi's efforts to bring up her brothers and her little sister and to care for her sickly father who, though still in work, was likely to lose it at any moment with, they feared, his life. Mhairi Diack was most worthy of employment and, they agreed privately, it would keep her from temptation until such time as she married. Besides, at the time the minister put Mhairi's name forward there were no other suitable applicants, those few who did apply being really more suited to the poorhouse or to parish charity.

Mostly, Mhairi worked at home, for the committee had had satisfactory reports as to its cleanliness and suitability. But on occasions she was required to go to the Society's sale room in Marischal Street, to undertake alterations or repairs, or to help check the stock. The committee had early discovered that Mhairi was intelligent, quick, honest, that she wrote a neat hand and had a good head for figures. When, as now, the Society held a sale of accumulated stock, Mhairi was an invaluable helper. As a special token of their appreciation, she was offered an extra discount should she wish to purchase from stock. Mhairi had matured in the last year, grown taller and more shapely. She knew she was not ill-favoured and she longed to dress herself in pretty clothes, to make the most of herself, to be elegant and ladylike and attractive, but though in the six months she had worked for them she had often seen garments she yearned to buy for herself, she never did. Her mother's few clothes could be made over, and there were the boys and Annys to keep neat and clean. Besides, they all had to eat, and on top of that she needed money for the school fees and her father's Balsam of Aniseed.

'Look after them all,' her mother had said, and Mhairi was doing her best. But it was an endless battle against want and despair. Occasionally, in her darkest moments, she would open the lid of the clothes kist and gaze at Fergus Adam's folded linen handkerchief with its embroidered monogram, symbol of that other life of cleanliness and comfort which her mother's death had put beyond her reach for ever. She had not glimpsed Mr Adam since that day, not even in St Nicholas church, and had it not been for the evidence of that folded scrap of best hemmed linen, might have thought the whole incident no more than a dream. As her whole life before her mother's death seemed a dream, a happy, trusting dream from which she had been brutally woken into cold reality.

Now, she had little time for dreams. Her whole energies were taken up with making ends meet, holding the family together, comforting Annys, watching that Lorn and Willy didn't go off the rails, keeping them all clean and neatly clothed, seeing that Tom and her father had food enough for hungry working men (though her father's appetite was meagre enough), maintaining some semblance of cheerful normality and always worrying . . . Was she doing what her ma wanted? Was she bringing up Annys right? Most of all she worried about her father. Keep them all from the poorhouse, her ma had begged, but suppose her father were to die . . . ? I'm doing my best, Ma, she would plead, knowing with simple faith that somewhere her mother could hear her. Tell me what else to do and I'll do it, gladly. But she saw no comforting visions, heard no voices . . . except that memory of her mother's words, pounding over and over like her own heartbeat, 'See none of them go to the poorhouse.' She and Tom earned little enough. Without their father's wage, what would they do? So she watched over her father with all the anxiety of a mother for a sickly, precious child and dreaded the day which she knew was approaching with inexorable, deadly tread.

Her father rose as before, uncomplaining, at five; washed, ate his porridge, gathered his tools and left with Tom before dawning, to walk the two miles to Silvercairns. But whereas Tom returned weary, ravenous, but physically satisfied with his day, her father came home from work grey-faced and drained, hardly spoke, and spent the evening curled over his coughing chest at the fireside, staring into the embers. Once, when she caught him unawares, she saw tears glistening on his cheeks and knew that he still mourned his wife's passing though it was more than a year now since her ma had died. Her brother Tom had lost much of his cheery optimism since his mother's death and almost overnight had grown more serious and mature, while Mhairi herself felt as worn and weary as any middle-aged housewife, without even the comforting companionship of a husband's love. Once she had caught Tom's eye above their father's bent head and knew that he felt as she did: Cassie Diack was already wearying towards his wife's land o' the leal and one day soon the responsibility for the family would lie entirely on their shoulders. She knew Tom would not fail her, but he was still only an apprentice and, Oh Ma, she cried in silent anguish, however will we manage when Da's gone?

So she worked at her sewing for the Ladies' Working Society in every available moment and in spite of the long hours spent stitching at tucks and gussets and plain calico seams, Mhairi enjoyed her work. It brought in little enough, to be sure, but as the ladies of the committee justified it, 'the Parish rarely offers such poor females more than a shilling a week', and it was a connection, though a tenuous one, with that other life of ladylike, untroubled ease. Besides, it was a pleasure to sew the crisp, new material though it was only plain flannel or cotton and never satin, scotch velvet or the latest velours d'Orient.

'Slave labour, that's what it is,' said Lizzie scornfully, dropping in one afternoon, as she often did since Mrs Diack's death, on her way to or from some errand for her mother. 'I wouldn't do it if it was me.'

Mhairi didn't answer. There were plenty of things Lizzie did that Mhairi would never dream of doing, but there was no point in mentioning them. Besides, it wasn't just the money. How could she explain that with the little ones at school, her father and brother at work, and the room to herself, Mhairi had found that the soothing occupation of her sewing enabled her to push her anxieties aside for a while and retrieve a little of those childhood dreams, though since her mother's death, she knew them to be what they were: impossible dreams, as far out of her reach as the brightest star?

Sometimes she would imagine that her cramped tenement room in the wilderness behind the Guestrow was a sewing-room at Silvercairns, in the west wing perhaps, up an attic stair, with a view over flower gardens and rolling pastures; or possibly a room off the family nursery with chintz-covered chairs and sunlight. She would imagine she was sewing petticoats for the young lady of the house, or a walking dress for when Miss Lettice went out in the carriage. Another day she would be in a turret room of the Adam town house, stitching a ball gown for Miss Lettice to wear to the winter Assembly. Once, daringly, she even imagined herself stitching a monogram on a gentleman's linen handkerchief, but when imagination led her on to that gentleman's shirt she thrust the idea quickly aside, with mingled embarrassment and shame. But she sang quietly to herself as she stitched and for a while would manage to forget the noise and the overcrowding and the constant battle against dirt and disease.

'Slave labour,' repeated Lizzie, with satisfaction. 'One day they'll have to pay decent wages, or they'll get no one to work for them, Eppie says. There was a third o' the servants not engaged last Feein' mart and no wonder wi' the wages offered. I wouldna work half a year for one pound.'

'What would you do?' asked Mhairi, not really listening. 'Starve?' She bit off her thread and inspected the finished tuck. It was neat enough for Miss Lettice herself, though it was only destined for someone's housemaid.

'Nae me,' boasted Lizzie. 'I'll get a job wi' real wages, in a rich house in the West End and nae as a scullery maid, neither.' Lizzie had had a brief and turbulent job in a Broad Street scullery from which she had been dismissed after less than a week, for helping herself liberally from the ale barrel and the raisin jar. 'Well it's plain daft,' she had protested, 'expecting folk to work on an empty belly wi' all that food and drink going to waste. I was showing them their Christian charity, that's all.' Her employers had not seen it that way, nor her own father who had promptly beaten her, 'for disgracing his name'. 'Some disgrace,' Lizzie had boasted bravely through her tears. 'A handful of raisins indeed! I could disgrace the bastard good and proper if I put my mind to it – and I will one day, if he doesna stop mistreatin' me. Serve him right.'

Now, Lizzie watched Mhairi thread her needle afresh and begin on the next tuck. Then she said, 'No, I'll not starve. I'll do all right for myself, one way or another. You'll see. Even for folks without jobs there's soup kitchens and the like and plenty o' rich folk wantin' to feel good by giving away what they've finished with to the likes of us. Besides,' she added, deliberately to shock, 'there's always the quay. That Maggie Henderson had a new gown last week, wi' velvet trimming and three rows o' tucks to her skirt. She's a pair o' new shoes too and ye dinna buy them wi' slave labour – leastways only *white* slaves – and Bess Pirie's got a cloak wi' real fur. Easy work, too,' she added as Mhairi bent her head over her sewing and made no answer. 'Do it lyin' on yer back, nae bother.'

'Lizzie!' said Mhairi, shocked into speech. 'You'll not speak about such things in my house.'

'My house! Hark at her ladyship!'

'And in front of children, too.' Whatever would her ma have said? Mhairi looked quickly over her shoulder to where Annys was curled up on the bed in the inside room, thumb firmly in her mouth and fast asleep. 'I hope you never mention such wickedness to Annys and the little ones, because if so I'll . . . I'll . . .' Mhairi searched for a suitable threat.

'What? Take her with you to your precious ladies and lose your job?'

'No. I shall go upstairs and discuss the matter with your father.'

'You wouldna dare, Mhairi Diack!' But Lizzie's bravado deceived neither of them. Mhairi knew the one thing Lizzie feared was her father's anger. 'Anyway,' Lizzie went on lightly, 'I wouldna dream o' mentioning yon filthy quines in front o' my wee ones. I look after them proper. Real educational our days are. Ask any o' them.'

'Annys told me about the fruit woman,' said Mhairi and

Lizzie had the grace to look shamefaced. 'At least she learned the price of an apple. But you'd best be careful, Lizzie. You don't want to be jailed.'

'Silly cow,' said Lizze with feeling, and added hastily, 'Yon wifie, nae your sister. Anyway,' she went on airily, 'I'll likely emigrate to Australia one o' these days. Folk can get rich real quick there.'

The most likely way that Lizzie would emigrate, thought Mhairi grimly, was on a convict ship, though she did not say so aloud.

'How's Tom?' asked Lizzie, after a suitable pause. 'I havena seen him lately.'

'You wouldn't. He's busy at the quarry. Mr Fergus has put him on to blasting the new seam they're opening and it's all to be done before the frosts come.' Mhairi liked to hear about Mr Fergus: though she had not seen him since the day her mother died, she still thought of him with gratitude and a secret, wistful tenderness. In memory, he had behaved like a prince, and treated her like a lady. Didn't she have that folded handkerchief to prove it? Now, apart from her dreams, Tom's stories were her only contact with Silvercairns. 'Apparently it's real tricky work,' she went on. 'You have to find just the right place to put the powder or the stone falls the wrong way and could kill someone.'

'Dangerous work, quarrying,' said Lizzie cheerfully. 'My da knew a man was killed, just lookin' at a rock. They'd been hammering at it, seemingly, and it hadna budged, then one man went to fetch a bigger hammer or something and this other mannie stood waitin' and lookin', idle-like – and it upped and squashed him flat. Just like that. But I reckon your Tom's nippy enough to get out the way, sharpish, and yon quarrying certainly builds a man's muscles. Your Tom looks real well on it.' She paused, watching Mhairi's unsuspecting face, and added slyly, 'So does that Alex Grant. You fancy him, don't you?'

'Of course not!' But in spite of herself, Mhairi blushed. 'He is a family friend, that's all.'

'Family, is it? You'd best watch he doesna give you a family of your own then, because from what I hear he knows how to go about it real well.'

Mhairi started with shock, pricked her finger and cried out

in alarm as the bead of blood touched the cloth. 'Look what you've made me do,' she cried. 'That Mrs Wyness's sure to see.' She scrubbed hastily at the spot with cold water, her back turned. She was scandalized by Lizzie's revelation, shocked, shamed, excited, and above all consumed with an urgent curiosity, but pride, and modesty, forbade her to ask questions.

'Aren't you going to ask how I know, then?' taunted LIzzie, delighted with the effect of her words.

'I might, if it was of any concern to me,' said Mhairi, her back still turned and holding the cloth up against the light for inspection. 'There, I think that's out.' She took up her sewing again and went on with as much nonchalance as she could manage. 'But I expect you'll tell me anyway. It's obviously what you came for.'

'Well, I won't,' snapped Lizzie, annoyed by 'yon Diack lass's silly airs and graces' as she told her ma later. 'And if you want to know you can twiddle your thumbs!' With that she slammed out of the room and Mhairi was left in a turmoil of confused questioning and speculation.

Lizzie must have made it up. Alex would never . . . surely? But he was no longer a boy. He was a fully-grown man, near enough, and a good-looking one, too. Girls fancied him. Look how that crowd at the pump called after him, teasing. An awful thought struck her and she blanched. Not Maggie Henderson or Beth Pirie? But if not one of them, then who? It couldn't be Lizzie herself, of course. Lizzie was too young. At least . . . no, that was impossible. But then how did she know? . . . If she did know?

Mhairi was still speculating when Lorn and Willy arrived home from school, Annys woke up and her quiet was broken by the usual evening clamour for food and attention. There was her da's and Tom's meal to put ready, the fire to see to, hot water to boil, Annys to feed and soothe – she'd been fretful ever since her ma's death – and the boys to feed. She wrapped her sewing carefully away in its protective sheet so that it should not come to harm till all her tasks were done and she might safely take it out again. And all the time she thought over and over what Lizzie had said, sometimes believing, sometimes knowing it to be a lie and the more she thought of it, the more unsettled she became. Alex Grant was no longer her brother's friend, a boy she had known all her life, but suddenly a grown man and a stranger. She was still thinking of it when Alex himself appeared, with Tom, in the doorway and in spite of herself she blushed.

Tom threw down his bag of tools and said, 'Da's called in to see Mackinnon on his way home. He'll not be long.'

'Aye aye,' said Alex cheerfully, ruffling Willy's hair and giving Lorn a friendly push. 'And when are you two joining us at the quarry?' They both blushed with pleasure – Alex was one of their heroes – and began to boast about their various deeds of prowess till Mhairi told them to hush their noise and eat up before their broth got cold. Obediently Lorn, Willy and Annys took their places on the bench at the scrubbed deal table, each with a steaming wooden bowl in front of them and a hunk of bread. Firelight danced over the scene, touching the three bent heads with gold, and the room was warm with the scent of baking.

Since their mother's death all the children had accepted that Mhairi had taken her place and that Mhairi's word was law. Authority had given her new stature and in the momentary silence as the children dipped bread into broth, it seemed to Mhairi that Alex was looking at her in a different way too, as if he could read her thoughts. For the first time in his presence she felt awkward and embarrassed. For something to do as much as anything, for the firelight was bright enough, she took a taper from the jar on the mantelshelf, touched it to the fire till the flame took hold, then, carrying it carefully in front of her, shielded from draughts by her cupped hand, she crossed to the dresser, removed the glass from the oil lamp, turned up the wick and lit it.

'Where's Donal?' she asked, her back to the room, as much for something to say as out of interest, though it was unusual to see Alex home without his brother. Carefully she adjusted the wick, replaced the lamp-glass, adjusted the wick again, till the flame burnt clear and strong.

'We dropped him off home first,' said Tom, reaching for the loaf and hacking off a chunk. 'Want some, Lackie?'

'Donal's working on some new design,' explained Alex, with a hint of pride in his voice. 'Besides, Tom and I have things to do.' He took the offered bread and bit hungrily into it.

Mhairi resumed her seat, took up her sewing and, with Lizzie's words still loud in her ears, was wondering just what 'things' implied when Annys spoke up in her clear child's voice.

'Why did the man hit Donal?'

'*What?*' Alex spoke scarcely above a whisper, but the suppressed violence in his voice seemed to fill the room. Mhairi looked up, startled, and found Alex looking not at Annys, but at her. She raised an eyebrow, shook her head, knowing his unspoken question and the anger behind it. 'What man, Annys?' she asked gently. The child's head scarcely reached above the edge of her wooden broth bowl and above its rim her solemn eyes were large and troubled.

'The man with the horsie. Why did he hit Donal?'

'Did you see him?' 'Where was it?' 'Who were you with?' As they bombarded her with questions the child's eyes brimmed with tears and Mhairi said hastily, 'Leave her be. She's only a child.'

'Can't you tell us, Annys?' asked Alex, coaxing, but as no one had answered her question, Annys ignored theirs and, rubbing her eyes with the back of one hand, she returned to the slow and careful business of spooning broth into her mouth without spilling it.

'She wasn't with us,' whispered Willy to Alex.

'Must ha' been with that Lizzie Lennox,' Lorn confided to Tom behind his hand.

'Then we'd best find out,' said Alex, 'and the sooner the better.' He moved for the door. 'Coming, Tom?'

'No!' cried Mhairi, scrambling to her feet. 'Wait. There's no call to . . .' but Alex interrupted her.

'No one lays a hand on my brother and gets away with it!'

'But she's only a child. Perhaps she got it wrong?' Mhairi clutched Alex's arm to hold him back. 'Please?' she pleaded, her eyes dark with fear. 'At least, wait till I have spoken with her? She will tell me, I know she will.'

'When? Tomorrow? Next week? Or never?' But he put his hand over hers, where it still gripped his forearm, and his eyes searched her face. 'Don't worry, Mhairi. I'll not lead your Tom into harm. But you do understand, don't you? *I must know.*' Then he loosed her hand and said, in a lighter voice, 'Find out what you can. Meanwhile, I'll make my own inquiries.'

'You'll not find Lizzie in,' cried Mhairi. 'She's away out with her ma.'

'We'll track her down. Are you coming or not, Tom?'

'I'll not be long, Mhairi,' said Tom, thrusting the last of the bread into his mouth and joining Alex in the doorway. 'I'll likely be back afore Da.'

'Take care.' But as she watched the two young men leap down the tenement stairs two at a time and stride across the yard towards the archway into the street, her heart trembled with a new dread. A man on a horse, Annys had said. Surely that could only mean a gentleman? And if Alex found out who and confronted him, Mhairi had no illusions as to which of them would win. Alex was healthy and strong, and powered by righteous anger, but the gentleman, whoever he was, had the power of birth and wealth and influence behind him, and the solid bastion of the law of the land.

What was she to do? If she found out what Alex wanted to know and told him, she was terrified what retribution he would seek on Donal's behalf. Alex was not a violent man. On the contrary, he was usually the peacemaker in any dispute that arose, and because he was known to be both physically strong and no coward, his word was often effective. But peace-loving though he was, he had one blind spot: anything touching Donal, the brother he had protected all his life, loosed an anger primitive in its violence and totally implacable. Suppose Alex killed somebody? Or was killed? The thought stopped her heart with momentary terror.

Yet if she found out and didn't tell him, he would surely know she was concealing something and would condemn her for it. But if, out of cowardice, she made no effort to find out, there was no saying that Alex would not track down the information for himself.

That last thought brought all her fears rushing back with renewed anxiety and as the evening dragged on and neither Tom nor her father appeared, her imagination ranged unchecked. Already Alex and Tom might have sought out Lizzie or the Henderson boy or another of Lizzie's brood and extracted the information. Alex might even now be on his way to vengeance . . . the tolbooth . . . transportation . . . even death.

'Where did you see the man hit Donal?' she asked Annys, as

she brushed the child's hair before bed. She had not meant to ask, but the words burst out of her, unbidden.

'On his back,' said Annys and added indignantly, 'Hard.'

'Poor Donal.' Mhairi brushed in silence for a moment before saying carefully, 'Was the man old?' She knew it was a stupid question the moment she spoke, but it was too late. All grown-ups were old to Annys.

'Yes,' said the child. 'Old and horrid.' She added tremulously, 'Why did he hit Donal? Lizzie said Donal wasn't naughty.'

'Because he was a horrid man,' said Mhairi firmly, scooping the child up and carrying her to bed. 'Now, if you promise to forget all about him, I will tell you a story before you go to sleep.'

But Mhairi herself could not forget. When Annys was at last asleep, and Lorn and Willy too in their beds, she sat on in the firelight, waiting for her father and Tom to return and going over and over in her mind what Annys had said. Lizzie had said Donal was not naughty, therefore Lizzie herself had been there. Lizzie had seen the incident, if incident it was, and when Alex tracked her down, Lizzie would tell. Might already have told . . . Oh God, she prayed over and over, keep Alex from trouble, keep Alex safe.

When her father and Tom eventually arrived home together, her father for once almost merry after the company of Mackinnon and several glasses of ale, and Tom cheerfully untroubled, her fear still ate away like a constant pain inside her.

'Did Alex find out anything?' she whispered at the first opportunity, but Tom merely shrugged.

'Not a thing.'

Apparently Lizzie, when challenged, had denied all knowledge of the incident. 'Wee Annys probably dreamt it,' she had told them cheerfully. 'In one o' yon nightmares she has.'

There was an element of possibility in the suggestion; Annys did have nightmares and often Mhairi was woken in the night by her little sister's sobbing and would cuddle and soothe and comfort her in the bed they still shared until Annys slept again. But Lizzie, unlike Mhairi, was an accomplished liar.

Her facility had been developed through years of evading her father's anger and she had learned at an early age how to wriggle out of the tightest of corners with an expression of wide-eyed innocence and the smoothest of falsehoods. In her world there was no such thing as truth, merely expediency. It was a philosophy she brought to all aspects of her young life, especially those areas which involved contact with authority, and she was adept at lying, with every semblance of truth.

So that while Alex and Tom did not entirely believe her, they did not disbelieve her either. When Alex asked Mhairi what Annys had told her, to her shame, she lied. Annys had told her only that the man was old and horrid. No more than that. And Alex had to be content. When those of Lizzie's ragged brood that they managed to track down and question claimed to know nothing, whether from ignorance, idiocy or natural caution, even Alex let the matter rest.

Only Mhairi knew, with the instinct of a lifetime's companionship, that Lizzie was lying, though why she was lying Mhairi could not imagine. But she was, and whereas Mhairi was glad that Alex's anger had been soothed, and that, for the moment anyway, the danger was past, Lizzie's motives both baffled and disturbed her. Lizzie did not lie for nothing, but whatever did the girl hope to gain?

April at Silvercairns was a beautiful month. In the distance, to the west, snow still lay thick in the Cairngorms, catching the sunlight in a sparkling undulation of hills. Blue-white, blush-white, golden-white as the day passed and the sky changed, they lay like fallen clouds on the horizon above an awakening countryside of fresh-tilled fields, thrusting shoots of grass and undergrowth, and green-budding trees. The Dee moved wide and full with its burden of melting snows, overlapping its banks here and there so that blue-glinting patches spread over low-lying fields and shrank again as the sun rose higher. The winter-white silver birch trees shimmered in a haze of fresh green, and in the scrubland at the edge of the quarry the first harebells appeared.

Servants moved out from the town house to whisk off dustsheets, light fires, sweep cobwebs, air beds and generally prepare the house for occupation, and Miss Lettice paid a visit especially to oversee the garden. The new Dutch hyacinth bulbs she had persuaded her father to buy from James Roy's last autumn, to plant under the terrace, showed no sign of appearing yet, though she found two separate clumps of snowdrops in the home meadow and the daphne at the corner of the kitchen garden was in lusty bloom. She visited the dairy and the brew-house, gave orders for herbs and spring vegetables, inspected the hothouse, reminded the gardener that once in residence she would require a constant supply of flowers for the house. Then she went inside to inspect the bedrooms, the guest-rooms, the public rooms, and even tested the grand piano for accuracy of tone. Aunt Blackwell could not understand her niece's apparent attack of domesticity and secretly marvelled. They were to move back to Silvercairns in mid-April and celebrate the opening of the summer season with a house party.

It was five months since that Temperance meeting at which Hugo had disgraced himself and Lettice had first seen Hamish Dunn. Since then, in spite of Hugo's teasing, she had attended every meeting in the immediate neighbourhood at which he was a speaker, and in the long absences when he was travelling elsewhere, she had followed his career as best she could through the newspapers and the local branch of the Temperance Society. This she had not officially joined, as too many of her friends were of the opposite persuasion and she herself could not see the virtue of total abstinence from anything so pleasant as claret, champagne or Sauterne. She was aware of the degradation and poverty which alcoholic excess could lead to among the lower classes – too many of Hamish Dunn's fellow speakers had given too many horrific examples for her to remain long unaware – but in her own circle it was different. For the wealthy and well-educated there was no harm in enhancing the pleasures of a social occasion by lavish hospitality in drink as well as food and her father's cellar was rightly renowned. But Lettice remained intrigued by Hamish Dunn, intrigued by his conviction, intrigued though unconvinced by his arguments, and emotionally stimulated as she had never been before. Had it not been for Hamish, her interest in Temperance would have evaporated when she left the hall with Hugo on that first disastrous afternoon, for none of the other speakers, then or since, could spark any enthusiasm in her. They were worthy, honest men, no doubt, with worthy, honest beliefs for the promotion of the good of their fellow men. But they were worthy, honest bores. If they were the product of Temperance, then uncork another bottle, quick.

Hamish Dunn, on the contrary, was a man of fire and humour. His reforming zeal was tempered with a vigorous enthusiasm which was both infectious and beguiling. A meal with him, she felt, would be entertaining if they drank only spring water, whereas the best claret at her father's table had often bored her to distraction. And now, before the end of the month, she would actually find out. For the unimaginable had happened: Hamish Dunn was to be called to the living of St Ninian's at Silvercairns.

Lettice had not followed the rumblings of the Disruptions that had split the Church of Scotland so violently three years before. They had something to do with the choice of ministers, that she knew: one half declared they were prepared to let the powers that be choose their ministers for them as of old, and the other half, the Free Church, that they were not and would choose their own. Congregations had been split on the issue, ministers been ousted, or resigned of their own accord. It was a matter of deep principle, but it had now been solved and St Ninian's vacant pulpit was to be filled.

Old Man Adam, as local laird and patron of the church, had been instrumental in the choice – 'A fine preacher, that young man. Just what our tenants need.' Mungo Adam was wholly in favour of temperance for the working classes and if Hamish Dunn could produce that, then he would have Adam's full backing. It seemed in no way incongruous to Adam that he should invite the Reverend Dunn to a welcome dinner at which he planned to serve a succession of the best wines the Silvercairns cellar could produce. For the Reverend Dunn was neither the only nor the most important guest. There were business contacts, old and new, including the Macdonalds, Burnetts and Forbes, and a new man who was reputed to be something big in railways. Old Man Adam was shrewd enough to foresee the huge benefits the railways could bring to the building trade and meant to be there in the forefront to collect them. He also intended that, if necessary, his offspring should forward his business success by judicious matrimony and with that in mind had included various younger guests in the invited company. Both Fergus and Lettice were of marriageable age and eligible.

Lettice was fully aware of her father's plans, though when she went over the guest list and seating arrangements with him, it was with only one guest in mind. She did not need her father's reminder of the excellence of the wines to make her plan the best dinner their cook could provide and she spent unusually long spells poring over recipe books and consulting those of her friends whom she considered to have a modicum of culinary taste. It did not occur to her that a reforming minister of Hamish Dunn's particular convictions might not appreciate such refinements. All men enjoyed a good meal and the more lavish the offerings, the more intricate and ornate the presentation, the better satisfied her guest would undoubtedly be. Lettice admitted to nobody, particularly not to herself, that she wished to impress Mr Dunn, to interest, captivate, even enthral him. But the truth was that beside her reforming Highland minister, young men such as Niall Burnett and his circle seemed juvenile, shallow and effete. She had grown beyond them and felt herself worthy of better company. So, when her preparations for the beguiling of Hamish Dunn's stomach were complete, she set about a similar campaign with regard to his eyes and thence his heart.

She ransacked her wardrobe, ruthlessly rejecting anything she felt was *passé*, or *risqué*, or just plain dull. She summoned Miss Roberts and ordered three new dresses, a manteau Infanta of black velvet in Spanish style, with a large collar trimmed with lace, several fetching little bonnets, a silk parasol, and finally half a dozen new petticoats, all to be ready by mid-April or Miss Lettice would take her custom elsewhere.

The distracted Miss Roberts (of Crown Court, Union Street, 'Parisian millinery, Cloaks, French stays, Sewed Muslin gowns etc., etc.'), leaving by the back stairs, bumped into Eppie Guyan and confided the impossible task. 'And where I'll get the help to finish in time the good Lord alone knows, with the Farquharson wedding and the Forbes dance and the whole town set on new clothes of one kind or another. But you know what Miss Lettice is like and I daren't say no. She wants tucking on the petticoats, too . . .' Eppie tut-tutted in sympathy and said if Miss Roberts was that busy her cousin had a friend who would run up the petticoats, no bother, and make as neat a job of it as a body could wish. She'd maybe help with some of the plain seams, too, and be glad of the money, poor lass, with no ma and a family of hungry kids to see after. And if ever Miss Roberts had any wee bits of trimming, ribbons and suchlike, that she was not wanting, then Eppie herself would be right grateful . . .

So it was that the overburdened Miss Roberts called upon Mhairi Diack in the Mitchell's Court tenement, inspected her work, and engaged her on the spot to sew half a dozen petticoats in double-quick time.

'You'd best not let on to they wifies i' the Ladies' Working,' warned Lizzie, 'or they'll give you the sack. You're nae supposed to work for anybody else if you work for them.'

'I don't at the moment,' said Mhairi calmly, though her heart had begun to beat uncomfortably fast. 'They have too much stock and we are not to sew any more till they've sold it.' In fact, Miss Roberts' order had been a godsend, for the Ladies' Working, as Lizzie called it, paid piece rates.

'It's right fine material,' said Lizzie, fingering a length of soft cotton. 'I wouldna mind a petticoat o' that.'

'Put it down,' said Mhairi sharply, and added, 'I'm sorry, but it marks so easily and I'm terrified that Miss Roberts'll make me pay for washing or something.'

'Old bag,' said Lizzie automatically. 'If she tries, just rip it through in front of her face. That'll teach her.'

Mhairi was appalled at the very thought. 'I couldn't! Besides, it's lovely.' She felt the smoothness of the material against her cheek and for a brief, blissful moment imagined the delicate garment was hers. 'It would be wicked to tear it.'

'Nay so wicked as some folks having six o' them at once when folks like us have flannel or nought.' Lizzie lay back in the chair and stretched one sensibly shod foot high in the air so that her rough woollen skirt fell back to expose a length of threadbare stocking and said, admiring her own shapely leg, 'You'll see. I'll be as well dressed as yon Miss Lettice any day now. Lettice! What sort o' daft name is that for a body anyway? Might as well be called Carrot or Neep.'

Lizzie Lennox had grown in the last year and, though still shorter than Mhairi, had a nicely rounded figure and knew how to flaunt it. Her thick mop of fiery hair was tied back with a strip of blue rag, but the curls invariably escaped in a cloud around her face and her startling brown eyes were always alive with some mischief or devilment or, as now, with lively indignation.

'Tell you what,' she said, suddenly sly. 'When you've sewn them things, real neat and pretty, I'll take them round to Miss Carrot myself. I'll say that Old Bag Roberts wanted me to bring them round the moment they was done and she'll maybe give me one o' her cast-offs. I right fancy one o' they smart gowns, Mhairi. I see myself in blue silk, or maybe taffeta, wi' flounces and frills. That'd make the boys wink, eh?' and she gave Mhairi a knowing nudge. 'And I'd maybe lend it to you now and then, when I wasna needin' it myself, seeing as how you're doing all the sewing. But if I dinna manage to get a dress,' she went on, warming to her theme, 'I fancy a rake around yon Adam house anyway, to see how the other folk live. Eppie says it's real comfortable, though old-fashioned like. Silvercairns is much smarter, seemingly.' She paused, watching Mhairi's busy hands, and added airily, 'I'll maybe work there one day.'

Mhairi didn't answer. She was not entirely sure that Lizzie was joking about delivering the petticoats. It was out of the question, of course. Miss Roberts would collect and deliver them herself. But at the same time the idea of one of Miss Lettice's dresses was a beguiling one. Mhairi saw herself in a lovely gown of silken flowing material, blue as Lizzie said, or soft French pearl. She'd put it on one evening, before the men came home, with her hair brushed neat and shining, and be elegant as any lady. Alex would be lost in admiration and wonder . . . But Lizzie's next words shattered her brief dream.

'I think that's a right good idea o' mine,' she said with deceptive indolence. 'I'm surprised at you, Mhairi Diack, for not jumping wi' joy. Here's me offering you shares in a blue silk gownie and all you do is sit there like a lump o' cold porridge and say nought. It's a right fine plan o' mine and you'd best agree, or I might just tell that Alex o' yours something you wouldna want him to know.'

Mhairi stared at her friend in shock as the implications of Lizzie's words took shape and solidified till she knew, with dreadful certainty, what she meant. Little Annys, up the stair with Mrs Lennox so Mhairi could get on, had been right about what she saw all those months ago. It was not a dream, and Lizzie, as Mhairi had always suspected, knew who Donal's assailant was. But if she told Alex, so long after the event, would he react? Surely what happened five months ago was past and done with? Could she be sure of that, though, where Donal was concerned?

Lately, Alex had taken to coming home with Tom after dropping Donal first at the house where they had lived, with an uncle, for most of their lives. Alex joined them at the fireside like one of the family, chatted easily to Lorn and Willy, helped wee Annys with her slate, chopped wood or carried coals for Mhairi, asked her father about the old days of quarrying, or of the croft where he was born, and spun the usual dreams with Tom of a yard of their own one day, with a quarry of their own so they could be entirely independent. Ships had been added to the daydream, to transport their stone to London or Liverpool, Naples, Marseilles, even Brisbane, in Australia. The Christie ships were reliable enough, but their own would be better. Their own team of horses, too, in their own stables. And always at some point in the evening, Mhairi would look up from her sewing and find Alex watching her, and when she caught his eye he would smile. Sometimes she smiled back, sometimes, blushing in spite of herself, she hastily resumed her sewing, but the evening would be lightened for her and when he left, he always found the opportunity to take her hand.

One day soon, she thought with a quickening of the heart, when there was a holiday, he might ask her to walk out with him . . . and perhaps she might accept. It was not quite what she had dreamed, but her mother's death had banished such dreams to the land of make-believe where they belonged. Alex was a lifelong friend whom all her family liked. He was honest, hard-working and handsome, much sought after by the girls of the neighbouring tenements, yet it seemed he was interested in her. If Mhairi remembered that other loving face which had bent over her in her fainting dream, she pushed the memory firmly aside. What was the use of yearning for the unattainable? Alex was no prince and could offer her no palace, but she liked him, he was a fine stonemason and one day would do well. They would have a house together, with their own front door. A loving husband and a home of her own, Mhairi told herself, would be both prince and palace to her . . . and now Lizzie Lennox was threatening to destroy even that small dream with enmity and violence.

For Mhairi knew that five months was no time at all to Alex where Donal was concerned. Orphaned early in life, the two boys had been taken in by an unwilling bachelor uncle, a journeyman carpenter of morose and retiring habits. He had given them house room and the bare necessities, and for the rest they had been left to fend for themselves. Alex had taken full responsibility for Donal from an early age, had seen that he attended the Deaf and Dumb Institute to learn all they could teach him, and when the time came, with the help of Mackinnon, had found him occupation at Silvercairns. Mackinnon had known the pair for most of their lives, living as he did on the same stair and, as he said privately, feeling sorry for the poor orphaned laddies. Mrs Mackinnon looked in now and then to see the place was 'kept proper' and slipped the wee lads home-baked biscuits or black bun, but could find only praise for the way Alex 'mothered' his poor wee brother. And though Mackinnon had warned Alex more than once about keeping his temper, the older man confided to his wife that you couldna blame the lad when he saw folk tormenting Donal and if he was in Alex's place he'd likely do the same.

So Mhairi knew that if Alex heard, however long after the event, he would storm round to confront the culprit on the spot, and Alex was a grown man and strong.

'Well?' taunted Lizzie. 'Cat got your tongue?'

The expression reminded Mhairi of the girls at the pump, calling after Donal, and she said carefully, though her face was white as the linen in her hands, 'I don't know what you're speaking about.'

'Oh, yes, you do, Mhairi Diack. I'm speaking about your Annys's "nightmare", only it wasna a nightmare, was it? And I know the name o' the mannie on the horse. When I tell Lackie he'll get real angry, that he will. Reckon he might even kill yon mannie. By mistake, o' course, but it'll be too late then and ye canna tell yon magistrates ye killed a body by mistake as they'll nae believe you, specially when gentry's involved. Always side with gentry, magistrates do. So I'll take yon petticoats round myself. Come to think of it, I'll maybe get mysel' a job in the

Adam house at the same time. I could always say I helped wi' yon stitching . . .'

She was grinning now, delighted with her strategem, and Mhairi could have wept with anguish and fear. Gentry, Lizzie had said, and that had the awful ring of truth. But rank would not stop Alex. Nothing would where Donal was concerned. She knew it was hopeless to argue with Lizzie, hopeless to try to explain. Lizzie was incapable of seeing right and wrong, let alone distinguishing between them. Lizzie had thought of a way to benefit herself and that was that. Mhairi with her scruples and her loyalties and her fear for Alex, was helpless to resist her.

'The petticoats are not finished,' she said, 'and they won't be as long as you keep interrupting me in my work. Anyway,' she added, to steer Lizzie away from the subject of Alex, 'I thought your Eppie was going to get you a job.'

'So she is. But I'll maybe hurry her up a wee bittie.' She swung to her feet, grinning, and walked jauntily out of the door. On the stair she turned and called, 'Are you wantin' your Annys back yet? Or will ye wait till Alex comes, so she can tell him what new she's seen the day?'

In the event Miss Roberts asked Mhairi herself to deliver the petticoats and to Silvercairns. 'So that should there be the slightest alteration required, you can do it on the spot,' explained Miss Roberts. 'I will pay you for your trouble, naturally. Oh and you may tell Miss Lettice I will bring the rest of the order myself, before the end of the week.'

So Mhairi, choosing her moment with particular care for it would not do to meet Lizzie Lennox on the stair and be forced to explain her errand, set out one bright April morning, a covered basket over her arm, to walk the two miles to Silvercairns. Lizzie would be furious when she found out, of course, but it would be too late then, the errand safely done.

Mhairi had not visited Silvercairns since the morning of her mother's death, some eighteen months ago, but little had changed. There were new houses in the western part of Aberdeen, in new grounds, with new hedges and gates, but when she reached Hirpletillam the smithy was the same cheerful meeting place for horseman, farmer, stable lad and idler. Mhairi cast a quick eye over the company to see whether Donal was among them, for she knew it was one of his tasks to take the horses to be shod, but he was not there. Even so, she lingered a little with the others, feeling the warmth from the furnace and watching the sparks fly, while she got her breath. Although it was April, there was an edge to the air and the wind from the sea blew chill. But the rowan trees beside the path were thrusting with leaf, the grass was fresh with new growth and there was a scent of spring in the air. Oyster-catchers wheeled and mewed overhead and a clutch of herring gulls, tossed inland by the onshore wind, squabbled noisily over a new-ploughed field. Mhairi pulled her plaid tighter round her shoulders, hitched up her basket and, her cheeks pink from the furnace and the exercise, set out on the last stretch to Silvercairns.

She was walking, as slowly as she dare without actually dawdling, along the tree-lined path which led to the gates of the big house, when she became aware of a horse some way behind her, but undoubtedly coming her way. The path led nowhere else but Silvercairns: first the house, then the quarry. She wondered idly who the horseman was and hoped it was not Old Man Adam. But her errand was legitimate. She had every right to be where she was, on the way to the house which she could see now, through a gap in the trees, etched clearly against the skyline. Smoke hurried westward from a dozen chimneys to be snatched up and dispersed by the freshening breeze and the sunlight flashed from a double row of windows. She saw the tall granite pillars of the entrance, white as marble columns and as elegant as any palace, above its gardens and its sweep of green. Alex said the house of Silvercairns was built entirely of granite from the quarry and would last for generations. 'Unless some fool plants a charge too close and blasts the house to pieces, with the quarry wall.' But no one would do that, surely? The house of Silvercairns was far too beautiful.

She had slowed her pace even more, not for the hill which was gentle enough, but in order to feast her eyes on that fairy-tale building, when she realized that the horse was close behind her now. She turned her head, stepped back on to the grassy verge of the track in order to let the rider pass, and, with a rush of heart-stopping agitation, saw that it was Mr Fergus, in tailored tweed riding jacket and pale woollen breeches, his leather riding boots gleaming like metal in the sunlight, his gloved hands loose on the reins. He wore a smart black hat and a white stock at his throat and Mhairi, lowering her eyes quickly after the first wondering glance, marvelled that she had ever considered him ordinary. On horseback, in the sunlight, he was . . . But she could not think of an appropriate word. Only that her heart was thumping suddenly faster and that her eyes were thirsty to look at him again, to capture every princely detail and hold them, precious, in her memory. She stood, eyes lowered, impatiently waiting for him to pass so that she could safely raise them and drink her fill, when she realized why the sound of her own heart was so uncomfortably loud: the steady beat of hoofs on hard-packed road had ceased and there was only birdsong and the soft soughing of the wind. He had reined in his horse. Startled, she looked up, saw him studying her, and looked quickly down again. Then he spoke.

'Are you going to the house?'

'Yes.' Her mouth was unaccountably dry. She added, belatedly, 'Sir.'

But he was looking at her with a strange intensity. 'You do not work there? Though I believe we have met?' It was half statement, half question.

Again she said, 'Yes,' and added, because his eyes were looking deep into hers and she could not look away, 'I came to your office, with a message for my father. More than a year ago. You were very kind.'

To her wondering astonishment he swung his leg over the saddle and dismounted, to stand on the path beside her. 'Your mother was ill, I remember.'

'She died.' Mhairi spoke with a quiet dignity that went straight to his heart.

'I am sorry.' He looked embarrassed and to her surprise Mhairi pitied him, faced as he was with a situation requiring some sort of comment and yet one of which he knew nothing. Less than nothing, and how could he? For death in a tenement in Mitchell's Court would bear no resemblance to death in the great house of Silvercairns.

'Oh, we are used to it now,' she said, attempting cheerfulness. 'Such things happen and it was long ago. We manage.' He looked at her without speaking, studying her with an attention that made her increasingly unsure. Had she been impertinent? Too familiar? Was he expecting her to say something else? Or did he feel, as she did, the deep, unspoken bond between them? She was suddenly overcome with embarrassment and an acute awareness of their physical proximity. Her cheeks flamed and she looked down at her hands, which clutched the handle of the wicker basket and held it like a barrier between them. She had folded the petticoats neatly and covered them with a layer of clean cotton so that no speck of dust should tarnish their perfection. Gathering courage from the sight of her own handiwork, which she knew to be good, she looked up into his face and said, 'Please excuse me, sir. They will be waiting for me at the house.'

He made no move to mount and ride on, as she had expected him to do, but continued to stare down at her, barring her path. He stood barely two feet away from her, head and shoulders taller than she was, his booted feet slightly apart, his hands clasped behind his back. His young face was grave, and though his dark eyes looked straight into hers, she felt he hardly saw her. It was as if he were disputing with himself, weighing the pros and cons of an unknown argument. Then he said, suddenly smiling, 'I am going to the house myself and my horse has had a weary morning of it.' Here he patted his horse's neck with obvious affection. 'It would be a kindness to him if I went the rest of the way on foot. Besides, your basket must be heavy.'

'No,' she protested, clutching it to her breast. 'It is only petticoats, for Miss Adam.'

'Then it is sure to be heavy, if I know my sister. Two of everything where normal mortals make do with one? No doubt she ordered solid gold thread for the stitching?'

Before she could speak, his hand closed over hers on the handle of the basket. For a moment she stood rigid as the warmth of his flesh spread through the soft kid of his glove and his eyes looked solemnly into hers. Then he smiled, she half smiled in answer, and a moment later he had taken the basket from her and attached it somehow to his horse's saddle. Then he took his horse by the reins and set off up the track, obviously expecting her to follow. Wonderingly, as in a dream, she did.

* * *

'What on earth were you thinking of?' demanded Lettice of her brother when, her new petticoats tried on and pronounced 'adequate', which in Lettice's parlance meant she could find no fault, she eventually tracked him down in her father's library. He was sitting in a high-backed chair beside the fire with an open book in his hand, though she could have sworn he was not reading it. He had an abstracted look on his face, as if he were somewhere else and it puzzled him. But his very abstraction annoyed her. 'Well?' she challenged. 'What were you doing? Walking up the drive with a *servant*?'

What had he been doing? Lettice's question only echoed his own and he could find no answer, though he had been going over and over the same question in his head ever since he had parted from the girl in the stable yard. No, before that, when they had walked in silence the length of the drive. No, before that still. When he had stood on the path beside her and been unable to remount and ride away. Yet when they had walked together, he had found nothing to say to her and she had not spoken. Had she been a girl of his own social set he would have been tortured with embarrassment, for though outwardly assured, he was still shy and diffident in female company, but strangely, it had not mattered. To him or, he was certain, to her. It had been enough that they were on the same path together. Earlier, he had seen her ahead of him on the track from Hirpletillam, and when he had recognized her as the girl who had fainted in his office and who had haunted his dreams for months after, he had known he must dismount, though why he could not say. Looking back, he realized it had seemed not only natural but inevitable. A prologue. But to what? Their paths were hardly likely to cross again.

'I saw you,' accused Lettice, breaking in on his thoughts. 'From my bedroom window. I could hardly believe my eyes.'

With an effort, Fergus returned his attention to the library and his sister's needling. 'Spying again?' he said pleasantly. 'What a busy life you must lead.'

'Ha, ha!' retorted Lettice. 'Most amusing. But then you always were a witty fellow.' It was a pity Eppie had brought up the petticoats herself: she would have liked to take a closer look at Fergus's servant girl, but had not thought to send for her until too late. 'What were you doing, anyway?' she finished, abandoning sarcasm in the interests of curiosity.

'Nothing. Merely exercising a little old-world chivalry.'

'On a servant? What a waste. You would do far better to exercise your charms on Flora Burnett.'

'As you do on her brother?' said Fergus, eyebrow raised.

'Niall is a loathsome, spineless, sneering, arrogant *toad*,' said Lettice, 'and quite impossibly juvenile.'

'Whereas you are a world-weary sophisticate of staggering maturity?'

'Well, I'm a good deal more sophisticated than you are, brother. Walking up the drive with a servant girl for all the world to see, and carrying her basket. You know what they'll say, don't you?' When he did not answer, but ostentatiously took up his book and turned the page, her eyes flashed with mischief and she said slowly, enunciating each word, 'They will say that it was obviously because she was carrying something of yours. Under her apron.'

'I cannot imagine what you mean,' said Fergus with cold dignity, but his cheeks had flushed all the same. 'My horse was lame, I decided to walk, overtook the girl on the path and merely offered to relieve her of her burden so that she might execute *your* errand with all speed.'

'How very kind,' teased Lettice, delighted to have annoyed him. Fergus was always so strait-laced and dull it was a positive triumph to have managed to ruffle his worthy feathers. 'Or was it merely so that she would be free the sooner, for a little errand of your own? To the hay loft, perhaps?'

'Lettice! I am beginning to wonder what sort of antics you get up to when Father's back is turned. No nice girl would even imagine such things, let alone speak of them.'

'Oh, don't be such a pompous old bore!' snapped Lettice, tiring of the contest. Fergus was a cold fish, without an ounce of lusty blood in his veins. If he came upon a bevy of naked nymphs cavorting in the woods, she reflected sourly, he would remain as righteously unmoved. She crossed to the window and glared out across the terrace to the short strip of parkland and the winding thread of the drive. To her right, through the screening trees which marked the boundary of the grounds, she could just glimpse the roof of the quarry office. It reminded her of another annoyance.

'If you must fraternize with the workers, Fergus, you might at least choose someone useful. The frost has cracked the terrace wall again in two places, and if it falls, as it threatens daily to do, my flower border will be ruined. I wish you would send someone from your precious quarry to mend it, preferably before the dinner.'

Fergus had no need to inquire which dinner she meant – there had been talk of little else for the past month – but it was not concern for social appearances that made him say, 'Of course. I cannot promise when it will be, but I will send someone, as soon as a man can be spared.'

'Thank you,' said Lettice, and added, with rare apology, 'and I am sorry for teasing you. But I desperately want this dinner to be a success. Shall I show you the terrace wall now?'

Fergus shook his head. He did not need to inspect the damage to know that it was not frost that had caused it, but blasting operations from the quarry itself. How long would it be before the walls of Silvercairns suffered a similar fate? He did not want to look at the terrace wall lest the answer be there in the cracks for him to read. And his father had ordered another massive bank of rock to be blasted with all speed.

'Later,' he said. 'After dinner, perhaps,' and resumed his book.

In the quarry at Silvercairns, Alex Grant was happy. That last seam they had opened had been a good one. He enjoyed working with rock, enjoyed the strength of his arm as he wielded the hammer, enjoyed the sunlight glinting off quartz crystals and mica as the rock broke apart. He enjoyed shaping the blocks to the required size and dressing the surfaces with hammer and chisel, and he enjoyed the challenge and the thrill of boring fuse holes in the rock for the fireman to fill and prime. When a new seam of rock was blasted open, it was a pleasure to him to study the new-born granite, exposed for the first time to the light of day – and to men's eyes. Alex was not an imaginative man, yet every time new rock was blasted, he regarded it with a touch of awe and remembered its primordial origins. Made from molten lava, they said, compressed and cooling under the earth's surface for thousands of years, and now exposed for the first time. And his eyes were the first to look upon it.

Lately, he had tried to explain something of his wonder to Mhairi Diack who, since her mother's death, had grown into a maturity which he found both soothing and exciting. She had shouldered her new responsibilities with calm acceptance and though he suspected she worked too hard and too long, she never gave a hint of complaint. Moreover, she had grown into a fine-looking girl, with hair like polished jet and startling blue eyes. She was good to Donal, too, not as some folk were out of cold and conscious charity, but from the warmth of her heart. That was important, for where Alex went, Donal must go too, and he could never marry anyone who would mistreat his brother. And Donal liked her. Alex found that his own heart was not indifferent and was confident she felt the same towards him. He had been with other girls, of course, it wouldn't be natural otherwise, but he knew instinctively that none of them would do for more than an evening's pleasure, and when he married he wanted a lifetime's companion . . . When he had worked out his apprenticeship, which wouldn't be long now, then Tom and he would find the money somehow and start up on their own. And he would marry Mhairi. He had said nothing yet to Mhairi about his plans, but he spent most evenings at the Diack house now, among the family, and was accepted not only as Tom's friend, but, he was almost sure, as Mhairi's too.

'If you look closely,' he told Mhairi, trying to explain to her the wonder of a newly opened seam of rock, while her brothers Lorn and Willy fixed their eyes on his face with rapt attention, 'you can see the different crystals glinting and sparkling. Black mica, white mica, felspar, quartz. In Silvercairns they are fairly evenly mixed, and finely grained. When they get to the polishing yards, our stones take a beautiful polish, which not all stones do.'

'Some are a prettier colour,' put in Annys, her eyes on Alex's face. 'Like Ma's stone with Donal's little birdie.'

At the mention of Donal Mhairi's heart turned over with sudden fear, lest Annys revive the question of the man on the horse, but she need not have worried. Alex the stonemason was speaking now and the subject totally engrossed him.

'Aye, Annys. That's from Corrennie where the felspar's pink and the Peterhead rock's the same. All granite's different, you see, depending on the mix o' the crystals . . .'

As Alex talked on a new fear crept up and clutched out of nowhere at Mhairi's heart. A man on a horse, Annys had said. A gentleman. Could it have been Fergus Adam? It was possible. Donal worked for the Adams, after all. But Mr Fergus had been courteous and kind, taking her basket for her, treating her like a lady. On that long walk up the drive of Silvercairns, although they had not spoken, they had walked together as equals. Almost, she thought yearningly, remembering the warmth of his hand on hers and the intimacy of his smile, almost as friends . . . or lovers. Then common sense brought her sharply back to reality. Fergus Adam had gone in by the front door, she by the back. That was the way of things and how it must always be. But in spite of such social differences, Donal's man could not possibly have been Mr Fergus. He was a little aloof perhaps and proud, but incapable of cruelty. It had obviously been someone else. Reassured, she brought her attention back to Alex.

'. . . Some rocks are best for building and no good for monumental work, others are fit only for roads, but ours', he finished with pride, 'are fit for anything, even a palace for the Queen.'

'Maybe she'll visit Scotland again one day and build herself one?' said Tom, whittling away at a stick. He was making a new spirtle for Mhairi as Annys had accidentally dropped the old one into the fire.

'Then I hope she waits until we've a quarry and yard of our own so we can put in a tender wi' the rest o' them,' said Alex. That reminded him. 'Word has it that Old Man Adam's after a big contract at the moment. No one knows for certain what, but wi' the railways coming nearer, I reckon he's got his eyes on a contract for all the viaducts and bridges in Scotland, and maybe the stations too.'

'Is there enough granite for that?' asked Mhairi.

'Aberdeenshire's made o' granite,' said Alex with a grin. 'If you mean does Old Man Adam own enough of it to build the railways single-handed, we'll soon find out. He's given orders to blast a whole new section o' the quarry in double-quick time and he's whipping Mr Fergus along like a flagging horse to get it done. I feel almost sorry for the lad.'

'Sorry for him?' said Tom. 'When he's son and heir to the best quarry for miles around? You're soft i' the head. It's us you should be sorry for. When Mr Fergus has made up his mind where to start, we're the ones who will have to bore the holes and a full day wi' an eight-pound hammer is no picnic. Besides, you can bet your life if Old Man Adam is driving Mr Fergus, then Mr Fergus will drive us twice as hard. He's feart of his father and Mungo Adam's a hard man.'

'He wouldna have got where he has done, else,' said Cassie Diack from the fireside and there was a moment of surprise. Cassie rarely spoke these days. 'Granite's a hard rock. I reckon it takes a hard man to work it.'

'But, Da,' protested Mhairi, 'you're not hard, nor Tom, nor Alex.' Nor Fergus Adam, she added under her breath. He was handsome and courteous and kind . . . She looked up, caught Alex's eye and unexpectedly blushed, not for the partiality of her words which had obviously pleased him, but because for a moment she thought she had spoken that last name aloud.

'Maybe not, lass. But we dinna own quarries.'

'I reckon we will one day, Cassie,' said Alex, with the confidence of youth and resolution. 'And we'll nae need to be hard neither. Except when it comes to boring that rock. But we'll have muscle enough for that, however hard Mr Fergus drives us, eh, Tom?' He rolled up his sleeve, placed his elbow on the table and lifted his hand in open invitation. Tom pushed up his sleeve too, swung a leg over the bench and sat down opposite him, placed his elbow in the correct position and gripped Alex's hand in his. A moment later, to yells of excited encouragement from Lorn and Willy, the Indian arm-wrestling was in full swing, Silvercairns and its management forgotten.

Mhairi, busying herself with preparations for the evening meal, thought again of Fergus Adam on horseback and how beautiful he had looked: like an illustration in a book of fairy-tales. She remembered his elegant, tight-muscled thighs firm against the horse's flanks, his gloved hand warm over hers: she could still feel the touch of it against her skin. But at the same time she could not help noticing how strong and firm the boys' arms were, as they locked in contest, both knotted with muscle, both rippling with taut strength. The skin of Alex's arm was tanned brown by the sun, the dusting of hair bleached blond, and as he strained to force her brother's arm flat on to the table, his neck muscles stood out strong and firm as tree roots. Under the rough cloth of his shirt she saw his shoulder muscles move and his back looked broad and strong enough to bear the heaviest burden.

The sweat stood in beads on Tom's forehead but he would not give in until, with a final, quivering clash of strength on strength, Alex's hand forced Tom's down, inch by quivering inch till, suddenly, resistance snapped and he conceded defeat. Alex looked up, smiling with triumph, and saw Mhairi watching him. The moment seemed timeless, though it was in reality only a matter of seconds, but long enough for Mhairi to see that Alex was offering himself for her approval and for him to see that she gave it.

'Best of three!' cried Tom. 'And I swear I'll get you this time.'

'Big words,' grinned Alex, 'from a little runt,' and dodged the blow Tom aimed at his head.

'You'd best drink this first,' said Mhairi, smiling. 'It promises to be a long and thirsty contest.'

She put one mug down beside Tom, then moved round the table to Alex's side with the other. 'Thank you,' he said, taking it from her with one hand while he put the other around her waist and kept her pinioned till he had drained the mug. Then he said, 'Thank you,' again, winked, gave her waist a squeeze, and released her.

As they took up position for the second bout, Mhairi knew that the arm-wrestling was irrelevant now. Alex had declared himself, and she had not refused him. Alex was no prince on horseback, with no country mansion, but he was upright and honest, strong-limbed and healthy, with a lusty, youthful vigour about him that stirred her blood. When he walked beside her at least they would enter the house by the same door. As she watched the two men pitting their strength against each other, saw their young muscles harden and their jaws set with resolution, she quivered with a new and secret excitement.

Suddenly she wanted to feel that warm hand at her waist again, to touch and be touched . . . Tom was her brother and she owed him loyalty, but she hoped the victor would be Alex Grant.

Fergus Adam frowned at the shimmering face of granite and wished that Mackinnon was still with them. The new man was competent enough, but he did not have Mackinnon's flair and something more than competence was needed if the next layer of rock was to be blasted with anything like success. It was no good ramming in a quantity of dynamite and taking cover. That would shift the rock all right, but in shattered fragments fit for nothing but road metal. For the engineering work his father had contracted for, it must be a carefully planned powder and fuse operation so that the granite fell apart in unspoilt blocks. They had tried a small preliminary blast to find the points of least resistance, but Fergus felt little the wiser. The explosion had been too mild to show them anything at all except smoke and a few small cracks. Perhaps Mackinnon could have read them: Fergus certainly could not and he doubted his foreman could either, though George Bruce tapped and studied, stood back and frowned, periodically laying his hands on the rock as if to feel the lie of the 'posts'. Unlike in Cornish quarries, the joints in the quarries of Aberdeen were irregular and found by experience, of which Fergus had next to none. He must rely on Bruce. He saw Bruce kick the solid wall of granite in futile annoyance, and found himself wishing again for Mackinnon's return. Approach the granite in a spirit of deference, Mackinnon had told him, and it will reward you. There was too much bad temper and too little respect in Bruce's boot.

But temper was understandable, thought Fergus, trying to be fair. He felt angry and frustrated himself, and who wouldn't after two whole days of trying to find the exact points for the fuse holes, of testing and rejecting and moving on, while in the background Old Man Adam was fuming and foaming at the mouth with impatience for results.

But this time they were not just blasting another few blocks along the existing section: they were quarrying the next layer down. Production for years to come might depend on the outcome and Fergus could not afford to get it wrong. Nor could he afford, he thought grimly, to find inferior rock below the existing, or, worse, no granite at all. Perhaps it might be better to blast deeper into the wall of the quarry, extending the work horizontally rather than vertically? But that would mean encroaching further into the grounds of Silvercairns house, and weakening the structure even more. Briefly, he remembered Lettice's terrace wall which he had promised to have repaired and had so far done nothing about: fortunately, he thought with irony, for it would no doubt need repairing further after the next attempt. Unless they could lease the adjacent land, for they were already near the outside limits of their property. But when Fergus had suggested the latter alternative, Old Man Adam had turned apoplectic.

'With our own quarry scarce touched, boy?' he had roared. 'You must think we've money to burn. There's good enough granite out there in the hole we've got without digging another. We've hardly skimmed the surface.'

When Fergus ventured to suggest something of the difficulties he was encountering, his father waved them aside. 'You've a foreman and trained men. What more do you want? When I started that quarry I had only determination and my own wits to help me. So get back out there and dig! With your own bare hands if necessary. I'll wager you anything you like there's solid granite half a mile deep in that quarry.'

'But Father, we must consider the position of the joints and . . .'

'Then consider them and don't waste my time! I want the quarry deepened and I want it done *now*! You've powder enough – and if you haven't, order more. If it's hard to shift, use a larger fuse. But blast it out somehow and quick. I've a contract lined up that will make us all a fortune as long as the supply holds out – and it's up to you to see that it does.'

Remembering his father's orders, Fergus made up his mind. 'That spot seems as good as any for taking the first fuse. Collect your boring teams and go ahead, Bruce. And tell the men to speed it up. We haven't all day.'

Oh, God, he wished it was Mackinnon instead of Bruce. Suppose it was the wrong spot? Suppose the blast dislodged the rock inwards and crushed them? Suppose the charge was too great and the impact cracked the quarry wall? Suppose the vibrations reached the house and, like an earthquake, shook it to pieces? Or suppose the fuse went off like a wet squib and nothing happened at all so that when he faced his father that evening over dinner he would have nothing favourable to report? How he wished it was still winter, that he still had Silvercairns to himself, that the road to Aberdeen was blocked, that the quarry was blanketed seven feet deep in snow, that there was no pressure to produce twice what the quarry was capable of in half the time. Most of all he wished his father had not arranged that house party which he knew was to be the occasion of signing the big contract Old Man Adam had spoken of. But before the signing, a delegation of interested parties would visit the quarry and if Fergus did not have the new seam to show them, heads would roll – his own being first into the basket.

He watched George Bruce collect his teams, watched him delegate each three-man group to a particular spot, watched them begin the slow process of boring the holes which would take the powder fuses. The steady hammer blows jarred and bounced off the quarry walls, assaulting his ears with the discord of metal on stone, and the penetration of the steel rods into the granite seemed infinitesimal. Tension and the incessant noise were increasing the early morning headache which he had hoped fresh air would disperse. The claret last night had been particularly plentiful.

After twenty minutes, the man holding the rod against the rock took a turn at the hammer, a new man took his place and the jarring, rhythmical succession of blows went relentlessly on. At the second change-over, Fergus inspected progress. Oh, God, fifteen inches, perhaps less? And each bore hole needed to be at least eighteen feet deep. There must be a quicker way. One day, surely, there would be. But in the meantime his father was pacing the floor at Silvercairns, awaiting results, and Fergus could not even begin to produce them until those men had hammered those iron rods eighteen feet into solid rock. And each blow seemed to split his head in two.

He nodded to the men to continue, said to George Bruce, 'How long?'

Bruce shrugged. 'Tomorrow? Depends if there's a frost.'

Although it was April, the nights were still cold, and after a spell of hard frost the quarry floor could be bitter. That could as much as halve the progress of the drilling teams . . . and he *must* get the blasting under way.

Anxiety and frustration, not to mention a sore head, made Fergus irritable and when he looked around him at the various groups of workmen on the quarry floor and saw one man squatting on his haunches, apparently doing nothing more vigorous than warming his hands at the brazier, he strode over to the spot.

'You! What's your job?'

'Causeyman.'

'Well, I don't pay you to waste my time. Get back to your work!'

'I was just getting the feeling back into my fingers, sir, so that . . .'

'Hard work will do that quicker than idleness,' snapped Fergus. 'I'll hear no excuses. Next time I see you idling my time away, you're out!'

Cassie Diack rose wearily to his feet and returned to the heap of granite setts which he had been trimming to rectangular proportions since first light. The skin of his frozen hands was split and bleeding, the shafts of his hammer and chisel like ice, but he took them up and resumed his work with the uncomplaining resignation of despair. Since his wife's death a year and a half ago he had wanted only to follow her to the peace of the grave, but unaccountably he endured. His chest was as choked, his breath as short, his heart as desolate and tired of living, yet every night when he went wearily to bed, longing to pass over effortlessly to that land o' the leal his wife had sung of, he woke again in the drear of early morning to yet another day.

Even his family could not rouse him from his torpor, though he loved them dearly. They would manage well enough without him. Tom was shaping into a good mason, developing both strength and skill, with an ambition Cassie had never had. He and Alex Grant had great plans together. Yes, Tom would do well. In another three or four years Lorn and Willy would follow him. He need have no worries on their account. As for the girls, Mhairi was practically grown-up now. She was a good girl, as pretty as her ma had been at her age, and a fine little housewife, too. One day she would marry, but he knew she would continue to care for Annys and the others, as she did now, like a mother. He need have no fears for any of them. As for money, he earned little enough anyway. They'd get by without him, somehow. He looked at the pile of granite setts beside him, the other pile of untrimmed blocks still waiting to be dealt with. Other men could do his job: he'd not be missed. From somewhere across the quarry came the steady hammering of iron on steel where Tom and Alex and the others were driving the boring rods steadily into bedrock. They were young men, on the threshold of life. They had ambition. But his life was over. He'd spent more than twenty years in the quarry, and since his wife's death nothing mattered any more. He was ready to go . . . but his dust-choked lungs still breathed, his heart still beat, in spite of all his longing. It would not be long though, surely? And they'd manage fine without him. He took up another block and paused, chisel in place against the stone, searching for anything he might have overlooked.

'I warned you, causeyman,' said an angry voice at his back. 'We've no place for idlers here. You can take your tools and go.'

Cassie looked up at Fergus Adam in blank incomprehension. It was a good two years since Mr Fergus had taken over the management of the quarry but, apart from that brief meeting in the office on the day of his dear wife's death, today was the first time he had spoken to him. George Bruce paid the men, hired and fired them, gave them their orders. Mr Fergus, in his country tweeds or city suit, stayed aloof, or, when as now he came among them, communicated through the foreman, Bruce.

'Did you hear me?' demanded Fergus. 'I said go.'

Slowly, Cassie straightened and looked Fergus Adam straight in the eyes. 'I heard you,' he said quietly. 'I just couldna believe what I heard, that's all.'

'Is anything the matter, Mr Fergus?' asked George Bruce, joining them.

'There most certainly is. This man seems to think we pay him for daydreaming and when I dismiss him, he refuses to go.'

Bruce raised an eyebrow, caught Diack's eye and looked away. 'Perhaps we'd best go to the office, Mr Fergus, and discuss the matter there.'

'There is nothing to discuss. This man leaves. And you, Bruce, get back to the work in progress. Or have you forgotten I want that section blasted by tomorrow evening?'

But it was two more days before the fuses were in place, the quarry cleared of men and the charge lit. When the dust and debris settled, Fergus and George Bruce inspected the results in gloomy silence.

'I'm afraid we'll have to bore again, Mr Fergus,' said Bruce, shaking his head. 'I reckon they fuses were not strong enough.'

'Then they damn well should have been,' snapped Fergus. 'Mackinnon would not have made that mistake.'

'Mistake you may call it, Mr Fergus, but I call it caution. Unless you want your precious granite shattered into road-metal.' George Bruce had a quick temper and a craftsman's pride. He may not have old Mackinnon's instincts and experience, but he knew the technicalities of his job well enough and a deal better than young Mr Fergus did. 'It's bedrock granite we're dealing with and it fair takes some shifting. But when we do, it'll be beautiful. Just look at that colour.'

Obediently, swallowing his anger, Fergus looked. The rock had been split open, though not enough to work as yet, and where the fresh rock showed it gleamed a rich, clean silver-blue.

'That'll be the best building rock in the country, Mr Fergus, and polished it'll be superb.'

With that thought to comfort him Fergus had to be content. At least it was something positive to tell his father. He gave orders for the resumption of work in the quarry and for fresh boring teams to begin and made his way back up the spiral track to the surface and the quarry office. There, he found a visitor awaiting him.

'I'll not keep you long, Mr Fergus,' said Mackinnon, 'and I'll not sit down. I just came to say that I'm ashamed o' ye, Mr Fergus, I am that. You shouldna need an old man to tell ye what's right, but I couldna rest easy in my bed till I'd told you to your face that what you did was wrong.'

'I don't know what you are talking about,' protested Fergus angrily. 'Anyone could get the first blast wrong and . . .'

'It's men I'm talking about, lad, nay rock. You just listen to me, laddie, and I can call you laddie if I choose as I dinna work for you now, so there's no need to go red i' the face and splutter like that. You can have all the book learning in the world, and more, but ye'll never be a good manager if ye dinna know your men. Diack's a good workman. He makes more cassies in one day than anyone else in this quarry and maybe in the whole o' Aberdeen. And if he warms his hands it's because a good workman knows how to care for his tools. What's more, Diack's given your quarry twenty years o' loyal service. If he's slowing down – and I've only your word for it that he is – it'll be because he's nae as young as he was and you should have found him a lighter job in the yard or up at the house. He didna deserve what you did to him.'

'How I run my quarry is my business,' said Fergus, though his face was red, 'and none of yours.'

'I'm thinking, Mr Fergus,' said Mackinnon sadly, 'that you've a lot to learn. You dinna even know who it is you've sacked. A man who's worked in this quarry ever since you were born, whose son is one o' your best apprentice masons, whose daughter came running two miles to fetch him when her ma was dying, whose wife left him wi' five bairns to bring up. It's nay wonder things are not going smoothly for you in the quarry. You must treat granite wi' respect – and that goes for the men who work it, too. Now I've said what I came to say, so I'll not trouble you further. Goodnight, Mr Fergus.'

He turned and went out into the brisk April evening, leaving Fergus deflated and ashamed.

But how was he to know who the man was? He wasn't the only worker in the quarry by a long chalk. And anyway, whoever he was, he was still not entitled to get paid for doing nothing. Then, suddenly, the import of Mackinnon's words struck him hard, in the heart. 'Oh, God.' *Whose daughter came running two miles to fetch him*. . . A distraught and striking girl, with startlingly blue eyes, who had fainted in his office, lain senseless and limp in his arms, then, recovered, had driven home in the dray cart with her father and brother. And later had walked with him, in trust, to the doors of Silvercairns. He remembered the soft blue of her eyes and the sense of intimacy he had felt when he touched her hand. Recalled her dignity as she had said, 'We manage.' And now he had sacked her father for no more reason than his own bad temper and condemned her to manage on even less. Mackinnon was quite right. He should have remembered. Should have expressed sympathy when the man returned to work, should have asked after his family and noted his name. Should have recognized him and recalled his circumstances. And most of all, he should not have sacked him. He had taken out his own frustration on the first man he saw for no more reason than a few minutes' rest and had been patently, flagrantly unjust. Even then, he could have set matters right. He could have let George Bruce deal with it, as Bruce had suggested. Should have done so. Bruce knew the men, being one of them himself.

Fergus sat at the office desk, his head in his hands, and let the whole force of his shame wash over him. Perhaps Mackinnon was right. Though he was an old man, perhaps old-fashioned too, everything he had told Fergus in the past had proved true. Suppose he was right about the quarry, too? About Fergus himself?

Yes, Fergus admitted, he did have a lot to learn. But so did everyone at his age and he was trying to learn it. He read books, studied. Lettice accused him of burying himself in the library when he should have been out riding or dancing or paying social calls. It was true that he did not go out much: he wanted so desperately to make a go of running his father's quarry and the need to win his father's approbation had taken precedence over everything else.

And now, if Mackinnon was right, it seemed all his work had been futile. Perhaps he would have done better to fritter his time away at parties after all? He thought briefly of Flora Burnett, the sister of one of Hugo's friends. He knew she liked him and he could have been attracted to her had he allowed himself to be so, but always Silvercairns had come first. Suppose he had joined in the social dance, taken a box at the theatre, attended the Assemblies, gone to house parties? Played cards and gambled? Flirted and joked and laughed? But that was Hugo's scene, not his. Fergus was serious-minded, quickly bored by frivolity, and no good at all at flirtatious small talk. He would not have made a success of the social whirl either. Perhaps he was incapable of making a success of anything?

He sat for a long time, immobile, while the light faded and outside the sky to the west was streaked with dying gold. The yard lay in shadow, and in the quarry, the braziers were extinguished, the last wagons loaded, the tools packed away and work ended for another day. Horses laboured slowly to the surface, followed by weary, plodding men. For the most part they were silent, saving their strength for the journey home, and from inside the office their passing sounded like the passing of a herd of docile cattle. But they were not cattle. They were his workmen, with wives and homes and children about which he knew nothing. Their lives were their own, and no business of his, as his was no business of theirs, except that their paths crossed every working day of the week when they came to Silvercairns.

Mackinnon had said Fergus would never be a good manager until he knew his men. And that the quarry would know it and react accordingly. It was fanciful, of course, but not altogether impossible. Mackinnon had had an affinity with the granite, had treated it as an ally and a fellow-workman. Whereas to Fergus it was an adversary. The thought was a startling one, but true. He realized he was afraid of that solid wall of granite, afraid of its power and weight. Afraid he would not measure up to it . . . and worst of all he had dismissed one of the quarry's workmen who was blameless and whose family would suffer in consequence.

The light had completely faded from the evening sky and the office was in darkness before Fergus found a path out of his troubles. Though he knew in his heart that he ought to reinstate Diack, apologize, and admit publicly that he had been wrong, it was more than his pride would allow. So he persuaded himself that to do so would undermine his authority and instead resolved to send the man a month's wages in thanks for his services. That would ease the family's burden and salve his own conscience. Of Diack's daughter, he refused to think. But from tomorrow, he would try to memorize at least some of the workmen's names.

The first stars were bright overhead when Fergus, well pleased with his decision, locked the office door and made his way towards the lights of Silvercairns.

* * *

They were eighteen at table and the long dining-room at Silvercairns sparkled for the occasion. Candelabra, flowers, shimmering crystal and silver, crisp damask linen and mirror-polished wood: surveying the product of all her nagging efforts, Lettice was well pleased. And pleased again when she glimpsed herself in the huge gilt-framed mirror over the mantelpiece and noted her own porcelain skin and beautifully dressed flaxen hair which her gown of cerise taffeta set off to perfection. She was less pleased when, glancing to her left, she saw Hamish Dunn wave away the excellent white wine which her father had selected specially to accompany the turtle soup and ask for plain water instead. It disconcerted her to see someone so apparently impervious to the blandishments of the Adam table and she felt her confidence falter. Perhaps he would be equally impervious to hers?

In the drawing-room before dinner she had thought everything went superbly well. Hamish had arrived a little late, but she had met him herself at the door of the drawing-room and extended her hand. 'So pleased to hear of your appointment Mr Dunn. I have been a devoted follower of yours ever since I first heard you speak, when my brother behaved so disgracefully . . .' (here she had given a pretty little deprecating smile inviting his indulgence) '. . . and now I look forward to hearing you speak with equal forcefulness from our own little pulpit at Silvercairns.' Here she had released his hand, as if aware that she had held it too long, and lowered her eyes in modesty before saying with a timid smile, 'We are all delighted you were able to come tonight.'

He had thanked her for her kind words, and apologized for his late arrival. He had been detained, he said, by the beadle and Lettice had earnestly hoped that nothing fatal threatened the fabric of the church.

'I hardly think one would call a blocked gutter fatal, Miss Adam,' he had said, with a smile, but before she could hoist the conversation on to more promising levels her father had removed Mr Dunn to introduce him to Mr Ainslie Sharp who was 'something big' in railways. But it was a promising beginning and the whole evening still stretched ahead of her, with infinite possibilities.

Mr Dunn's hair was redder than she remembered, or perhaps

it merely seemed so against the black correctness of his clothes, and at close quarters his skin was more freckled, his hands larger and squarer, and his jaw positively pugnacious. She had known him to be a tall man, but there was also something rugged and almost primitive about him, in spite of his clerical garb, which gave the impression, she thought daringly, of a savage tribesman, tamed. His eyes were lively and intelligent, his voice mellifluous and strong, with that delightful Highland lilt which had so intrigued her the first time she heard him speak. If she had been looking for a contrast to that insufferable Niall Burnett whom her father was always pushing in her direction, she could not have found a better. When he took her hand in welcome she had felt the masculine power in his warm, firm grip, and now just to be close to him sent a pleasant little *frisson* up her spine. But for the moment her father had commandeered him and Lettice began to circulate as she had never circulated before, smiling, complimenting, making her guests feel warmly welcome, introducing one to another, and now and again she would glance in Hamish's direction, hoping he would notice. Once she caught his eye, he answered her quick smile, and she sparkled afresh, determined to do herself proud in the role of hostess. For were not ministers' wives required to do such things? To mix and mingle with any company, to play a sort of ecclesiastical lady of the manor? Lettice was not closely acquainted with ministers' wives, their own minister for so many years having been a widower with a perfectly competent though uninspiring sister who offered dry shortbread and tiny glasses of Madeira to any visitors brave enough to call. Whether the sister called on her brother's parishioners and what she took with her if she did were unknown to Lettice. But the business of parish visiting could come later. For the moment it was enough to show herself to him as the assured and solicitous hostess. She had been so engrossed in her part that she had not noticed whether Hamish Dunn held a glass in his hand and if he did, what was in it.

Now, seeing that reproachful glass of water, she wished she had had the foresight to refuse wine too. But the idea had never occurred to her.

'Do you never drink wine, Mr Dunn?' she asked, regarding him solemnly with artless eyes. The seating plan had been overseen by her father, but by sacrificing herself to Widower Burnett on her right she had managed to keep Hamish Dunn on her left. Similarly, though Fergus had been saddled with Widow Macdonald on one side, he had Fanny Wyness on the other, though in his case, she suspected, he found each equally boring, but no doubt either lady would do for a bride as far as her father was concerned.

'I am surprised at you, Miss Adam,' he said, though from the twinkle in his eyes she took it to be teasing. 'Surely you expect me to practise what I preach?'

'Yes, of course, but I thought . . . I mean . . . surely Temperance does not always have to mean total abstinence, but merely the avoidance of excess and one small glass . . .'

'Is not excessive? No. But then the wine is so delicious and the hostess so charming that one glass becomes two, then three, perhaps more. At what point, Miss Adam, would you draw the line between moderation and excess?'

Hugo, who had been placed further up the table on the opposite side, overheard. 'At the point where you fall under the table!' he called cheerfully and promptly emptied his glass. 'Damn good vintage, this.' He tipped back his chair and summoned the butler for a refill.

'I rather think that proves my point,' said Hamish Dunn. 'Even your brother, with all his mathematical genius, loses count when it comes to wine.'

'I say,' said Hugo, good-humouredly enough, 'that's a bit below the belt, old chap. Though I did set you right about your road of bread it was only in fun.'

'I don't think "old chap" is quite the way to address your new minister, Hugo,' said Lettice gently, but the glare she gave him was far from gentle. Why didn't he shut up and talk to the Macdonald girl like a dutiful son?

'Oops, sorry your reverence. No offence. Here's your very good health,' and he raised his glass to Hamish Dunn, bowed solemnly across the table, and drank.

Lettice was furious with her brother and immediately set about mending matters. 'You must forgive Hugo,' she murmured confidentially. 'He is very young still, and since our mother died . . .' She left the sentence unfinished, hoping for sympathy perhaps, but Hamish Dunn said, 'Think no more about it, Miss Adam,' and returned to his soup. A moment later he turned to Flora Burnett on his other side and soon they were deep in conversation about the troubles of crofters in the Highlands.

Damn Hugo. Why couldn't he learn when to shut up?

'May I say, Miss Adam, how utterly charming you look tonight?' said a smooth voice on her right and she turned to find Flora's widowed father, Archie Burnett, regarding her *décolletage* with obvious appreciation. 'Like a blushing damask rose, if I may say so without impertinence, "and fair as is the rose in May."'

'Thank you, Mr Burnett, for that generous compliment.' But she did not want his compliments, or the gallantry which he unleashed with gathering eloquence as the meal progressed. She did not know which was worse: Niall Burnett's arrogant and needling antagonism or his father's excessive attention. But she knew she wanted neither. She wanted only to engage Hamish Dunn's interest, which, however hard she tried, she failed to do. He was polite, attentive, courteous, but always after exchanging a few sentences with her, he turned to his other neighbour and redressed the balance. In vain she told herself he was merely being the well-bred guest, that others were doing the same, that no one at a dinner table was expected or allowed to monopolize one guest over another. But she wanted Hamish Dunn's attention wholly for herself. She wracked her brains in vain for some comment she could make which would intrigue him, make him look at her with different eyes, and in her frustration emptied her glass and allowed it to be refilled, twice.

He refused the claret. So did Flora, but then Flora only drank white wine anyway. That meant nothing. Across the table Hugo was making up for their abstinence, and she saw Fergus accept a glass too, though whereas in Hugo's case wine induced frenetic high spirits, in Fergus it seemed to have no effect. He was making no effort at all to talk to poor Mrs Macdonald, who was a pleasant enough woman and not unattractive for thirty-eight, and as for Fanny, apart from offering her the salt cellar, he had ignored her throughout the meal. Fanny was used to that, of course, having known Fergus since childhood, but it did not excuse his behaviour all the same. When he was not staring at his plate, he was staring across the table at Flora and Hamish

Dunn with an expression of equal despondency. He had been preoccupied all week, brooding over his blessed quarry. Too preoccupied to do anything about her terrace wall anyway, even though he had promised, and he was obviously still brooding . . .

Lettice glanced quickly to the head of the table: if her father noticed Fergus's behaviour he would be in trouble. But her father seemed deep in some no doubt technical conversation with the railway expert and impervious to everything else around him.

'Fergus,' she said, leaning across the table and trying to see through the leafy barrier of her tasteful floral display. 'Why don't you tell Mr Dunn about the new quarry workings. I am sure he would be interested.'

'Why should he be? Besides, nothing to tell.' Too late Lettice realized that Fergus's leaden silence was the direct result of the circulation of the wine, and that he had had far more than one glass.

'I would certainly be most interested, Mr Adam,' said Hamish cheerfully. 'Especially as a number of your workmen attend my church and I hope to recruit many more. For instance, how many workmen do you employ and in what capacity? Do you have any sort of accommodation for them or must they live in town? Is there any sickness provision or compensation for the victims of accidents? Or any help for their widows and children? I am, as yet, woefully ignorant of such things.'

'So am I,' said Fergus morosely. 'Ignorant as sin. Sacked a fellow last week and didn't even know his name.'

Hamish Dunn looked startled and Flora Burnett said gently, 'Oh, dear. Was his offence very heinous?'

'I thought so at the time. He didn't, of course, and neither do I now, but it's too late.'

'Oh, Fergus, I am sorry.' Flora looked at him with genuine sympathy and for the first time Fergus attempted a smile.

'My own fault,' he shrugged. 'Try to do better next time. Do you know, I have resolved to learn the names of three of my workers every day?'

'A noble resolution,' she said and added playfully, 'I'll wager two of every three will be Alexander something, anyway.' Then she turned back to Hamish Dunn and the Highland clearances.

'Three a day,' repeated Fergus, to no one in particular, and once more relapsed into silence, but it was a different silence as he watched Flora Burnett across the table. He remembered why he had been attracted to her: she was sweet-faced, intelligent, sensible, the sort of girl one could feel at ease with and yet at the same time admire. Like that other girl, in a way . . . the same dark hair, the same soft eyes, though the other girl's eyes were a deeper, more passionate blue . . . But that was ridiculous. He shook his head with quick impatience to clear it of such inanities. How could they be similar? One was a nobody, the other old Burnett's daughter, with an ancient family estate, and a lineage long as your arm.

Flora's dark hair was done up in a particularly attractive way tonight, he noticed, with curly bits and little velvet flowers, and that dark green silk stuff certainly emphasized the curve of her bosom and her neat little waist. It changed the colour of her eyes, too, making them green instead of whatever they usually were. Blue, was it? Or grey? He realized, with returning despondency, that he did not know.

If only the quarry did not occupy so much of his time, he would pay court to her, and gladly – that was one thing of which his father would approve – but, waking and sleeping, he found himself wholly preoccupied with the business of granite. It was like an obsession, a disease, and he knew that until he had blasted this new seam, opened up the next 'bank' of rock, and set production successfully in motion, he would have time for nothing else. Even Flora. Watching her through the fronds of asparagus fern and hothouse carnations, he resolved that by the summer he would have beaten the quarry into submission and be free. Then he would ask her . . .

At the far end of the table his father, too, was thinking of the summer. 'Two months from now, Mr Sharp, I can promise you we will be producing double what we are at the moment. We'll have stone enough for a hundred viaducts and as many bridges as you choose to build from Edinburgh to Inverness.'

'You will have to make your prices competitive, Mr Adam,' warned Sharp, a smooth-faced gentleman with colourless hair and small, round glasses which, however, failed to mask the shrewdness of his eyes. 'We've had offers from quarries in the Edinburgh area which we'd be foolish to refuse.'

'And equally foolish to accept,' countered Adam, 'with all the transport costs and delays, not to mention inferior stone. You don't want a viaduct that's going to collapse under your trains, do you?'

'Nor one that's going to cost so much it will never get built,' retorted Sharp. 'We have shareholders' money to consider, remember, and shareholders expect dividends.'

'You are just the man to tell us, Mr Sharp,' put in George Wyness from across the table, 'is it to be the Great North of Scotland plan or the Perth, Inverness and Elgin one?'

'All I can tell you at the moment, gentlemen,' said Sharp smoothly, 'is that the railway will come to Aberdeen. It will undoubtedly extend further northwards, but I understand the exact route is still under discussion.'

'Very diplomatic,' grumbled Wyness, 'but no help to a man when he's choosing where to put his money.'

'Why not give it to me, George,' called Duncan Forbes, 'and I'll guarantee to keep it safe for you in my bank.'

'That reminds me,' said Adam. 'You should take a look at the new bank in Castle Street. Then you'll see what Aberdeen granite can do. There's nothing to beat it. Edinburgh quarries indeed! Rubbish. That's what you'll get from them. In this world you get what you pay for, Sharp, and if you buy cheap, you buy shoddy.'

'All this talk of money and business,' twittered Aunt Blackwell anxiously. 'I'm sure we ladies would much prefer to hear what plans are afoot for the Queen's birthday celebrations this year.' But Old Man Adam was not to be diverted.

'You can see with your own eyes in the morning, Sharp. I'll take you to the quarry and show you myself what we have to offer. If it wasn't for the dark, I'd take you this minute, by George. When you've seen our stone I guarantee there'll be no more talk of Edinburgh granite!' He drained his glass and looked round angrily for more, but in contrast to Old Man Adam's obvious agitation Ainslie Sharp remained apparently unmoved.

'Certainly, Adam, I would be most interested to see it, but I am afraid it must be on another occasion. I catch the Defiance for Perth in the morning.'

'Did I hear you say Defiance, sir?' said Niall Burnett. 'The best-conducted coach in the kingdom and I defy anyone to deny it.' He leant back in his chair and hooked well-manicured thumbs into brocaded waistcoast pockets as if waiting to be challenged.

'Niall is right,' said Hugo. 'Aberdeen to Edinburgh, regular as clockwork for sixteen years.'

'Fifteen, dear,' said Aunt Blackwell. 'I remember distinctly because it was the year your dear mother . . .'

'Sixteen,' interrupted Niall smoothly and smiled in that supercilious way he always did, thought Lettice, when he had been impossibly rude and expected no one to take offence. On the contrary, one was expected to grovel and be grateful. He was an arrogant, self-opinionated ass and she, for one, was not going to worship at the shrine of his carefully curled hair and his ridiculous waistcoats. The Burnett estate was a large and prosperous one, and she knew her father had asked Niall particularly in order that he might look Lettice over, but she would rather die an old maid than marry him.

The talk diverged into various channels all of which flowed round Lettice without involving her. She sat silent, picking at her roast sirloin without appetite. It was proving to be a dreary dinner, nothing like what she had expected, and she had gone to such trouble, too. It was not fair. She tried once more to engage Mr Dunn in conversation, about the theatre this time, but with no more success than before, and she bit her lip with mingled disappointment, annoyance and affront. How dare he take no notice of her? And at her own table?

'You are very fetching, Miss Adam, when you pout like that,' said the smooth voice on her right. 'Like a little girl who cannot get her own way. Or perhaps one who has had a spanking and wants a kiss to make it better?'

'I don't know what you're talking about,' snapped Lettice, but when he asked whether, one day next week, she would allow him to accompany her to the theatre where he had engaged a box for the season, she grudgingly said yes. No doubt Niall would be of the party too, but two could play the arrogance game and she would merely ignore him. Besides, Hamish Dunn was hardly likely to take her, and it was reputedly a good play.

The gentlemen sat a long time over their port and when they eventually joined the ladies in the drawing-room, Lettice noticed that Fergus and Hamish Dunn seemed the best of friends. The card tables were set out for those such as Mrs Macdonald and Aunt Blackwell who wished to play, but Mr Dunn took no part. Flora and then Amelia played the piano. Fanny Wyness sang. It was the usual, tedious, uneventful evening, and she had had such splendid, romantic hopes . . .

'Is anything troubling you, Miss Adam?' asked Hamish Dunn, sitting down beside her on the cream upholstered sofa. 'You seem a little melancholy.'

She looked up at him for an unguarded moment with the eyes of a thwarted child before the mask of rich Mr Adam's lovely and accomplished daughter slipped back into place.

'Do I? Then I am sorry. I expect I am a little tired.'

'Then I must not intrude upon you any longer. You must be longing for your guests to go home.' He smiled, with that mischievous look she remembered, and suddenly the evening was not quite so unrelievedly bad.

'Oh, no, I did not mean that. At least, not in your case. Though to be truthful, perhaps in some . . .'

'Believe me, I understand. The demands of hospitality are sometimes onerous. But to relieve your burden at least a little, Miss Adam, I will take my leave. If I am to be up as early as your brother in the morning I had better seek my bed.' For a wild moment Letticc thought Hugo must have challenged him to some sort of wager, then he said, 'Fergus has very kindly offered to show me over your quarry. If I am to minister at all adequately to my flock I had better find out all I can about their pastures, don't you think?'

'In that case, Mr Dunn,' said Lettice daringly, 'would it not be more convenient for you to stay the night? There is a bed made up in readiness and it will be no trouble.'

'And no trouble to me to ride a short mile home. But I am grateful for your offer.' In the doorway he took her hand and raised it to his lips with a gesture of old-world gallantry which took her breath away. 'Farewell, Miss Adam. Until we meet again.'

'Well!' said Lizzie Lennox in astonishment. 'And him a minister o' the cloth. Would you credit it?' She had been sent by cook to fetch more eggs from the dairy, ready for the morning breakfasts, and seeing the light from the open doorway as she crossed the yard, had slipped round the corner to spy, out of lifelong habit. Now she stood in the shadow of the stable wall and watched the stable boy lead the minister's horse to the steps. The minister mounted, touched his hat, and rode off down the moonlit drive towards the gates while that Miss Carrot stood looking after him as if she expected him to turn round any minute and ride back again. But he didna. Just kneed his horse into a trot and vanished into the night.

'Five guineas my horse can trot to your place and back in an hour,' cried a voice behind her and she whipped round to see that several men had appeared from the back regions and were milling about the stable yard in a cheerfully drunken fashion.

'Not now, Hugo old chap. It's too dark.'

'My horse can see in the dark, no bother, can't you, old fellow,' and he lurched towards one of the looseboxes where a handsome chestnut with a white star on its forehead looked disdainfully over the company. 'Ten guineas he can do it in the dark, there and back, in under an hour.'

'Not with you on his back, Hugo old man. You'd be in the ditch before you'd gone a mile.'

Lizzie recognized the voice as that of that supercilious Niall Burnett, the one she'd flashed her bum at in Belmont Street that time, and the other was Hugo Adam. She'd seen him about the place of course, but not face to face yet, what wi' Ma Gregor the cook being such a battleaxe, wi' eyes in the back of her head and wanting to know what Lizzie was doing morning, noon and night. But Lizzie had been lucky to be offered the job and luckier still to get her da's permission to take it and then only because Old Man Adam was known to be a God-fearing man and a patron of the kirk, who saw that his servants said their prayers proper, and she wasna going to lose it till she'd done well for herself, one way or another, so she'd smarmed and simpered and done what the old bag wanted, and bided her time. But, she thought gleefully, this might just be that time.

She ran quick fingers through her hair, tugged at her apron, tightened her belt, set her head at a jaunty angle and, the basin of eggs in her arms, set off across the stable yard on a course that could only run through the middle of the group.

That arrogant Niall Burnett didna look at her, of course, just went on talking and pretending she wasna there, but she made sure Hugo Adam saw her. 'Good evening, Mr Hugo,' she called out when she was so close he couldna help but hear and when he looked around, she smiled at him real pretty and dipped a curtsey.

'Good God!' said Hugo, his face a picture of dawning wonder. 'Who the devil are you?'

'Lizzie, sir. Lizzie Lennox.' She turned away, with a demure look over her shoulder and the smallest, almost accidental wiggle of her hips.

'Just a minute. Not so fast.' Hugo lurched forward and grabbed her arm, horse, trotting race and guineas forgotten.

Deliberately, she dropped the wooden basin so the eggs spilt out and shattered on the cobbles. 'Oh, sir! Look what you've made me do! Cook'll kill me!'

'Oh, lor.' Hugo looked at the glutinous mess with an expression of comical dismay.

'That was your breakfast, sir, all them eggs. Now I'll have to fetch more and they're counted every last one o' them and how I'll explain that there's a dozen missing I canna think.' She feigned a trembling lip and looked up at him with reproach. 'You shouldna have jogged my arm, sir, not wi' me carrying eggs.'

'Impudent hussy,' said Niall. 'Send her packing.'

'No . . . my fault . . . must put things right. Tell you what, Niall,' said Hugo, putting his arm round the other's shoulder, 'forget the trotting wager. Too dark anyway. Why don't you take the others to the billiard room and set up the brandy, while I have a quick word with Cook? A brace of shakes and I'll join you.'

'Is that what they call it now?' drawled Niall, shrugged, said, 'Rather you than me, old boy,' and led the others away towards the house.

'Now, Lizzie,' said Mr Hugo, looking down at her with a particular gleam in his eye. 'Why don't I help you fetch more eggs from the dairy, then . . . later . . . I'll make things right with Cook?'

'Mr Hugo!' she said, feigning shock, but not too convincingly in case he thought she meant it. Before the promising exchange could develop further they heard an irate voice from the kitchen calling, 'Lizzie! Where's them eggs?'

Hugo swore, squeezed her waist, whispered, 'Fetch more and leave it to me,' gave her a playful smack on the rump, then strode forward towards the lighted kitchen regions. 'My fault, Cookie,' he said cheerfully. 'I am afraid I commandeered them – a little wager of mine. Have you ever juggled with eggs? No, you wouldn't have, I suppose. Not altogether successful, I admit. Anyway, not the girl's fault. I sent her for more. Who is she, by the way?' he asked conversationally when the cook pursed her lips and made no answer.

'My new kitchenmaid and no business of yours, if I might be so bold, Mr Hugo.'

They heard hurrying footsteps behind them and Lizzie appeared with a fresh supply of eggs. 'I'm ever so sorry, Mrs Gregor, that I am, but . . .'

'Juggling with eggs indeed,' interrupted Cook. 'Whatever next!'

'As you say, Mrs Gregor, whatever next?' Hugo turned to leave the kitchen and winked at Lizzie behind Mrs Gregor's back. She could not acknowledge it, as Mrs Gregor was going on at her, face to face, but she didn't need to. That was one young man Lizzie knew she would see again.

When she finally lay down for what was left of the night in the attic room she shared with three other girls, she went over in her mind the events of the evening and was well pleased.

She had been at Silvercairns almost three weeks, ever since Eppie had sent word that the kitchenmaid had measles, the scullerymaid had disappeared and the parlourmaid been found in the family way and dismissed, all in one week, and with the household just newly moved to Silvercairns and everything at sixes and sevens, if Lizzie wanted a job, now was the time to go for one. Lizzie had gone, and to her momentary disappointment, been taken on. She'd fancied getting her own job, wi' those petticoats Mhairi had sewed, and a bit o' blackmail, just to make it exciting, like. But Mhairi Diack had swicked her. Lizzie frowned with remembered affront. Sneaked off without a word and delivered them herself, and Lizzie only finding out later, by chance. She owed Mhairi one for that. But Lizzie still had that useful piece of information, and Mhairi Diack couldna swick her on that. At least Lizzie was in the house now, and could rake around all she pleased, as long as no one caught her.

Not that she had abandoned the idea of that threat; she'd merely saved it up for future use. Now, as she lay on the edge of sleep, she wondered if maybe she wouldna waste it on Mhairi after all, but use it on someone else instead. She hadna seen the last of Hugo Adam and if she played her cards right, she could maybe do very well for herself there, one day.

Fergus Adam was striding down the Gallowgate some weeks later when he saw her, a slim, dark-haired girl with striking blue eyes. For a moment, his head still full of the bargaining details for the barrels of blasting powder he had just ordered from Cruikshank's – 'And see you deliver them in double-quick time!' – he noted her merely as a remarkably pretty girl: then, with a rush of shame and embarrassment and something else he refused to acknowledge, as the girl in the lane, the daughter of the man he had so summarily dismissed. She saw and recognized him at the same moment, but, instead of lowering her eyes and avoiding him, as he had expected, she came straight on up the Gallowgate, challenging him to step aside.

'Good morning, Miss Diack,' he said, and bowed, astonished at his own behaviour. He was according her all the courtesy he would have given Flora Burnett, yet she was no one in his social acquaintance, merely the daughter of a sacked quarryman.

'Good morning, Mr Adam,' she replied, with cold courtesy, but her eyes challenged him, as an equal, to speak, to justify himself, even to apologize.

He saw the cloth of her bodice tighten as her breathing quickened, noted the two pinker patches on her cheeks and the proud tilt of her head. Her neck was white and achingly slender, her hair thick and gleaming dark as jet. He noted that she held a small girl by the hand, her sister no doubt, for the child was regarding him with the same disconcertingly direct eyes. He ought to have stepped aside, to let her pass. Instead, his heart beating suddenly faster under the blue intensity of her gaze, he said, ridiculously, 'How is your father?'

'Out of work and ill. But I thought you would have known

that, Mr Adam. It was, after all, your doing.' Her eyes met his with unflinching accusation.

'I am truly sorry, Miss Diack. It was unfortunate that . . . that . . .' he floundered, unaccountably at a loss.

'Unfortunate that my father lost his job? Oh, yes, Mr Adam. Unfortunate for him and for his family, but not, I think, for you.'

She made to pass him, but he put out a hand to restrain her. 'Please, Miss Diack.' He could not let her go until he had justified himself somehow. 'If there is anything I can do to . . .' He had been going to say 'make amends' but she interrupted him.

'*You?*' The single word held surprise, contempt, disgust. 'Haven't you done enough?' He dropped his hand and she moved on with a dignity that would not have disgraced a duchess. Fergus Adam felt humiliated and angry and doubly ashamed. He should never have spoken to the girl in the first place. The daughter of a man he had dismissed. What had he been thinking of? She might have sworn at him, spat in his face, flown at him with tooth and claw . . . Except that he could not imagine her behaving with anything but ladylike decorum.

Ladylike? He was madder than he thought. But instead of turning his back and moving on, Fergus watched her walk away up the Gallowgate, and as he noted her trim waist, her threadbare but spotless clothing, the protective way she guarded her little sister from the buffetings of other pedestrians, and her brave dignity, he felt an overwhelming urge to comfort and protect her. He wanted to clothe her in soft silks and cashmeres, give her gloves for her work-roughened hands, take the anxiety from her pinched young face, put flowers in her hair . . .

But that was ridiculous. Whatever was he thinking of? Money would be of far more use to the Diack family. But if he sent money to the house, he knew she would reject it. Diack had accepted the extra wages as only his due, but any more money Fergus sent would be seen as charity – or conscience money. Remembering her scornful '*You?*' he flushed again with shame. She had had no business to speak to him like that, of course, but in his heart he knew he deserved it. Besides, when they were together, it was as if they had known each other all their lives. It had been so from the moment he first saw her, on that day in the quarry office . . . Impatiently, he shook his head. He was being fanciful and maudlin, even downright absurd. She was little more than a child, seventeen at the most, and a nobody, whereas he was son and heir to Mungo Adam of Silvercairns.

The thought of Silvercairns reminded him firstly that he had further business to transact on the quarry's behalf, and secondly that Diack also had a son who, he presumed, still worked at the quarry. Fergus has been perfectly genuine in his resolution to learn his workmen's names, but when it came to the point he did not seem to have the facility. Hamish Dunn, on the other hand, seemed to have it to excess. During that trip around the quarry, he had asked endless though pertinent questions, spoken to several of his parishioners by name and inquired after their respective families, introduced himself to as many more, tackled first George Bruce, then Fergus himself about the hours worked and the wages paid, demanded what would happen if, say, a man was killed or injured by a rock fall, and while making no comment, approving or otherwise, had left Fergus with the uncomfortable feeling that he had fallen short, somehow, in his duties, both as an employer and as a Christian. He had also left Fergus with the certainty that the Reverend Dunn had committed all those names, facts and figures to memory and could produce them again, effortlessly and without fault, at the drop of a hat. And now Fergus could not even remember what the Diack boy looked like, let alone whether he still worked for him or not.

A good workman, he seemed to remember someone saying. Mackinnon perhaps? And he had added, 'One o' your best apprentice masons.' Fergus would see what he could do to increase the boy's wages, without laying himself open to suspicion, of course. A bonus payment, perhaps, when the new seam was fully opened up? That would help the family out a bit. Or, better still . . . He remembered that promise to his sister to get her terrace wall repaired. Of course! The Diack lad must do it. He would speak to George Bruce. The order would come better from him. But Fergus himself would see that the lad was paid generously for his trouble.

Pleased with his decision, he turned into the doorway of William Glass's shop to cast a critical eye over the new consignment of shooting gaiters which, the proprietor assured him, were absolutely impervious to wet. And while he was there, he might as well buy himself new spats. With work at the quarry going so well, he might soon have time for a little social life, and Flora Burnett.

'How dare he?' fumed Mhairi, over and over, as she hurried up the Gallowgate with Annys trotting obediently beside her. She was trembling now with the shock of her encounter: but the moment she had seen Fergus Adam, she had determined to speak her mind. For weeks now, in the two poor rooms they called home, her father had sat silent and defeated, hour after hour, staring at nothing, like a hopeless, broken man. Hasn't he had grief enough? she cried, with silent, helpless anguish. With his job the only dignity left to him, how dare Fergus Adam take it away? And to think she had secretly admired him, had held dear the memory of his chivalry and kindness and his apparent friendship, had cast him in her dreams as a prince . . . And now, she thought with returning fury, he sacks my father for no reason at all except his own bad temper and then has the nerve to ask if he can do anything to help! I'll never forgive him for that. Prince indeed! He is a heartless, arrogant, supercilious . . . but she ran out of suitable adjectives and had to content herself with yet another 'How dare he!'

That evening, as he had taken to doing, Alex said lightly, 'Want to see me to the end of the street, Mhairi?' Annys, as usual, begged to go too, but this time when her father suggested Annys stay at home with him, Mhairi agreed. 'Da will tell you stories about the countryside,' she soothed, 'and I'll not be long.' Though she would not admit it to herself, she wanted the reassurance of Alex's uncomplicated honesty and love. At the foot of the tenement steps, he put his arm around her waist and when they reached the darkened archway off Galen's Close where they usually stopped, to laugh and talk idly together before parting, he drew her into its shadows, as she had hoped he would, and kissed her. Not the chaste goodnight kiss which Annys's presence demanded, but a deep and satisfying lover's kiss.

'I've wanted to do that for so long,' he murmured, his breath warm against her cheek. Alex was kind and good and he loved her. He would never be gratuitously cruel, to her or to her family. Not like . . . She twined her arms tight round his neck, found his mouth with hers, and sought to obliterate all memory of that other in the sweet communion of flesh with flesh. There were carriages in the Castlegate, not ten yards away, lamplight, and a knot of city businessmen in the doorway of the Lemon Tree tavern, but Alex and Mhairi might have been alone in the wildest desert for all the notice they took of their surroundings. Until he slipped a hand inside her bodice and caressed her breast. With a small moan, she tried to twist away, but he held her tight and as the sweet sensations flooded through her body, filling her with melting need, she knew that she loved him, wanted him with all her trembling being.

Then out of nowhere the image of her mother, bleeding to death in premature childbirth, flashed terrifyingly before her eyes and she struggled to push him away. 'No . . . please . . .'

Abruptly he turned away from her, leant his head against the cold stone of the arch and groaned. In memory she heard her mother's anguished voice saying, 'Never marry, lass. It isna worth it.' And she knew now what her mother meant – squalor and poverty and struggle and children. But when Mhairi married, she thought fiercely, it would not be like that. She would have that house she dreamed of, for herself and her husband alone, so that when the children came, as she supposed they inevitably must, there would be space and cleanliness and peace.

After a moment, when he did not speak, she said timidly, 'I am sorry,' and added, in propitiation, 'I love you.' He turned then, clasped her against his chest, buried his face in her hair and said, 'I know, and I love you too, Mhairi. I'm sorry if I . . . oh, God, Mhairi, I want you so much . . . but what are we to do?'

'Wait, and hope.'

There was a long silence before Alex said, with vehemence, 'I'll succeed one day, Mhairi, I promise you. When I've served my time, I'll set up on my own and then in no time at all I'll be rich as Old Man Adam. I'll build you a palace, big enough for all of us . . .'

'I know you will,' soothed Mhairi, 'one day.' She remembered her mother all that time ago, saying 'Never lose hope' and she was right. Hope made anything bearable. Besides, with her father out of work and her motherless family to feed and care for hope was all they had. She clung to that thought for comfort as they kissed and parted, unsatisfied, he to his uncle's tenement, she to Mitchell's Court.

Since her father's dismissal life had been harder than ever in Mitchell's Court, and with his breathing bad and his spirit broken Cassie was not likely to find work now, had he the energy to seek it. Tom's wage as an apprentice was minimal and what Mhairi managed to earn by her sewing was little more. When they were not at school Lorn and Willy did their best, gathering driftwood and selling it in bundles, for kindling, to the rich houses in the West End, and hanging around the Plainstanes in the hope of earning the odd penny by holding a gentleman's horse, carrying a lady's basket or running a message. Mhairi was grateful for their efforts, but anxious.

'See you get into no trouble, mind,' she would warn them, over and over. 'I'll not have you pinching apples and the like, or handkerchiefs from gentlemen's pockets. I know what Lizzie Lennox used to let her kids get up to, but those sort of tricks are not for the Diacks. There was a lad transported only last month for thieving and I'll not have that happen to any of mine. So remember what I'm telling you. No trouble!' And they would promise her solemnly to stay on the right side of the law.

But Mhairi still worried, as she worried about Lizzie Lennox. She had smiled with relief when she heard of Lizzie's job, for though the petticoats were safely delivered, she did not trust Lizzie not to think up some other threat to hold over Mhairi. She might still do so, but at least she was two miles away and out of sight, in Silvercairns.

Miss Roberts had been so pleased with Mhairi's work that she had promised to give her more. Mhairi was more than grateful though Miss Roberts paid as little as the Ladies' Working, for the latter were still apparently selling off old stock and had given Mhairi no work for several weeks.

However, this year the Queen's birthday was to be celebrated with more than usual splendour for it was also the day chosen for the laying of the foundation stone of the new harbour works, to be known as Victoria Dock. There were to be processions, bands, fireworks and grand dinners, both public and private, and as the day was a public holiday, everyone would take part. All the Masons' Lodges would be in the procession in ceremonial regalia or fancy dress and Mhairi had promised to take Annys to see her brother and Alex, while Lorn and Willy would go whether Mhairi took them or not. Miss Roberts had brought Mhairi a heap of sewing to finish before the grand day, for she had more orders than she could deal with for ball dresses, soirée gowns and evening cloaks, as well as under-petticoats and stays.

Mhairi stitched and sang and felt excitement bubble up inside her as the great day drew near, and had it not been for her father's silent despair, and her constant worry about making ends meet, she would have been almost happy. Alex and Tom were to be in the procession, too, and she had promised to stitch a bear's head for one and a wizard's hat for the other. Somehow or other she would manage it, in time snatched from Miss Roberts' work or from her own sleep. She would have sat up all night, if necessary, to get the work done, and when the procession was over, Alex and she would watch the fireworks together and later, perhaps, slip away somewhere, secretly . . . Whenever she thought of Alex, which was most of her waking hours, she felt a quivering, yearning excitement which was both joy and pain, for always, inevitably, in their meetings there came the moment when she said 'no', though each time, as their bodies grew more in tune, it became more difficult. Sometimes, in the twilight hours before sleep, when she lay alone, remembering his caresses, an insidious worm of fear would creep into her brain to eat away at her confidence. Fear that she would lose her resolve and afterwards regret it, that he would grow tired of waiting, turn elsewhere for his pleasure. She remembered Lizzie Lennox's gleeful hints at Alex's sexual prowess, and at the thought of where he might go for solace when she refused him, burned with jealousy and pain.

Suppose, in spite of all protestations, he ceased to love her? Even if he did love her enough to wait and marry her, suppose their happiness did not last? In the bleak, small hours she frightened herself with fears that he would fall ill, that there would be some dreadful accident at the quarry, that she would lose him . . . And always, under her anxieties and her happiness, was the fear of Lizzie Lennox. For, though it was months ago now, Mhairi knew her too well to think she would forget about her threatened blackmail and Alex, for all his gentleness, had a blind spot of violence where his brother Donal was concerned. Of Fergus Adam she hardly thought at all.

The harbour works were a major undertaking and Mungo Adam had done well to secure a contract for a good section of the pier foundations. It was not every granite that was suitable for underwater work, where not only hardness and durability were required, but great specific gravity as well in order to withstand the constant buffeting of the breakers. A good, heavy, compact granite was ideal and Mungo Adam had managed to convince the harbour authorities that Silvercairns could supply what was needed. Now, with that advertisement to his credit – and the celebrations on the Queen's birthday, with the official laying of the foundation stone, would provide an ideal forum at which to draw attention to Silvercairns – he hoped to do better. For Mungo Adam had spoken only the truth when he had told Fergus there was enough granite in the hole they had without digging another. The new 'bank' Fergus had opened up was, if anything, richer than the old and there was enough stone there to pave every street in London, rebuild Aberdeen, carry a railway from Land's End to John o' Groats, raise bridges over every river in the country, and provide enough slabs for polishing to bury the entire Scottish nation besides. Or so claimed Mungo Adam.

But Ainslie Sharp had proved a hard nut to crack. He was quiet, courteous, shrewd, and gave nothing away. The railway works were reported to be making rapid progress from the south towards Aberdeen. The piers for the arched viaduct from the terminus, near Market Street, to Polmuir were already half built and the digging and pile-driving were going on apace. At the point on the river bank where it was proposed to cross the Dee preparations for the foundations of the railway bridge were well under way. All this activity provided constant employment for the labouring population of the city, but the quarrymen were less pleased. In the spring at Silvercairns, Sharp had mentioned the lower tenders of the Edinburgh quarriers, and it seemed, frowned Old Man Adam, that the cheap and shoddy lobby had won.

But tenders had been called for eight more viaducts south of the city, and he had submitted estimates for all of them. By the end of the day, he hoped to have secured at least some, if not all, for Silvercairns. But the railway would not stop at Aberdeen. It would thrust on northwards and when it did, there was no reason why Silvercairns should not benefit again. Whichever route was finally chosen, there would be stations and bridges and railway hotels to be build and Old Man Adam meant to win the contracts for as many of them as possible. His quarry was in full production already, but there was no reason why young Fergus should not increase the output, open another new seam, extend the quarry, horizontally as well as vertically if need be, and double the profits. No reason at all.

When the Queen's birthday celebrations were over and he had the new contracts under his belt, he would summon Fergus and tell him so.

It was a glorious day. There had been thunderstorms the day before, with lightning and torrential rain, but by morning the sky was a clear, untroubled blue and the steaming puddles rapidly shrank and soaked away in the gathering sunlight. The northern summer night was almost at its shortest and a bare four hours after bedtime Annys was awake and demanding to be dressed in her holiday clothes.

The town was still sleeping, the pale night sky barely tinged with pink, but Mhairi was as excited as her little sister. 'You must wash, first,' Mhairi whispered, so as not to wake the menfolk, 'and brush your hair. You must be quiet as a mouse, then if you are very good and promise not to spill anything you may put on your new dress.' This Mhairi had made herself out of an outgrown one of her own, and trimmed with scraps of ribbon she had saved from Miss Roberts' sewing. For herself, Mhairi had what had been her mother's best dress, a plain blue garment of fine wool which she had adapted to fit. When her father saw her in it, some time later, his eyes blurred with emotion and Mhairi hugged him with quick compassion. 'I'm sorry, Da. I didn't mean to remind you. But it's all I have to wear and I thought . . .'

'Nay, lass, dinna mind me,' he said, brushing his eyes with the back of his hand. 'It's just that you look the image of your ma, and when I saw you standing there you could have been my Agnes when we was courting.'

'Oh, Da', protested Mhairi, but she blushed with pleasure before saying briskly, 'Now it's your turn to look smart, Da. I've brushed your Sunday suit and your best shoes. Hurry and get ready for the bells will be ringing soon and we dinna want to miss anything.' Tom had gone hours ago, to whatever rendezvous had been arranged for those taking part in the procession.

'I'm thinking I'll just sit here at home, Mhairi. I dinna like crowds.'

'Nonsense. I can't keep an eye on Lorn and Will as well as Annys. I'm needing you to help. There's no saying what mischief they'll get up to if they think no one's caring. Isn't that right, boys?'

'Yes, Da, you must come! Please. It willna be the same, else.' Wearily, reluctantly, Cassie Diack consented to be helped into his best suit, Mhairi brushed his shoulders, dabbed at a spot on one lapel, gave his shoes yet another rub with a duster, and pronounced him perfect. Then she turned her attention to her brothers until finally, hair combed, faces scrubbed, collars neat and hands clean, she deemed them fit to be seen out in the streets.

'Come on, Mhairi!' wailed Annys, hopping from one foot to the other with impatience. 'It'll be starting without us.'

At that moment the clock on St Nicholas kirk struck the hour and simultaneously every bell in the city began to ring with an air of holiday jubilation that made even Cassie Diack smile. 'Come on, lass,' he said, offering Mhairi his arm. 'I reckon Annys is right and we wouldna want to miss anything.' With wee Annys on his other side and the two boys skipping along behind, Cassie Diack led his family out into the street, to join the general celebrations.

Union Street was more crowded than on any market day and growing more so by the minute. The mail and stage coaches each disgorged their contribution of revellers and the Velocity steamer from Peterhead brought scores of Buchan lads and lassies to join in the fun. By noon the city streets were crammed. Every vessel in the harbour was decked with bunting, and there were Union Jacks all over town as well as greenery and streamers and any other adornment the townsfolk could think of to add to the general air of festivity. All the shops were shut for the day, but their fronts were suitably decked with patriotic emblems and all along the procession route the windows and balconies were crowded with those lucky enough to have secured a bird's-eye view. At noon more bells sent the pigeons flying and a contingent of scavenging seagulls that had been screaming and swooping over the milling crowds scattered in loud indignation. The royal salute of twenty-one guns boomed out from the Castle Hill barracks and was echoed sporadically for the rest of the day by crackers and fireworks of one kind or another from all over town. Willy lit a squib before Mhairi spotted him and earned himself a smack on the ear, but it was a half-hearted smack. It was, after all, a holiday and it was a long time to wait till evening and official firework time.

The procession was to start from Albyn Place and travel the length of Union Street before turning down Marischal Street to the quay and the site of the new works, and Mhairi had spent several anxious days deciding which would be the best vantage point for she wanted to see Alex – and Tom, of course – for the longest possible time before the crowds closed in again. In the end, she had settled for the steps of the Assembly rooms, for then Annys and the boys might be able to see over the heads of the crowd. But when she and her father finally fought their way to her chosen spot, in company with at least a hundred other people, Lorn and Willy promptly burrowed their way under elbows and past knees to the front of the crowd and a ring-side seat. Annys begged to be allowed to go with them, but Mhairi feared that if she did, she would be lost for the day, and preferred to heave her sister up in her arms instead, for she feared that Annys's weight, little though it was, might prove too much for her father, with his labouring chest . . .

But even her father seemed to forget his troubles when they heard the thunder-roll of drums in the distance and the high skirling of pipes, which changed as they listened to the steady marching beat of the first of the bands. The mile-long procession had begun its splendid progress through the centre of the city.

The Masons' Lodges marched in full regalia, beginning with the seven lodges of Aberdeen itself, then the Provincial Grand Lodge, and the whole hierarchy of members, while the bands crashed out their marching music and the banners proudly waved. There were gold and ermine, scarlet and silver, furs and velvets and glittering emblems, uniforms, masonic regalia, fantastical costumes and every kind of outlandish fancy dress. Captain Barclay, as head of the City Constabulary, cleared the way on horseback and the cheering echoed and re-echoed as the glorious procession passed.

Annys saw Alex first, in the St Nicholas contingent, and squealed in excited recognition. 'There's Lackie's bear-hat. Isn't he lovely!' And Tom. Tom! Tom!' she cried, waving and struggling in Mhairi's arms till she almost dropped her. But Annys was right. Alex looked superb and Annys's squeals had apparently penetrated the general hubbub for he turned his head and looked in their direction. Mhairi clutched Annys with one arm and waved till he looked away again as his section of the procession moved on. But Mhairi was well satisfied. After the procession, she was to meet Alex at the Market Cross and they would have what remained of the day together.

Momentarily, she wondered what had become of Donal. But no doubt he was with his uncle, or with Mackinnon who lived on the same stair. With the thought of Alex to keep the smile on her lips, she gave herself up to enjoying the day.

Donal Grant watched the procession from behind the granite façade of St Nicholas kirkyard. Or, it would be more accurate to say, he escaped the procession. He would have liked to see the colourful costumes, the horses, the marching bands and the splendidly bedecked officials at close quarters, but crowds had always frightened him and the crowds today were the worst he had encountered in his life. He felt the earth jar under his feet and the air throb, knew they were shouting and blaring their incomprehensible noises all around him, saw mouths gaping, feet stamping, drumsticks beating against stretched hide, bagpipes breathing, everywhere a frenetic, frightening, silent exuberance from which he was excluded. He felt his own isolation close around him with the icy grip of midwinter frost. He was a goldfish, looking out: or rather, they were the happy, rejoicing fishes cavorting in their crystal bowl and he was the outsider. Go with Mackinnon, Alex had told him. Enjoy yourself. But he had not enjoyed himself, there in the throng by the Market Cross. Mrs Mackinnon had smiled and held his arm, Mr Mackinnon had done likewise, but at the first opportunity he had made them understand that he wanted to go home. Then he had gone, moving as best he could through the crush, accepting shoves and pushes without protest, till he had reached the comparative emptiness of the back of the crowd.

But he had not gone home. He had sought out the one place where he felt at no disadvantage: St Nicholas kirkyard. Here was peace, and a silence to match his own. Here he could find gravestones going back almost three hundred years, marking the resting place of people long dead and all as silent now as he. But that was not the only reason he sought out the kirkyard. There was Mrs Diack's grave and the headstone which he, Donal, had designed.

He was pleased with the stone, well satisfied with its execution. But looking down at it now he wondered whether perhaps a different style of lettering might have suited the pink-hued stone better? He looked around him for a similar, noting the different shades of granite – the Rubislaw, the Corrennie, the Peterhead – the different polishes, the different styles and patterns of decoration, the different cutting of the letters. He took out a pencil and folded paper from his trouser pocket and soon was completely absorbed in copying the shape of a stone here, a carving there, and adding his own elaborations and notes. He drew birds and flowers, the geometric complexities of Celtic decoration, crosses, angels, skulls. He drew letters in Roman capitals and in Greek, his own name, Alex's and finally with infinite, blushing care, that of 'Mhairi Diack'.

'How peculiar,' said Lettice Adam, looking down from her vantage point at the Macdonalds' first-floor window. 'Someone is drawing pictures of graves!'

The windows of the Adam town house, being in the Guestrow, did not command a view of the procession, but as Widow Macdonald and her daughters occupied a more strategically placed house on the corner of Back Wynd which did, the Adams, in company with the Burnetts, Wynesses and Forbes, had ridden in from their various summer retreats to join the Macdonalds in their upstairs drawing-room from where they could watch the proceedings in comfort.

However, the gentlemen of the party, having safely delivered their ladies into Mrs Macdonald's care, had dispersed at an early stage in the day, the elder to take up official positions on the quay where the stone-laying ceremony would eventually take place, and the younger about their own unspecified business, but with promises to return shortly, and certainly in time for dinner.

The dinner was to be an informal and regrettably female affair, as the more senior gentlemen were attending the grand town dinner in the Assembly rooms, but Lettice had suggested that Mrs Macdonald invite Mr Dunn and his nephew Andrew to go a little way towards redressing the balance. Now, she felt restless and impatient for Hamish Dunn's arrival. Since that welcome dinner at Silvercairns she had attended regularly at his church, listened with all appearance of rapt attention to his sermons, lingered as long as she dared in the church porch, snatching at anything to prolong a conversation, but still she felt no closer to him than before they met. He was courteous, friendly, cheerful, even jocular, but always elusive, as if there were an invisible barrier between them. She had explained it away to herself as his consciousness of her position, his responsibilites as a parish minister, even his shyness. Surely he could not be entirely unaware of her invitation? Or impervious to her charms? She knew she had never looked better, or been gayer company. Any other man of her acquaintance would have succumbed long ago. She could not understand it. But his elusiveness both challenged and excited her and made her all the more determined to win. Today, in the informality of this public holiday atmosphere, without the intimidating presence of her father and his contemporaries, perhaps at last the barrier would fall and he would allow himself to cross from acquaintanceship to something closer? She certainly meant to use every feminine wile in her repertoire to see that he did.

But the dinner hour was not until six and already the day was dragging. The first part of the procession had passed beneath their open window ten minutes ago, with all the dust and noise and odour of a heated multitude in a confined space. The thumping and blaring of the band had made Lettice put her hands over her ears until it had moved on up the road, but the interminable crocodile still flowed noisily past beneath their window and Lettice, growing bored with the spectacle, had moved to the side window for a breath of fresh air and a different view. This window overlooked the kirkyard of St Nicholas with, to the right, the row of elegant granite columns which separated it from Union Street. These partly obscured her view of the street itself but she could just see, through their screen, the backs of the processing revellers, the leading band's music receding with them towards the corner of the Castlegate and the road to the harbour, while behind her she could hear the approaching thump, thump of the next contingent. It was a warm June day and the windows were open to the street, but at the side window Lettice caught less of the crowd's heat and noise and more of the deserted peace of the kirkyard. If she was to be a minister's wife, she thought dutifully, then this view was far more appropriate for her than that thronged and secular street.

The grass was rich green between the headstones and flowers grew here and there, but it was the man's figure which had caught her attention. A solitary figure, in his Sunday best today like everyone else, but, unlike everyone else, apparently taking no notice of the procession. Instead, he was drawing! In a churchyard. There was something vaguely familiar about him, though she could not think what and after a moment's half-hearted effort to remember, she gave up. He would be some workman from one of the granite yards, perhaps, unrecognizable without the tools of his trade. Or a session clerk, taking notes. She was rather vague about the duties of session clerks and made a mental note to ask someone – not Mr Dunn, of course, for that would show too much ignorance. Aunt Blackwell, perhaps. Of course he might not be a clerk at all, she mused, watching the solitary figure, but someone whose relative had died. A good minister's wife would be expected to know such things and to say a few well-chosen, comforting words, but the idea of memorizing all those names was a daunting and rather depressing one. Fergus was certainly finding it so at the quarry. But when Hamish Dunn had gone round the place with Fergus he had had no such trouble. Perhaps if she tried really hard she would find it easy, too? For instance, where had she seen that young man before?

'That is Donal Grant, I believe,' said a soft Highland voice at her back and she whipped round to see Hamish Dunn, the noise of whose entry had been quite drowned by the noise from outside. 'Forgive me, Miss Adam, but I thought I would presume on my invitation to dinner to arrive early. It is hot work pushing through those crowds.' He took out a large handkerchief and began to mop his neck and face which, Lettice noted with slight dismay, was as red as his hair, and glistening with perspiration.

'Oh, yes,' she said brightly, 'and one really sees so much better from above. Besides, why suffer with the crowds when one can escape into peace and quiet with . . .' but she saw that he was not listening to her. Instead he was studying that figure in the churchyard.

'Poor young man,' he said quietly. 'Condemned to a life of silence, whether he chooses or not. And today, of all days, with such celebrations everywhere. I must go to him. If you will excuse me,' and he turned for the door.

'But, Mr Dunn, you have only just arrived!' She laid her small, white-gloved hand on his arm and smiled coaxingly up at him. 'Stay at least for a glass of something refreshing before you hurry away? Mrs Macdonald has some excellent Chablis, cooling specially . . .' She bit her lip on the mistake, and hurried on, 'for the *others* and a jug of raspberry cordial which I know you will enjoy. Besides, you said yourself the heat and the crowds . . .'

'I assure you I will return,' he interrupted, disengaging his arm with, she thought afterwards, unnecessary brusqueness. 'I cannot say when, Miss Adam, but certainly for dinner.'

'Then I shall come with you,' she announced, taking up her silk shawl from the sofa where she had discarded it earlier and draping it elegantly over one arm. 'It is so boring here, with that incessant noise under the window, and I can think of nothing nicer than a stroll in the peace of the kirkyard.' When he did not answer, she glanced up, saw that his troubled eyes were still regarding that figure below, and added gaily, 'And I will talk to him too, Mr Dunn. Together we will lift his sorrows . . .' She slipped her hand into the crook of his arm, and coaxed him with her prettiest smile. 'Shall we go?'

'No, Miss Adam. I will go. You will stay here, where you belong.' He looked at her steadily, and after a long moment her own eyes dropped and she withdrew her hand. She heard his steps on the stairs, then the slam of the outside door.

She could have stamped her foot with frustration and fury, or wept with humiliation. Instead she bit her lower lip, hard, in thought until she saw the black-clad form of Hamish Dunn appear in the street below and, after a few minutes, enter the kirkyard by the gate and approach that solitary figure. He did not run away, as Lettice half expected, but stood obediently waiting, as if he knew and trusted the minister. They sat down together on a convenient stone and she saw Hamish Dunn's hands moving, gesticulating. After a moment, she turned away, baffled and frowning. How dare he prefer the company of some dreary nobody to hers? If the man was in need of cheering, then she could have smiled and made conversation too, and surely the attention of a beautiful and solicitous young gentlewoman would have cheered him far more than what looked from this distance like a sermon. Mr Dunn must learn not to take life so seriously, and to cultivate the social graces more. It had really been quite rude, leaving her in that cavalier fashion, especially when she had done him the favour of offering her company. Lettice Adam was not used to being rebuffed.

But perhaps it had been the wrong moment? He had been, on his own admission, hot and tired of the crowds. Irritable too, probably. And that creature was plainly one of his parishioners, in need of comfort or advice. He had obviously thought to despatch the matter more quickly without her company which would, of course, have diverted his attention. That was the explanation: conscientiousness towards his work and solicitousness towards her. A minister's work was never done, of course. She must get used to that. And when Hamish had given the creature ten minutes or so of his time and discharged his burdensome duty, he would return, to the Macdonald drawing-room and to her.

But it was several hours before Hamish Dunn returned and then barely in time for dinner. His nephew Andrew had arrived an hour before, with Hugo, and even Fergus had had the manners not to be late. Lettice had to fight hard to conceal her annoyance, and harder still when she found herself placed at table at the opposite end from the minister, who had been given Flora Burnett and Amelia Macdonald for company. She had to be content with nephew Andrew who was dull, as usual, and Niall Burnett who was worse, and there were far too many women. Her temper was further tried when she noticed Flora Burnett smiling at something Hamish Dunn had said and it took all her control to preserve a modicum of good manners and social aplomb. She would not have bothered to try were it not for Mr Dunn, for it had been a tedious and disappointing day with the prospect of worse tedium to come. But Mr Dunn should see that she knew how to behave in the most adverse circumstances, and behave she did, though at times the effort almost choked her.

But at last the interminable meal was over, the ladies withdrew, and after a commendably short time the gentlemen joined them, for coffee in the drawing-room. Lettice lost no time in seeking out Hamish Dunn, her excuse a china demitasse of fresh-poured coffee.

'For you, Mr Dunn,' she said, 'to restore you after a gruelling day.' He took it, thanked her, and stirred it in silence. But Lettice was not easily daunted. 'That poor man in the churchyard,' she began, 'how is he? You were able to help him, I trust?'

'I believe so, Miss Adam. Inasmuch as anyone can help him.'

'Oh?' She added lightly, 'Is he so far steeped in sin as to be irreclaimable? Or has he succumbed to the demon drink?'

'Neither. His troubles are not of his own making. But I thought you would have known that, Miss Adam. He is, after all, one of your father's workmen.'

'Of course!' she cried, and gave a self-deprecating little laugh. 'How silly of me. I knew I had seen him somewhere, but then in those unfamiliar clothes . . . But now you mention it, of course I remember him. A pleasant young man and an excellent worker.' Rashly, she elaborated, 'Why, only the other day we met on the Silvercairns road and exchanged a few amicable words on this and that.' She waited for his approval, but instead saw that he was looking at her with an expresison that was almost pitying.

'Hardly, Miss Adam. Donal Grant is deaf and dumb.'

To her consternation, Lettice flushed a deep and humiliating red, but before she could think of a reply, Hamish Dunn said quietly, 'Miss Adam, I hope you will not be offended at what I am going to say, but it has been on my mind to say it for some considerable time.'

For a wild, astonished moment she thought he was going to propose to her! Then he continued, 'Why do you persist in striking attitudes and pretending to be what you are not? Surely you cannot really be so shallow and selfish and spoilt? Somewhere inside that brittle exterior I am sure there is an honest, honourable and loving young woman. Please give her the chance to emerge, before it is too late. You owe it to yourself, and to God.' Then, with a quick bow of the head, he left her. A moment later he was talking with Flora Burnett as if nothing untoward had happened.

Lettice stood immobilized by shock, while that incriminating blush gradually faded and a cold and venomous fury took its place. How dare he speak to her like that? How dare he insult and humiliate her, when it was her own father who had given him his job – and could as easily take it away. How dare he?

'Oh, dear,' said a soft voice at her side. 'Whatever did the holy man say to offend you, Miss Adam? Been stealing the collection again?'

Lettice whirled on Niall Burnett with the full force of her fury. 'Why don't you go to hell!'

'I expect I will one day, Lettice dear,' he drawled. 'Shall we arrange to meet?' But Lettice turned her back. She wanted only to go home. To hide her humiliation and lick her wounds in the privacy of her own bedroom. But of course that was out of the question. She would not give that odious man the satisfaction of thinking he had ruffled her. Instead, she held her head an arrogant inch higher, sought out her hostess, complimented her on her dinner and, when someone mentioned cards to while away the time until the fireworks, said there was nothing she herself would like more. Out of the corner of her eye she saw that Mr Dunn was still talking to Flora Burnett, in the window, but when the card tables were brought out he took that as a signal for him to leave. No doubt he considers whist as wicked as whisky, thought Lettice and defiantly took up a pack of cards and began to shuffle them. But if she had known he would leave, she would not have committed herself to partnering Mrs Wyness. Now, there was no getting out of it. It was one more sin to be laid at the man's door.

Fergus Adam noted Hamish Dunn's departure with a relief in which there was not a little nervousness. He had waited ever since dinner for an opportunity to speak to Flora alone, but she had been commandeered by one person after another until finally Hamish Dunn had steered her towards the window seat and had spent the last twenty minutes, as far as Fergus could see, practising his worthy and no doubt tedious sermons on her. Flora had listened and nodded and even smiled once or twice, with every semblance of interest, but then Flora was a kind-hearted, tolerant girl and far too polite to do otherwise. She must, however, be as relieved as Fergus that the man had finally gone.

Carefully he placed the brandy on a convenient table, adjusted the cuffs of his evening shirt, straightened his shoulders, and threaded his way between card tables, sofas and other impedimenta to the window seat and Flora's side. 'May I?' he said, and, without waiting for an answer, sat down beside her.

'I have been waiting all evening for the opportunity to speak to you, Miss Burnett,' he began, as he had rehearsed, over and over. But it sounded so stilted and formal. Taking courage from that last, most generous brandy, he lowered his voice to an intimate murmur and said quickly, before his courage failed, 'Flora, there is something I want to say to you. Have wanted to say for many months.'

'Oh, dear.'

It was not at all the reaction he had expected. Shyness perhaps, but that 'Oh, dear' held no timidity. It sounded more like pity, and regret. His confidence faltered, but having begun the proposal, there was no drawing back.

'Surely it comes as no surprise to you, Flora? You must know how I . . .' but before he could express the depth of his admiration and love for her she had interrupted him.

'Before you say anything you might regret, Fergus,' she said quietly, looking at him with honest, unwavering eyes, 'I must tell you that Hamish Dunn has proposed to me and I have accepted.'

Fergus was stunned to the core. *Hamish Dunn?* That odious, red-faced bull of a minister? That pompous, teetotalling clod-hopper with the manners of the bothy and hands like slabs of meat? That . . . that . . .

'I am so sorry, Fergus dear.' She laid a gentle hand on his arm. 'But Hamish and I . . .' He did not hear the rest for the shame and fury that filled his whole being till he wanted to burst out of the house, race after the fellow and smash the sanctimonious smile from his face. By the time he had regained some semblance of control, she was murmuring something about waiting so long, and if only he had spoken sooner.

'My time, alas, is not my own, Miss Burnett.' To his own ears he sounded admirably cold, dismissive and correct. 'But no matter. Let me be one of the first to wish you and your . . . your future husband all happiness.' He bowed, offered to fetch her more coffee and when she refused, said, 'In that case, perhaps you will excuse me if I seek out a cup for myself?' With what he hoped was perfect aplomb, he drank not only one, but two cups though the effort almost choked him, circulated briefly but courteously among the older women, and took his leave as soon as he could discreetly do so without giving rise to comment. Fortunately, there was enough going on in the town that night for his plea of another engagement to be instantly believed.

The grand dinner in the Assembly rooms lasted several hours, but with nineteen tureens of green turtle soup to be disposed of, not to mention seventeen dishes of roast lamb, nine of beef, thirteen ornamented hams and as many tongues similarly adorned, with a succession of ducklings, chickens, kidneys stewed in champagne, Madeira wine jellies, lobster salads, numerous vegetables, ratafia baskets of pastry and an assortment of ices, it was not surprising. When champagne, sherry, claret, port and punch were added to the burden of obligation it was a wonder the dinner reached the speeches stage at all, and more of a wonder that anyone was in a fit state to make, or listen to them. But the occasion was universally applauded as a pronounced success and the various contented guests debouched into the city streets in time to witness the splendid display of fireworks arranged by the Council, and the many rival displays provided by individual revellers.

Mhairi and Alex stood, arms entwined, by the Market Cross and watched the sunburst of coloured stars lace the evening sky with light. Cassie Diack had taken Annys home to bed, Tom and his young brothers were somewhere in the crowd and Donal, said Alex, was working. Apparently that new minister at Silvercairns had met him in the kirkyard, taken him home to the manse and lent him a book about lettering from his own library. Donal was copying designs from it now, though if Alex knew his skinflint uncle, he'd be measuring every drop of lamp oil burnt and charge him for it after. But Alex wasn't worried. Donal was safe at home, and happy, and for once Mhairi too was without attendant worries. It was bliss to stand with Alex beside her and to know she need think of nothing and no one else for a precious, blessed hour. Alex moved, readjusted his arm and drew her closer, so that she was held warm against his chest, his strong arms shielding her from the press of those around them. For they were not the only ones at the Market Cross. Half Aberdeen seemed to have gathered in the Castlegate to see the fireworks and a good part of them were variously distributed about the pedestal and steps of the cross, but they might as well have been so many sheep as far as Mhairi was concerned. Her world was bounded by Alex's strong arms, the muscles hard and firm under his unaccustomed coat, by the strength of his body, where she leant against it, by the pulse-beat in his wrist, where his hand folded over hers, and she heard only his breathing, his voice in her ear when he bent his head and whispered, 'I love you.'

Reds and greens and fizzing whites coruscated overhead in a succession of oohs and aahs, against a background of crackling squibs, but Mhairi heard none of them. Her head on Alex's shoulder, she heard only the steady beat of his heart, and her own happiness, like a song inside her. Soon, they would slip away into the shadows of some convenient close and explore each other's bodies with yearning hands, while their lips clung sweetly, achingly together until, at the edge of that forbidden land, they recollected and drew back. For Alex had promised, and said he understood. Remembering certain aspects of their private loving, Mhairi's eyes grew bright with anticipation, her full lips soft and moist. But for the moment they lingered, watching the Queen's fireworks with the rest of Aberdeen. Then, in the darkness between one rocket and the next, he bent his head and kissed her, and when the rocket shot aloft to explode directly overhead, neither of them noticed.

'Well!' said Lizzie Lennox in mock outrage. 'Look at that Mhairi Diack carrying on like a dockside whore and wi' half the town to see her, too. Her ma'd turn in her grave if she knew, that she would. Some folk have no shame!'

'Disgusting,' agreed Maggie Henderson and gave a high cackle of laughter, echoed gleefully by Beth Pirie. 'It's nae ladylike!' Both were in their most garish street clothes, with fur tippets and rolled parasols, bright taffeta sashes and hats 'like a dish o' dead birds, wi' greenery' as one of the Diack boys later reported. Normally it would have been beneath Lizzie's dignity to be seen in the public street with them, especially if her father was anywhere in the vicinity, but her father, for once, was dead to the world in Ma Gibbs' tavern and tomorrow she'd be safely back at Silvercairns. She could do what she liked tonight. Besides, there was safety in numbers and she reckoned it might be exciting to see how the pair o' them went about it, like. Lizzie didn't have to join in, not that they'd be likely to let her if it meant her taking money they'd consider rightly theirs. So Lizzie Lennox, free for the day like most of working Aberdeen, and dressed, like them, in her Sunday best, with the addition of various elegant touches new to her friends, had escaped her own family early in the evening and when she spotted Maggie's purple feathers, had decided to tag along, for a lark.

'Ooh, Lizzie Lennox, where'd you get that necklace?' cried Maggie, with envy, and Beth had added, 'And them gloves are right pretty. You got a gentleman friend then?' and she had nudged Lizzie in the ribs, with a suggestive leer.

'If I had, I wouldna tell you, would I?' And the banter had continued in similar fashion as they cruised, arms linked, along Union Street, apparently delighted with their own company, but each one with a wary eye open for anything interesting in trousers.

Lizzie spotted them first: a group of young gentlemen, evidently tipsy, and equally evidently on the look-out for female diversion. In top hats and tails, fresh from some nobs' dinner party by the looks of them, they stood out from the generality 'like a flock o' silly penguins,' as Lizzie jeered from across the street.

But she was summarily jerked almost from her feet as Maggie on one side of her and Beth on the other swaggered across the cobbles towards where the group of young men were now leaning against the splendid columns of the new bank, watching the fireworks and apparently arguing about what to do next.

'They'll do,' said Maggie gleefully. 'Plenty to choose from and enough for all. Bags me the one wi' the malacca cane.'

'Oh, lor!' groaned Lizzie, momentarily taken aback. Her hand flew to the necklace at her throat.

'What's the matter, Lizzie? Lost your nerve? It's only men.'

'Aye,' said Lizzie, 'but one o' them's Mr Hugo, from Silvercairns.'

'So what? You're on holiday today, remember. Besides,' Maggie winked, 'now's your chance.' Then she loosed Lizzie's arm and strolled up to the group. 'Enjoying the fireworks, then?' she said, giving the nearest what Lizzie recognized as the message. 'Like a bit of excitement, do you?'

'Don't we all,' drawled one young man and turned away.

'Me now, I like a nip o' stout wi' my fireworks,' said Beth, 'and I know a real cosy place to find it.'

'Do you indeed?'

'Come along, Hugo. We've other calls to make,' said a supercilious one with a silly eye-glass on a string, but another, a young, freckle-faced lad not much more than eighteen, said, 'I say, hang on a moment, Niall. Don't be so damn rude. This lady's talking to us.'

'Not to me she isn't.' But at that moment Hugo spotted Lizzie.

'I say, if it isn't Lizzie Lennox! The red-headed glory of Silvercairns! Are these lovely damsels friends of yours, Lizzie?'

'Well, not what you call friends exactly, more acquaintances, like.'

'Some friend you are, Lizzie Lennox,' hissed Maggie, with

venom, then simpered 'Such a tease, our Lizzie. We was brought up practically next door, wasn't we, Beth?'

By this time Beth and Maggie had somehow insinuated themselves into the centre of the group, and each had her chosen victim by the arm. There was a good deal of banter and giggling, Lizzie saw a male hand pinch Beth's bottom and a black-sleeved arm was across Maggie's purple bosom. Hugo moved to Lizzie's side.

'And do you know this cosy place your friend mentioned? Where we could have a drink together?' He slipped a tentative arm around her waist. Lizzie bridled with mock affront.

'Kindly take your hand from my waist, Mr Hugo. The idea!' He grinned, folded gloved hands over silver-topped cane, bowed, and said solemnly, 'Miss Lennox, will you do me the honour of favouring me with your company for an evening stroll?'

'I might,' she said, looking at him with speculative eyes. 'Then again, I might not.'

'She's learning!' 'You tell him, Lizzie.' Beth and Maggie were well established now, apparently happily set up for the evening.

'We could visit the Coffee Rooms, Miss Lennox, for a late supper?' Hugo offered his arm with grave courtesy, but his eyes were dancing with mischief as he looked down at the fiery-haired, exuberant girl he remembered first seeing, immodestly flouting that pompous ass Burnett outside Corbyn's dancing school. He had been right about her: she had grown into a damn fine filly, and a spirited one too.

She looked at him now with open challenge, and he added slyly, 'With a glass of chilled champagne?'

'In that case, Mr Hugo, I might just be able to spare the time.' Gleefully, she linked her arm through his, her gloved hand lying just like a lady's on his black sleeve, and set off with prancing elegance towards Market Street. Those other two could do what they liked. She'd always wanted to eat in them Coffee Rooms, and with Miss Lettice's necklace and gloves to give her confidence, she knew she was dressed a real treat.

* * *

Tom Diack was wandering aimlessly across the Plainstanes when he saw her and his face flushed with anger. He had had a long and arduous day, first the procession, then various celebrations with a succession of groups of friends until his head was spinning with the unaccustomed noise and gaiety. He had lost Alex hours ago, barely glimpsed his small brothers, but knew that Mhairi would be keeping a good eye on both them and their father. Tom felt a twinge of guilt about his father: he ought to have tried harder to make him join the lads for a drink, but since his dismissal his father had shunned all company but the family. Remembering, Tom felt the familiar anger churn and bubble inside him. How dare they treat his father so? How dare that smooth-faced Mr Fergus break a man out of sheer ill-temper? Tom himself still worked at the quarry, but since the day of his father's dismissal his ambition had concentrated into a driving urge to complete his apprenticeship and leave. Then he would set up in opposition to the Adams and one day, somehow, teach them the lesson they needed.

Tom had been a mild-tempered and cheerful boy; his mother's death had saddened and matured him, but without bitterness; now, his father's treatment had poisoned his optimism and left a simmering, vengeful anger which could find no outlet. The fact that his father accepted his treatment, as he accepted his illness, with weary resignation and without complaint only increased Tom's anger. He saw his father's health deteriorate as his spirit failed, and every day vowed revenge on Silvercairns. If he could have seized Mr Fergus by the throat, shaken the arrogance out of him, forced him to reinstate his father and to grovel in abject apology, he would gladly have done so. But the law would have stopped him before his hands reached that well-dressed throat and he would have been sacked on the spot. If he did manage to touch the man, he would be summarily jailed, transported or hanged. And now that his father had no work, Mhairi was relying on Tom to help her provide food for them all and school fees for the little ones. On that last point she was adamant. She had promised her mother, and the school fees must be paid. But, little though these were, they made a hole in the budget before the week began, and with Cassie Diack's Balsam of Aniseed her next priority, there was little enough left for housekeeping.

So Tom contained his anger and continued to work at the quarry, and, when ordered to do so, in the grounds of the house, though to his way of thinking a drystone dyker would have been more use. It practically choked him to have to rebuild that wall which was no use to anyone as far as he could see, except to make extra work for the gardeners. But that was the Adams all over. A huge great house with rooms enough to house the whole of Mitchell's Court and to spare – and most of them empty half the year – and a huge great garden laid out like some sort of pretty picture when it could be put to far better use feeding cows or growing vegetables for the people of Aberdeen. But however much he simmered with resentment and anger, when told to do the work, he obeyed. Mhairi needed the money and George Bruce paid him well. But every working hour he brooded and planned for the day when he could leave and set up, with Alex Grant, on his own. Then he would show the Adams that they were not the undisputed lords of the earth. He would beat them at their own game, drive them to bankruptcy and ruin. For though it had been Fergus Adam who had dismissed his father, Tom knew that every Adam was the same. Arrogant, black-hearted, oppressive, whatever the rights or wrongs of a case, they would close ranks against all outsiders, and the rest of their class would line up in support behind them. They thought they were impregnable . . . but Tom would show them, one day. He would revenge his father and put the Adams in their place.

So when Tom, meandering across the Plainstanes on that holiday evening, saw Lizzie Lennox on the arm of an Adam, the long-latent anger and the ale combined to fill him with rage. How dare Lizzie disgrace herself with one of the gentry, and an Adam at that. She was behaving like that Henderson girl. Lizzie Lennox! Mhairi's friend who Tom had known just about all his life. If Mhairi knew what she was up to, she'd stop her soon enough. Anyone would. Lizzie was flighty maybe, and high-spirited, and not always as honest as she ought to be, but she wasna *like that*. If he were Lizzie's brother, he'd soon put a stop to it. But Lizzie didn't have a brother, leastways not a grown brother, only a drunken, bible-spouting, self-righteous old fool of a father who was worse than useless and who, if he was here, would likely beat Lizzie for wanton wickedness and beg the

Adam fellow's pardon. Then Lizzie looked up into the man's face and laughed, and something burst in Tom's head.

He leapt after them, seized Lizzie by the arm, wrenched her bodily away from her escort and when the fellow took a swing at him with his cane, Tom caught it in one hand and snapped it like matchwood. Tom had not swung a mason's hammer for nothing and he had more strength in one hand than that runt had in two.

'Tom Diack!' cried Lizzie, furious. 'You stupid loon. Look what you've done to my dress!'

'I'll do more than that, if you don't behave yourself, Lizzie.'

'Take your hands off her, this instant,' ordered Hugo, with the confident arrogance of the lord to the servant. 'This lady is with me.'

'Oh, no, she's not!' Still gripping Lizzie with one hand, Tom pushed Hugo hard in the chest with the other.

'How dare you, you scum!' Hugo's stick was broken and it was against every principle to engage in open fisticuffs with anyone but a fellow gentleman, but when Tom knocked the top hat from his head it was too much. Besides, the fellow had manhandled Hugo's little lady and the lady herself was watching. So Hugo lunged back with his gloved fist and would have flattened Tom's nose had Tom not jerked aside in time.

'Go on, feller, give it him!' 'Good one, Gloves! Give him another!' People gathered instantly from nowhere to watch this rival entertainment and already the three were hemmed in by a jostling, inquisitive crowd, like spectators at a cock-fight. In spite of her screaming abuse and her struggles, Tom still held Lizzie firmly in his left hand while fighting off Hugo Adam with the other and Hugo circled and danced, fists raised in boxer fashion, trying to find an opening through which to demolish this impertinent intruder and reclaim his lady without felling her in the process. Had Hugo been coldly sober, he would no doubt have summoned the town police to deal with things, but he was not sober and normal rules of decorum did not apply. Besides, the lady in question looked more desirable by the minute, with her splendid hair all over the place and her eyes blazing. She was a spirited filly and worth fighting for. It was a matter of pride now to distinguish himself in the eyes of Lizzie Lennox, as well as to prove to the world that no one laid hands on an Adam and went unpunished. So they circled and sparred, with Lizzie fighting her own battle between them, while rival factions cheered encouragement to one or the other. Someone retrieved the battered top hat and stuck it on his own head, while overhead the fireworks continued to burst and sputter and shriek in a panoply of brilliant colour.

Then from across the square came a warning shout, 'The Watch!' Instantly, the crowd fell apart, Tom and Hugo Adam stood in a startled moment's suspended animation and, from a lifetime's habit, Lizzie twisted out of Tom's grip and ran. Before Hugo could collect his thoughts, Tom leapt after her shouting, 'Lizzie! Come back here you little . . .' and both were swallowed up in the crowds.

Tom caught up with her on the corner of Broad Street and pinned her, panting, against the wall. 'You keep your hands off me, Tom Diack,' she spat at him in fury. 'Interfering where you're not wanted. I was all set for a right fine evening, wi' champagne and all, till you came poking your nose in and spoilt everything.'

'Everything? And what is that supposed to mean?' Tom was out of breath too, chest heaving, face flushed with anger and exertion, eyes very bright.

'Not what you think, neither. Mr Hugo was taking me to supper at a real restaurant. Not that you'd be acquaint wi' such places, of course, being bred in the gutter wi' manners to match.'

Lizzie was as flushed as Tom, her dark eyes glinting, her hair a fiery cloud about her head. The tight stuff of her dress rose and fell over her rounded breasts and it was as he looked at them, with a sudden stirring of a different excitement, that Tom saw the necklace.

'Where did you get that?' he demanded, reaching out to finger it. Seeing her advantage, she ducked to twist away and he seized her hard by the forearm. 'Oh, no, Lizzie Lennox, you'll not escape me that easy. Not till you tell me. You never bought that in a month of Sundays. Who gave it to you?' When she didn't answer, he said softly, but with deadly precision, '*Was it him?*'

For the first time, Lizzie felt a stir of unease. Tom was

looking at her in a way she hadn't seen before and it made her nervous. 'Course it wasna him. Why should he give me anything?'

'He was going to give you supper, you said, at a real restaurant. *Why?*'

'Why not?' countered Lizzie, blustering. 'He was just being friendly, like.'

'And how "friendly" were you going to be in return?'

'I don't know what you mean, Tom Diack, and I'll thank you to get out o' my way and let me go home.'

'Oh, yes, you do know,' he said, ignoring her protests. 'You know fine how a servant girl thanks a master who gives her presents.'

'I'll not be insulted by the likes o' you, Tom Diack,' cried Lizzie and slapped him, hard, across the face.

With a gasp of pain and fury, Tom seized her wrists, forced them up and back against the wall till she was held, helpless, in a position of apparent surrender, and when she kicked and squirmed in futile rage, he pinned her to the wall with the weight of his own body. 'And I'll not be insulted by the likes o' you, Lizzie Lennox,' he growled. 'Do you think I'm stupid enough to believe your lies? Look at you! Dolled up to the nines, like yon Henderson tart. Gloves. Jewels. And you expect me to believe you got those for nothing?'

'Yes!' screamed Lizzie in impotent fury. 'Because it's the flaming truth!' She glared defiance into his furious face which was mere inches from her own, while the warmth of his body pressed hard against hers. Then as he said nothing, but continued to look at her in a way that both frightened and excited her, she said, with unconvincing nonchalance, 'It was that Miss Lettice. She gave them to me.'

Tom looked down at her through narrowed eyes and said slowly, 'I do not believe you.'

'Don't then. It's all the answer you'll get.'

'Is it?' He still held her arms back against the wall and his grip tightened as his face came closer until, suddenly, he kissed her, his mouth hard on hers. She twisted her head this way and that but after the first half-hearted protest, ceased to struggle.

'Well?' said Tom softly, when at last he released her, 'I'm waiting for that answer . . .' But there was a note of exultation in his voice. Lizzie grinned, but only for a moment, before she looked away, tossed her head and said defiantly, 'All right, then, if you must know. I borrowed them.'

'You did *what?*' Tom was appalled. This time there was no question of Lizzie lying, except possibly in the choice of verb. But borrow or steal, the result was the same and he knew she spoke the stark and awful truth. 'But if you get caught you'll go to jail.'

'Who says I'll get caught? That one has so many jewels she doesna know one from another, and the gloves was old anyway. Besides, I'll put them back tomorrow. She'll know nought about it.'

'Oh, Lizzie, Lizzie. You shouldna do such things. You really shouldn't.' Lizzie had always been reckless, daring, light-fingered, but now she was grown she ought to know better. She was so full of life and vigour it would be dreadful if . . . Tom laid his forehead against the cold stone wall and closed his eyes in despair.

This time, though he had freed her hands, she did not try to escape, but began to put her clothes in order, smooth her hair, straighten her unaccustomed gloves. 'Don't see why not,' she said after a moment, though her voice had lost some of its bounce. 'Folk are entitled to a bit o' finery on a holiday, surely, and if some folks have none and others too much where's the harm in sharing, like?'

'None,' groaned Tom, 'if you ask first.'

'Ask? You must be soft in the head. If I asked she'd say no, wouldn't she? Then where'd I be? Oh, come on, Tom Diack. I'm fed up wi' this arguing. As you've sent my young man packing I reckon the least you can do is buy me a drink yourself.' When he made no answer, she slipped her arm into his and said coaxingly, 'Let's you and me go and look for Mhairi and Alex. Mind you, I dinna suppose they'll want to be found, but I reckon it's time someone kept an eye on them, afore they get themselves into trouble.'

'And what have you been up to?' demanded Lettice crossly of her brother Hugo when he arrived back at the Adam town house as midnight struck. The family had intended to spend the night in town before returning to Silvercairns the next day, though Fergus unaccountably left the Macdonald dinner early and declared his intention of riding home to Silvercairns that same evening. He had been in an abominable temper, too, and now here was Hugo looking black as thunder, with no hat and his shirt front all anyhow.

'Nothing,' snapped Hugo, slamming the door behind him and throwing himself into a chair.

'It must have been a very aggravating nothing to put you into such a temper. You look decidedly cross.'

'And wouldn't you be if some lout had had the nerve to pick a fight with you, in the public street?'

'Really, Hugo? Do tell.' Lettice perched on the arm of his chair and began to put his shirt front in order, smoothing the creases and straightening his bow tie. 'Please?'

'Nothing to tell, really,' said Hugo, mollified by his sister's attentions. 'He pushed me in the chest, knocked my hat off, but the police are never where they're wanted so I had to retaliate. Matter of honour.' He glowered into the fire, regretting that he had not drawn blood.

'But why, Hugo dear? Why did he pick on you?'

'Why not?' said Hugo evasively. 'Jealousy, I expect. He was a drunken, low-bred lout.' Then remembering the crowds who had witnessed the incident and the possibility that some version of the story might eventually reach Lettice's ears, added, 'He had a girl with him. Maybe he thought she fancied me.'

'Hugo, you are impossible! Not every girl you meet fancies you, you know.'

'Don't they?' drawled Hugo, 'You disappoint me.'

Lettice laughed, then said, 'Well, go on. What happened? Did you knock him down?'

'No, more's the pity. The Watch arrived on the scene and everyone fled, including the arch lout. But if I ever set eyes on him again, I'll teach him a lesson he'll not forget in a hurry.'

'Of course you will, Hugo dear. But I do wish you had hit him tonight.'

'So do I, Lettice, old girl. So do I. All in all,' he added morosely, remembering lost opportunities and that delicious Lennox girl, 'it was a disappointing evening.'

'Yes,' agreed Lettice with feeling, but Hugo was too taken up with his own thoughts to notice and on the whole Lettice was glad. She had no wish to share her humiliation with anyone and until she could rearrange her memories into a less hurtful pattern she would keep them to herself.

For the plain truth of the matter was that Mr Dunn had rejected her. He had told her, most insultingly and to her face, to stop play-acting and to be herself, then had spent the rest of the evening talking to that odious Flora Burnett. It was insupportable. She had a good mind to report him to her father and have him removed from Silvercairns church.

But what could she say to her father? That she had thrown herself at the minister and he had rejected her? Like Hugo, she stared into the fire, and reviewed the humiliations of the evening until they heard Mungo Adam himself at the outside door and sped hastily upstairs to bed. Neither of them wanted to be questioned on the doings of the day until they had had time to sift through their memories and discard the mortifying and the inconvenient.

Fergus Adam glared into the darkness ahead with a black and awesome fury. He had left the lights of the town far behind him, with the fireworks and the celebrations and the empty social twitterings, and the road ahead lay empty and open to the summer night sky. The trees on either side were dark masses which stirred and whispered at his passing, somewhere an owl hooted its mournful warning and from far away came the sharp bark of a fox. But the loneliness and the solitude were balm to his battered spirit and his horse knew the road well enough. The animal could have found its way home were he dead drunk across its saddle and, remembering the humiliations of the evening he wished he were. But he would not give the affianced of that odious man the pleasure of seeing him the worse for drink, however much he longed to blur his pain with brandy. At home, in Silvercairns, he would pour himself a bumper measure and drink damnation to the pair of them.

The night breeze was cool on his cheek and overhead stars prickled the pale velvet of the sky. It was almost midsummer and the night hours were short and barely dark. They said in the Arctic regions there was no night for weeks in the summer – and no day in dead of winter. That would not do for Fergus, for night meant no work in the quarry and with his father taking on more contracts than they could handle, they needed every daylight hour there was.

The smithy at Hirpletillam was shrouded in darkness, its windows shuttered, even the dog asleep, though there was the familiar scent of smoke in the air and the familiar warmth as he rode past. Then he was on the last stretch of the journey, with Silvercairns a silhouette on the horizon and the dark maw of the quarry just a little way beyond. Was it imagination or was the ground between the two shrinking? What did it matter anyway, thought Fergus with bitterness. His father did not care. Lettice would marry and leave. And Hugo . . . Hugo lived only for irresponsibility and pleasure. As for himself, the house would probably last his lifetime and after his death, who would care what happened to it? Not Flora Burnett certainly. Recalling her treachery he flushed yet again with mortification, then swore viciously and regularly in rhythm with his horse's hoofs until the pain had eased.

He had made such a damned fool of himself. He wished he'd never gone to the damn dinner, never sought out Flora Burnett, never edged her into that corner by the window and whispered those things to her, never laid himself open to such a rebuff. But it had not once occurred to him that she might refuse. He was, after all, an Adam. *I am so sorry, Fergus dear.* He could hear the words even now, searing his heart with shame. *If only you had spoken sooner* . . . Mere blarney, of course. She knew he was up to his ears in work all the time. Besides, if she had really cared for him she would have waited, wouldn't she? Instead of which, she had promised herself to that fortune-hunting, sanctimonious, hypocritical teetotaller of a minister without a penny to his name. Briefly, he wondered what old Burnett would have to say about the matter, or Niall, come to that. The thought of their united outrage was the only chink in the night's gloom.

But even that chink vanished when he remembered his own father's plans. The Old Man would be furious when he heard. He would berate Fergus for missing his chances and letting that minister walk off with a fortune, while no doubt the minister himself was crowing like the cock o' the north with triumph. How Fergus would endure to sit through another of his ranting sermons he did not know, but it would be useless to refuse to go. The Old Man required the Adams in force in the family pew and the Old Man must be obeyed. Unless, of course, his father managed to remove the fellow? But Fergus doubted his father's influence stretched that far unless the minister committed an actual felony and marrying one of the richest heiresses in the neighbourhood hardly constituted sin.

But the thought of his father reminded Fergus that Old Man Adam was out to bag a brace of contracts today. If he succeeded, there would be more blasting, a new seam to be opened, and enough work to blot Flora Burnett completely from both their minds. After all, she was not the only heiress in Scotland and there would be time enough for marriage when the railway work was complete. For the first time since his disastrous proposal, the cloud of depression lifted a cautious inch and by the time Fergus reached the gates of Silvercairns, his heart was several degrees lighter. To complete the cure, he decided to ride on past the gates and have a look at his quarry in the moonlight before he went to bed.

The quarry at night was an eerie place. Where the moonlight fell, the stone was an iridescent, ghostly silver and at the fringe of the quarry the grasses and wild plants were a monochrome of tangled greys. But when Fergus urged his horse to the top of the spiral path which led down to the quarry floor and looked into the darkness a hundred feet beneath, the half that was in shadow was black as a bottomless pit. He felt an almost primeval fear as he looked from that pit to the moonlit face of unbroken stone, at whose foot lay the fallen blocks which his men had blasted only yesterday, and the air was filled with sudden silence. No night sounds, no surreptitious squeakings or rustlings, no owl or fox or distant barking dog. Not even his own horse whiffling softly through velvet nostrils. Only a timeless, throbbing silence . . .

It was as if the rock accused him of violation, spoliation, rape. As if the rock itself was threatening revenge. Unaccountably he shivered, drew in his horse's reins and turned his head for home. The quarry safely behind him, he dug in his heels and took the last stretch at a satisfying canter, but even the speed and the rushing wind in his face could not quite dispel his unease. He handed over his horse to the stable lad, strode in through the kitchen entrance, ordering a fire to be lit immediately in the library, though it was mid-June and almost midnight, and summoned a bottle of his father's best brandy.

Half an hour later, comfortably installed in his father's leather armchair before a blazing log fire, with the firelight dancing over the dark oak panelling and picking out the gold lettering on the leather bindings of his father's books, Fergus at last felt his tension slip away in the contemplation of his second brandy. A sense of well-being gradually crept over him and it was not until he was refilling his glass for the third time that he remembered Flora Burnett. A silly girl. Didn't know what she was missing. He'd been mad to consider her in the first place. Far better fish in the sea.

Out of nowhere came the picture of a girl, running across the quarry yard, her hair flying behind her and her face distraught, and another picture of that same girl, proud and accusing, in the Gallowgate. He must remember to do more for her brother when that wall repair was finished. Perhaps the new contracts would provide the opportunity?

Lettice Adam returned to Silvercairns subdued and thoughtful. She had not forgiven Hamish Dunn nor that scheming Flora, whose fall from grace Aunt Blackwell had recounted to her with shocked relish. 'And not a penny to his name, apparently. What Mr Burnett will say I cannot imagine, but she is of age and he cannot prevent it. He could disinherit her, of course, and no doubt will, but she is already most adequately provided for and her money is her own, as everyone knows. No doubt the minister knew it too, but who are we to criticize a man of the cloth? And I had so hoped dear Fergus would have married her.'

'Oh, no, Aunt Blackwell,' Lettice had corrected her. 'Dear Fergus has other things on his mind. He does not mean to marry for many years, if at all.' Lettice had no basis for her statement, but she did not intend Aunt Blackwell to spread the tale all over town that her brother had been jilted by the Burnett girl, or bested by Hamish Dunn. As for that reptile, she would show Mr Dunn that he could not insult an Adam and go unpunished, but for the moment she could not think how.

Meanwhile she would merely avoid or ignore the pair of them. But in spite of her indignation, her pride still smarted most uncomfortably, so that when her father summoned her to his study and told her that he planned a dinner at which Ainslie Sharp was to be the chief guest and that he wanted her to go out of her way to make him welcome, she seized the opportunity with enthusiasm.

'Remember, Ainslie Sharp's high up in the railway business, Lettice, and I'm relying on you to make him welcome. We want him to feel one of the family, so when he sees the tenders on the desk in front of him, he takes ours. Do you understand me?'

'Yes, Father. But I thought you already had the railway contract?'

'One of them, yes, but not the one I want,' said Adam, frowning. 'This time it's for north of Aberdeen, and we're best placed to supply their needs, not like that lot in Fife, with transport charges and all.'

'But surely they could use their own railway, Father?' said Lettice innocently and gave Mungo his idea.

'They could,' he said slowly, 'when they've built it, my dear. But it will not be open for another eighteen months. Meanwhile . . . But that is my business. Yours is to make our guests welcome.'

'You can rely on me, Father' said Lettice, demurely.

'I hope so. With your brothers a pair of fools, one way and another.' She knew he was thinking of Fergus and of the Burnett opportunity lost, but was surprised at the lack of outrage in his voice. She had expected him to take badly the loss of the Burnett match, but after the predictable outburst on first hearing the news, he had merely shrugged and turned to other matters. Now he fixed her with stern eyes and repeated, 'I hope so, Lettice.' It occurred to her, briefly, that her father might be transferring the obligation of acquiring the Burnett money to *her*. If he was, she would have to disoblige him, though she had no intention of telling him so. But her father's next words dispelled that particular fear, at least for the moment.

'You are to pay *especial* attention to Ainslie Sharp, do you understand me?'

'Yes, Father. I promise I will do all in my power to make Mr Sharp welcome.' She dipped an obedient curtsey for good measure, and hurried gleefully upstairs to her room to review her wardrobe. If, as she suspected, Mr Dunn was to be included in the party, and it would be beneath her dignity to ask her father to exclude him (quite apart from the awkward questions such a request would produce) then she would show him what an elegant, witty and accomplished prize he had lost. And if her father's Mr Ainslie Sharp benefited, so much the better. At least her father would be pleased.

Later, on a tour of inspection of her garden, in case the need should arise for her to take Mr Sharp for a romantic evening stroll, she came across an unknown young man with his sleeves rolled up to the elbows, his shirt undone at the neck and a dusty leather apron bound with rope. He appeared to be demolishing her ornamental wall.

She stared at first in astonishment, then in affront. The first thing a servant learned was to keep out of sight, whether indoors or out. She had certainly never come across any of the gardeners in such an unexpected fashion.

'What are you doing in my private garden?' she demanded.

Slowly, the man straightened to his full height and looked down at her. He was holding one of the stones from the wall in his hands. It was a large and heavy stone, of Silvercairns granite, but apart from the bulging muscles of his biceps, he showed no sign of strain. 'I would have thought it was obvious,' he said, with no trace of deference or respect. He was dark-haired, she noticed, his skin weather-tanned, and his eyes surprisingly blue. They did not lower as she glared her annoyance.

'Who gave you permission to invade my privacy?'

'I did not know I needed permission,' said the man with remarkable insolence. 'I was told to do a job of work and I'm doing it. That is, when I am not being prevented by those with no work of their own.'

'How dare you!' began Lettice, then, because the young man's eyes were challenging her to lose her temper, and because he was really quite handsome for a servant, she said haughtily, 'See you make a good job of it, that's all. At the moment, it looks worse than it did before.'

He looked at her steadily, in silence, then deliberately dropped the rock. She squealed and jumped back as it thudded into the ground between them, to set the earth quivering with the impact of its weight.

'Perhaps you would like to show me how to do it, *madam*?'

For once in her life, Lettice was lost for words. She was trembling with shock and outrage, yet at the same time strangely excited. 'Certainly not,' she managed after a flustered moment. 'Just see that the wall is finished as soon as possible, that's all.' With that she swept past him with what remained of her dignity and made her way to the little, octagonal doocot in the south-west corner.

Here, there were steps to a stone archway and inside a sort of summer-house, with seats, while overhead the doves purled and cooed and preened their plumage in a dozen miniature doorways in the grey-domed roof. Yellow stonecrop carpeted the flagstones, pansies and forget-me-nots and night-scented stock crowded the neighbouring flower border, with delphiniums standing guard behind them and flamboyant hollyhocks knee-deep in love-in-a-mist. A tea-rose, full-blown and opulent, scented the air with its old-world fragrance, and the path at Lettice's feet was strewn with its ivory petals, soft as satin. It was a lovely, tranquil corner in the evening sunlight, and Lettice, after a moment's uncertainty, mounted the steps and sat down on one of the seats in the summer-house till the thumping of her heart slowed to its normal steady pace and she regained composure. But, though she felt once more in control, of her world and of anyone she might meet in it, instead of continuing her walk, she stayed where she was, in the doocot summer-house. She told herself she was reconnoitring for her Welcome-Ainslie-Sharp campaign, but in reality she was watching the stonemason, through a gap in the yew hedge which separated this part of the garden from the rest. His back was towards her, and she noted the broad strength of his shoulders, the ease with which he took up a stone, tested it, tossed it aside or set it in place. He bent and turned and lifted and bent again in a continuous rhythm which had its own beauty of movement and when he paused, straightened, turned half towards her and rubbed the sweat from his brow with the back of a forearm, she realized that he too had a kind of beauty. In fact, he was decidedly handsome. That is, if a stonemason and a servant could be called handsome. He was certainly better looking than most young men of her own social circle – that effete Niall Burnett, for instance, and his chinless friends. As for Ainslie Sharp, she remembered him as a colourless weasel of a man with a long nose . . . It was a pity really . . .

She watched the young stonemason until the sun sank behind the doocot roof and the summer air struck suddenly chill. Then she stood up, smoothed her skirts, adjusted her bonnet to its most becoming angle and strolled back up the path towards the house.

'Goodnight,' she said graciously, as she passed him, but he did not answer.

'I'm pleased for you, Mhairi, love,' said Cassie Diack, giving his daughter a kiss. With the end of his apprenticeship in sight, Alex had approached Cassie for his official permission and now Alex and Mhairi were handfast. When Alex's term of apprenticeship was over, in September, he and Mhairi would marry. She would live with Alex – and Donal, for where Alex went, his brother must follow – but not too far from Mitchell's Court so that she could look in every day to see the family were managing. If ever Mhairi remembered those other dreams of palaces and princes, she discarded them as childish fantasy. All she wanted was a home of her own, with the man she loved, and when Tom and Alex left Silvercairns and set up in business together, as they fully meant to do, she would have both. As long as they worked for the Adams, their lives were not their own, but once they were free, there would be no limit to what they could achieve. Alex loved her, and he had promised . . .

'Aye,' said her father, interrupting her thoughts. 'Alex's a good lad. He'll look after you when I'm gone.'

'That'll be a long time yet, Da,' said Mhairi, as cheerfully as she could manage, but it was true enough that with the coming of summer his chest seemed to have improved and his breathing was easier. He'd really enjoyed the holiday for the Queen's birthday, too, and since then had gone out of the house more often. He and Mackinnon had taken to meeting of an evening now and then, for a drink or a chat, and her father even talked of keeping an eye open for casual work as long as it was not too far away. 'For I'm nae fit for walking the miles I used to, Mhairi love, and it wouldna do to arrive at my work wi' no energy left to lift a hammer.'

Mhairi was glad to see him more cheerful, but in no hurry for him to find work. They were managing well enough at the moment, with the extra work Miss Roberts gave her and the pennies Lorn and Willy earned. Willy had found himself a job for the summer, sweeping the shop floor for old man Abercrombie of Abercrombie and Sons Emporium and Lorn had gone with Donal one day to the Wyness yard and persuaded old Wyness to take him on as a yard boy, clearing away the slurry from the polishing sheds and keeping the yard tidy. They handed over all their meagre wages with such pride to Mhairi that there were tears in her eyes as she thanked them. Then only last week Tom had come home with extra pay. 'For rebuilding a wee bit wall at the big house,' he said morosely. 'Seemingly I made too good a job of that cracked terrace and Madam thought she'd like the little wall around her croquet lawn "improved". Though if it hadna been that we need the money I'd have pulled it down around her arrogant ears. Patronizing bitch.' It appeared he was referring to Miss Adam.

'Tom!' cried Mhairi in horror. 'You must not say such things. Especially about your employer.'

'And why not? It's the plain truth. Prancing up and telling me how to do my work, spying on me from behind hedges when she thinks I canna see her. Counting every minute, no doubt, and deducting time for breathing! They're all the same, yon gentry. Expect folk to work for them all hours o' the day and night for pittance wages and be grateful for the honour. Lizzie says her time's not her own from one day's dawn to the next.' The only advantage that Tom could see in that building job at the big house, apart from the extra money of course, was the opportunity it gave him to keep an eye on Lizzie Lennox. For all her spying, Miss Adam couldna stop his calling at the kitchen door, for a glass of water or cool ale when the thirst took him, and since that scene in the Castlegate when he had rescued Lizzie from young Mr Hugo he had not been easy in his mind about her living in the same house as him. But Ma Gregor had reassured him, not in as many words, but by the impression she gave of having every minute of Lizzie's day arranged for. As for the nights, he knew for a fact she slept in a communal dormitory with the other maids and would be safe enough there. Nevertheless, he remained uneasy. He didna trust Mr Hugo, or his sister, come to that. She had given him a right funny look when he dropped that stone to frighten her, silly cow.

'And not satisfied with a plain, drystone dyke,' he went on indignantly, 'and as well-built a dyke as you'd find in all Scotland, she's sent to say she wants fancy coping on the top. But George Bruce told her she'd have to wait for that as we've a big drilling job to do.'

Mhairi was not quite quick enough to hide her disappointment – the extra money would have been a godsend – and Tom grinned.

'If you're thinking I've lost a good bonus, you needn't grieve, Mhairi. There's to be extra money for the drilling, seemingly, though it's not been heard of before.' He went on to explain, with mild astonishment, 'Word has it that Mr Fergus is that keen to blast the next bench of rock that he's offering extra pay to the men who drill the quickest.' There was no need for questions – they all knew that would include Tom.

'The quickest way isna always the best,' said Mackinnon when he heard. 'I hope Mr Fergus knows what he's doing.' Mackinnon had not visited Silvercairns quarry since Cassie Diack's dismissal though he knew well enough what was going on from Tom and Alex and others. 'A quarry isna just a hole in the ground: it needs to be treated with respect or it can play a man false.'

But whatever the wisdom or otherwise of Mr Fergus's approach, it would put extra money into the Diack purse and Mhairi was glad. She did not want her father worried on their behalf, did not want him to feel guilty for having no work and for sitting idle at home. And now of all times she wanted to be able to save just a little, week by week, to put against her wedding.

'As soon as I have my papers, Mhairi, we'll be man and wife,' murmured Alex, his arms folded tight around her and his cheek resting on her silken hair. She brushed it a hundred times a day, as her mother had told her the gentlewomen did, and she knew it was as sleek and beautiful as any lady's.

They had escaped from the tenement, after the evening meal, to stroll along the canal path and snatch a brief time alone together, without the constant demands of Mhairi's family to intervene. Now that it was summer, the long, light evenings and the softer air meant that they could look beyond the archways of the town for privacy and move further afield, to the Links or the shore or, as now, the lush green of the canal bank. Behind them rose the dark hump of Castle Hill, shutting out the town. On their right the long straggle of buildings which edged the Quay stretched away to the harbour mouth while to their left the man-made canal wound its tranquil way northwards between town and green fields. This was the packman's track to the Aulton two miles further north and provided a more leisurely route than the city streets, with watering places for the horses and green places for their owners to rest, or camp around a cheerful fire. Often the sound of fiddle music drifted along the canal bank of an evening, with singing and, now and then, the wail of bagpipes. In the daytime there would be barges carrying coal or other freight northward to Inverurie and other barges bringing produce from the country into town, but now, in the twilight of a soft summer evening, the only water traffic was a family of moorhens scurrying in the reeds on the far side. The water lapped gently against the canal bank and it was very quiet.

'At the end of September,' said Alex as they wandered slowly along the path, stopping every few steps to embrace.

Across the canal bank, the land stretched eastwards towards the sea, with the dark block of the gas works an alien island in the green swath of the meadow, and the Queen's Links beyond, before the bent grass, the fringe of golden sand and the grey German sea. There would be races on the Links in September.

'Can you wait until then, my handfast darling?' His lips moved to her ear, her neck, the corner of her mouth.

'I must.' She twisted away, laughing as excitement bubbled up inside her and overflowed. 'And so must you.'

He caught her to him and kissed her, teasing. 'Must I?'

'Oh, yes. You promised. It is only five weeks away, after all.'

But when she lifted her face to his and kissed him with the sound of distant laughter in her ears and the first summer stars overhead it seemed that September was a thousand years away. Suddenly fear gripped her.

'We will have that little house of our own, won't we? I don't think I could bear it if . . .' She stopped on the edge of the nightmare which had crept upon her increasingly in recent weeks. When they married, she knew their home would be no Silvercairns with a dozen plumed chimneys and a dozen silver dishes on the breakfast sideboard, perhaps not even a cottage with roses round the door and a little garden, merely a but-and-ben somewhere beside the land which would be their polishing yard, or a simple bothy. But Tom and Alex hadn't found their land yet, and suppose it was not even that? Suppose it was the same rooms in Mitchell's Court with the same noisy, quarrelsome neighbours, the same stench on the stairs, and her family, much as she loved them, still crowding round her, making the same demands for food and clean clothes and for her constant attention until she felt she were being torn into little pieces?

'Of course we will have our house, Mhairi,' soothed Alex. 'Haven't I promised you?' When she did not answer, but bit her lip and turned her head away, he took her face in his hands and made her look at him. 'What is it, my love? Don't you trust me?'

'Oh, yes, but . . .' How could she explain that it was not him, but fate she feared?

'No "buts",' he said softly, and as he began to kiss the tears from her eyes, with lips as light as a butterfly's wings, his arms strong around her and his confidence sure, her fear receded into the shadows behind them until Mitchell's Court seemed a world away. Here, on the twilit canal bank, there was only beauty and silence and peace, with nothing and no one to come between them.

'One day you will have your house, my darling,' he murmured. 'Haven't I given you my word?' He led her, unprotesting, into the shadow of the bridge, spread his coat for them on the soft grass and drew her down beside him. *One day* . . . When he murmured, 'Must we really wait until September?' she found no answer, except to kiss him with a kind of yearning despair. 'You are so lovely, so desirable and soft and welcoming and . . . oh God, Mhairi, I want you to be all mine, now, here, in our secret heaven under the stars. Please, my handfast darling? If you truly love me?'

Common sense and prudence are cold counsellors and Mhairi hardly heard them. All she heard was the pleading hunger in his voice and the thudding fear in her own heart. 'One day,' he had said. But when would that day come? Suppose their marriage bed was to be her mother's bed in the tenement, with the family only a wooden partition away? Suppose tonight was their only chance of privacy? Suppose they were destined never to be alone together again? Suppose . . . she shut her eyes tight against the fear. 'Please?' he murmured, his lips close against her ear. 'My love, my sweet one.' He began slowly to kiss her throat, her shoulder and the warm skin of her breast, while his hands caressed and teased, until the last shred of her resistance melted into fire. She forgot virtue, caution, everything but the all-consuming need to lose herself completely in the glorious, thrusting strength of his love.

The canal water lapped softly against the bank, mere feet away, and beyond the shadow of the bridge moonlight brushed the water with shimmering silver. Overhead the stone arched black and gleaming as if to guard their privacy and the scent of grass was fresh and clean. 'If you love me,' he had said, and later, as they lay together, drained and languid and deliciously replete, she knew that she did, with all her joyful, overflowing heart. They were handfast and September almost here. Surely nothing could prevent their wedding now?

On that bright summer morning Lettice Adam had ordered the carriage and driven into town, with Eppie in attendance, to make various purchases and to pay a few social calls. She would be gone for several hours.

When Lizzie had finished her tedious and mostly unnecessary tasks – in her opinion, anyway, for what was the use of blackleading the stove every day when it would only get spoilt again? – she busied herself with rubbing up the hearth tiles, running a cloth over the brass jelly pans and generally pretending to be occupied while she kept a watchful eye on Cook. Mrs Gregor was partial to her food and even more to her daily glass of port and with the heat of the kitchen and the need to take the weight off her feet, she usually nodded off in the basket chair for half an hour or so in the afternoon, before regirding her loins for the challenge of family dinner. This evening there were to be visitors, but the worst of the preparations were already over.

The kitchen was a long, stone-flagged room with a high ceiling and a vast slab of a kitchen table in the centre. The deal table-top was three inches thick and scored all over with knife marks and the dents of the chopper where Mrs Gregor was used to decapitate poultry and game. It was one of Lizzie's daily tasks to scrub the surface of this table spotless and she hated it. As she hated peeling endless vegetables, scouring endless saucepans, and generally cleaning up after Mrs Gregor and the others. Fanatical, that Ma Gregor was, as if a bit of honest dirt did anyone any harm. But today Lizzie was finding tasks to occupy her, deliberately, until she was certain Cook was well away. The other servants were about their various tasks in other parts of the house, for the kitchen at this hour was sacred to Mrs Gregor, and Lizzie had no worries on that score. They wouldn't care what she was doing. But Ma Gregor seemed to regard Lizzie as her property, and every hour of Lizzie's life as hers to order and dispose of. Lizzie would have admitted it to no one, but she had a sneaking respect for the cook, and was a little in awe of her.

The clock ticked solemnly on the mantelpiece above the vast cast-iron stove and the vast black kettle simmered obediently on the hob, while Ma Gregor's generous chin sank lower on her well-upholstered bosom. Lizzie paused in her aimless dusting and studied her from under carefully lowered lids. Ma Gregor had been known to spring alive from the seeming dead and pounce on some trivial misdemeanour like a hawk on its prey. But the heavy figure had collapsed into the welcoming comfort of the chair, as if her corsets had split, giggled Lizzie in silent glee. The cook's mouth was slightly open, and one plump hand had slipped from her lap to hang, drooping, over the side of the chair.

Surely now it would be safe to go? As Lizzie hesitated, she heard the first soft snore and grinned in decision. She should be safe for half an hour. Carefully she eased open the heavy kitchen door and slipped through into the passageway, then she tiptoed along the stone-flagged passage past china room and butler's pantry and game pantry and laundry, from which came a burst of smothered laughter and the chatter of female voices, until she reached the back stairs. Then she mounted to the ground floor.

At the baize door which led to the front regions of the house, she paused, listening. She knew what was on the other side of the door, for though she was forbidden to leave the kitchen regions she'd managed to escape Ma Gregor's eye and look. She wasna going to live in a house and not know what it looked like, was she? On the other side of the door, instead of stone floors and bare walls, there were carpets and panelling, and ceilings in pink and blue and green, with white cornices and big white ornamental bits in the middle, with chandeliers hanging down. There were paintings on the walls and little statues on shelves which looked to have been scooped out special like, and some of them as naked as when they was born. It was disgusting really, and some of they pictures were as bad. Not the portraits, though they were an ugly-looking lot for the most part, wi' long noses for looking down on folk with and bad-tempered expressions, but the other ones. Folk with no clothes on, prancing about in fields with bits of drapery fluttering. Lizzie wouldn't have them in her house, not if you paid her. There was a dining-room, cold as charity, wi' a table big enough to lay out a family of twelve wi' room to spare, and a drawing-room full of mirrors and gold paint. It had the biggest piano Lizzie had ever seen in her life, but when that Miss Carrot sang and they listened on the kitchen stairs, she didna sing near as well as Mhairi Diack's ma used to do. There was the master's library, too, full of books that nobody read, and his study, and another room they called the breakfast room though why they couldna eat breakfast in the same place where they ate dinner was beyond her.

But now, as she stood with her ear to that baize dividing door, Lizzie heard no sounds of movement. Mr Fergus was at the quarry, she knew, and Old Man Adam was likely with him. Or asleep, like Ma Gregor, in his study. Reassured, she sped on upstairs to the second green baize door which led to the corridor in which lay the family bedrooms. Lizzie knew which was Miss Carrot's because once, when the family were safely in the drawing-rooom after dinner, Eppie had shown her. She had asked Lizzie to give her a hand with the ironing, there being extra with the Queen's birthday coming and all, and they had gone together to put Miss Carrot's clean linen back in her press.

Eppie of course would be horrified if she knew what Lizzie was up to – Eppie had always been a prude and was growing worse in her old age – but Eppie wouldn't know. She was safely in Aberdeen with her precious Miss Carrot, wasn't she, and Lizzie had the place to herself. So she pushed the door slowly open, listened, stepped through, listened again, and let it slowly close behind her. She stood at a right-angled corner where the west wing met the main block, and the corridor stretched carpeted and silent in a dark red line to her left and straight ahead of her, white-painted, panelled doors to either side. Mr Fergus's room, Mr Hugo's, and that Miss Blackwell's were in the west wing, she remembered, and a spare room or two, but the best rooms were over the drawing-room and dining-room, in the main block. Hesitantly she tiptoed forward past the master's room, his dressing-room, and then, she was almost sure, Miss Lettice's. Almost, for in memory there had not been so many doors. She stood for a moment, listening for the slightest sound, and when she heard none, put out her hand and slowly turned the handle on the door.

Pink walls, white-painted wood, polished floor with Indian carpets, windows with chintz hangings and through them a view of meadowland and the long sweep of the drive. That was handy. She'd see the carriage coming. But it was a real pretty room. She'd forgotten how nice it was, but then she'd had Eppie with her last time, fussing and hurrying. The bed was a huge four-poster, with a canopy and hangings of chintz stuff like the curtains. It looked real comfy. Daringly, Lizzie crossed the room and lay down on it, her head on the satin-covered pillow and her eyes staring up at the canopy with its pale blue and yellow flowers and its gold threadwork. And the little curtains were pretty, too. You could climb into bed, draw them round you and be real private, not like at home where you had to share the bed with half a dozen kicking and whining kids. Mind you, it would be real cosy to share this bed with someone . . . the right someone. Lizzie giggled, sprang off the bed and pranced across to the great wooden press which contained Miss Lettice's clothes. She remembered to listen again, just in case, before opening the doors, but after that she forgot everything in the wonder of what she saw. Blue, green, yellow, pink, shot purple and violet, silver, every rainbow shade you could imagine hung there in front of her, waiting for her to handle, fondle, lay against her cheek, and finally try on.

Miss Lettice was taller than Lizzie, unfortunately, and some of the dresses were a bit tight across the bosom, but then that Miss Lettice hadna the figure Lizzie had, poor creature. Nor the hair. That whitey-yellow hair was awful insipid compared with Lizzie's red. She tried on a blue dress, then a pink, then her eyes lighted on a ball dress with lace on the shoulders and a huge yellow artificial rose at the waist. 'Oooh, yon gownie's lovely!' she breathed in awe.

Her own serviceable shift showed under the low-cut bodice, and her woollen stockings and heavy working shoes looked glaringly out of place, so she slipped them off and tried on the dress again, with nothing but her cotton drawers. Her own drab garments lay scattered and forgotten on the floor, but Lizzie was beyond caution now, and quite caught up in the fairy-tale wonder of Miss Lettice's clothes. Then she noticed that there were silver-backed brushes on the dressing-table and a collection of cut-glass phials with enamelled stoppers. Lizzie sat on the tapestry-covered stool at the dressing-table and unscrewed them, one by one, sniffing. Eau-de-Cologne, lavender water, rose water . . . She dabbed some of each behind her ears and over her front, then picked up the silver brushes and began to brush her hair. But the bristles seemed to get tangled in her curls and after a moment's tugging she tossed the brushes aside and decided to explore the little drawers instead. When Eppie took her into Miss Lettice's bedroom that time, before the Queen's birthday holiday, Lizzie had spotted the necklace lying on the floor under the dressing-table and had managed to pocket it without Eppie seeing. As to returning it, in spite of her promise to Tom she had done nothing about it, reasoning that as no hue and cry had been raised to her knowledge, the thing had not been missed. It was safely stowed away under her mattress in the attic and, she vowed, would stay there. After all, wasn't finders keepers? Besides, she'd given back the gloves, which were too small anyway, dropping them on to the washpile in the laundry, so she reckoned that ought to do. And the necklace was real pretty.

But now, as she pulled open the first little drawer, she saw an Aladdin's cave of wonders which made that simple necklace seem like a child's bauble, and, forgetting caution, she breathed a long and heartfelt, 'Cor!'

After holding up two or three necklets to her throat to try the effect, she selected a diamond and a ruby one, clipped it in place and turned her head this way and that to see the effect. 'Cor!' she breathed again. 'That's beautiful, that is.'

There was a pier glass between the two long windows and Lizzie was standing in front of it, admiring herself in the lemon yellow ball dress with the white lace shoulders and the artificial yellow rose, which set her hair off so well, and that lovely ruby sparkle on her front, when she heard a sound at the door and froze in horror.

'Lettice? Are you in there?' She stared, transfixed, into the mirror, saw the door reflected behind her and the handle of that door slowly turning. In the space of a moment she had considered and rejected hiding under the bed, in the wardrobe, anywhere, for though the dishevelment of the clothes press and dressing-table might just be blamed on burglars, her clothes still lay scattered in glaring evidence on the floor. There was nothing for it but to brazen it out, and as the door opened she turned, like an animal at bay, to face her doom.

'Well, well,' he said softly, 'if it isn't little Lizzie, looking lovelier than ever.' He stepped into the room and closed the door behind him. 'And in my sister's clothes. Her jewellery, too, I see, and from the smell of it, most of her scent.' Lizzie licked dry lips and sought wildly for an answer while he continued to stare at her with obvious enjoyment at her plight. He looked down at her splayed bare feet and said, grinning, 'Her shoes, I suppose, were not your size.'

Her face flushing with a mixture of embarrassment and anger, Lizzie pulled her feet quickly under the concealing folds of the dress and said defiantly, 'Well, why shouldn't I try her things on? It does her no harm and I was going to put them all back, real neat, so she'd never know.'

'Were you now?' Hugo was grinning at her in a way that both

confused and infuriated her. 'And I suppose you were going to put the perfume back into the bottles, too?'

'Don't be so daft! And stop staring at me.' Suddenly aware of the expanse of naked flesh which the ball dress revealed she crossed her arms protectively over her chest and said, 'If you was a gentleman you'd go away and let me put my clothes on in peace.'

'Would I? And miss what I am sure is a delectable sight?'

'Well, you're nae seeing it, so get out.'

Hugo leant back against the door, crossed one ankle over the other and folded his arms across his chest. 'Get out?' he repeated. 'And leave you with all my sister's jewels? How do I know you wouldn't steal them? Oh no, my dear, I feel it is my duty to stay. My solemn, delightful duty.'

Lizzie fumbled furiously at the clasp of the necklace and flung it back into the open drawer. 'There. It's back safe, wi' the others.' She slammed the drawer closed, screwed tops back on to an assortment of bottles with fingers that trembled in spite of her efforts, rearranged the hairbrushes and turned to face him. 'There,' she repeated defiantly. 'That's everything like it was.'

'Except the dress,' he said softly. 'Why don't you come here, Lizzie, and let me help you with the fastenings. I wonder if you have borrowed my sister's underwear, too. I do hope so, as I greatly look forward to helping you remove it again.'

'You keep your hands off me, Hugo Adam, or I'll tell someone something you wouldna want him to hear.'

'Oh?' But in spite of his apparent nonchalance, Lizzie detected a sudden wariness in his voice.

'Ah-ha! That took the smile off your face, didn't it? Well, when my friend hears that you've laid so much as a finger on me he'll sort you out, he will.'

'I assume you mean your ill-bred friend of the other night?' said Hugo, with obvious relief.

'Well, I don't, so you can take that smirk off your face for a start. Though I reckon he'd be glad enough to lend a helping hand, now you mention it.' She grinned briefly at the memory of Tom's kiss. He was nae a bad lover and she'd fair enjoyed the evening after, wi' more where that came from. 'No,' she went on with growing confidence, 'this is another man, who wouldna like to hear of how you treated his brother.'

But Hugo was unimpressed. If that town lout reappeared he'd soon send him packing and his friend with him. A touch of the birch would not come amiss there. Now, had she threatened him with information for his father, it might have been a different matter – But she had not and Lizzie Lennox, with her breasts bursting out of his sister's dress and its skirts practically tripping her up, looked delectably ripe for the picking. Besides, a quick glance over the garments which littered the floor made him practically certain that she had next to nothing on underneath. He felt behind him with one hand, turned the key in the lock, and pocketed it.

Lizzie blanched. 'You take a step nearer and I'll scream,' she threatened. To lead Mr Hugo on as she had planned to do that time in the stable yard was one thing: to find that he had the upper hand was quite another.

'Come now, Lizzie, would I hurt you? You're a fine-looking girl, do you know that? I knew it that time years ago when you behaved so delightfully outside Mr Corbyn's dancing class. That girl, I said to myself, would look the equal of any lady in the dance, were she dressed as they were. And here you are, in a dress of Lettice's that looks ten times better on you, and you won't even let me admire you. I call that ingratitude, I really do. I think,' he said with mock sadness, though he was grinning openly now, 'that I shall have to tell my sister all about it, and possibly that dear Mrs Gregor too. What a pity. We could have come to such a friendly arrangement.'

'I don't know what you mean,' she temporized, searching helplessly for some way out of the appalling situation.

'Well, suppose you step out of that dress and hang it back in the cupboard, Lizzie, while I try to explain.'

'Promise not to move from that door?'

'I promise.'

'Promise not to look?'

'I promise to stare straight ahead of me,' he said solemnly, 'until you are fully clothed again.'

'God's honour?'

'God's honour.'

Lizzie snatched up her clothes piecemeal, opened the door

of the clothes press and stepped behind it. Then she wriggled out of the loathsome ball dress and let it fall in a heap on the floor.

'As I thought,' said Hugo softly. 'Absolutely beautiful,' and Lizzie spun round to find herself reflected full length in that wretched mirror, bare to the waist and with only her cotton drawers to cover her shame. Hugo's teasing eyes met hers in the mirror and she clapped her arms across her breasts and opened her mouth to scream, but he put a finger to his lips and said, 'Hush! My father is asleep, next door.' It was a lie, but she was not to know it and it stopped the scream in her throat. But only for a moment. 'If you lay a finger on me, Mr Hugo Adam, I swear I'll scream till the whole house hears me.'

'And what will they think, Lizzie dear, when they see you flaunting yourself, naked, at poor, defenceless me?'

'I'm nae naked! I've got my drawers on.'

'More's the pity.' He took a step towards her.

'Don't you dare,' she warned, backing away from him, her arms still crossed tight across her naked, bouncing breasts. 'Lay a finger on me and I swear I'll kill you.' It was an empty threat and they both knew it. Suddenly she changed tack. 'Please Mr Hugo, go away till I've got my clothes on? I daren't stay up here any longer. Ma Gregor'll be looking for me and if she finds me here, I'm for the chopping block, sure as eggs.'

'Suppose I do,' said Hugo slowly. 'Will you meet me later? Somewhere safer and more private?'

'Yes, if you want me to. Anything. Only please hurry. I know she'll be after me.'

'All right. But first, a kiss?'

'Not without my clothes on!' cried Lizzie in outrage.

With the toe of his shoe, Hugo lifted the nearest garment from the floor, caught it in his hands and, grinning, offered it to her, like a toreador taunting a bull. She snatched at it with one hand, her other arm still clutched across her front, missed, stamped her foot in fury as he held it just out of reach, his eyes teasing her and a look on his face that filled her with excitement and a pleasurable shiver of fear. Then, without warning, he tossed the garment aside and made a grab at her, she dodged and a moment later they were playing a bizarre and gleeful game of cat and mouse until, panting and exultant, he cornered her between the window and the four-poster bed.

Laughing softly, arms spread to bar her escape, he took a slow step towards her.

'Mr Hugo,' she squealed, 'don't you dare!' but her eyes were laughing and her cheeks pink with the chase. She glanced quickly over her shoulder, judging whether to attempt escape across the bed, then back – and beyond his shoulder, saw a movement which took the colour from her cheeks and froze her blood. 'Oh, lor!'

He turned his head, following the direction of her eyes through the bedroom window, and saw the carriage in the drive. 'Quick!' he said, in quite a different voice. 'Dress as fast as you can.' She scuttled across the room, snatched up her bodice from the floor and thrust her arms into it while he collected her various other scattered garments and crossed to her side. Then he hesitated, bent his head and kissed her quickly on each unprotected breast, before thrusting the clothes into her arms. Lizzie was too startled, and too agitated, to protest. She scrambled into her bodice and shift all anyhow, dragged her regulation blue drugget dress over her head and topped it with the overall apron which marked her kitchenmaid status, while he crammed Miss Lettice's ball dress back into the wardrobe and attempted clumsily to set the skirts to rights.

There was no time to put on her stockings so she bundled them into her apron pocket and thrust her bare feet as they were into her shoes. Hugo dropped to one knee and tied one of the laces for her while she tied the other and when they both finished at the same time she looked up to find his face a mere inch away. He smiled, winked, said, 'Thank you for the private viewing,' and dragged her to her feet with one hand while unlocking the door with the other.

'Will you tell?' managed Lizzie, with an attempt at composure.

'I don't think so . . . yet. But we can talk about it later, behind the dairy. At ten? Remember to be there, or I might change my mind.' Then he opened the door, peered out to make sure there was no one in sight, and pushed her out into the corridor, with a parting smack on the bottom. Lizzie gathered her scattered shreds of pride and sped down the corridor, reaching the baize door just as the front door opened below and Miss Lettice arrived home.

She did not go straight to the kitchen, but took temporary refuge in the china cupboard, among the shelves of Spode and Sèvres and Wedgwood, to readjust her clothing and put on her stockings. It was while she was retying her apron strings that she noticed the smell. She reeked of that Miss Carrot's scent bottles! She scurried through the kitchen, behind Cook's back, and out into the yard where she scrubbed her face and neck at the outside pump, until Mrs Gregor's voice called imperiously from the kitchen, 'Lizzie! Where's that dratted girl got to now?'

Deliberately, Lizzie trod in a steaming pat of horse dung and walked it into the kitchen. 'Yes, Mrs Gregor. You wanted me?'

'Good God, girl, what's that dreadful smell? And look at yon floor! Get out of here and clean yourself up and next time look where you're stepping. Then you'll get down on your knees and scrub my floor so clean the Queen herself could eat off it and take no harm . . .'

With Ma Gregor's grumblings and scoldings buzzing in her ears, Lizzie happily did as she was told. If she smelt of anything now it was horse dung and brown soap and no one would connect that smell with Miss Lettice's bedroom! She had escaped and Mr Hugo wouldn't tell. He wasna a bad lad after all and it had been real kind of him to tie her shoe like that. Mind you, he shouldna have looked in the mirror and spied on her in that underhand fashion, shouldna have chased her round the bedroom half-naked, though she had to admit it had been fun, and as for kissing her *there*, she blushed to think of it. All the boys she'd kissed, not that there were many of course as she wasna that kind of girl, had kissed her on the mouth, or tried to, but never anywhere else. Remembering, she felt an unexpected thrill of excitement. He'd said nice things, too. She reckoned she'd best meet him behind the dairy, just to make sure he wasna going to tell on her, but he needn't think he'd get anywhere with her, just because he'd seen her half-naked, like those women in the pictures. If he tried anything, she'd send him packing soon enough. But she couldn't help wondering what he would try, if he did, and how he'd go about it. Not that she'd let him, of course, but it might be interesting to lead him on a bit, just to see . . . Singing happily to herself, she dipped the scrubbing brush into the soapy water and attacked the floor.

'*My love is like a red, red rose that's newly sprung in June* . . .' sang Mhairi happily as she thumped the flatiron on to the spread linen and held it, steaming, over the dampened cloth. For once it was not a piece of sewing for the Ladies' Working or for Miss Roberts, but a new petticoat for herself, with ribbons saved from Miss Roberts' commissions, and a scrap of broderie anglaise on the bodice. Mhairi was delighted with it and when she had pressed it carefully, aired and folded it, she would put it away in the press with a sprig of lavender until the wedding.

The wedding. Mhairi whispered the words to herself over and over, savouring their beauty and their promise. Alex was a good man, hard-working, loyal, kind: he would be kind to her father and brothers and her little sister, as she would be kind to Donal. And he loved her. Remembering how he loved her Mhairi held the iron suspended while the warmth and ardour of those private memories brought the faintest flush of pink to her cheeks and a secret smile of pure elation. He loved her. And within a month they would be man and wife, for ever and always, world without end . . .

'Oh, Ma,' she breathed, 'I wish you were here, to share my happiness. I know you would like him, Ma. You always said he was a nice lad when he was little and now . . . oh, Ma, he's so handsome and brave and good. And he loves me, Ma. He really does.' From somewhere in the depths of memory a voice came, anguished and despairing, 'Don't ever marry, lass. It isna worth it.'

But her ma had said that only because she was ill and frightened. She hadn't really meant it. She couldn't have, not with her and Da being so fond of each other. Look how her da had grieved, and still grieved, for her ma. That was true love, like she and Alex felt for each other. If her ma were still alive, she would not say such things. She would be glad for them.

Reassuring herself thus, Mhairi set the flatiron on the stove to reheat and took up the second which was already heated through. She would let down the hem on Annys's dress next. The child was growing so fast now that Mhairi could hardly keep up with her and she was doing really well at school. Mhairi wouldn't be surprised if Annys won a prize this year.

The schools had been back a month now and though both Lorn and Willy had protested fiercely Mhairi had insisted that they return to school for one more year. 'Ma said you were to be educated properly and I intend to see that you are,' she told them. 'And don't think to skive for I'll soon find out if you do and then you'll be in real trouble.'

It was hard at first without the boys' contributions, small though they had been, especially with the school money to be found again, but Mhairi had saved a little over the summer and somehow they would manage. And Alex approved, as he approved of everything she did since that precious, private night on the canal bank. Already he behaved like a responsible older brother to the little ones and one day, when he and Tom had established their yard together, Lorn and Willy would work in the family business, with Alex's brother Donal. One day . . . Smiling to herself she ironed flat the opened hem of Annys's dress, then carefully turned up and pressed a newer, narrower hem for added length. Tom and Alex were still looking for that piece of ideal land, but there was time yet and they would find it. Hadn't Alex given her his promise?

'The canal?' repeated George Wyness, feigning surprise. 'Aye, we're nae far from the canal. Fine and handy it is too when we've blocks to be sent to the harbour for shipment.'

He was in the office of his granite-polishing yard, where he had been summoned by an agitated nipper-boy who had informed him that Mr Adam was waiting for him in the office and had told him to fetch his master right quick. When the lad found him, Wyness was in the cutting shed, explaining to his chief cutter the precise dimensions he required for a plinth they were making for a statue, and when he heard the message he had taken particular pleasure in first asking the lad to tell him how many blunt tools he had collected so far that day and from whom, and when he thought the smithy would have them ready, then speaking to every cutter in the shed, to the saw-boy who fed the sand and water into the cutting groove and to the slurry boy who swept the floor, before eventually making his deliberately slow way out into the yard. Even then he spoke to a joiner who was cutting templates for a headstone and another who was knocking together a wooden crate, to a mason chipping away at a funeral urn, and to two apprentices who were dressing a block that had come in only that morning from Dancing Cairns. He had an unnecessary word with his foreman, and another with the yard boy who had replaced young Lorn Diack before finally making his way to the front office. Here he had found Mungo Adam, even blacker of brow than usual, his coat-tails raised to catch what meagre heat there was from the coal-fire in the tiny grate and his expensively shod feet rapping the worn hearthrug in increasing impatience.

Without waiting for the normal civilities Adam had said, 'I told that lad to fetch you at once. If he was mine, I'd sack him for incompetence. But you're here now, Wyness, though not before time, so I'll state my business. I believe your land abuts the canal?'

Wyness had kept his face expressionless as he answered, though his mind had already leapt ahead to what was coming so that when Mungo Adam spoke again, he was well prepared.

'The railway, I believe, is planned to pass this way, too.'

'Oh, aye?' Wyness was enjoying himself. It had been immediately obvious to him that Mungo Adam was after something and Wyness meant him to sweat for it, whatever it was, and to sweat hard. Already Old Man Adam was suspiciously red about the gills and holding in his temper with difficulty. That proved he wanted something, otherwise he'd have shouted his rage to the world, as he usually did. Carefully Wyness kept his face expressionless and repeated, 'Oh, aye?'

Mungo Adam's choler increased. 'Oh, aye?' was a particularly annoying rejoinder, typical as it was of local wariness, local hostility, and the propensity of so many of these fellows to play their cards so close to the chest it was a wonder they could see them themselves, let alone know what tricks they held. George Wyness, however, held a trick that, though he might not know it himself, Adam not only wanted, but was determined to get.

Mungo Adam did not relish the position he found himself in. The need to be conciliatory was abhorrent to him, especially when he had been used to treating Wyness with the high-handed disregard which was all the fellow deserved. But that dinner with Ainslie Sharp had been productive in more ways than one. Lettice had made herself particularly agreeable, as he had told her to do, and Adam reckoned that Sharp had not been unaffected. Not that the man himself was worth much of a fortune, leastways not as far as Adam had been able to find out, but Sharp was in a position to put very lucrative business in Adam's way. In return, Adam could introduce Sharp into society, give him a bit of good shooting, a dance or two perhaps, and a few well-chosen house parties. It would be, at the very least, useful if Lettice made a match there. But more important than that possibility was the Wyness connection.

Angling, as usual, for a contract for the railway work north of Aberdeen, Adam had mentioned, in the sort of throw-away aside that was designed to catch his quarry's attention and lodge in his brain for later perusal, that a business partner of his had premises most advantageously positioned for the transport of building materials north which would, of course, greatly reduce the tender which Adam could offer without reducing the quality of the stone supplied. It was, he implied, a magnificent opportunity for all concerned, and all concerned, including Sharp and the railway company, would be stupid not to take advantage of it. He was almost certain that Sharp had bitten, swallowed, and willingly digested the bait and Adam expected the contract daily. Now all that remained was to prepare Wyness for his new status as business partner and to extract from him the most favourable terms. It was, after all, an honour to be allied with the Adam enterprise, and if, as he might have to do, Adam allowed his name to be bracketed with Wyness's over the Wyness premises, then that alone was worth a fortune in itself. The use of Wyness's yard and canal access for transport purposes ought to be, if not actually free, then certainly at a peppercorn rent. Slowly, as to an idiot, and with all the diplomacy at his command, which after a life of unchallenged tyranny was minimal, Adam pointed out to Wyness the benefits of his plan.

Unfortunately, George Wyness refused to see it in the same light. In fact, he was proving remarkably obtuse, both as to the honour being offered him and the ease with which the transaction could be carried through without inconvenience to anyone concerned.

'Good God, man,' burst out Adam, his puny attempts at diplomacy abandoned. 'Do I have to draw you pictures? Any fool can see it's the opportunity of a lifetime.'

'So,' said George Wyness slowly, looking at Adam across the marked and pitted office table with eyes which were not in the least foolish, 'I am to save you a fortune in transport costs by giving you free run of my yard and my canal access in return for the privilege of putting your name above my door. Is that it? And what am I to do with my monuments when your carts are unloading your building blocks all over my yard? How am I to ship my best polished headstones by canal barge to the harbour, as I usually do, when my barge is full o' your bits and pieces o' rock that could go just as easily and always have done afore by horse and cart to town?'

'You do not understand, Wyness,' said Adam testily. 'My building materials are to travel north, not south. Your barge will go north with my materials, then come back to load again with your materials to take them south. I see no problem.'

'Well, I do. Who's to say that when my stuff's ready for shipment my barge will be waiting at the canal bank to take it? It'll be up Inverurie way with your stuff and I'll have to wait around for hours till it comes back and then, like as not, you'll expect to load it up again with your stuff and nae mine. I reckon you'd best buy your own barge, Mr Adam, and leave me to mine.'

Mungo Adam opened his mouth to swear, thought better of it, fumed and snorted in impotent fury until he felt able to speak, then said, through clenched teeth, 'A fair point, Wyness. A separate barge might be more sensible. But that could be arranged.'

'Then while you're at it,' said Wyness, enjoying his advantage, 'you'd best arrange a separate landing stage, too, and a separate approach road, for mine's awful busy and nae big enough for two. There's land at Constitution Street that'd do you fine, if you've a mind to pay for it, like, and you'd easy build a wee road and landing stage and all. There's other folk after it, of course, with it being so handy, but I know the party selling and I could put in a word for you, maybe?'

George Wyness kept his face straight as he propounded his outrageous suggestions, knowing Constitution Street was the opposite side of town from Silvercairns, knowing Adam's tightfistedness, his arrogance, his expectation that everyone should jump to his bidding and be glad of the privilege, knowing his belief in his own power to get whatever he wanted, when he wanted it, or sooner. The idea that George Wyness should have influence where Adam did not was guaranteed to blow the top off Adam's temper and unleash every insult known to the English-speaking world, with more, no doubt, of Adam's own invention.

Wyness waited for the result of his calculated baiting with particular, if expressionless glee. His grievance against Mungo Adam had increased over the last year to the point where he no longer felt the need to ingratiate himself or curry favour. The business Adam put his way was minimal now and Wyness had long since given up expecting preferential treatment when he wanted a special type of block for his thriving monumental trade. That design of young Donal's had brought him new business and his own men had elaborated and built on it till he had a steady stream of orders and not just from Aberdeen. He'd sent a headstone to London only last week and had orders for two more. As to stone, Silvercairns was not the only source. There were plenty of other, smaller quarries more than willing to oblige him and he had found he could manage very well without Mungo Adam, thank you very much. If he did want a piece of Silvercairns rock and nothing else would do, then he had a good friend in Donal Grant, who passed the word to his brother Alex and together they'd choose him a fair piece. Then he'd have a word with George Bruce, the foreman, and though it cost him that wee bit extra, naturally, it was easier than asking Mungo Adam and having his request shot to the bottom of the list.

Besides, he hadn't forgotten that dinner party when young Fergus Adam had sat next to poor little Fanny and hardly said a word to her all evening. It was one thing for Old Man Adam to snub Wyness himself, but when it came to his son snubbing Wyness's daughter, then Wyness was not going to stand for it.

They could keep their quarry and their money and their high-falutin' snobbery for those who liked that sort of thing. Give him honest folk like the Diacks or that Grant boy any day. They may not be rich, leastways not yet, but you knew where you were with them. Honest, hard-working folk who'd not be looking every minute for the next way to do a man down. That wee Diack lad who'd worked for him all summer had been a bright lad, too, taking an interest in all that was going on, learning what he could, and that day he'd found a penny in the yard he'd taken it straight to the office and handed it in. Not many lads his age would do that. They said young Hugo Adam had debts all over town, but that wouldn't stop his attending the race meeting on the Links next week and running up as many more. No, thought Wyness, narrowing his eyes, the Adams might think they were God's gift to Aberdeen but there were plenty folk who'd disagree and he was one of them.

But Old Man Adam did not, as Wyness had expected, explode into a torrent of oaths. He went purple in the face for a minute or two, 'wi' steam coming out of his ears like a boiling kettle wi' two spouts' as Wyness reported later, but he kept his temper. It was unheard of, and Wyness took good note. Old Man Adam must want that share of Wyness's yard real bad, which meant, among other interesting speculations, that Wyness, for the moment, had the upper hand. He waited politely for Adam to speak.

'Does that mean you are not prepared to consider my offer?' demanded Adam, reserving his temper for the table which he thumped with his clenched fist.

'You havena told me what the offer is yet,' pointed out Wyness. 'And watch you dinna spill my ink or I'll charge ye for it.'

Mungo Adam decided to laugh, though it was an empty travesty of mirth. 'Always the businessman, Wyness, right down to the inkwell on your office table. But that's the way to get on in the world and you are quite right. I'll have my lawyer draw up an offer and send it round for you to look over in a few days' time.'

'He can send what he likes,' said Wyness cheerfully, 'though I dinna promise to look at it. I'm that busy these days . . .' He stood up, indicating the interview was over.

'I hope you will look it over,' said Adam ominously, 'because if not . . .' He had been going to threaten Wyness with some unspecified disaster, when his eye was caught by a silhouette portrait in a little oval frame and a different idea came to him. 'If not,' he finished lightly, 'you'll lose the chance of a lifetime. By the way, my son Fergus is planning to take a party to the theatre and asked me to ask your permission to invite your daughter Fanny.'

'He can ask her,' growled Wyness, 'but that doesna mean she'll go. She's a popular girl, wi' lots of engagements.' But as Wyness held open the door for Adam to leave, he knew that Fanny would go, and Mungo Adam knew it too.

'The theatre, Father? With Fanny Wyness?' Fergus Adam was astonished. He couldn't remember when he had last attended the theatre, though he had planned to take Flora Burnett, before she rejected him for Hamish Dunn. They were married now, after what Aunt Blackwell had described as a 'suspiciously short engagement' though in what the suspicion lay Fergus could not imagine, neither party's behaviour suggesting anything but the most virtuous of courtships. He found, to his surprise, that he could think of Flora without pain, or if he felt any lingering twinge it was in his pride rather than his heart which, he realized, had never been lost to her, except in his imagination. If he felt anything for her now, it was a comfortable indifference and when she came to dinner at Silvercairns, which he supposed she would inevitably do, he knew he would be able to meet her without distress. But the prospect of an evening in Fanny Wyness's company was far more daunting. What on earth could he find to say to her? He regarded his father with ill-concealed dismay. 'Whatever for?'

'Because she's young and unmarried and rich, you dolt, and because, for a number of urgent reasons, I want her father's yard. It will be ideal for the northern railway construction, or have you forgotten it's practically on the canal?'

'No, Father, but would it not be better to wait till you actually have Sharp's contract before committing me to that particular fate?'

'Good God, man, you don't have to propose to her on the

spot. As to the contract, Lettice and Ainslie Sharp will be joining you at the theatre. All I require of you is to keep the Wyness girl happy till her father has signed the agreement.'

'And suppose he doesn't sign it?'

'He will.'

'But Papa, he never spoke to me once the last time we met and I sat beside him all evening.'

'He was maybe shy, lass, like all young lads are sometimes. You just be nice to him and he'll soon get his confidence. He wouldna ask you if he didn't want to take you, would he?'

'No,' wavered Fanny, who was not convinced. She still admired Fergus Adam, of course. All the girls did. In fact for years, like them, she had had a secret, passionate, and hopeless crush on him, but in his presence she was invariably tongue-tied and he, in turn, found nothing to say to her. Her ardour had decidedly cooled since that last dinner and the idea of spending a whole, silent evening with him was not an attractive one. Theatre or no theatre, she would rather stay at home. But her father had ordered her to accept the invitation and she had no choice.

As for George Wyness, he had seen through Mungo Adam's plan from the start. Adam wanted control of Wyness's yard and wanted it badly. That could only mean money and not just the saving of a few pounds on transport. No, there was more to it than that and Wyness meant to find out what. But, providing he knew what was at stake – and that meant knowing as much as Mungo Adam and preferably more – then an alliance of that kind with the Adam family might not be a bad thing after all. There had been a time when he'd actually wanted it, but then when Mr Fergus had behaved so churlishly and the rest of the Adams with him, Wyness had had second thoughts. Now he was reconsidering. His yard was flourishing, with all the business it could handle and more, and for some months he had been thinking of expanding, moving to larger premises perhaps, or buying extra land. With the Adam money he would be able to do that, and he'd have what he'd hankered after for years – his own quarry. Well, not his own exactly for it would have to be 'Wyness and Adam', but at least the Adam part of it would be his son-in-law and he had no son of his own to carry on the yard when he'd gone. There'd be grandsons, too, one day. He'd not have Fanny hurt, mind, and it was her decision, but he knew she admired Fergus Adam and if Fergus actually proposed, then he'd maybe look again at that piece of paper the Adam lawyer had sent round. But of one thing he was certain: it would lie untouched and unread until Fanny had the Adam boy's engagement ring on her finger and the first banns were called in St Nicholas kirk.

The graveyard of St Nicholas was deserted on that late September afternoon when Cassie Diack made his way, as usual, to his wife's grave. Mhairi, bless her, was hard at work sewing for that Ladies' Working Society though they paid little enough for the hours she put in stitching away at interminable seams. But she didna seem to mind. She was happy these days, singing away to herself, just like her ma used to do. *But sorrows sair are past, John, and joys are coming fast, John* . . . The words seemed to come from the air around him as he stood looking down at the polished granite stone, pink as sunrise in the afternoon air. She would have liked yon stone. Donal Grant, for all his limitations, had a rare touch when it came to a headstone. That wee dove was perfect. And a week from now Donal Grant would be one of the family, for Mhairi's wedding was fixed for Saturday next, the day after Tom and Alex completed their time.

It would not be a grand ceremony, but the minister would marry them, proper like, and the hall was booked for the dance after. All the tenement folk had been asked and Tom's and Alex's mates from the quarry, and there'd be others like Mackinnon and George Wyness who Mhairi had been shy of asking, but Alex said why not when he'd been so kind to Lorn all summer and to Donal too . . . and certainly he'd said he'd be right glad to come. But it wouldna be much of a wedding for Mhairi for all that. He wished he could have given her a fine kist of new clothes like his own Agnes had had for her wedding, or at least a wee leather bag of money, to put by for the future when she'd likely need it, but he had nothing. A slow anger towards the Adams stirred inside him as he thought of the injustice of his dismissal. If it had not been for Mr Fergus and his bad temper, Cassie would still have had his job at the quarry, still have been earning a weekly wage, and would have been able to give his daughter the wedding she deserved. She was a good lass, a man couldna ask for a better daughter than she had been to him, and now when he wanted to give her something to show how he valued her, he had nothing. And when the poor lass was married, unless Tom and Alex found that place they talked of before the week was out, she'd likely come back to the same house with the same family to look after and two more mouths to feed. And though they'd bring two more wages, it wouldna make Mhairi's work any the less.

Cassie Diack stood looking down at his wife's grave and spoke to her, as he often did, unburdening his troubles as he had done when she was alive. 'I'd like fine for her to be able to set up house proper like, just as you and I did, Agnes love, with her man to herself and no one else to consider till her own bairns come along. But I havena the money to help her.'

As he looked down at his wife's grave, pondering the problem and wishing yet again that he still had his job at the quarry, it seemed to him that he heard her soothing and comforting him, and her soft voice singing of peace and everlasting joy in a land where there were no more troubles . . . Until he was startled from his reverie by a step behind him, and the familiar voice of Mackinnon, the old foreman from Silvercairns.

'I thought I'd find you here, Cassie, so I came here first afore going to your home. I've just been talking to a friend of mine, a man from the viaduct works at Ferryhill. He says they're a man short and whoever can get down there first thing tomorrow can have the job. I thought of you straight off, with Mhairi getting married and likely needing a wee bit extra. What do you say, Cassie? Are you game? Or shall I find someone else?'

'I'm game,' said Cassie, beaming, for was not this the startling, miraculous answer to his prayer? He would have money for Mhairi, and afterwards . . . afterwards did not matter. Standing there beside her grave he knew beyond a doubt that his Agnes wanted him to do it, willed him to do it, not only for Mhairi's sake, but for hers too. With the haunting notes of her singing still clear in his mind, he turned, jubilant, for home.

'Are you sure you're well enough, Da?' protested Mhairi anxiously when her father told her his news. 'You haven't worked since the spring and you know your breathing's not strong.'

'It's strong enough for a labourer's job on a viaduct, lass. And it's only for a few days, till the other man comes back. He's strained his leg, seemingly, so Mackinnon says, but when it's mended he'll want his job back and I wouldna want to keep it from him. I'm right looking forward to a bit of work again after so many months and I'll manage fine. And I'll maybe give you a wee bit extra for your wedding, Mhairi love.'

'Da, you are not to take a job just for me. We've managed fine all summer and we'll manage fine now.' Mhairi was worried for her father, worried by his coughing, his breathlessness, and, conversely, by his eagerness to work. It was not like him, for he knew as well as she did that a mason needed strength and stamina. But something seemed to have got into him to make him reckless and he brushed aside all arguments.

'I'm away to my work in the morning, lass, so see and have my piece ready and my flask of ale. It wouldna do to be late or someone else will take my place. I'm determined to give my eldest daughter a wedding gift and no one's going to stop me.'

He was up before dawn the following morning, and Mhairi heard him singing to himself as he washed and dressed in the shivering chill. It was not until he had picked up his bundle of tools and his lunch pack, kissed her on the cheek, waved to her from the tenement steps, and walked off into the half-light, turning again to wave from the corner into Broad Street, that she realized what it was he had been singing: *I'm wearying awa', John, like snow wreaths in thaw, John, I'm wearying awa' to the land o' the leal* . . . With a shiver of apprehension she turned back into the crowded tenement room where Tom, too, was donning his outdoor clothes ready to leave for work and Lorn and Willy crouched bleary-eyed over their morning porridge, while Annys struggled with the tangles of her thick hair and chanted, 'Seventeen-eighteen-nineteen' as she brushed.

'Here, let me help you, Annys love,' said Mhairi, but even the satisfaction of ridding her sister's hair of every tangle till it gleamed like polished cedar could not rid her own mind of anxiety. Why had her father sung that particular song? It was her mother's song, not his, and the last time her mother had sung it . . . But Mhairi shied quickly away from that particular memory. She was being over-imaginative and silly. Her father sang because he was happy to have a job at last, after so many months, that was all.

Determinedly she pushed anxiety away and took up the day's sewing.

The railway works were advancing apace and already several of the arches of the viaduct had been cast, but for the past ten days the centrings of three of these had been unfinished. Now work was to concentrate on completing these three as the viaduct advanced from the planned railway station at Ferryhill towards Market Street and the centre of town. Cassie Diack was to report at the far end of the workings, near Devanha Brewery.

It was not far from the tenement in Mitchell's Court, and a mere quarter of the distance he had been used to walk when he worked at Silvercairns, but Cassie felt himself growing out of breath with the excitement and the unaccustomed exercise before he even reached the foot of the Shiprow and had to make himself slow down. The cobbles glistened underfoot and the tenements on either side were still shuttered and in darkness though from several of the arched entrances silent figures emerged, carrying work bags as he was, and muffled against the early morning cold. There was a hint of night frost in the air and the breeze from the sea blew chill.

But it was good to have the prospect of work again, with wages at the end of it to give to his family, good to have a part to play, however briefly, good to be out in the half-shadows of early morning, with the other workmen, making their several ways as he was to their several occupations.

He paused on Trinity Quay in the half-darkness to watch a ship make ready for sailing. There was a light at the Weighhouse further along the quay and already the shore-porters were at work, trundling barrows of merchandise to the gangplank or shouldering barrels on to the quay. Sailors moved bare-footed about the deck, calling to each other, and there was a smell of tar and clean rope in the air. A cat prowled, low-backed, through the shadows by the Christie office where already there was a light in a first-floor window.

In the harbour, many of the roosting ships still carried riding lights which were reflected in broken ripples on the water and there were different lights in the shipbuilding sheds on the Inches where someone was at work already though the sun had yet to rise. Across the water came the noise of hammering and the busy rasp of a saw. To the east the sea was patterned with the first flush of gold and the sky above the horizon lightened as he watched to turquoise streaked with trails of pink. The fishing fleet would be well out to sea by now, though he saw one latecomer, a solitary black shape bobbing in the path of the sun. Behind him the spires of the town showed black as silhouettes against the lightening sky and from somewhere in the Castlegate came the steady clop of horses' hoofs on cobbles. The dray horses were on the move as well as the shipbuilders and a steady stream of dark-clad figures flowed over the streets around the harbour as fish-gutters, fish-porters, fish-curers and merchants went about their business. Others converged from the country road, with baskets of produce to sell, and the busy life of the town resumed for another day.

Though there were still heated and acrimonious disputes concerning the planned route north of the city, the agreed route of the railway coming from the south to Aberdeen was to cross the Dee from south to north above Wellington Bridge and thence to follow the river bank, by means of a viaduct, to the foot of Market Street. That would bring it close both to the centre of town and to the upper dock, thus making it convenient both for passengers and for freight. It was a well-conceived notion and a noble undertaking on the part of the shareholders, who had been called upon to contribute another five pounds a share at the beginning of the year with no hope of dividends for months, if not years, to come.

But as Cassie Diack strode along the riverside road he had no thought for the shareholders, only for the beauty of the morning and the different, man-made beauty of the viaduct, whose half-completed arches he could see ahead of him on the right of the river. The tide was out and the mudflats on either side gleamed pink in the strengthening light, the darker thread of the river shimmering bright between them. Herring gulls wheeled overhead or squabbled over debris, oyster-catchers, correct in their black and white plumage, strolled in the mudflats or rode the ripples of the ebbing tide, and suddenly, the crowning glory of his morning, a skein of grey geese mewed and chattered high overhead in a long, untidy 'V'.

Cassie's heart was full as he reached the building site, his voice cheerful as he introduced himself, received his orders and took up his position at one of the three half-finished arches. He was one of a dozen men on that particular stretch of the viaduct, some masons, some labourers, but the work was familiar to him and he set to with a will. It was a change from chipping away at the endless causeway stones as he had done at Silvercairns, but he was master of many skills and the building of the viaduct arch, while hard and heavy work, was satisfying. The river flowed cheerfully past them beyond the road, the sun rose higher, the stone under his hands lost its chill and in a nearby tree a blackbird sang while the leaves blazed in golden glory overhead.

Although the stone he was working with was granite, it was not the granite he was used to. Strange, for he had heard that Old Man Adam was all out to get every contract there was for railway work, but this granite had not the same look to it as Silvercairns's: the crystals were different, the colour different when it caught the light. No doubt Old Man Adam had been out-bid for the work. Cassie did not care. He had given his loyalty unstintingly to Silvercairns for over twenty years and would have done so still had not Mr Fergus summarily sacked him and severed his connection. But the connection was broken now, and if the Adams had lost a valuable contract it was nothing to him. Tom still worked there, of course, but not for long. He'd leave the moment his apprenticeship was over and set up in business with Alex Grant. Silvercairns would have to manage without the Diacks and good luck to them. The thought of Tom brought a fleeting frown to Cassie's face. Tom was a good lad. He would do fine. But where would he and Alex find the money to set up on their own, as they planned to do? They could scarcely scrape together the money to lease a plot of land, let alone buy the tools and equipment they would need. Then the frown vanished again in the happiness of the morning. A good workman could set up on his own with practically nothing, Mackinnon always said, and make a go of it, and Tom was a good workman all right. There was no doubt of that. As Cassie was himself. Feeling the skill and competence of his own hands as he dressed the granite block to fit the curve of the arch, his doubts vanished. He would help the lad himself, as long as he could, and when he couldna . . . well then, Tom would manage fine without him. As they all would. But first, Cassie would earn a wee bit pin-money for Mhairi to buy herself a ribbon or two. He stripped to his waistcoat as the sun rose higher and the sweat ran, but he did not once pause in his work. His breathing was fine in the clean September air and his heart was light, as if in happy expectation.

The men stopped for a break and Cassie took out the bread and cheese that Mhairi had given him and bit into it with the first real hunger he had felt for months. He drank the ale with equal enjoyment, wiped his mouth on the back of his hand, and at the foreman's signal took up the mason's tools and resumed work. Through the gap in the unfinished arch above his head he could see a patch of sky, the intense blue of an Indian summer day, and the new granite block he was setting into place sparkled silver in the reflected light. Somewhere nearby a fellow workmen whistled and Cassie felt simple happiness wash over him and bear him up like a bobbing boat in the path of the sun. *But sorrows sair are past, John, and joys are coming fast, John, the joy that's aye to last* . . . As he sang and worked he heard his wife's voice singing in duet with him, and she was still singing when the first ominous crack sounded overhead. The crack became a rumble, then a crashing thunder roll and as Cassie looked up to that scrap of perfect sky the blue shattered into a thousand stars as the arch crumbled and loosed an avalanche of falling masonry. In the space of a moment Cassie and his fellow workers were buried under a mound of granite blocks. As the last stone fell and the last rumble died away, her voice was the only sound in his head, gently, sweetly calling him, till he followed her singing into the distance . . .

Mhairi heard the thunderous crash from the Castlegate where she had gone to do the daily marketing and her heart beat fast with sudden fear. 'The railway works!' 'It's the viaduct!' Wild messages sped through the town: an explosion, an earthquake, the entire viaduct had collapsed, hundreds had been buried and killed. From all over the town people flocked to the scene, to see the disaster for themselves and to help where they could, and Mhairi, ashen-faced and trembling, went with them, stumbling, running, pushing her way through the press as best she could, to fight her way to the front of the crowd and to see the worst for herself.

Provost Blaikie was one of the first on the scene and by the time Mhairi arrived was already directing operations for clearing away the fallen masonry and 'rescuing' the buried men. But Mhairi needed no one to tell her there was little hope of finding anyone alive under that tumbled pile of stone. On either side like treacherous, truncated arms the torn ends of the viaduct hung jagged overhead and between them, where three arches should have stood, was their dropped burden of masonry: huge dressed blocks of granite, with smaller blocks and rubble, heaped higgledy-piggledy where they had fallen, and over all a fine powdering of dust. *Dust unto dust* came involuntarily into Mhairi's mind as she stared at the terrible scene, then she felt a hand at her elbow and turned to see Mackinnon, as grey-faced as she was, and full of concern.

'Was Da . . .?' she began and could not finish the question.

Mackinnon nodded. 'There's twelve men under there,' he said quietly, 'and your da's one o' them. It's my fault, Mhairi lass, and I canna say how sorry I am.'

'Your fault?' repeated Mhairi. 'How can it be? It was the arches . . .'

'But I found him the job, lass. If it hadna been for me he'd have been safely at home.'

'He was happy this morning,' said Mhairi, trying only to comfort the old man, but as she spoke she realized with growing certainty that it was true. 'Happier than he had been since . . . since Ma died. He was singing when he left the house.' Then, remembering what he was singing, she added, to herself alone, 'And I believe he knew . . .'

They stood in silence, watching as workmen from the length of the viaduct strove to lift and move the granite blocks, to lay them aside and clear a space under where the arch had been, while others took and stacked them further away and the burial mound shrank until the first piece of clothing was sighted and the first body found. The crowd was silent now, watching in reverence, as the body was laid gently on the bare earth, a doctor bent over him, put ear to chest, felt wrist and neck, and finally shook his head. Someone brought a blanket but before it could be spread, a woman broke through the crowd and fell on the prostrate figure, weeping. A minister laid his hand on her shoulder but she shook him off and he stepped back a pace to stand in silent prayer. Another body was brought out, and another, both lifeless. Then, on a gasp of indrawn breath from the crowd, one of the rescuers, from the pile of rubble, called urgently for a doctor and stretcher bearers. One of the buried men had been found alive. The rock had fallen in such a way as to leave a cavity beneath and though the man was injured, he had not been crushed. Another was brought out from the cavity, also alive, and the mood of the crowd changed to hope. Five found, seven still to come, but death no longer inevitable.

Mhairi clenched her hands to still their trembling and bit hard on her lower lip, while beside her Mackinnon made restless, impatient movements and tried yet again to be allowed to help. Yet again he was held back: there were younger, fitter men in plenty without adding to the casualties, said the policeman in charge of holding back the crowd and Mackinnon had to be content. Half an hour had passed since the accident: to Mhairi it seemed like half a lifetime and still the slow, careful rescue work went on while overhead the sky was as blue and the sun as bright as before, and in the chestnut tree the blackbird still sang.

Another man was brought out alive, but badly crushed; he was strapped into the horse-ambulance and sent immediately to hospital. Then two more, dead. Four left to find and the brief hope that had flickered up with the finding of the first breathing casualty was fast fading. Mhairi was light-headed now with fear and swayed on her feet. Mackinnon took her arm to steady her and in silence, they waited.

Two more dead, then, miraculously, a man not only still alive, but conscious. Now there were seven silent, blanket-covered figures laid out on the grass, and when the last poor, stone-battered mason was lifted from the wreckage of the viaduct Mhairi needed no one to tell her that it was her father, and that he was dead. She broke from Mackinnon's grasp and ran forward, trying to wrest his body from the rescuers in her anguish, but they treated her with kindness and compassion, easing Cassie gently on to the ground and straightening his crushed and shattered limbs so that he looked almost normal, except for the gash on his forehead and for the dust which coated him and filled every crease and fold of his clothes. Blindly, for the tears were coursing freely now, Mhairi endeavoured to brush the dust from her father's clothes, to straighten his waistcoat and fasten the shirt buttons which had burst open. She took a handkerchief from her pocket and wiped his face, saying over and over, 'You shouldn't have done it, Da. I know you did it for me and for my wedding, but I didn't want the money. Oh, Da, I promised Ma I'd care for you and now I've failed her. She'll be so angry with me, and sad . . .'

'He wasna sad,' said Mackinnon gently. 'Look at his face. I reckon he was happy to go. He was happy to be able to work for you, lass, afore he went, but I reckon he knew he'd not long left. And I reckon he was happy at the end, in spite of everything. Happy to go to his Agnes . . .'

'In the land o' the leal,' managed Mhairi through her streaming tears. But, looking down at her father's face, she knew that Mackinnon was right. Her father was happy. *Sorrows sair are past, John, and joys are coming fast* . . . but she choked on the words as she tried to sing them, and buried her face in Mackinnon's shoulder.

'Come away, lass,' he said gently. 'You'd best let the men see to things.' Now that the full complement had been accounted for, the dead were being moved, with reverence and solemnity, to their respective homes, each with an accompanying crowd of sorrowing relatives and friends. As if from nowhere, her own neighbours had materialized, for word had spread through the tenements – and to the schools, too, apparently, for Mrs Lennox appeared with Annys and the boys, and not long after Tom arrived, to take his place beside her and escort his father home for the last time. Alex and Donal joined them, in silent sympathy, with George Bruce and a score of fellow workers from the old days at Silvercairns and the crowd made its slow, lamenting way back through the afternoon streets, all normal work suspended in common sympathy for the bereaved and respect for the dead.

Already the Director of Railways had summoned Mr Cubitt,

the consulting engineer, and had let it be known publicly that the railway company would pay all funeral costs and grant temporary assistance to the widows and families of the dead. That was brief comfort and provided for immediate needs. But after that?

As she walked behind the litter which bore her father home, Mhairi felt the cold wind of responsibility blowing at her back. If she had thought to escape with Alex, if only for a little while, that time was gone for ever, with her father. She and Tom had been thrust into adulthood and had become, with the falling of a bridge, the older generation. As she felt Annys's timid hand in hers and heard her tearful voice ask, 'Who will look after us now, Mhairi?' she answered, unhesitatingly, 'I will', and Tom beside her said, as solemnly, 'And so will I.'

It was late that night, when Annys had at last sobbed herself to sleep in Mhairi's arms and Mhairi herself was weary with weeping, before she remembered her wedding. It was to have been on Saturday. That was out of the question now, unless she wanted to combine a wedding with a funeral.

Part 3

The funeral was a sombre, dignified affair with so many mourners that Mhairi's heart overflowed with gratitude: not a neighbour was absent, not a quarry worker, past or present, and the entire workforce of Wyness's yard, with George Wyness himself at their head, stood in respectful silence as the coffin passed. There were others Mhairi did not recognize, railway officials, town councillors and the like, even a representative from the Ladies' Working, and when Mhairi looked among the pews reserved for the gentry, she saw the pale, preoccupied face of Mr Fergus Adam, ordered no doubt by his father to attend, though Silvercairns had been in no way involved in the viaduct disaster. Remembering his treatment of her father, Mhairi's indignation boiled inside her. How dare he come, uninvited, to parade his false sympathy and sorrow? Her anger served to keep her grief in check and though she knew it was unchristian, she both welcomed and encouraged it. Beside her, she knew Tom felt the same and the knowledge strengthened and sustained her as the harrowing service progressed.

Fergus Adam, glancing in her direction, sensed the anger and knew the cause. It was unjust, of course, irrational prejudice, yet at the same time there was a certain dogged logic to it which his own lingering guilt made him acknowledge. But he had done his best to make amends, had paid good money to her brother for tasks that were less than essential and would continue to do so for as long as he was able without laying himself open to question. He would have liked to offer her his sympathy, to wipe the tears from her eyes with his softest handkerchief, to . . . He caught himself up short before imagination led him into further indiscretion. And if he offered his sympathy, would she throw it back at him, as she had done that time in the Gallowgate? Here, in the full public eye and as representative of Silvercairns, he dare not risk such humiliation. He would not stay for the interment, but slip unobtrusively away. Yet in spite of his resolve, his eyes strayed in Mhairi

Diack's direction more than once before the service was over, and afterwards he lingered on the fringes of the crowd in the kirkyard until the brother stepped forward to sprinkle the first handful of earth on the coffin. Only then did he turn abruptly away.

Mhairi saw him go, but as she watched her father's coffin laid to rest beside his wife's, even her anger at Fergus Adam's apparent heartlessness could not check her tears. The late September sunlight sparkled from granite headstone and frost-laden grass as the sombre group gathered in silence round the heap of new-turned earth, while in the street beyond that dividing row of elegant granite columns, the rest of the town went about its daily business. Gentlemen on horseback, riding in from the country on business, maidservants on foot with loaded message baskets, countrywomen with produce to sell, townswomen gossiping, dogs and children and horse-drawn cabs. All the cheerful bustle of living, while inside those dividing columns were only stillness and death.

Then Mhairi felt a hand in hers and looked up through her tears to see Donal Grant beside her. He was signing to her with intense anxiety, a look of yearning compassion on his face.

'Donal says he will design a special inscription for the headstone,' explained Alex who, with Lorn and Willy on either side of him, stood close beside her. Mhairi held Annys's hand tight in hers and Tom held the child's other hand, 'like a pair o' responsible parents,' commented Mackinnon to his wife, in a voice gruff with emotion, and added, 'Poor lassie, wi' her wedding planned and all.' Since Cassie's death, Mackinnon had felt almost a guardian's responsibility for the orphaned family.

George Wyness, from across the graveside, also noted the tight-knit little group, the protective way they guarded the wee girl, the set of the younger lads' shoulders, and the sombre determination on the face of the eldest, saw their genuine, loving grief and felt his own eyes moisten. 'Old fool,' he told himself impatiently, fumbling for a handkerchief, but it did your heart good to see honest, hard-working folk bound by honest family affection. Not like some families he could think of, aye squabbling and backbiting. They deserved better luck than fate had dealt them so far and if ever it came his way to be able to help them, then by George he'd do it.

'I'll make it up to you somehow, Tom lad,' said Mackinnon, when the funeral was over and the family had returned to their rooms in Mitchell's Court, where Mrs Lennox and the other women from the tenement had set out refreshments for those friends who cared to come. Of these there were plenty, for Cassie Diack had been a man of no malice, with a good word for everybody, and the family was well liked. 'I can't say how at the moment, Tom, but somehow, I promise.' Mackinnon was still wracked with guilt for the part he imagined he had played in sending Cassie Diack to his death.

'There's no need,' sighed Tom, for the umpteenth time. 'It wasna your fault, Mr Mackinnon. If it was anyone's it was the railway company's.' Or Mr Fergus Adam's, but Tom kept that particular grievance firmly to himself. 'With the railway money Mhairi and I will manage, and with Alex's help . . .' but his voice trailed into silence at the memory of their splendid plans. They had been going to collect their papers and leave Silvercairns, walk out into a glorious future, with a yard of their own. They'd heard tell of one the very day his father died, but now . . . Responsibility weighed heavy on Tom's shoulders. He'd best stay at Silvercairns where he had steady work. Free of his apprenticeship, he'd earn a mason's full wages and he owed it to Mhairi and Annys and the others not to jeopardize his own and the family's future by throwing that security away.

'What are your plans now, lad?' asked Wyness, joining them. 'Are you and that friend of yours still planning to start out on your own? Lorn was telling me all about it.'

'Fairy-tales,' said Tom, with an edge of bitterness to his voice. 'Dreams. With my father gone, I reckon I'd best stick to the quarrying for a while, leastways till the young ones are grown.'

'And by quarrying you mean Silvercairns?' said Wyness, eyeing him shrewdly from under thick, untidy brows.

'It's where I work.' But he did not forgive the Adams for what they had done to his father, and would not, as long as he lived. If Mr Fergus had not sacked him, his father would never have taken that job on the viaduct. The Adams were responsible. It was not their viaduct, not their granite even, yet they were responsible, as surely as if they had sent Cassie Diack themselves to the railway works. Something of his anger must have shown on his face, for Wyness said, 'Aye, lad, meantime. But there's other quarries than Silvercairns, and other owners, and not all of them made in the Adam mould. Remember that.'

'More whisky, Mr Wyness?' offered Mhairi, and Annys, who had clung to her sister closer than ever since Cassie's death, held up a plate of oatcakes and managed a gap-toothed smile. She had lost the first of her milk teeth, but the new ones were a long time coming and the result was particularly appealing.

'Thank you, lass, I will. And I'll take one of those oatcakes to go with it, little lady.' He smiled at Annys who promptly hid her face in Mhairi's skirt. 'If you'll not think it disrespectful to the dead, Mhairi,' he went on gravely, 'I'll drink to your future happiness with that man of yours. One day.' He raised his glass and drank and Mhairi lowered her eyes and clenched her teeth hard to keep back the tears. Her wedding was to have been tomorrow, and afterwards that little house her man had promised her, for the two of them alone. Now she didn't know when it would be. She and Alex had hardly spoken alone together since her father's death, but when they did, tonight perhaps, what was there to say? Her future stretched bleak and comfortless ahead of her and she could see no light . . .

'Nay, lass,' said George Wyness kindly, 'life's not that bad. You've a fine, hard-working brother to help you and that Alex o' yours waiting to marry you as soon as is seemly. You may be orphaned, but you still have family and friends. There's folks with ten times your wealth and not a tenth part of your good fortune. Remember that.'

'I'll try, Mr Wyness, and thank you.' She added bravely, 'Thank you for attending the funeral. My father would be honoured and . . . and we are very grateful to you for your kindness.' Before he could speak, she went on, with an obvious effort at good manners, 'How is your wife? And your daughter?'

'They're well enough, thank you. Gadding about as usual, here, there and everywhere. Fanny's attending the theatre next week.' Wyness frowned momentarily at the thought. Fanny couldn't be much older than Mhairi Diack and through no fault of either girl's one had everything and the other nothing. But that was life, after all. 'Don't really hold with theatres,' he went on, 'except, of course, the building of them. Now if someone was to build a new theatre here in Aberdeen I'd be right glad to do the pillars and porticoes and any kind of fancy trellising in my own yard, and maybe throw in a free statue of the benefactor into the bargain. What do you say, Tom lad? Do you reckon you've learned enough at Silvercairns to be able to tackle fancy stuff like that?'

'Aye,' said Tom, without hesitation. 'I reckon I could put my hand to anything. That's not to say I'd do it, mind. There's some jobs that's a waste of a man's time.'

'Craftsmanship,' said Wyness. 'Think of it that way and any job is worth while if it lets you prove your worth.'

'Even a useless coping on a useless bit of garden wall?'

Wyness looked at him shrewdly for a long moment, then nodded. 'Aye, lad. Even that.' Then he grinned. 'Providing, of course, that you're well paid.'

Tom would not have done it except for the money, would have refused to be patronized and inspected like some sort of entertainment in a circus. Would have downed tools and walked out. Except that his father was dead and he must behave responsibly.

The Monday after his father's funeral, George Bruce sought him out at the quarry face and told him to report at the big house as soon as his work was finished for the day. 'There's more work to be done in the garden, seemingly,' the foreman explained and when Tom did not immediately answer, said, 'You'll be well paid.'

Tom did not have to go, of course. He was his own man now, and his time after work was his own. But he could not afford the luxury of refusing, not while his family relied on Silvercairns for their daily bread. He could, however, refuse to answer silly questions, refuse to be diverted from the job in hand, refuse to act like some sort of performing bear for Miss Lettice's house guests. So when he heard a girl's footsteps on the terrace and a girl's voice, apparently speaking to him, he did not immediately look up from his task.

'That's a lovely little wall. I like the coping bits.'

Tom had been going to ignore the voice, as he always ignored Miss Lettice when she tried to engage him in conversation, then he realized with faint surprise that it was not Miss Lettice's voice, but another, less arrogant, even timid one. He straightened slowly and saw, on the terrace above him, a pleasant-faced girl with brown ringlets and an anxious expression. Behind her rose the splendid pile of Silvercairns house, its many chimneys plumed, its rows of windows catching and reflecting the evening sun. The terrace stretched from the imposing front entrance the length of the south elevation and around the corner to follow the line of the west wing. From the low, flat-topped wall which bordered the terrace and on which urns of geraniums overflowed with trailing scarlet blossoms, the garden fell away in a series of graceful steps through clipped hedges and herbaceous borders, secluded lawns and rose arbours, herb gardens, a lily pond, till the final wall which separated garden from meadow and at the south-west corner of which stood the doocot summer-house from which Lettice Adam had watched Tom Diack at work.

The wall which Tom considered unnecessary, and on which he was now working, was one level down from the terrace, and designed to separate the path from the square of grass Miss Lettice called her croquet lawn. The grass was no longer lush, but fading with autumn and patched here and there with moss. Last week the croquet hoops had been pulled up. The first wall Tom had been called to mend, being the retaining wall of the terrace and dangerously cracked, had been a worthwhile job. This one, in his opinion, was not, being designed for no purpose that he could see except to get in the gardener's way, and when the coping was finished, no one would even be able to sit on it, which might otherwise have justified its presence. Tom resented what he regarded as a misuse of his talents in spite of George Wyness's advice to think only of the workmanship, and if, as he suspected, Miss Adam's next idea would be for him to build miniature gateposts in the central gap, then she could look elsewhere. He was a quarryman, not a builder of garden follies for the idle rich.

But the girl on the terrace above him had none of the arrogance of Miss Lettice. On the contrary, her voice held a note of nervousness and when he straightened and looked at her she glanced quickly over her shoulder as if to make sure she was not being followed before saying, 'Coping is the right word, isn't it?'

She wore a dark red dress and carried a muff and after a moment he realized why she reminded him of someone. She must be George Wyness's daughter, Fanny.

'Aye,' he said. 'It's a coping, though to my mind a drystone dyke looks well enough without.'

'Yes,' agreed Fanny, comparing the finished section with the unfinished. 'It's a lovely wall. But I like the other bits, too. Like little stone tents.'

In spite of himself, Tom grinned. 'I hadn't thought of it like that, but I reckon you're right. Tents for the futrats, maybe. Weasels,' he added in explanation as she looked puzzled. 'They like a good wall.'

Fanny shuddered. 'Oh, dear. I hope there aren't any weasels here. They are so fierce. They kill things.'

'Not human beings,' he said kindly, 'only frogs, voles, fieldmice and suchlike.'

'How horrid.'

'Not at all. They have to eat, like the rest of us, and they're brave little beggars. If cornered, they dance about on their hind legs, hissing and spitting, and they can give a wicked bite. I've known one kill a rat twice its own size.'

'Really? To eat?' Disgust and admiration struggled in her voice. Fanny was terrified of rats.

'Oh, aye. Well, maybe in self-defence first, but they'd not let it go to waste after. Sometimes,' he continued, warming to his theme, 'they climb bushes and steal eggs or baby birds from the nest, so my father used to say. He was country-born and knew all about such things.' He paused, with remembered sadness, before continuing, 'They'll even tackle a rabbit, given they can catch it. But only when they need food,' he added hastily, seeing the obvious distress in her face. 'After all, they have to feed their families somehow, as we do.'

'I suppose so,' she admitted, not entirely convinced, but Tom had remembered he had a job to do before nightfall and turned back to his work. He realized, with some astonishment, that he had actually been talking without resentment to one of Them. He'd even mentioned his father. Except that George Wyness was not really one of Them, in spite of his money, and to listen to his daughter speak, she wasn't either. At least, if she was, she hadn't adopted their autocratic condescension.

'Oh, dear,' she said now, breaking into his thoughts. 'I've just realized. You must be Tom Diack? I was so very sorry to hear of your father's dreadful accident. Papa told me all about it and then Lettice said you were working here and . . . and I really am very sorry. You must miss him dreadfully.'

She sounded genuinely sympathetic and he was grateful. Miss Lettice had not bothered to mention it. Now he said gruffly, 'Thank you,' and turned back to his work.

She watched him for a minute or two in silence, then said, 'I hope you don't mind me watching you? I'll go away if you'd rather.'

'No, that's all right. As long as you don't mind if I keep on working. I want to finish this section before nightfall.'

'Thank you. I really ought to be inside with the others, but I wanted a breath of fresh air and to escape for a little. We've just had dinner you see, and now we are going to the theatre, when everyone is ready.' She did not sound enthusiastic and Tom said nothing.

She watched him test the weight of a stone in his hand, discard it, choose another, set it in place, then said innocently, 'Is it hard, learning how to do that? I am always surprised at how clever Papa's workmen are. They make such beautiful things every day out of the plainest pieces of stone.'

'No, it's not hard, leastways the learning of it isn't, though hammering a bore-hole through bedrock can be hard enough. It's more a question of practice and having the right tools and the right teacher. I've been learning for seven years so I ought to have got things right by now. But there's always more to learn, different stone handles differently, you see, and . . .' He stopped at the sound of approaching footsteps, several pairs.

'Oh, dear,' said Fanny nervously. 'I think they're coming for me.' She made it sound like an impending arrest. She added, with touching naïvety, 'I don't really want to go, but . . .'

'Fanny!' called an imperious voice, which Tom recognized instantly as Miss Adam's. He continued to work on the low wall as if no one had spoken and he was alone in the garden. 'Fanny!' The voice was nearer, almost overhead. 'You wretched girl. We've been looking everywhere. What on earth are you doing, hiding out here?'

'Admiring the wildlife, apparently,' drawled an unknown voice and a girl giggled. 'Niall, what a thing to say!'

'I was not hiding,' said Fanny, and added bravely, 'I was enjoying the evening air and waiting for you. I have been ready for ages.'

'And how were we supposed to know that when you disappear into the woodwork like a . . .'

'Futrat in a dyke?' suggested Fanny and smiled in Tom's direction, but he was not looking at her, or at any of them. Head down, he was working away at the half-built wall as if they did not exist.

'I say, is that the master mason you were telling us about, Lettice?' said a cheerful male voice, slightly slurred with drink. 'The one with the rippling muscles?'

The same girl squealed, 'Oh, Hugo, you are dreadful!'

At the hated name, Tom's patience snapped. He straightened, with slow and menacing purpose, to find himself staring straight into the wine-flushed face of Hugo Adam. His own face was white with fury, his powerful fists clenched, and as they confronted each other, one smooth-cheeked and debonair in evening finery, the other weather-tanned, workman's shirt open at the neck, mason's leather apron dust-caked after a day's work in the quarry, Tom squared his shoulders with a gesture that even Lettice recognized as dangerously threatening. Another moment and he would be across the intervening space and at Hugo's throat.

'My brother did not mean to be offensive,' she said hastily. 'Did you, Hugo?'

'Yes, I damn well did,' said Hugo, as recognition dawned through the happy haze of his father's claret. He was on home ground now, surrounded by friends, instead of alone on the alien territory of the Castlegate, and he had an old score to settle. Not this time with fists, but with a horsewhip and horse-trough till the fellow begged, on his knees, for mercy. 'That's the lout who . . .' But some innate caution fought through to the surface of his fuddled thoughts and stopped him completing the sentence. His intrigue with Lizzie Lennox was his own affair and he was not going to risk giving the game away to anyone, least of all to this fellow. Besides, the knowledge that the delicious little lady was his for the picking was victory enough for the moment. Another time, another place, and he'd thrash the man as he deserved.

'Who what?' prompted a pale, supercilious gentleman in a tail-coat and immaculate striped trousers. He wore a shiny black opera-hat, tipped very slightly over one eye, and carried an ebony cane.

'Who repaired those dreadful cracks in the terrace wall I told you about, Ainslie,' said Lettice, taking his arm. 'Do come along, Fanny. You have kept us all waiting long enough and Fergus is champing at the bit with impatience. He is sure we are going to be late, as if it mattered. Our box is paid for so there is no reason why we cannot come and go as we please. Take Fanny's arm, Hugo, and for goodness' sake, Amelia, stop staring in that vacuous manner. Have you never seen a workman before?'

But Tom was not working. He was standing belligerently upright, like a weasel at bay and just as fierce, thought Fanny with anxiety, as obediently she linked her arm through Hugo's. For though Tom was stronger than any of his tormentors, they far outnumbered him, and they had the strength of wealth and privilege on their side. She looked back over her shoulder as they reached the corner of the terrace and saw him still standing, fists clenched and glaring defiance after the departing group.

Tom was quivering with suppressed fury as he watched his despicable tormentors leave the field, the women trailing silken skirts in the dust with no thought for tomorrow, the men whose kid-gloved hands had never known a day's honest work. He despised the lot of them. Spat on their patronage and their condescension. How dare they talk about him like some sort of household animal. How dare the Adam woman discuss his muscles. He caught up his hammer and brought it smashing down on the nearest stone, to shatter it to fragments. He saw the Adam woman start and turn her head. Deliberately he swung the hammer again and this time brought it down on the newly completed section of the wall. Hurriedly, the group turned the corner and disappeared.

Tom was tempted to bring down the hammer again and again, until he had demolished the whole of his evening's work. It would give him the greatest satisfaction to destroy the entire, useless wall and defy her to ask for his wages back. But in the act of swinging the hammer, he remembered and with a groan of defeat dropped it, useless, to the ground. He stood, hands hanging loose, shoulders drooped in defeat. He knew something of what his father must have felt when he talked wistfully of the country he had left behind him. Families brought responsibilities which could not be shed on an impulse of defiance. Mhairi and the others needed the money and until his brothers were grown, he was trapped. He stood a long time, immobile, while the shadows lengthened and the air grew chill, and the anger drained slowly out of him. What was the use of anger? He was trapped, as his father had been trapped . . .

He would tidy up, collect his tools, and leave. And when George Bruce ordered him, he would, inevitably, come back. But he would take no insults from anyone, and if Hugo Adam so much as showed himself over the horizon, Tom would not give a farthing for the man's chances.

It was as he thought of Hugo Adam that he realized what had been niggling away at the back of his mind ever since the encounter. There had been a look in the man's eye that was more than antagonism. A private look of amusement. No, of triumph! Remembering the cause of their confrontation in the Castlegate he saw that there could be only one explanation. Tom snatched up his tool bag, slung his coat over his shoulder and strode purposefully towards the house.

He found Lizzie Lennox in the scullery, elbow-deep in suds and scrubbing away at the first of a pile of dirty cooking pots. She looked flustered, angry and hot.

'Well, what do you want, Tom Diack? You can see I'm busy. Or are you come to do my work for me?' Derisively, she held out a scrubbing brush, its bristles caked with food and dripping soap suds on to the scullery floor.

'Lizzie!' bellowed a voice from the depths of the kitchen. 'If I've tellt ye once, I've tellt ye . . . Oh, it's you, is it, Tom Diack?' Ma Gregor appeared in the doorway which led from scullery to kitchen and smiled. She had a soft spot for the lad, him being a polite and helpful sort of fellow, always willing to lift a sack of oatmeal for her or carry coal when he had no call to help at all, being an outside worker and not really staff. So when he called at the kitchen door for a glass o' water on a hot day, she gave him ale and a slice o' slab cake, or maybe a fresh-baked scone. A growing lad needed feeding and he was a handsome boy, with lovely blue eyes and a winning smile. So now, seeing who it was who had interrupted that minx of a scullery maid, she said, 'Finished for the day, are you, Tom?'

'Yes, Mrs Gregor, but I just wanted a quick word with Lizzie, if that's all right. A message from her ma. Nothing urgent, just news of the family. It can wait if you'd rather.'

'Bless you, no, lad. You go ahead. Only mind you don't keep her long, she's a lazy baggage!'

Ma Gregor returned through the connecting door to her kitchen and the comfort of her fireside chair, not to mention the glass of port she regarded as no more than her due after cooking and serving a dinner for ten above stairs and almost as many more below. Behind her back, Lizzie put out a derisive tongue. 'Old bat!' she said, with feeling. 'Well, what is it, then? What does Ma want now? Or is it Da, with another load o' Bible tracts?'

Tom glanced quickly beyond her to the kitchen regions and lowered his voice. 'The message is from me, Lizzie, and it's this. *You can tell Hugo Adam to keep his filthy hands off you or I swear I'll teach him a lesson he'll not forget.*'

Caught off guard, Lizzie blanched momentarily with shock. She bit her lip, looked over her shoulder, then, with a great show of righteous innocence, began to scrub busily at the saucepan, splashing water wholesale in her zeal. 'I don't know what you're on about, Tom Diack, that I don't.' Her colour was beginning to come back and with it her indignation. 'It's insulting, that's what it is, coming in here wi' your threats. And if I did know,' she countered, changing tack, 'I reckon it's no business of yours.'

'Oh no? Well, I reckon exploitation *is* my business, and when the likes of him exploits the likes of you, for his own fleeting pleasure, then he deserves everything he gets.'

'You're mad, Tom Diack,' blustered Lizzie. 'Soft i' the head. I reckon you was dropped when you was a baby, or the sun's got you, working all day in yon quarry.'

But Tom saw the evasion in her face, the flushed cheeks and restless eyes which would not meet his and an awful suspicion gathered inside him, to choke the words in his throat. He gripped her wrist, hard, regardless of the slippery suds and her futile struggles. 'You listen to me, Lizzie, and listen well. If I find out that Hugo Adam has laid so much as one finger on you *I swear I'll kill him.* That's the message. See he gets it.'

Before she could answer, he turned on his heel and strode out into the gathering night.

'Well, Fanny?' said her father, over family breakfast. 'Did you enjoy your evening?'

'Yes, thank you, Papa.' She picked up her teacup and drank. Then, as he seemed to expect more from her than ritual politeness, she added, 'I saw Tom Diack at Silvercairns, building a little wall.'

'Did you, indeed?' So the lad was taking all the work he could get, in spite of the indignity. Between mouthfuls of Mrs Wyness's excellent porridge, which she invariably supervised herself so that the oatmeal was sufficiently soaked and the cream sufficiently thick, Wyness took good note. He had his own reasons for watching the Diack lad and his friend Alex Grant, but for the moment he was keeping those reasons to himself. 'But it wasna the Diack boy I was asking after, Fanny,' he said, laying down his spoon and wiping his mouth on a starched linen napkin. 'I thought you'd been to a theatre, but maybe I'm mistaken?'

'Oh, the theatre. Yes, we did go. It was very pleasant.'

'Is that all you can say? Come, Fanny love, you can tell your old father. Was he nice to you, that Adam lad?'

'Do you mean Fergus, Papa?'

Wyness caught his wife's eye across the loaded table and raised his own eyes to the ceiling in silent exasperation. Mrs Wyness calmly reached for the silver teapot and refilled his cup, then lifted the lid from a silver chafing dish and served him a succulent and steaming Finnan-haddie from which butter oozed in mouth-watering golden droplets. 'There you are, dear,' she said, placing the plate in front of him. 'You'd best not be late this morning, remember. You said yourself you wanted to see that man about the railway.'

'So I did, my dear.' He laid a hand absently on his wife's plump one and squeezed it before taking up his knife and fork and attacking his breakfast haddock. But after the first pleasurable mouthful, he remembered Fanny's unsatisfactory answer with returning irritation. Carefully, and with exaggerated patience, he said, 'Of course I mean Fergus, Fanny, as it was Fergus asked you!' When she did not immediately speak, but sat looking down at her plate on which lay a half-eaten slice of thin toast, he sighed, laid aside his fork and said, as if to a child of meagre understanding, 'Who was in your party?' Fanny told him. 'And were there others at the dinner beforehand?'

'Only old Mr Adam and Miss Blackwell.'

'And it was a lively evening, was it?'

'Yes, Papa.'

'Well, from what you've told me so far it sounds about as lively as a soirée in a morgue,' said Wyness in exasperation. He returned to his haddock and when he spoke again it was between one mouthful and the next. 'Did he say anything to you?'

'Who, Papa?'

But, even from a much-loved daughter, this was too much for Wyness's patience. 'The Archbishop of Canterbury!' he exploded, slamming down his knife and fork and spattering the table-cloth with melted butter in the process. 'Who do you think?' Then, as the tears gathered in her eyes, he said, more gently, 'Just tell me what you talked about, love, what that Fergus lad said to you, whether he treated you right. Please?'

'He was very polite,' said Fanny, looking down at her hands, anxiously twisting this way and that in her lap. 'He offered me a programme. He asked if I was enjoying the play.'

'Did the evening yield any other such pearls of conversation?' said Wyness with ill-concealed sarcasm. Fanny searched her memory desperately for something to cool her father's temper and came up, in all innocence, with, 'Oh, yes, Papa. Tom Diack told me about weasels. They are called futrats and are very interesting. They can even kill rats.'

'Really?' sighed Wyness, and added, under his breath, 'I give up.' But later, replete with an excellent breakfast to which freshly baked rolls and home-made marmalade had added the final, satisfying touch, Wyness went over in his mind what his daughter had told him, and asked himself why Tom Diack's information about weasels should have been the highlight of

Fanny's evening. The answer was not reassuring. On the evidence of the theatre-party, that document of Mungo Adam's would remain unread.

'Alex,' said Mhairi one evening, three weeks or so after her father's death. 'About our wedding . . .'

They were in the tenement in Mitchell's Court, Lorn and Willy at the table, poring over their school-books which Mhairi insisted they study every evening, 'Or you'll not be allowed to leave that school, for another year!' and Annys beside them laboriously copying a bible text into an exercise book in almost perfect copperplate. For a child of six she wrote a beautiful hand and Mhairi was as proud of her as if she had been her own daughter. Donal, too, was with them this evening, sitting in the chair that had been her father's, an open book on his knee. It was a book about architectural design which Hamish Dunn had lent him and which to Mhairi's eyes looked very complicated. Tom was not yet home, but as it was almost dark now, Mhairi expected him at any minute. As usual, he had been called upon to put in extra hours at the big house. 'But not for much longer,' he had told Alex. 'I'm fair sick of it. I'll be right glad when the family moves back into town.' It was well into October and past the normal time, but Old Man Adam had arranged a party specially for that Sharp fellow, and till it was over, they were staying on.

Mhairi worried about Tom. He was looking tired these days, and preoccupied with thoughts that were obviously sombre ones. She knew he mourned his father, knew he took his responsibilities hard, knew he hated working at the big house and did it only for her, but though she had told him over and over that they could manage well enough without the extra, he refused to listen. It worried Mhairi. He was a young man, barely twenty-one, and he deserved some happiness. She wished he could find a girl, a nice, honest, hard-working girl who would love and cherish him as a man ought to be cherished. She wondered sometimes if it was a girl that caused that frown on his face, and his air of restless tension, but if so, she could not think who it could be. Now, she crossed to the hearth, signalling with her eyes for Alex to follow her, lifted the lid of the simmering pot, and stirred the contents.

'Mmmm, that smells good,' said Alex, coming up behind her and slipping his arms round her waist. 'What is it?'

'Only broth,' she said, lifting the spoon to her lips and tasting. 'But with a good mutton bone in it.' She added salt from the wooden salt box, stirred, tasted again, and replaced the lid. 'About our wedding . . .' she began again, not looking at him.

'Don't worry, love,' interrupted Alex, still holding her by the waist. He tightened his arms and held her close against him, dipped his head and murmured close to her ear, 'You know I love you, Mhairi, and one day we'll marry. The minister understands and so do I. With your father dead . . . it's natural you want to wait a bit, out of respect, but we'll be married in a month or two. After Christmas maybe, or in the New Year. I'll wait for you, love, and by then maybe we'll have sorted something out. I haven't given up that idea of a yard of our own and nor has Tom. It's just that it will be a wee bit more difficult now, with your father gone. It's not the money so much, for your da wasn't earning, at least not regularly, but we'd been relying on him to help, like, with the new venture. Besides, with him gone and you responsible for the young ones, we'll need to find a bigger house. I haven't forgotten I promised you. Still, we'll work something out, you'll see. I was talking to Mackinnon only yesterday and he reckons . . .'

'No, Alex,' interrupted Mhairi quietly. 'Please listen.' She stared unseeing at the cooking pot and the firelight flickering at its blackened edges while she sought for the right words in which to tell him. Behind her in the shadowed room the boys talked quietly to each other and Annys sang, half under her breath and frowning with concentration, as her small hand formed the letters. From the corner of her eye she saw that Donal's attention was all on the book in his hands, and though he could not hear, she was glad. What she must say was for Alex alone and she must say it now, before Tom came home. 'Please listen.' She spoke with a quiet despair that caught all Alex's attention. 'I think we had better marry soon, that is, if you still want to.'

'Of course I want to, you daft wee . . . Soon, did you say?' Suddenly Alex was very still, even his breath suspended, as the underlying message of her words sank home. Before he could stop himself, he breathed an agonized 'Oh, God . . .' He strove at once to cover his dismay, to reassure and comfort her, but it was too late. She had heard his first, unguarded reaction and though it had also been her own, when the knowledge dawned that she was pregnant, she had dreaded to hear it echoed by Alex. Her chin tilted in pride, her eyes fought against threatening tears, and she shook off his embrace with an anger that made Alex ashamed. 'Listen, Mhairi,' he pleaded, his voice low and urgent. 'I'll see the minister tomorrow. No, tonight,' he amended, but she had turned away and, deliberately shutting him out from the family group, she bent over her sister and said, 'But that's beautiful, Annys. I couldn't do better myself.' She pulled up a chair and sat down beside the little girl. 'While we wait for Tom to come home, shall I show you how to do a lovely pattern of loops and crosses for a border to the page?' Her back was to Alex and its unbending rigidity said as clearly as any words, 'I have no more to say to you. Go home.'

After a moment's indecision, Alex crossed to Donal, signed to him to stay where he was till Alex fetched him, and strode out of the room. A moment later, Mhairi heard the outside door slam.

Lorn looked up from his book. 'Where's Alex gone?'

'I don't know. To meet Tom perhaps.' But in spite of her outward control, Mhairi was trembling with fear and hurt and outrage. 'Never marry, lass, it isna worth it,' her mother had said, and now Mhairi might not even have the chance. Oh, God, what was she to do? All her years of striving for ladylike respectability had been for nothing. She, like any other poverty-stricken tenement lass with more lust than sense, was expecting an illegitimate child. What would they think of her? What would her family think of her? What would she tell Annys, whom she had promised her mother that she would bring up 'right'? Worst of all, what would her mother think of her, in her land o' the leal?

And now, when she needed him most, Alex had deserted her. As she bent her head over the page of childish handwriting, it cost her all her will-power not to weep.

* * *

Alex Grant was appalled – at Mhairi's news, at his own reaction, at the prospect ahead, at the whole, bleak, uncompromising world which was closing round him with relentless pressure. And why had she told him there, with her family all around her? Why not when they were alone? Except that since Cassie Diack's death they were rarely alone. Annys clung to Mhairi even worse than before and with Tom working late, she dare not leave her. Mhairi took her responsiblities seriously and he would not have it otherwise, but he could not help wishing sometimes that she would forget them for a while and think only of him. And now, before they were even married, there was yet another responsibility to be considered. He wanted children, naturally, and one day he would love a son to work beside him in the yard, to learn his skills, to add his name to the nameplate over the door and one day to take over from his father and in turn teach his own sons . . . One day. But not now. Not yet. He wanted to find that bit of land, start up his own business, see Donal provided for in case he himself was injured or killed, as Cassie Diack had been, and most of all he wanted, for a while, to have Mhairi to himself.

Except that because of Cassie's death he could never have Mhairi to himself: even if he found that little house, she could not shed her family responsibilities, as he could not shed Donal. There were Mhairi's little brothers and wee Annys to bring up to adulthood, let alone Tom and Donal to feed and care for. When he and Mhairi married, they would not be a young couple, alone together as they had dreamed, but a household of seven. Surely they had responsibilities enough already without collecting more? And yet . . . and yet . . .

He had had no fixed purpose when he strode out of the tenement in Mitchell's Court, except to escape the accusation in Mhairi's face and the guilt of the hurt he had unwittingly caused her. But once in the street, with the cool night wind fresh in his face and the lights of the houses in the Guestrow spreading patches of golden light along the darkness on either side of him, he had some vague idea of seeking out the minister. But then again, perhaps it was not the hour to do so and if he did, what should he tell him? Merely that they wished to be married at once, or was it necessary to confess the reason? Their marriage had been arranged and postponed through no fault of their own. It was only natural they should wish it to take place once sufficient time had elapsed since the funeral, and they were not gentry. They could not aspire to a year's black crape and the elaborate social conventions of mourning. Mhairi had loved her father and he had died. The fact that she wanted to marry so soon afterwards in no way diminished that love or the sincerity of her grief – and there was no need to confess the reason. Besides, they were handfast: surely the sin of fornication did not apply?

By the time Alex reached the end of the Guestrow he had decided to postpone his visit to the minister till tomorrow. He would go to Ma Gibbs' for a different kind of uplift and forget his troubles in the pleasures of male company and good ale. But before he was half-way there, he had changed his mind again. Poor wee Mhairi. It was not her fault, after all. All she had done was love him, and because of that she was carrying his child. She had not chosen it any more than he had. It was fate, that was all. The least he could do was to see the minister now, at once, and fix their wedding without delay.

But she had looked so angry, so hurt and defiant and proud. Perhaps he had best speak to her again, reassure her and ask her forgiveness, beg her to choose the date of their wedding herself, as soon as she thought fit? He turned away from Ma Gibbs' and yet could not persuade his feet to go further than the Plainstanes and the Castlegate. Later, he told himself. He would go later, when he had sorted things out properly in his own mind.

So, impervious alike to his surroundings and his fellow townsmen, Alex walked aimlessly to and fro in the darkening streets, while he argued and talked to himself and went over and over the question of where they would live and how they would live, with ever more mouths to feed – for one baby would not be the end of it. If he loved Mhairi, and he did love her, there would be more, and he could not condemn her to a life of increasing squalor in a tenement in Mitchell's Court. He had given his word. Then there was Tom and his hopes for the future. What would he have to say about the unborn child?

The unborn child. His child. A son, perhaps? He stopped suddenly on the corner of Broad Street and stood motionless, full of a new and dawning wonder. For the first time the idea was something more than an appalling inconvenient mistake. His son. His own little new-born son. Excitement stirred deep in his heart and with it the first flickerings of pride . . . But when his son was born he wanted to be able to offer the child a future that was more than merely working, day in day out, for a callous employer who skimmed off all the profits like cream from the milk pail, and left only the thinnest of whey for his workers to share. *He wanted his own yard.*

'Oh, God,' he cried aloud in futile protest, turned the corner – and collided, hard, with a portly gentleman with grey side-whiskers and an angry expression, dislodging his hat and striking most of the breath from his well-covered body.

'Sorry, sir,' said Alex hastily, retrieving the hat from the gutter and dusting it off on his sleeve. 'I'm afraid I wasna looking where I was going. I didna mean to walk into you.' Then, as lamplight fell on the other's furious face, added hastily, 'Mr Wyness, sir.'

'I should hope not, by George,' roared Wyness, taking out the evening's fury on the nearest scapegoat. 'But if I thought you did I'd have the Watch on you, you idle, drunken . . .' He stopped, studied Alex in the light shed by the helpful street lamp, and said in a different voice, 'Well, well. Alex Grant, isn't it? Donal's brother? And what are you doing out in the streets at this hour, mowing down old gentlemen without so much as a by-your-leave? Swearing, too, unless my ears deceived me. Did they?'

'No, sir,' admitted Alex. 'And I am sorry I walked into you. But I assure you I am not drunk. Just disturbed in my mind about something.'

'Aye, lad, so am I, so am I.' George Wyness looked at him shrewdly for a long moment, noted the honesty in his face, the obviously troubled expression, and, remembering the service his brother Donal had done the Wyness yard with that design for Mrs Diack's headstone, said, 'I was about to go home, but they'll not miss me if I stay another hour or so, and the Lemon Tree's a fine, relaxing sort of place. Leastways, when it's not full of folk who think nothing of stabbing their own grand-mothers in the back for a piece of cheese.' He paused with remembered affront before saying, 'But I reckon you'd best come back inside wi' me, lad, and let me buy you a mug of good ale. It'll do us both good. Then, while you drink it, you can unburden some of those troubles on to me. That is, if you'd like to and if they're not too private?'

'Thank you, Mr Wyness,' said Alex with relief. 'I'd like that.'

'And in return, when you are your own man again, you can listen to a few problems of mine and maybe help me to decide what to do about them. In confidence, of course.'

'Of course,' agreed Alex, with a stirring of interest. What was Headstane Wyness up to?

'I wouldna' want word to reach Silvercairns, mind.' Suddenly, Wyness chuckled with private glee. 'I want to see their faces, when I tell them myself. The devious, scheming . . . but enough o' that. Your troubles first, lad, over a jug of the Lemon Tree's best.'

When Alex eventually returned to the tenement in Mitchell's Court, he found Donal still waiting, asleep at the fireside, and the Diack family in bed – all but Mhairi, who sat straight-backed and defiant, stitching a plain seam by the light of a single candle.

She put a warning finger to her lips, but no amount of caution could keep the excitement from his voice. 'It's going to be all right, Mhairi,' he said, pushing aside her sewing and pulling her to her feet. 'Another week, and it's all going to be all right.' Then before she could protest or question, he kissed her, with a confidence and jubilation that swept aside all misunderstanding and left her trembling with new joy and hope.

They were twelve at table. 'A round dozen,' as Old Man Adam said more than once, with an effort at jocularity which fell uncomfortably flat. There were too many uneasy undercurrents in the company that evening, too many unknowns.

It was to be the last dinner at Silvercairns before the household returned to town, though as always rooms would be kept open for such of the family as needed them. For a shooting weekend, perhaps, thought Lettice idly, or for fishing. This year she was less eager for town life, finding the autumn colours of the countryside and the spacious comforts of Silvercairns for once more appealing than city entertainments. Besides, there was Ainslie Sharp. Studying him across her elegant drawing-room before dinner she had remembered the uncouth strength of Hamish Dunn with lofty distaste. How could she ever have thought such rough-cut simplicity attractive? Recalling the man's red, perspiring face and redder hair on that humiliating day in June, Lettice shuddered afresh with revulsion. How could Flora Burnett bear to touch him?

Ainslie Sharp, in contrast, was cool, urbane and invariably immaculate. The colourless hair and pale complexion which she had once thought effete seemed now to Lettice the height of elegance, and the sharp lines of nose and cheekbone took on an arrogant and classical precision. If he was not well-born, and no one had been able to ascertain the fact one way or the other, he had every air of being so. That, combined with his undoubted business acumen, his sharp mind, and his subtle air of aloofness and unattainability, had gradually transformed him in Lettice's eyes from a mere duty urged upon her by her father to an interesting possibility and finally a positive challenge. She did not delude herself that he loved her, as she did not love him – at least, not yet – but he did not shun her company. Sometimes she suspected that he read her father's mind to the last footnote, that he knew she had been ordered to make herself pleasant and knew perfectly well why, that he enjoyed the advantages such an interest brought and intended to make the most of them, and that throughout he was smiling his superior smile at them, behind their backs. Strangely, the thought did not annoy her: instead, she saw it as an extra challenge which only made her the more determined to wear down his defences. She intended that Ainslie Sharp should propose to her, and when he did . . . but she had not quite made up her mind on that score. Meanwhile, it had become a contest in which, for the first time, she felt herself pitted against a worthy adversary. Sometimes she even thought he knew she knew and that they were both acting out some devious, intricate game. But it was a game she had grown to enjoy and one she meant to win, not merely to placate her father, but for her own satisfaction and triumph. With that in mind she had decided to play the accomplished hostess to perfection and had thrown every effort into making tonight's dinner the best yet.

Now, casting that hostess's eye over the table, Lettice could not fault the napery, the silver, the discreet flower-arrangements or the crystal. The long mahogany table gleamed with a mirror-finish in which she could see her own face reflected, should she choose to do so, and the firelight mingled with that of chandelier and silver candelabra to add the final touch of comfortable opulence to the scene. Yet the assembled company held no answering sparkle, in spite of the succession of excellent dishes and even more excellent wines. Something, somewhere, was wrong.

Lettice surveyed the company surreptitiously more than once, trying to identify the cause of the unease. Aunt Blackwell was her usual twittering, silly self. Hugo idiotic, as ever. Amelia Macdonald as gigglingly appreciative. Mrs Macdonald and Mr Burnett were conversing with the ease of long acquaintance and as it had been decided that Flora and her new husband should not be included there was no cause for friction in that quarter. For once the odious Niall was not of the company either, so she could lay no fault at his door, and even Fergus, under his father's watchful eye, was making some effort at conversation with his neighbours, though he and Fanny Wyness, on his right, seemed to have as little to say to each other as ever.

Perhaps that was it? She noticed that George Wyness was also watching Fergus, with a look of speculation which seemed to weigh up and judge every word he spoke, or did not speak, to Fanny. And when he was not watching Fergus from under those bristling grey brows, he was studying Old Man Adam himself, with an air of private anticipation which Lettice found both baffling and disturbing. Something was in the wind. Both Wyness and her father knew it, she realized, and whatever it was made for uneasy company. She glanced quickly round the table to see if anyone else might be involved in whatever private mischief was brewing and encountered her father's warning glance. Hastily, she remembered her duty.

'How are your plans for the railway progressing?' she asked, with cool assurance, of Ainslie Sharp on her left. After a dozen dinners together and as many social engagements of one kind and another she had abandoned the flirtatious manner she employed on lesser prey in favour of more serious conversation, as between equals. What he felt about the change she did not know, but she herself found it surprisingly enjoyable, as she did the necessary background reading in her father's library. 'I trust the various squabbling factions have fought it out at last and decided which towns are to be favoured with a railway station?'

'I leave such squabbles, as you so delightfully designate them, Miss Adam, to the shareholders,' said Ainslie smoothly. 'My task, I am afraid, is merely to build the line.'

'Aye, lad,' pounced Wyness from across the table, with the air of a man seizing the booty he had been waiting for all evening. 'That's all very well, but you're not going to tell me you've no idea where that line will go, because I'll not believe you. Yon air of holy innocence maybe comes with your job, as a guard against bribery and suchlike, but underneath I'd wager a hundred guineas and more that you know fine what's what and which way the wind blows. Am I right?'

Ainslie Sharp leant back in his chair, reached for his glass with a well-manicured hand, exposing as he did so an immaculate starched cuff and monogrammed gold cuff-link, and said, with a tolerant smile which did not, however, reach his eyes, 'I am merely an engineer, Mr Wyness. How could I be expected to know the secrets of the boardroom?'

'Right enough,' said Wyness unexpectedly. 'How could you know? Unless, of course, folk told you.' There was a moment's pause in which Wyness looked straight at Old Man Adam, then Aunt Blackwell said, with her nervous social laugh, 'What does it matter, anyway, which way the line goes north? For my part, I am far more interested in travelling south. What about you, Mrs Wyness? Are you planning a journey south when the railway finally opens? To Edinburgh, perhaps or even London, to see the Queen?'

But George Wyness was not to be deflected. 'I heard', he said slowly, 'that a certain railway company was going to be wound up and that another railway company was taking over the shares. I heard that compensation would be paid to folk whose land was needed for the railway line. I heard that as the canal didna make sufficient profit one way and another it might be taken over for a railway line instead, one day. Maybe I'm wrong,' he said, looking straight at Mungo Adam. 'But if I'm not, then folk with land like mine stand to make quite a bit of money, one way and another. And folk who try to get their hands on it, wi' tales of transport difficulties and suchlike, are no more than scheming, devious crooks. Wouldn't you say so, *Mungo?*'

The use of his Christian name was insult enough, but it was not that that made Old Man Adam go a deep, incriminating red, while his mouth opened and shut and no words came. After a moment, he managed, with scant courtesy, 'I don't know where you get your information, Wyness, but it is pure balderdash.'

'Is that so? Well, well. You should spend more time in the Lemon Tree, Mungo, then you'd maybe learn the difference between balderdash and truth. Tell him, Mr Sharp. Repeat that conversation you were having the other night with your engineer friend, at the next table to mine, only you didn't notice that, did you, because you were too busy talking about the best way to feather your own nest and discussing all those boardroom secrets of which you know nothing. Old Man Adam is on to a good thing there, you said. Stands to make a pretty packet, you said, *with that yard of his, by the canal* you said. And more, about the daughter's prospects, which I wouldn't soil my lips by repeating. Except to say that a fellow who discusses his host's daughter as if she were a heifer at the mart is no gentleman and never was, for all the fancy airs he gives himself. As for you, Mr Mungo Adam, I'll just say this, and you'd best listen, for I'll not say it again. It is *my yard* and now that I know just what you were after when you offered your so-called partnership, I reckon I'll keep it that way. Unless, of course, you care to make me an offer I can't refuse? And I don't mean your name over my door and permission to kiss your arse whenever I feel like it, neither.'

There was a moment's awful silence in which half the company looked firmly at their plates and the other half at Old Man Adam, then Lettice, with creditable aplomb, pushed back her chair and stood up. 'Aunt Blackwell? Mrs Wyness? Shall we leave the gentlemen to their discussion . . .?'

But before the ladies could join her, George Wyness was also on his feet. 'As far as I'm concerned, there's nought to discuss. I've said all I came to say, so if you'll tell the lad to send round the horses, I reckon we'll go. Get your cloak, Fanny. You too, lass,' he said as his wife laid a hand on his arm. 'I reckon it's best. We're none of us wanted here and they can savage our reputations better behind our backs.' With that, he ushered his womenfolk out into the hall.

'Well, well,' said Ainslie Sharp softly, though his cheeks, for once, were almost pink and he avoided Lettice's eyes. No one else spoke. Amelia Macdonald gave a nervous giggle before her mother removed her smartly from the room. Aunt Blackwell followed. As Lettice closed the dining-room door behind them, she heard her father swear profusely and Mr Burnett say, 'Not worth the effort, old boy. Forget the bounder and pass the port.' She would have given anything to linger at the keyhole, to hear how Ainslie Sharp extricated himself, to see his guilty face. Instead, with a serene self-possession worthy of Ainslie Sharp himself, she led her band of ladies upstairs.

'I am so sorry for that unseemly display at table,' said Lettice, pouring coffee in the drawing-room. Aunt Blackwell was much too agitated to pour anything without spilling half into the saucer. 'So ill-mannered to speak of business affairs at such a time.' Deliberately, she ignored that other affair of heifers and markets.

'Absolutely,' agreed Mrs Macdonald and, after a suitable pause, added 'Whatever do you suppose it was about?'

'That daughter of his most likely,' declared Aunt Blackwell, with loyal indignation. 'She has been setting her cap at poor Fergus for months and the dear boy too polite to send her packing. It's disgraceful.'

'But she hardly speaks to him,' protested Amelia. 'That time at the theatre . . .'

'That is neither here nor there,' pronounced her mother sternly and Amelia retired, subdued, to a corner to sip her coffee and wait for the gentlemen and to listen with growing awe to the accusations which were progressively laid at the Wyness door. No one, while Lettice herself was present, dared raise that other, far more interesting topic and in consequence George Wyness's reputation suffered double the battering.

Lettice listened to them in abstracted silence wondering over and over exactly what it was that Ainslie Sharp had said about 'the daughter' and that George Wyness had overheard. Something coldly calculating, certainly, for she had long since decided the man had no heart. Or if he had, there was no room in it for anyone but himself. He had probably speculated about the dowry he could expect and whether she was worth it. At first, she had been outraged, mortified, and as shamed as if her clothes had been stripped off her in the public market-place, or she had been offered for hire, like a common servant. It had been far worse than when Hamish Dunn had rejected her, for he at least had delivered his blow in private, but then, as a cold, contemptuous anger took the place of shame, she had felt exalted as on the crest of a triumphant wave. For the first time she had the advantage where Mr Supercilious Sharp was concerned. She would ignore the whole incident with supreme disdain, pretend she had not understood George Wyness and knew nothing of Sharp's plots and plans which, whether she knew of them or not, were far beneath her notice. That would baffle him and at the same time lay every burden of obligation firmly at his door. As for the business of the Wyness yard and her father's money, Sharp had been shown up, in public, in a most ungentlemanly light, and he knew it.

She wondered what he would do. Unless, of course, her father had already shown him the door, but on the whole she thought not. There were valuable contracts at stake. Then would he flee the field? But she thought him too shrewd to throw away so easily what social advantage he had won. No, more probably he would at this moment be drawing on every devious source of charm, persuasion and trickery that he possessed to re-establish himself in her father's favour, for if he lost the Adam patronage, Society would close ranks against him in her father's support and Ainslie Sharp would be finished, in this part of the country anyway, and such news soon spread. Gentleman Sharp would not like that. But port in the dining-room was one thing, coffee with the ladies afterwards quite another. Would he make an excuse to leave early? Avoid her? Or pretend nothing had happened and resort to bluff? When eventually they heard the dining-room door open and the sound of male voices approaching, Lettice was as excited as anyone to see what would happen, though she remained outwardly cool and composed.

Ainslie Sharp came straight to her side. 'I must apologize most humbly, Miss Adam,' he began, with every sign of sincerity. 'I should not have discussed your father's affairs in public and I should most certainly not have discussed other, more personal matters in such a place.'

'No,' said Lettice calmly, looking him straight in the eye. 'You should not.'

'It was ungentlemanly of me,' he said, before she could say it herself, 'and I can only plead the beguiling influence of good wine and a sympathetic ear. There are times, Miss Adam,' he went on, his fine-boned face grave and his voice a confiding murmur, 'when the burden of secrecy becomes too heavy to bear.'

'Really?' Lettice did not believe a word of it, but she gave him full marks for a superb performance. She could not have done better herself.

'Surely you must have some inkling, Miss Adam, of my sentiments towards you?'

'Must I?' Lettice was enjoying herself too much to give him the slightest help, though she could not resist adding, 'I know only of your sentiments towards my father's bank balance.'

'That was cruel of you, Miss Adam, though I deserved it.' He looked down at his hands which held between them a white china coffee cup whose gold rim, she noticed, perfectly echoed the gold of his cuff-links. She suspected he had noticed it too and that the pose of abject contrition was a studied one. Either that, or he was collecting his thoughts for the next round. Which, apparently, he managed to do, for he raised his head, looked at her gravely and said, 'Miss Adam, you and I both know the importance of money in this all too mercenary world. Only fools, romantics and those who have never known the lack of it claim otherwise. Surely it would be the height of irresponsibility not to consider such things before taking the most important step of one's life?'

But Lettice had no intention of letting him retrieve self-esteem so easily. Mr Immaculate Sharp had had the ascendancy for far too long.

'And by the same token, Mr Sharp, the height of irresponsibility to conduct one's *considerations* in a public ale house?' Before he could answer she said coolly, 'Excuse me. I must attend to my other guests, who are old and trusted friends.' She laid just the right amount of emphasis on the word 'trusted' and turned her back. A moment later she was talking with particular animation and much laughter to Archie Burnett and when he slipped a tentative arm around her waist and squeezed, she actually let him with every semblance of enjoyment.

If Ainslie Sharp felt excluded, so much the better. It served him right.

'It's all your fault, Fergus,' growled Old Man Adam when the guests had left and the womenfolk gone to bed. 'If you'd got the Wyness girl under control, like I told you to do, there'd have been none of this nonsense. We'd have got that blasted yard long ago.' Fergus did not trouble to answer. It would be useless to remind his father that his instructions had been only to 'keep her happy' till the contract was signed. It would never be signed now and he was glad. He was not interested in Fanny Wyness and she, he was sure, was not interested in him. The poor girl would be as relieved as he was that the whole, deceitful farce was over. But his father had not finished.

'As for that Sharp fellow, not knowing when to keep his mouth shut . . .' Adam paused, glowering into the grate where the last of the logs was slowly crumbling to ashes. The dinner this evening was to have settled the business with Wyness and also, he had hoped, with Sharp. Now both were in jeopardy. 'He'd best come up with that contract, or you can tell him from me there'll be the devil to pay.'

When Fergus still did not speak, but stared morosely into his brandy glass, his father remembered another grievance. 'Where's that ne'er-do-well brother of yours disappeared to?'

'His studies?' suggested Fergus with a sigh, though he had last seen Hugo heading in the direction of the stables and the darkened dairy. Adam senior merely snorted and both men relapsed into silence, each occupied with his private thoughts which they would have been surprised to learn were very similar, concerning as they did the future of the quarry.

The new seam had proved richer than the last and the rock that came out of it was as good as any granite in the land, 'And better than most,' as George Bruce boasted with pride. For weeks now the quarry had been in full production and Bruce had had to hire more men, by the day, to keep up with the boss's demands. Ton after ton of good building rock was needed for the railway viaducts and bridges, and more for the hotels, stations and private houses that followed in the railway's wake. Other firms than the Adams' were involved in the contracts, of course, but whatever the competition, Mungo Adam meant Silvercairns to stay out in front. He tendered for every advertised contract, large or small, and had even travelled as far as Newcastle in order to secure business. He inspected production himself every day and sometimes twice a day, and Fergus bore the brunt of his displeasure if the results fell short of expectation. Already he was talking of blasting a new 'bench' of rock, deeper and wider than the last.

'When we win the big contract,' Old Man Adam reminded Fergus, over and over, 'we'll need plenty in reserve if we're to keep up with demand.' But they had heard nothing of the contract and now that that bastard Wyness had let the cat out of the bag, brooded Adam, and Ainslie Sharp knew they had no conveniently placed yard by the canal, as Adam had claimed they had, would it make a difference? As it was, if they did get the contract, with the extra transport costs their profit margin would be woefully slim, and if they did not get it . . . with an uncomfortable jolt Adam remembered certain investments he had made which had proved less than satisfactory and certain moneys he had borrowed, at twenty-five per cent, to make up his losses. But, dammit, the quarry was a gold-mine, whichever way you looked at it, and the Silvercairns granite the best in Scotland. The man would be a fool not to steer the contract Adam's way. Besides, he was a shrewd and competent business-man. He had taken Adam's hospitality for months, eaten and drunk with him, strolled in the grounds with his daughter, and known perfectly well what was required of him in return. And then there was Lettice. They seemed to get on well enough, the pair of them, and he had no complaints where his daughter's behaviour was concerned. She could do a lot worse than marry the fellow, but Sharp had not declared himself, though he had had ample time and opportunity. In fact, one way and another Sharp was proving to be a thoroughly devious piece of work.

Adam tossed his cigar butt into the ashes and announced abruptly 'I'm going to bed. And you'd best do the same, Fergus, if you're to be up betimes in the morning. Remember there's the new blasting to set in hand.'

'Yes, Father. Father,' he called after him with sudden resolution as Old Man Adam reached the door, for it had been on his mind to say it for some days now, 'don't you think it is time for us to expand?'

'Dammit, boy, we are expanding! What do you think the new blasting is?'

'I meant literally, Father. Or if not that, then I thought we might lease another quarry. The Fyfe workings, for instance, on Donside, would be an excellent investment. Our quarry here is too close to the house already, and every time . . .'

'Nonsense,' interrupted his father angrily. 'I know what you're going to say and it's nonsense. The house is firm as a rock. I'll not spend good money leasing land we don't need and you've seen for yourself our granite goes down into the very heart of the earth. There's another hundred feet of it at least to be quarried, and another hundred after that.'

'But Father . . .'

'Don't argue with me, boy!' roared Old Man Adam. 'Go to your bed. And be up before I am in the morning or I'll have the hide off you.' He slammed out of the room.

But in spite of that parental threat Fergus smoked another, slow cigar and drank another, reflective brandy while the anger and frustration drained out of him, the last glow faded from the ashes in the grate and the house settled into silence. It was then, in the emptiness of the night, while his thoughts, as always, hovered about the quarry, that he remembered Mhairi Diack and wondered how she was managing, with her father dead and that pathetic family of orphans to support. It was time he did something more for her. Her brother, he remembered, was no longer an apprentice. Perhaps now would be the time to increase his wages? He would talk to George Bruce about it in the morning.

With that cheerful thought, he turned out the lamp and made his way upstairs. As he passed Hugo's door he noticed it was open, the room in darkness and the bed still neatly made. He wondered briefly whose bed his brother had chosen to share tonight, then shrugged in disgust. The boy was a fool, but

Fergus had more important things on his mind and it was no business of his.

It was Wednesday of the week that was to be Tom Diack's last at Silvercairns. Last night they had heard from Headstane Wyness and Mhairi could hardly contain her excitement as she packed her brother's lunch box and filled his flask from the ale jar. Only three more days and everything would have changed. They would be free – gloriously, splendidly free of Old Man Adam, Silvercairns, everything, even, very soon, of the shabby, overcrowded tenement in Mitchell's Court. All of them, free . . . Mhairi caught her breath with wonder and excitement and fear whenver she thought of it, which was almost every moment of her waking day, and had been since the night Alex gave her the unbelievable news. Wonder that such a thing should have happened to them, excitement at the prospect of such a splendid, undreamed-of opportunity, and fear that something might happen to snatch the prize away before Alex and Tom had a chance to prove they were worthy of it. And they were, she thought fiercely, both of them, whatever happened. But dear God, she prayed, please don't let *anything* happen.

She felt she could not bear it if her dream was taken from her yet again. So she prayed over and over inside her head, Please God, don't let Tom lose his temper with Mr Fergus, don't let him be rude to Miss Adam, don't let Alex find out who hit Donal, don't let there be an accident at the quarry, and please, please keep them all out of trouble till the week is safely over. Then, God willing, this time next week . . . but superstitiously Mhairi closed the door on that particular dream lest it vanish as the last had done, in tears and sorrow.

But there was no sorrow this morning in the Mitchell Court tenement. Even young Annys felt the excitement in the air as she and her brothers sat over their breakfast bowls at the scrubbed deal table in the chill half-light of an October dawn and Tom was positively beaming as he spooned up the last of his porridge, pushed back the bench and reached for his cap.

'You will remember to be patient, Tom,' she warned him anxiously. 'Promise? And whatever you do, don't lose your temper or you will give our secret away. And you know what

Mr Wyness said.' No one, particularly Old Man Adam, must suspect a thing until the deal was sealed and signed.

'Me? Lose my temper? I don't know what you're on about, Mhairi, and me always so cheerful and friendly.' He winked at her and grinned. 'I'm a model worker, I am. They'll be right sorry when I go.'

'Then don't let them guess that you're going, Tom. Promise me you'll be careful?'

'Don't fuss, Mhairi love. I'll not breathe a word. Mr Fergus couldn't be doing with all the men in tears at the thought of me leaving, could he? It might dampen his precious fuses and there'd be no blasting done.'

'Idiot,' said Mhairi, laughing. It was fine to see her brother cheerful again, and almost his old, optimistic self.

'It's no laughing matter, damp powder,' grinned Tom, then he winked. 'Leastways, Mr Fergus wouldna laugh, with his father breathing down his neck all the time demanding double the production every week. It's only my exceptional skill that keeps the quarry up to schedule. And Alex's too, of course,' he added, dodging the playful smack Mhairi aimed at his head. 'The quarry'll be right lost without us.'

'Then perhaps you'd better stay?' teased Mhairi, handing him his lunch box.

'I will – till Friday. Then I'll . . .'

'Don't say it!' she cried, her hand on his mouth. Then, shamefaced, she withdrew it. 'I'm sorry, Tom, but I can't help being superstitious. And you will be careful, won't you?'

'Haven't I promised? That man of yours is an idle beggar, Mhairi,' he continued cheerfully, swinging the heavy tool bag to his shoulder and turning for the door. 'I reckon I'll have to rouse him from his bed myself.' But at that moment there was the sound of steps on the forestair, the door burst open and Alex himself appeared, beaming, in the doorway, Donal at his back.

'Aye, aye,' he said, ruffling Willy's hair and giving Lorn a playful shove. 'Not coming with us this morning, then?' Before they could make any answer, Alex swung his tool bag from one hand to the other, put his free arm round Mhairi's shoulder, and kissed her. 'Not long now, my wee darling,' he murmured in her ear then he winked at Annys, said, 'What are we waiting for, lads?' and a moment later the three of them were striding purposefully across the yard towards the street.

Mhairi stood at the top of the forestair and watched until they reached the corner, turned, waved, and vanished into the early-morning city: and when they returned at the end of the day, that would be one day less to wait before everything was gloriously, splendidly different. She crossed her fingers quickly in childlike superstition and looked around her for suitable wood to touch against ill luck. But surely this time nothing could go wrong with their plans? She laid a hand on her womb, still flat enough to guard her secret from prying eyes, but in spite of that reassurance, felt the familiar fear. But Mr Wyness would not go back on his word to them, surely, and neither would Alex on his promise to her.

Nevertheless, when Lorn and Willy and even little Annys clamoured excitedly to know what would happen tomorrow and the day after, and whether they could leave school and help, Mhairi said sternly, 'Wait till tomorrow and you might find out.' Alex and Tom had been sworn to secrecy until Mr Wyness had his plans ready, but in spite of their precautions, the younger children sensed the excitement in the air and knew that something was afoot. Now, seeing their crestfallen faces, Mhairi relented and let them speculate unchecked until it was time to pack them off to school with the usual warnings to the boys not to dawdle and to work hard, though this time she added, 'So Mr Wyness will know the Diack men are to be relied on.' She had no need to admonish Annys who had long been star pupil of her year. But when they had gone, and she had the tenement to herself, although Mhairi tried her best to concentrate on the pile of sewing she had undertaken to do for the Ladies' Working, she found her thoughts following Tom and Alex on the road to Silvercairns. Suppose something went wrong? Suppose there was an accident? Suppose Mr Fergus . . . But she was being ridiculous. She told herself firmly to concentrate on facts rather than fantasies – and picked up the first of the flannel petticoats.

She had been sewing happily for perhaps two hours when she heard a sound at the door and looked up, startled, to see Lizzie Lennox on the threshold, her white face anxious and her red hair escaping in damp curls from under the dark plaid she had bundled around her.

'Can I come in?' Before Mhairi could answer, Lizzie had slipped swiftly inside and shut the door. 'There's no one here, is there?'

'No, but . . .'

'Thank God for that.' Lizzie shook off the plaid with a toss of her head and ran agitated fingers through her tangled hair before saying, 'I waited in the back close till I saw Ma go out. I couldna risk meeting her on the stair.'

'Whyever not, Lizzie, she's . . .' but Lizzie interrupted.

'Mhairi, you've got to help me. Da will kill me if he finds out and I daren't tell Ma. She'd likely let on without meaning to and . . . oh, God, Mhairi, what'll I do?'

Mhairi stared at Lizzie in growing horror as the implications of her words took shape. 'What have you done, Lizzie? You haven't been stealing again, have you? From Miss Adam? You haven't been caught?'

'Oh, I've been caught all right,' said Lizzie with a pathetic attempt at a laugh. 'But not the way you think. I'm pregnant.'

Mhairi went white with shock, her head a whirl of dreadful possibilities. Tom? Mr Fergus? But before she could ask the inevitable question, Lizzie answered it.

'I could kill that Hugo Adam,' she said with venom. 'And him supposed to be a gentleman. Do you know what he said when I told him? Sorry I can't help you, old girl, he said. Old girl! When only last week he was chasing me round the hay loft and bouncing me in the straw and calling me his little filly. That's a kind o' racehorse, seemingly,' she added with brief pride.

But Mhairi had found her tongue. 'Lizzie, how could you? It's immoral, it's . . .'

'Oh, it is, is it?' flared Lizzie. 'Immoral to have a bit of fun, is it? Well, of course, you'd know all about that, wouldn't you? You and Alex Grant. How many times have you been "immoral" with him, then, Mhairi Diack, and you no more married than I am? Fornication, that's what they call it. What's more, by the look in your eye you're likely as pregnant as I am, for all your high and mighty airs, only your man will stand by you, if you're lucky, whereas mine . . .' Suddenly her valiance deserted her and she crumpled into tearful despair. 'Oh, Mhairi, what am I going to do?'

Mhairi's cheeks were burning with the mortification of Lizzie's words. It was the truth, of course, no matter how she excused it to herself. And though she and Alex loved each other and Lizzie, by her own confession, was only 'having a bit of fun', Lizzie's words had scattered censure and left Mhairi humble and ashamed. And suddenly, heart-grippingly, as frightened as Lizzie herself, though for a different reason. Suppose Tom were to find out? Remembering her brother's fury on the night of the Queen's birthday when he had caught Mr Hugo and Lizzie Lennox together – for she had heard all about that incident, from a dozen different sources – and his threats of vengeance should it ever happen again, the thought filled her with terror. Tom would go looking for Hugo Adam and . . . oh, God. Mhairi knew that she would do anything to keep it from him. But Lizzie must not see her fear. She said carefully, 'You say you told him?'

'Aye, I told him, and much good it did me,' sniffed Lizzie, drying her eyes on her skirt. 'Mean bastard. I'm not fool enough to expect him to marry me, with him being a gentleman and all, but it's his bairn and the least he can do is pay up. Then it all comes out that he's been to the races, betting and suchlike, with his snotty friends. Rather strapped for cash at the moment, my dear, he says, all superior like. Then he remembers he has urgent business elsewhere and hops it. It'd serve the bastard right if I told Old Man Adam, only I daren't. He'd give me money, maybe, but he'd be sure to send for Da to fetch me home. And Da would kill me.' There was real fear in Lizzie's eyes at the thought. 'That's why I came to you, Mhairi. I thought you could go to Mr Fergus and ask for the money for me, private like.'

'But why don't you ask Mr Fergus yourself? It's the obvious thing to do.'

'Obvious to you, maybe. Not to me. I'm scared of him, Mhairi. His eyes seem to look right through you and you never know what a man like that's thinking. Besides, he'd maybe say I was lying. But he'll believe you. And you must make him promise not to tell my da. Please, Mhairi? And do it afore the week's out? I reckon I'll begin to show, else, and yon Ma

Gregor's got eyes like a buzzard's for spying out trouble. Besides, end of the week and we're moving back to town so it'd be right convenient. Then I could go away somewhere. Leith, maybe. I've always fancied a trip to Leith. Or Glasgow. You could tell Ma I've found myself a job in one o' the tobacco-merchants' castles.' Mhairi didn't answer, but continued to stare at Lizzie with hunted eyes, and in growing desperation Lizzie cast around in her memory for some suitable threat. She found it.

'You'd best help me, Mhairi Diack,' she said, a sly look in her eye, 'and you'd best do it quick. Or I might just tell your Alex about the day Hugo Adam hit Donal. Oh, I know it was a while ago, but I reckon it wasna the last time neither and you know what your Alex's like. When he hears he'll go straight round there and paste Mr Hugo to the walls and it'll serve the bastard right.' She grinned triumphantly at Mhairi, knowing she had won.

'All right,' said Mhairi quickly. 'I'll do it.' The fear of facing Fergus Adam on such an appalling errand was nothing compared to her fear for Alex. Why must it happen now? she cried with silent anguish. Now, with only three more days to go before . . . Then resolution came to her aid. Whatever she had to do, however she had to humble herself, she would make sure that nothing and no one snatched away the prize this time. She had required patience and tolerance and good humour from Tom and Alex, whatever the provocation, and had urged them to give only of their best. She could hardly require less of herself.

'I will do it,' she repeated, 'but only if you promise not to breathe a word to Tom or Alex or anyone. *Not one single word.* Because if I find you have,' she added, slowly, 'I shall go straight up the stair to your father and it won't matter whether you are in Leith or Timbuctoo, he will seek you out.'

'Aye, he would too,' agreed Lizzie, with a mixture of pride and apprehension. She glanced nervously over her shoulder.

'Do you promise?'

'God's honour, hope to die,' gabbled Lizzie hastily, then hurried on, 'You'd best see Mr Fergus in the quarry office. He'll likely have money there.'

'In the *quarry office*?' Mhairi was appalled. Somehow she had assumed it would be at the Adam town house. 'But suppose Tom or Alex sees me?'

'Tell them . . . oh, I don't know. Tell them anything. But they won't see you, will they? They'll be down the quarry, hammering rock. Leastways, they will if you pick your time right. Besides,' she went on as Mhairi hesitated, 'what would you be doing, seeing Mr Fergus at the big house? That would look right suspicious, that would. And aren't the wages paid in the quarry office?'

'Yes, but . . .'

'There you are, then!' said Lizzie triumphantly. 'Mr Fergus will be able to lay his hands on the money, no bother. He'll give it to you, then you can bring it to me at Silvercairns. Here,' she said, lifting her skirt and unrolling first one thick black stocking, then the other. 'Hide the money in these. There's plenty holes in them anyway and you can say you was darning them for me.' She grinned suddenly, with something of her old spirit. 'See you make a good job of it, mind. I canna abide lumpy darning. But I'd best go. I'm supposed to be scrubbing out the china cupboard in the Guestrow house so's it's clean for the family moving back. As if a bit o' dirt did anyone any harm.' At the door she turned, hesitated, then said, in a rush, 'Thanks, Mhairi. You're a good friend. And I didna mean it about you and Alex. You're good as married anyway.' Then to Mhairi's astonishment, Lizzie kissed her quickly on the cheek. 'Goodbye, Mhairi. I reckon I'll miss you, for all your stuck-up ways.' Then she scuttled out of the room and down the tenement stairs.

When she had gone, Mhairi fell back in her chair and let the whole appalling horror of the situation flow over and engulf her. But only for a moment, before she snatched up those dreadful stockings and began darning as if her life depended on it. Which it did. Or rather, Alex's did, and possibly Tom's, too. Then she saw the pile of sewing still waiting to be done for the Ladies' Working. She'd promised to finish it by four that afternoon. Oh, God, she could not risk falling behind with her work for the Ladies' Committee: suppose they would not give her any more? But it would be too late by the time everything was finished. The visit to the quarry office would have to wait till tomorrow. Tomorrow morning, as soon as she judged Tom and Alex were safely at the quarry face. But please God, let Lizzie hold her tongue.

By the time her family returned that evening Mhairi was white-faced with anxiety and emotionally exhausted.

'Hey,' said Alex softly, lifting her chin with his hand. 'What is it, my sweet? What's troubling you?'

'Nothing.' She bit her lip and turned away. 'At least . . . it's just that I can't help worrying,' she finished evasively. She dare not meet his eyes in case he read her secret.

But Alex was too full of happiness to suspect anything amiss. Instead he hugged her, told her to be patient, not to pluck worries out of thin air, and later, when the meal was over, he and Tom staged an Indian arm-wrestling contest, with bizarre handicaps such as plates on heads, which everybody entered and which Annys, to her squealing delight, won. There was much laughter and good humour and under everything a simmering excitement heady as good wine. When Alex finally left with Donal for his own home, Mhairi was almost calm again. There were only two days left to go. But when the others were in bed she remembered Lizzie's stockings neatly mended and hidden away in a dresser drawer and the errand she must do in the morning, and all her anxieties came rushing back. It was a long time before she slept.

It was strange to be walking the road to Silvercairns again. The last time, she remembered, had been when she carried that basket of petticoats and Mr Fergus overtook her. That was before he had sacked her father, and when he had dismounted and offered to carry her basket she had thought, in her innocence, that they were friends. Remembering her last sight of him, at her father's funeral, Mhairi's jaw set with new resolution. She despised him, as she despised his brother. They were as bad as each other, both arrogant parasites, rotten to the core. She forgot that she had ever admired the Adams, ever yearned for the many-chimneyed splendour of Silvercairns, ever cast Fergus Adam in the role of prince or woven dreams about Miss Lettice's clothes. They were no more than despots, all of them. Cruel, heartless despots. They thought they could do what they liked with their workforce – sack them, bed them, toss them aside without a thought for the suffering they caused. But then, with their privileges and their riches, what did they know of suffering? What did they care?

Mhairi deliberately fuelled her anger, so that her spirit might not fail her before she reached the quarry office. The silver birches beside the path were almost bare now, their bark flaking in gleaming disks and the soft ground at their feet layered with gold. The hedgerow by Hirpletillam had lost its scarlet berries, and the dusty bracken was brittle as straw. There would be a frost tonight. When she turned the last bend in the path and saw the stately outline of Silvercairns House against a crisp October sky, for a moment she forgot her anger and antagonism in the simple pleasure of looking once more on her childhood dream.

The house looked as gracious and as elegant as she remembered, the gardens as tranquil, the meadowland, though tinged with frost, as lush. A handful of black and white cows grazed picturesquely under a winter chestnut tree and on the scrubland between the grounds of the big house and the quarry the heather still gleamed with cobwebbed dew. Then from the yard at the back of the house came the distant sound of voices, the clatter of a milk pail and a sudden squawking of hens. Domestic, kitchen sounds which should have increased the pleasure of the scene, but which instead reminded Mhairi too sharply of what she had to do. What good was a beautiful shell if the inside was corrupt? She averted her eyes from what had once been her dream palace, and instead kept them determinedly on the jumble of wooden buildings in the distance, at the end of the quarry path.

It was two years since she had run, distraught and panting, along this same path: as through a window into a different land, she saw her sixteen-year-old self, an innocent, guileless and dishevelled child, stumbling heedless through the quarry yard and on to that forbidden path to fetch her father home. Then she had fallen and, afterwards, Fergus Adam had been kind. She still had that laundered linen handkerchief as proof. But that was long ago.

Ahead of her was the same square wooden outline of the quarry office roof, the same smell of horses from the stables, the same dust-choked grass beside the path, but she was no longer that innocent child. As Mhairi neared the yard, she straightened her back and lifted her chin with resolution. If her spirit faltered, she had only to remember Alex and what was at stake. The words she had rehearsed, over and over, pounded loud in her head with the thumping of her heart. Then she reached the door of the office and, with only momentary hesitation, lifted her hand and knocked.

He was sitting at his desk, pen in hand, checking figures in a ledger. At first he continued to run the pen down the page, pausing now and then to make notes on the pad beside him, but after a moment, sensing her silence, he looked up. 'Miss Diack!' He rose hastily to his feet. 'I am sorry, I did not realize . . . I thought it was my foreman.'

His feudal choice of words was a welcome reminder to Mhairi of what she had come to do. When Fergus Adam smiled and offered her a chair she refused, with a cold and scathing dignity of which any duchess would have been proud. 'I prefer to stand, Mr Adam. My business will not, I hope, take long.'

'Your business?' He looked puzzled. 'Does it perhaps concern your brother?'

'No.' Though Lizzie's plight, were Tom to know of it, might well affect him deeply. 'It concerns yours.' She was pleased with that reply, quite unrehearsed, for it washed the complacency from his face and left him shocked and cautious. He crossed to the door, opened it, looked out, closed it again, returned to his desk, and sat down behind its reassuring width. 'Perhaps you had better explain, Miss Diack.'

He had recovered his dignity, she noticed, and though he was pale, he betrayed no agitation. For a moment she regretted refusing that chair for her action left her standing like a servant awaiting rebuke while at the other side of that imposing desk Mr Fergus Adam sat like a judge at the bench.

'Well?' he said, when she did not speak, and the quiet question scattered her hesitation like dust in the wind. How dare he speak to her with such arrogant, patronizing, complacent . . . she ran out of adjectives in her choking anger. But she would not give him the satisfaction of seeing her lose control. A lady never loses her temper, she heard her mother saying all those years ago, and though she had failed her mother in so many ways, she would not fail her now.

'I came, Mr Fergus,' she said with icy hauteur, 'to inform you of your brother's wicked exploitation of an employee and to ask for justice. No,' she corrected herself quickly, 'not to ask for it. To require it.'

Fergus Adam did not speak, but continued to look at her, his eyes sombre, his expression grave, as if she were the only fixed point in the universe. Which, for the moment, she was: of his universe, anyway. He had forgotten how striking she was, how intense was the blue of her eyes, forgotten the straightness of her back and the pride in the tilt of her chin. Forgotten the way his heart behaved when he saw the glossy wings of her hair and the way her bosom rose and fell . . . Ever since her father's funeral he had put her determinedly out of mind, or if ever he found her pushing her way into his thoughts, had pushed her firmly out again. But now, here she stood in front of him, in glorious flesh and blood, and his eyes could not have enough.

Mhairi, seeing his unblinking stare, felt herself blushing in spite of all resolution. How dare he try to outface her by his lawyer's tricks? How dare he stare through her, as if she was not there? 'Do you have nothing to say, Mr Fergus? Or are you merely occupied with searching for the best way to evade responsibility?'

'That was both unnecessary and cruel, Miss Diack,' he said quietly and Mhairi felt brief shame. But only brief.

'Not as cruel as for a gentleman to take advantage of a servant girl in his employ and to refuse to pay for the inevitable consequences.'

Fergus started with shock and the blood drained from his face. He had somehow assumed her complaint concerned the quarry and a workman there, but 'to take advantage of a servant girl' could mean only one thing. His hands gripped the desk edge till the knuckles stood out white as bone. She had mentioned his brother and young Hugo was notorious where girls were concerned, especially servant girls. But the Diack girl was not in Silvercairns's employ, was she? Then he remembered that day on the quarry road when he had overtaken her on the way to the house. She had been working for Lettice then, she said, but . . . Oh, God, not Hugo and *her* . . .

When he could speak, he said in a voice he hardly recognized as his own, 'You have asked him for money?'

'I?' Then the implications hit her, hard. For the second time in a week she was being accused, but Lizzie's taunts had been harmless home-truths compared to this. Mhairi flushed scarlet with mortification, then a cold and deadly fury took the place of shame. How dare he assume, on no evidence at all, that she had tumbled in the hay loft with Hugo Adam, and in consequence had come begging on her own behalf? 'No, Mr Fergus,' she said, with commendable self-possession and a voice like broken ice. 'I have not asked him, but my friend Lizzie Lennox who is the employee in question has done so and was informed, with, I believe, some element of hilarity, that Mr Hugo had lost too much on the horses to be able to help her. Very sorry and all that, old girl, was, I believe, the phrase used. An illegitimate child may be a subject of mirth to gentlemen such as you and your brother, Mr Fergus, but I can assure you it is not so to the mother concerned. I would have thought common decency alone would require the father to contribute to his child's maintenance, but perhaps decency is too *common* a quality to be entertained in such exalted circles as Silvercairns?'

Fergus Adam was too overcome with relief to speak, or to take in the details of what she was saying. Hugo had not gone to bed with her after all. Beyond that, what else mattered? Then he realized she was waiting for an answer and made himself concentrate on the matter in hand.

'Do I understand you are here on behalf of a friend, Miss Diack?' he said with care.

'Of course. Surely you do not imagine I would come here otherwise?' She did not need to add 'after what you did to my father'.

'A friend who is a servant in Silvercairns? And of whom you say my brother has taken advantage?'

'Are you challenging the truth of my statement, Mr Fergus? Because if so I suggest you . . .'

'No, Miss Diack, certainly not. I am merely trying to marshal the facts.'

'Then allow me to help you. Lizzie Lennox is expecting your brother Hugo's child. Is that fact simple enough for you to understand, Mr Fergus? The second fact is that your brother has refused to give money to help her. My friend, for reasons of her own, would prefer not to approach your father on the matter – yet,' (Mhairi thought it prudent to put in that 'yet' though Lizzie would flee the country rather than confront Old Man Adam) 'and therefore has asked me, on her behalf, to ask you, on your family's behalf, to make suitable provision for the maintenance of the mother until her lying-in and for the upkeep of the child thereafter.'

'Admirably concise, Miss Diack,' he said, leaning back in his chair, and reaching for his pen. He took it up and began to doodle absentmindedly in the margin of the page. Then, because she had cruelly hurt him and the wound still bled, he added, 'But what proof have I that there is the smallest element of truth in this story?'

'You have my word!' she flared, her cheeks flushed and her eyes bright with anger. He had touched her on the raw and it showed in every proud line of her body, in the arrogant tilt of her lovely head. Then she said, deliberately, 'You could also ask your brother, though whether you can attach as much credence to his word, is another matter.'

Fergus, goaded beyond caution, pushed back his chair, sprang to his feet and the next minute had rounded the desk and gripped Mhairi by the forearm. 'How dare you, woman! You forget my brother is a gentleman.'

'I rather think he forgets it himself,' said Mhairi, looking him defiantly in the face, though his face was too close for her comfort and his hand too bruisingly hard through the thin stuff of her sleeve. 'As you do.' She looked down at his hand, still gripping her arm, and was rewarded by seeing Fergus Adam flush and look away. He loosed his grip and said quietly, 'I apologize. I forgot myself.' Another moment and he would have kissed her: the knowledge appalled him. He took a step back and said, 'Please sit down, Miss Diack, so that I may do so too. Besides, you look tired, and if I may say so, a little faint?'

His words reminded them both of that scene in this same office when she had fainted and he had caught her. There was a moment's silence in which both explored the intimacies of memory, then Mhairi said quietly, all animosity gone, 'Thank you, I will sit down. As you say, I am a little faint.' Without thinking she laid a hand across her waist and Fergus in a flash of revelation saw Mhairi Diack at her father's graveside, her brothers and sisters around her and a tall, well-built young mason, one of his own workers, at her side. The man had put his arm around her shoulders at one point and she had laid her head briefly against him before straightening again. Jealousy flooded through him like bitter bile and brought all the cold arrogance back to his voice.

'When you are recovered, Miss Diack, perhaps we might discuss the details of this necessary, if painful transaction? There must be safeguards, of course, and discretion. On both sides.'

'Of course,' said Mhairi, and knew that she had won. She ought to have felt relief, but instead felt only sadness. It was as if she and Mr Fergus were united in shame, he for his brother, she for her friend, but in a shame which, as well as uniting, set them further apart than before. The money was counted out, handed over, stowed away. The amount was entered into an account book – not the big quarry ledger but a smaller, private one – and Mhairi signed her name beside it, adding, on Mr Fergus's instruction, 'on behalf of L.L.' Then she thanked him, he held open the door for her, and closed it behind her as she stepped out into the yard. It was a joyless victory.

Outside, in the crisp air of the deserted stable yard, she was on the point of congratulating herself that she had accomplished her mission without detection from anyone in the quarry when she turned a corner and walked straight into Donal Grant. He was leading one of the quarry horses by the reins and indicated to Mhairi that the animal had cast a shoe. He must have come up to the surface especially to take the beast to the smithy, unless, she thought with sudden hope, he was merely going to stable it till later and use another. But whether she would have his company on the Hirpletillam road or not, it was too late now. He had seen her in the quarry yard and if he revealed as much to Alex, she would have to explain, and explain convincingly, if she was to keep Lizzie's secret safe. She laid a finger to her lips and endeavoured to tell Donal that she was not there, that he must not tell, that he had not seen her, that it was a secret, and at last he smiled, nodded, laid his own finger to his lips and she knew he had understood. There had been enough secrets during the last few days to make another one seem natural enough. 'Thank you, Donal,' she said and smiled with relief. Then she hurried on her way to the Silvercairns kitchens to hand Lizzie those incriminating stockings, before making her way home to Mitchell's Court and safety.

Fergus Adam was late home that evening, but though there was barely time left to change for dinner, he went straight in search of his brother. He found Hugo with Lettice and Aunt Blackwell in the drawing-room, a full brandy glass in his hand.

'Behold my brother, the working man,' said Hugo cheerfully, with an expansive wave of the hand, and Fergus did not need Lettice's wink to tell him that Hugo had been drinking, and copiously. 'Come in, Fergus, old chap, and join the happy drones. Life's too short to waste it working . . . isn't that right, Lettice, old girl? Far better things to do. Horses, f'rinstance. This afternoon . . .'

'Hugo,' interrupted Fergus, 'I would like a word in the library.'

'Would you now, brother mine? Well, I would not like a word, leastways not in the library. Cheerless places, libraries. All those accusing books. Drawing-rooms are far preferable: sweetness and light and lovely ladies, not to mention sustenance of a liquid kind. Happy to talk to you here, old chap, any time. Have a drink.'

'In the library,' repeated Fergus. 'Now, before Father comes down.'

Hugo sobered instantly to wariness. 'All right, if you insist. Excuse me, sweet ladies,' he said with an elaborate bow. 'Duty calls.' But he looked uncomfortably apprehensive as he followed his brother into the library.

'Why the cloak and dagger stuff, Fergus?' he blustered, as soon as the door was closed. 'Has someone pinched the quarry cash box?' But if he had hoped to divert Fergus from his purpose, he failed.

'The matter concerns Lizzie Lennox and your unborn child.'

'Who?' Hugo attempted a carefree laugh and failed. 'I don't know what you are talking about, old chap,' but his cheeks were flushed and his eyes evasive. Into Fergus's mind flashed the memory of Mhairi Diack saying, of his brother, 'Whether you can attach as much credence to his word is another matter' and with shame he knew that she was right.

In a voice whose quietness should have warned Hugo, he said, 'I think you do.'

'And if I did, would it be any concern of yours, brother?'

'It has to be someone's concern, and it is obviously not yours,' said Fergus angrily.

'And why should it be mine? If some forward little minx gets herself into trouble then it is up to her to get herself out of it.'

'But she did not get herself, as you so charmingly put it, into trouble. You got her into it, Hugo. Or do you deny it?'

'Oh, I'd deny anything for a quiet life,' said Hugo airily. Then Fergus hit him.

Taken unawares, Hugo staggered, blood spurting from his nose, then with a cry of pain and rage he launched himself at Fergus, with all the fury of a lifetime's jealousy. A chair crashed to the floor, Hugo's fist connected with Fergus's eye, Fergus retaliated with a sharp one to the jaw and split Hugo's lip. The brothers were well matched: the younger was taller and more nimble perhaps, but the older was stronger and more devious. Fists flew indiscriminately in a contest of silent hatred, until Hugo saw his chance and clutched his brother in a bear hug, pinioning his arms. He was trying to wrestle him off his feet and to the floor when the door behind them opened and a voice thundered, 'Stop!' In the moment's silence which followed, Hugo's grip loosened, Fergus broke away and both men attempted to straighten torn collars, tuck in shirts, and somehow retrieve composure under the black and furious glare of Old Man Adam himself.

'What is the meaning of this unseemly brawl?' he roared, then, in sudden contrast, and with far more chilling calm, he said, 'Go to your rooms and make yourselves respectable. I will see both of you here, after dinner.'

It was a long and for the most part silent meal, with Aunt Blackwell attempting the occasional idiocy, Lettice making a conciliatory remark or two in the interests of family harmony and the men monosyllabic. For once, Lettice did not know what was afoot, though it was plain that something was, and that both her brothers had incurred her father's displeasure. For Hugo that was commonplace, but not for Fergus. Besides, both her brothers had a vaguely battered look: Hugo's lip was decidedly misshapen and one of Fergus's eyes was bloodshot and half-closed. Surely they had not been fighting, she thought gleefully, remembering certain thumps and bumps from the direction of the library before dinner. If so, she wondered what it could have been about. Money? Certainly Hugo was always in debt. Perhaps Fergus had had enough of handing out money for nothing and wanted Hugo to pull his weight? Or a woman? But Fergus was such a cold fish she could not imagine him feeling deeply enough about any woman to fight over her. The only thing he felt deeply about was the quarry and, regretfully, Lettice decided that must be the explanation. When she and Aunt Blackwell adjourned to the drawing-room, her aunt agreed. Perhaps Old Man Adam had ordered Hugo to work in the family business at last and Fergus had objected? Or Fergus and his father were disputing as usual about the next area to blast, and Hugo had somehow got caught up in it too? But such speculation was too boring to continue for long. Aunt Blackwell took up her interminable embroidery and Lettice sat down at the piano and began absent-mindedly to play. She wondered what Ainslie Sharp was doing? And when he would next get in touch?

'Well?' said Old Man Adam in the sort of voice that brooked no evasion. Both Fergus and Hugo knew it of old and knew the futility of resistance. Nevertheless Fergus tried.

'It was my fault, Father. A disagreement between us, on a private matter, led me to strike my brother. I should not have done so and I apologize.'

'And what was this private matter on which you so violently disagreed?'

There was a short silence, broken this time by Hugo. 'Oh, what's the use? He'll get it out of us in the end. You'd best tell him, Fergus.'

Briefly, and in general terms, Fergus did.

Again there was silence, but only while Mungo Adam built up steam, to let it out in a stream of fury aimed at Hugo. Time-wasting, profligacy, betting, drinking, whoring, truancy, idleness, the accusations tumbled over each other in a crescendo of rage until Old Man Adam finally ran out of breath. 'One more misdemeanour on your part, my boy,' he finished, 'and it is the colonies for you. Do you understand?'

'Yes, Father.'

'Then get out of my sight! And don't think to escape to the fleshpots of Aberdeen. You'll go to your room and stay there and if you set so much as one foot over the threshold before morning, I will personally tan the hide off you. Understood? Now get out. And I expect to see you at breakfast, *early*.'

When Hugo had scrambled hastily out of the room and upstairs, Old Man Adam breathed more easily, poured himself a large brandy and as an afterthought offered Fergus one. Fergus accepted.

'It was time somebody thumped that boy,' muttered Adam after a few minutes' brooding silence. 'Suppose there's no doubt the child's his?'

'I think not,' said Fergus, then, remembering Mhairi Diack's accusations, added, 'None at all.'

'Pity. Young fool. Who is the girl, by the way? No, don't tell me. I'd rather not know.'

'Whoever she is, something must be done to help her, Father.' Fergus was beginning to feel the same anger rise as had prompted him to strike his brother. He had the uneasy impression that much of his father's censure of Hugo was bombast, lip-service to morality, and that secretly he regarded what the boy had done as more peccadillo than crime. Every word they spoke on the subject reinforced Mhairi Diack's criticisms that the Adams were arrogant, despotic, unfeeling. He felt impelled to redress the balance. 'Remember, Father, that the child, whether it is born in wedlock or not, will be your grandchild.'

'In wedlock or not? Surely the fool has not promised marriage?'

'Would it be so disastrous if he had? It would at least be honourable.'

'Honourable? To marry a servant? You are out of your mind. The boy's been a fool, but not such a fool as that, thank God.' He drank deep of his brandy, smacked his lips with appreciation and added, 'If any son of mine married into the servant classes, he'd take none of my money with him, I'd make sure of that.'

'Nevertheless, Father,' said Fergus, keeping his temper with difficulty, 'provisions must be made.'

'Then make them, for God's sake. A lump sum now, and more when the child is born. The usual. Only leave me out of it.' Angrily, he took up the newspaper and riffled through it for the stockmarket page.

'Yes, Father,' said Fergus, through clenched teeth. He forebore to say that he had already made arrangements. With equal caution he forebore to ask what 'usual' involved. It suggested aspects of his father's life of which he preferred to remain ignorant.

'And see you are down early to breakfast, too, Fergus. I want a word about the next blasting.'

Fergus sighed. Not about the early rising, for he was invariably the first one in the breakfast room, but at the prospect of yet another dispute about where to set the next fuse. His father would win, as he always did, and another crack would appear somewhere in the structure of Silvercairns, if not in the big house, then in the terracing or the outhouses. It was only a matter of time before . . . but Fergus turned away from that depressing avenue of thought. Time enough to think of that in the morning.

On the morning of the day that was to mark the end of the old life and the beginning of the new, Alex and Donal Grant called early at the tenement to collect Tom Diack. Solidarity must be demonstrated from the start and now, walking three abreast through the early-morning streets of the town, they felt invincible, the equal of any employer in the land.

It was a bright morning, the ground frost still crisp underfoot, the few leaves left on the trees which lined the road from Hirpletillam already glinting gold and russet in the early sun. Blackbirds exulted in the branches. Alex whistled as he strode up the familiar track, the rising sun at his back, ahead of him the block of Silvercairns house square-cut against the paling sky. Other early-morning workers trudged ahead of him and more followed, but whereas they, for the most part, reserved their energies for the day ahead and moved in dogged silence but for a grunted greeting and a nod of the head, he walked head high and whistling, every now and then breaking into song. Tom at his side looked equally cheerful, with a gleam of anticipation in his clear blue eyes and an air of suppressed excitement, and Donal, as tall now as Alex and almost as broad in the shoulders, had an air of quiet satisfaction which told any onlooker that he shared their secret and approved.

They were almost at the gates of the big house when they heard the hoofs. A horseman was coming fast down the drive of Silvercairns, a young man, low in the saddle, whipcorded knees gripping the rippling chestnut strength of his mount, gloved hands and snaking whip urging the animal faster. There was no pause in the drumming rhythm of hoofs on impacted earth as the horse swung out through the gates and into the quarry path, crowded at this early hour with workmen three and four abreast on their way to the Adam yard.

'The bastard,' gasped Tom Diack, in the forefront of the men. 'The arrogant, stupid bastard.' Then the horse was upon them, men scattering to right and left like the bow-wave of a ship as the hoofs thundered on with no slackening of pace. The white star on the horse's forehead flared, the gloved hand brought the whip down hard on heaving flank and raised it again. For a moment Hugo Adam's and Tom Diack's eyes met in recognition, and instead of leaping for the hedge like the rest of them, Tom lunged with an oath for the gleaming leather boot and felt the whiplash curl across his back. He heard Hugo laugh, before Alex grabbed Tom's arm to hold him back; Hugo Adam raised his whip again, Donal Grant flinched and flung up a protective arm as Adam lashed out indiscriminately, with a string of oaths. Another moment and he had fought through the milling men and was riding free. The last they saw of him was a cloud of dust on the Hirpletillam road.

'The bastard,' repeated Tom Diack with quiet fury. 'The arrogant, stupid bastard. But I swear I'll make him pay. After today, he'll not be able to touch me, and then I'll get him.'

'Don't be a fool, Tom,' warned Alex. 'The likes of him can always "touch" the likes of us. Remember you promised Mhairi you would keep your temper.'

'Aye, I did, but that was before . . .' Suddenly, with awful revelation, the full implications of the encounter hit him. It was too early for the likes of Hugo Adam to be abroad – unless *he had never been to bed at all.* Which meant, at Silvercairns, either a night spent gambling – which, with Old Man Adam resident, was unlikely – or a night spent illicitly in someone else's bed. With an animal cry of rage Tom started back down the track after his enemy, but again Alex restrained him. Besides, the workmen had closed ranks again to block the lane behind the disappearing horseman. Defeated and balked of his purpose, Tom shook off Alex's arm, raised his voice and bellowed after Hugo Adam, 'I swear I'll kill that bastard one day, with my own bare hands, and I don't care who hears it.'

There was a murmur of support from the men around him, but it was a cautious murmur. Already they were too close to the yard gates and it would not do for George Bruce or Mr Fergus to hear.

'Hold your tongue,' warned Alex, looking quickly round him to see if anyone of authority was in earshot. 'Do you want to ruin everything?'

'I'll get him,' repeated Tom obstinately. He knew in his bones that Hugo Adam had been with Lizzie Lennox. Why else had he ridden with such arrogance among his own father's workmen? It could only be because he had used one of their women for his own pleasure and thought he could do so again, unchallenged and unpunished, whenever he chose. 'But I'll make him pay,' vowed Tom through clenched teeth. 'He'll not harm those who can't help themselves and get away with it. I swear it.'

'All right, Tom,' soothed Alex, 'all right. But not now. It isn't fair to Mhairi and the others. Not today, remember? Wait till we're free.' But as Tom reluctantly unloosed his fists and relaxed from the muscle-taut belligerence which had gripped him, Alex felt his own unease grow. There was something in the encounter that had escaped him. That he had half seen and not sufficiently registered. Something he ought to remember, but which, however hard he sought to recall it, still escaped him. The happiness had gone from his day, leaving uneasiness and a sense of growing threat.

In the three-man boring team, Tom swung his hammer with almost manic speed and strength so that the sparks flew dangerously far and his partner could scarcely keep up with him. When it was his turn to hold the post steady he quivered so restlessly with impatience that he put the team off their stroke. Bruce the foreman told him twice to slow down. 'I thought Mr Fergus required speed at all costs,' challenged Tom with barely concealed sarcasm.

'Then you thought wrong, lad. And the way you're going you look set to blow the lot of us sky high if you send sparks flying the length you've been doing. There's powder in these parts, remember, and fuses which I'll decide when to light, not some hammer-happy idiot of a mason newly out of his swaddling clothes.'

But it did no good. The moment Bruce had moved on, Tom resumed his frenzied hammering with redoubled vigour. Fergus Adam, inspecting the progress of the various boring teams, commended him in person for being way ahead of the others. 'Tom Diack, I believe?' said Fergus, pleased to have remembered the man's name, and pleased to have his private plans so patently approved. For, though he scarcely acknowledged it to himself, he wanted Mhairi Diack's approval, an approval which yesterday's encounter had done little to increase. He had turned the matter over and over in his mind during the night's sleepless hours, remembering her accusations, refuting them or admitting their truth, until at last he saw his way clear. Nothing could blot out Hugo's shameful conduct, of course, but at least Fergus could show her that he, unlike his brother, did not exploit his workers. He would reward excellence where he found it, and should Old Man Adam object, would point out that such a system would spur on the workforce to ever greater efforts. And the extra money which Diack would take home would show his sister that Fergus Adam was a fair-minded and generous employer. That Diack would be so rewarded had gone without saying, and now here was the man himself, proving it for all the quarry to see. Fergus could give the man a bonus with no suggestion of impropriety. 'Well done. A fine job of work.'

Tom paused, looked him coldly in the eye, gave the briefest of nods, and brought his hammer smashing down on to the boring rod with a force that almost caught his team-mates unaware and made Fergus Adam jump hastily backwards out of range.

Alex saw the exchange from across the quarry and worried afresh that Tom would spoil everything by not keeping his temper. They had planned this day down to the last detail, with Mhairi's guidance and approval, but they had not allowed for any unexpected disruption such as Hugo Adam's behaviour on the quarry path. 'See there's no trouble, lads,' Wyness had warned them, 'or I might just change my mind. I've no time for trouble-makers.' Remembering the promises they had given him, and Mhairi, Alex was tormented with anxiety that something more would happen to break Tom's fragile control. As for himself, he worried over and over at that half-remembered scrap of something which he should have noticed fully and had failed to do. He knew it was important to him, knew that if he did remember, action would be required of him, but what and where he did not know and try as he might he could not school his memory to come up with the clue. By the end of the day he was as tired and as emotionally exhausted as Tom so that when the final whistle blew and Alex, with Donal and Tom beside him, lined up with the other daily-paid workers in the office yard, the moment they had anticipated with such pleasure in the early morning of Mitchell's Court seemed overlaid with threat.

As a result, when it was Alex's turn at the office desk, he faced the foreman not with the proud cheerfulness he had planned but with barely concealed impatience. Bruce counted out the day's wages and pushed the small pile of coins across the desk. Almost before he had withdrawn his fingers, Alex scooped up the coins and dropped them into his pocket.

'Thanks,' he said, 'and goodbye. I'll not be in again.'

George Bruce looked up in surprise. 'Oh? Why is that? If it's the wages I can tell you now that Mr Fergus plans to . . .'

'It's not the wages,' interrupted Alex, 'though they're little enough to my way of thinking, and if a man has a wife and family to support then they're a downright insult. But I've served my time now, I'm bound by no contract, and if I choose to take my labour elsewhere that's my business and none of yours. I do choose.' He turned on his heel, remembered, and turned back before George Bruce had got beyond opening his mouth. Leaning forward, his two hands flat on the desk and the muscles of his biceps bulging, Alex put his face close to the foreman's and said slowly and clearly, 'And that goes for my brother, too, Mr Foreman, *sir*. He canna tell you himself, as you well know, so I'm telling you for him. He'll take his money too and goodbye.'

The foreman looked from Alex's face to that of his brother Donal and though he knew the man could neither hear nor speak, said carefully, his eyes meeting the other's and enunciating slowly, 'Is this true Donal?'

Donal nodded with a look of mingled pleasure and excitement that filled the other man with curiosity.

'Aye, it's true,' said Tom, pushing his way through the queue to stand at Alex's side. 'We've had enough of working for pittance wages day in, day out, so that other folk can lie late in their beds and pick at fancy breakfasts that would feed a working family for a week, and squander their lives away in drink and gambling and loose living.' There was a rumble of interest from the other workers behind them and more than one, 'Aye, that's right, lad. You tell him.' George Bruce half rose in his seat and bellowed, 'Quiet! Unless you all want to be sent home without your pay!' In the instant's pause that followed the door to the inner office opened and Mr Fergus appeared.

'Is there some sort of trouble, Bruce?' he asked, looking over the assembled company with a quelling and authoritative eye. Then he saw Tom, across the desk from the foreman and in the forefront of whatever dispute there had been.

'Ah, Diack,' he said, stepping forward. 'I was hoping to have a word with you. Today's drilling was excellent. Really excellent. The best I have seen. I'll be adding a bonus to your pay at the end of next week if you keep it up.'

'Thank you, Mr Fergus,' said Tom with heavy sarcasm, 'for your boundless generosity. But if it's all the same to you, I'll take what's owing to me, bonus and all, today as I'll not be here next week.'

'And why is that, may I ask?' said Fergus with all the hauteur of the son of the house, though Tom's insolent tone had darkened his face with anger. He had offered the bonus in a spirit of generosity, for the Diack girl's sake, and to have it tossed back in his face was an insult and, from one of his own workmen, an open provocation.

'You may ask, Mr Fergus, till you're blue in the face, but as I dinna work for you any more, I'm not obliged to tell you. My pay, please,' he demanded of Bruce, holding out his hand.

'Just a minute, Diack,' said Fergus, a restraining hand on the foreman's shoulder. 'You'd best keep a civil tongue in your head or you'll find yourself in the tolbooth. And before you tell me what you're obliged and not obliged to do, let me remind you that you've learned all you know in this quarry. Seven years we've taught you until you're a qualified mason, and a good one too. You owe it to Silvercairns to give back something of what you've taken.'

'I do, do I? And what do you give back, Mr Fergus Adam, for all the rock you and your family have blasted out of Silvercairns and sold to line your own pockets? Tell me that.'

'That's enough Tom, lad,' said Bruce quietly. 'Take your pay and go.' He pushed a pile of coins across the table.

'And my bonus?' demanded Tom.

'I rather think you've forfeited that,' said Fergus, keeping his temper with difficulty. Only the memory of the Diack girl's sad face and her lovely eyes kept him from striking the lad. But her brother's eyes were the same clear blue, his hair as black, and he was, after all an employee.

'Right,' said Tom. 'Then I'll just go back down the quarry and fill up those bore-holes of mine with rubble and I'll pack it down so tight it'll take three men a day at least to clear it, I promise you.' He turned to push his way through the crowd, but Fergus was at the door before him, barring his exit.

'If you do,' he said with cold fury, 'I will have you up before the circuit court for trespass and wilful damage – and assault,' he added warningly as Tom took a threatening step towards him. 'Furthermore, if you are so disloyal as to walk out of your job here, after seven years, without even a day's notice, I'll see you find no other in the whole of Aberdeenshire, and that's a promise!'

'Will you now?' said Tom coolly, looking him straight in the eye. 'Well, well, I wouldna be so free with my promises if I were you, Mr Fergus, in case I couldna keep them. As for that bonus you so patronizingly offered, you know just where you can stick it, *sir*!' He looked over his shoulder, summoned Alex and Donal with a jerk of his head and walked out of the office. This time, Fergus made no attempt to stop him.

'Right, men,' called Bruce warningly, 'back in line. We'll have no more nonsense so see you keep civil tongues in your heads or there'll be no pay tonight.' Then, to Fergus Adam, 'We're well rid of them, sir. I'll find replacements no bother, and we can't be doing with unwilling workers. They cause nothing but trouble. A pity, for young Diack's a good mason and how his sister will manage now, I dread to think. But I'm surprised at Alex Grant. I'd thought him a good, steady lad.'

Fergus Adam did not answer. Instead, he left Bruce to it and returned to the inner office, closing the door behind him. The encounter had left him angry and uneasy. He had come into the room feeling nothing but goodwill towards Tom Diack and had had his friendship thrown back in his face. But it was not only the thought of Mhairi Diack's reaction when she heard her brother had lost his job that filled him with apprehension. It was the memory of the Diack boy's face as he had said, 'Will you now?' and advised Fergus not to make promises he might not be able to keep. What had Diack meant? The uneasiness of that dinner with George Wyness, followed by yesterday's disturbing encounter with Mhairi Diack and the subsequent disruptions of the evening at Silvercairns returned to fill Fergus's thoughts with nameless foreboding and he found it impossible to bring his mind to bear on ordinary quarry business. Something was amiss in the normal order of things: something which threatened to shake the comfortable foundations of Silvercairns. Not with quarry blasting this time, though his father's relentless pursuit of profit made that daily more likely, but with something more elusive and subtle and insidiously dangerous. One phrase of the Diack boy's rang over and over in his memory, like an accusing knell: 'What do you give back, Mr Fergus Adam, for all the rock you and your family have blasted out of Silvercairns?' It was a fair question, to which Fergus could give no answer.

'You go on home,' said Tom abruptly at the gates of Silvercairns. 'You can tell Mhairi I'll not be long.'

'Where are you going?' asked Alex. 'You're not after trouble, I hope.'

'I've business to attend to,' said Tom shortly.

'If you mean Hugo Adam,' warned his friend, 'remember your promises and *leave it.*'

'I don't mean him. I mean my work here,' lied Tom.

'Oh, I see,' said Alex with obvious relief. 'You mean yon wee garden wall you were always complaining about. Then I'd best come with you and give you a hand, so we can all go home together.'

Tom neither confirmed nor denied it. Instead, he said, 'Thanks, but there's no need. It'll not take long. You go on ahead with Donal and I'll catch you up.' Then, to forestall any further interference, Tom added, 'I've finished at the quarry. Now I want to finish my work here, too.' For a moment Alex hesitated, then he shrugged, grinned, said, 'Tell Lizzie I was asking for her,' and strode off down the road towards Hirpletillam, his brother Donal at his side.

When he was sure they would not turn back and follow him, Tom hitched his tool bag higher, turned into the drive of the big house and strode purposefully for the stable yard and the kitchen regions.

He traversed the gardens by a roundabout route, lest anyone see him from the windows of the house, but he need not have worried. From the look of things they were far too occupied with packing the house up for the winter, tying chandeliers in linen bags, throwing dustsheets over sofas, packing the best silver away in boxes to be taken back to town. The scullery was empty and when he went through the inner door into the kitchen he found Lizzie elbow-deep in straw and newspaper, the greater part of a Royal Worcester dinner service for twelve heaped on the scrubbed deal table and a large packing case containing a small number of carefully wrapped articles. Lizzie looked dishevelled and cross and when Tom appeared in the doorway she snapped, 'What are you after? Can't you see I've enough to do without folk coming where they're not wanted. And before you ask, no, you can't have a free meal and a mug of ale.'

'There's only one question I want to ask, Lizzie Lennox,' said Tom quietly, crossing the room in two strides and seizing her by the forearm with fingers that dug hard into her flesh.

'You take your hands off me, Tom Diack!' she flashed. 'Or I'll scream so loud I'll split your eardrums.'

Tom ignored her. His face close to hers and his hand bruising her arm with his strength, he said softly, 'I warned you,

Lizzie. I told you what would happen. And you took no notice, did you? Last night, you were with him, weren't you?'

'Mind your own business!'

'Weren't you?'

'If you know so much about it, you tell me, though as I was in my bed in the attic with the other girls and all of us sleeping the sleep of the just it'll make a rare fairy-tale.'

'You were with him,' repeated Tom with deadly accusation, as she struggled to break free. 'I swear it.'

'Swear away if it makes you happy, you daft . . . ow! Let go my arm, you're hurting!' she cried, as loudly as she dared with Ma Gregor sure to be somewhere around, lurking and ready to pounce. She twisted and fought to struggle free, then seeing her chance, she brought up her knee hard in his groin. With an indrawn gasp of agony, his grip loosened and Lizzie broke away, darting quickly round the table to keep its solid bulk between her and her accuser.

'You bitch,' gasped Tom, bent double and grey-faced with pain.

'Serves you right,' she retorted. 'No one tells me who I can see or not see in my own time, and you'd best remember that, Tom Diack. You're not my keeper!' but she sounded less angry and after a moment added, 'Sorry, Tom, but you shouldna have hurt me.'

There was the sound of footsteps in the passageway and Ma Gregor's voice called, 'Are them plates packed yet, Lizzie? The carter's waiting and we havena got all day.'

'They'll be ready directly!' called Lizzie bundling an ill-wrapped plate into the packing case and reaching for another. 'Now look what you've done wi' your interfering,' she hissed in Tom's direction. 'You've landed me in right trouble, you have. She'll be in here any minute and me nowhere near finished.'

'Were you with him?'

'For pity's sake, Tom Diack, will you stop your pestering and leave me alone!' She edged further round the table, keeping it safely between them, before adding derisively, 'But even if I was, I'd not be likely to tell you, would I, wi' you being mad as a bull wi' jealousy for no reason that I can see. So you can take yourself off, Tom Diack, and good riddance.'

'I'll go,' said Tom, the colour coming back to his face as his pain eased, 'when you've answered my question. *Were you with him last night?*'

Suddenly, Lizzie abandoned resistance. 'Me? With that bastard?' She spoke with heart-felt venom. 'I wouldna spend a night with him if he were the last man on earth. Now are you satisfied?' Tom looked at her, wanting to believe her, seeing truth in her momentarily defenceless eyes. Then the old Lizzie was back again, fighting her running battle with life. 'And if you've any sense left in that daft head o' yours, Tom Diack, you'll go now, before Ma Gregor catches you. Oh, I know you think she fancies you, but you'd best think again. She's in a rare temper today, what wi' the packing up to do an' all.'

'Just remember what I said, Lizzie,' warned Tom, edging towards the door as he heard Ma Gregor's voice raised in some sort of altercation with the laundrymaid along the passage. 'Because if I find out he's harmed you . . .'

'Who's talking about harm?' taunted Lizzie. 'I can take care o' myself, Tom Diack, or hadn't you noticed? I've another knee where that one came from and it's him as would be harmed if he dared try anything on wi' me. Hugo Adam!' She spat derisively on to the flagstoned floor. 'It's insulting, that's what it is, suggesting I'd have anything to do with that scum.' There was genuine disgust in her voice and Tom's wavering certainty increased. Perhaps he had been wrong after all?

'Well, what are you staring at?' she challenged, hands on belligerent hips. 'Don't you believe me? I'll swear on the family bible, if you like. I'll swear if ever that Hugo Adam tries anything on wi' me, I'll give him both knees, hard, where it hurts. Does that satisfy you, Tom Diack?'

Before he could answer, there was the sound of footsteps in the passage and a grumble of approaching voices. 'Quick,' said Lizzie, in a different voice. 'You'd best go before she catches you.' She pushed him towards the outside door, but on the threshold she said, with sudden urgency, 'There's nae need to be jealous, Tom Diack. You're worth ten of him any day, ye daft loon,' and before Tom knew what was happening, she had reached up and kissed him. 'Goodbye, Tom. You've been a good friend.' Had he not known her better, he would have sworn she had tears in her eyes. But at that moment the inner door opened and without waiting to see Ma Gregor and thus plunge Lizzie into further trouble, Tom slipped quickly through the other and outside.

In the sudden quiet of the yard he stood a moment, collecting his turbulent thoughts. Lizzie Lennox had sworn with every semblance of truth that he was wrong about Hugo Adam and her. And she had kissed him. Freely, out of the blue and for no reason. He was reminded of the night of the Queen's birthday when he had rescued her, against her will, from Hugo Adam and later they had kissed and laughed and forgotten Adam in their own enjoyment. But with that memory came others: her annoyance that Tom had done her out of a champagne supper, the way she had hung on the fellow's arm, smiling up at him. She had been happy enough to let the fellow touch her then. But now she swore she wouldn't let him near her. So what had happened between them? Something had, he was sure of it. Whatever Lizzie said to the contrary, he felt it in the marrow of his bones, knew it with every breath he drew. Had seen it that very morning in the arrogance of the fellow's face. Maybe Lizzie could take care of herself, when she chose, but suppose there had been times when she had not chosen? Suppose the fellow had beguiled her with his promises of champagne suppers and the like? Given her presents? And then grown tired of her? That would explain her venom now. Lizzie had always had a taste for pretty things.

And yet, she had offered to swear on the bible: no mean undertaking from a child of Bible Lennox. If Lizzie swore such a sacred oath, then even Lizzie's word was to be believed. Gradually Tom's tension relaxed. Perhaps he had been wrong after all? Had let his imagination run away with him? Had been making excuses for his own dislike of the fellow?

He was making his way across the stable yard towards the gardens when he heard the scullery door open behind him and Ma Gregor's voice raised in anger. 'I tell't ye *two* dozen eggs, ye daft quine. And when you've fetched them, mind and slice that ham for Mr Hugo's supper. Though with him in such disgrace wi' his father, there's no saying he'll be allowed any.'

There was more that he did not catch, but he had heard enough. Mr Hugo was in disgrace. The whole town knew that Old Man Adam and his younger son did not get on and that periodically sparks flew. But Old Man Adam still held the purse strings and young Mr Hugo had no choice but to obey. Afterwards, the town always knew it for Mr Hugo would take out his frustration, indiscriminately, on anything and anyone who got in his way. Remembering the scene in the lane that morning, Tom's brow finally cleared. So that was the explanation! Nothing to do with Lizzie at all.

Mind you, that did not excuse the fellow's high-handedness. He had no business to ride through his father's workmen, scattering them in his path like so many terrified sheep. But he, Tom Diack, was no longer one of the meek herd. He was his own man now and by God, he vowed, the next time he met Hugo Adam face to face, he would pay him back if it was the last thing he did. As he remembered how Hugo Adam had deliberately raised his whip to thrash Tom out of his way that very morning – he could feel the weal even now, sore against the rough cloth of his shirt – a thought occurred to him and he stood still, in the stable yard, looking around him. If the horse he sought was here, then the owner would be also and Tom was in the mood for tying up loose ends.

But the end stall was empty, the chestnut horse with the white starred forehead nowhere to be seen. It would be fruitless to wait. Ma Gregor had mentioned 'supper' but that could be at any hour and already he was late. But he'd not forget. Oh, no. Nor would he forget Mr Fergus's arrogance. The Adam family had a lot to answer for, one way and another, and one day, he vowed, he would see that they did answer for it. But not tonight, he admitted with regret. Tonight, he'd best go home and bide his time. Besides Mhairi would be worrying. She'd planned a special supper, to celebrate.

Tom was striding homewards through the gardens in the lengthening shadows of evening, making no attempt this time to keep out of sight, when he came across Lettice Adam near the doocot summer-house. She was apparently alone. Deliberately he ignored her, and made to go on his way but she called out, 'Stop. I'd like your advice on the summer-house. I see a new crack has appeared in the wall and it doesn't look at all safe. Have you a minute to look at it?'

Tom stopped, turned, looked at her steadily for a long

moment, then said with no trace of the deference due from a servant to a master, 'Miss Lettice, do you really want to show me a crack in a wall, or are you just finding excuses to keep me about the place so you can giggle with your friends behind my back and talk about my muscles? A working man is as good as a zoo animal for the likes of you, isn't he? And if you can watch his muscles, which I'll warrant you never see on your own peely-wally menfolk, and give yourself a daring little thrill at the same time, so much the better. I've seen you spying on me, waiting for me to strip the shirt off my back in the heat, hoping I'll take off my trousers too, no doubt, while you pretend to be lady of the manor, all innocence, picking flowers.'

'How dare you speak to me like that!' she gasped, while the blush spread upwards to engulf her face.

'I dare,' he said, 'because it's the plain truth. Deny it if you can. And before you go running to your father to have me sacked, I don't work for him any longer, nor for you. And to show you I'm as free a man as your own brother, I reckon I'll take a leaf out of his book.' Before she realized what he was going to do he had pulled her roughly towards him and kissed her, hard, on the lips. She struggled briefly, then stopped struggling as those muscular arms held her tight, crushed her breasts against the pounding strength of his chest, pressed her hips hard against his till she felt every intimate part of him as close against her own privacies as if they had both been naked. When he eventually pushed her away from him, saying, 'That's something else for you to giggle with your friends about,' she did not scream for help, as she had fully meant to do, but stood trembling with shock and arousal and uncertainty, waiting for she hardly knew what. But he merely swung his tool bag on to his shoulder, turned his back and strode on his way, whistling. That whistle told her as clearly as any words could have done that he considered her not worth a second thought.

How dare he! She was Lettice Adam, heiress of Silvercairns, and he was an impudent *nobody*. He should be grovelling abjectly at her feet. Remembering what he had said, and done, she blushed afresh with mortification. Nevertheless she watched until his powerful figure strode on past the summer-house and turned the corner out of sight. Then, stamping out the shameful excitement his kiss had aroused and which still quivered annoyingly inside her, she retrieved what was left of her dignity and made her way back to the house. There was no need to mention the incident to anyone else. It had been disgraceful, of course. There was no question of that. But understandable. Afte all, she was a most attractive young woman. Though that might explain his impertinence, it did not, of course, excuse it. But to bring the matter to her father's attention would only add to her humiliation and would do no good. Besides, the fellow had said himself that he had lost his job at Silvercairns so he could not be punished that way, and her father had worries enough on his plate at the moment. It might be best just to forget the incident. After all, they were to return to the town house in the morning. Ainslie Sharp had tickets for the theatre.

Suddenly she saw in vivid contrast Ainslie's pale, cold elegance and Tom Diack's rough-cut strength. He had surprisingly blue eyes, she remembered, and his skin had been firm and warm . . . Impatiently she pushed memory aside. He had behaved outrageously. She ought to report him to her father. Or to Ainslie? If she did, she wondered idly, what would Ainslie do? She could not imagine him squaring up to Tom Diack, man to man. No, he would be more likely to hire someone else to do it for him, so as not to soil his own beautifully manicured hands. Or to have the man arrested on some devious, trumped-up charge. Or would he merely ignore the whole thing as beneath his notice? Probably that, thought Lettice with disappointment. And, of course, he would be right. To ignore the incident was much the most dignified thing to do. Dignified, but unsatisfying.

Then she remembered: Ainslie himself had insulted her just as deeply and in public, and must not be allowed to forget it. It was out of the question to mention the Diack incident to him, had she ever seriously considered it. But the Diack incident, as she chose to call it, seemed wholesome and honest compared to Ainslie Sharp's cold-blooded calculation. Remembering George Wyness's revelations at her ill-fated dinner party, and Sharp's suave attempts to re-establish himself in her favour, she vowed to make Ainslie Sharp earn every minute of her company, twice over.

By the time she reached the terrace her self-possession was almost restored. She even stood a moment on the steps, admiring the way the setting sun splashed the sky to the west with vermilion and dying gold behind a tracery of autumn trees. The windows of the west wing cast back the colours in many panes of reflected light and her own shadow lay long across the grass. Below the terrace she could see the colourless patch of her croquet lawn and the dark line of the wall the Diack man had built. It was beautifully made. But then his hands were firm and sure. Abruptly, she turned her back, mounted the last step and walked briskly along the terrace towards the steps. The night air was chill and her father would be waiting, no doubt impatiently, for the cold meat she had ordered for their last night in Silvercairns. She hoped to goodness Hugo would have the sense not to be late home.

Tom was half-way down the track to Hirpletillam when he heard the horse – a single distant horseman, but approaching fast, the hoof-beats sharp in the night silence. He stopped, listened and, as he listened, felt a surge of excitement, heady as wine. Whoever it was, was coming in this direction and, apart from the forge, the track led only to Silvercairns and the quarry. Swiftly, in memory, Tom ran his eye over the stables: Hugo's horse had not been there but yes, he was almost certain, the huge black beast which carried Old Man Adam had been tethered in its stall. That left Mr Fergus and he, it was common knowledge, walked between quarry and house, unless of course he went on business into town. But Tom had had that brush with him in the quarry office only this evening. It might be a visitor, of course. Or the minister. Tom listened, ears straining into the evening stillness, and as he listened the hoof-beat changed, scrambled for a moment, then resumed more slowly, in a different, broken key. The animal must havc stumbled and cast a shoe. And if that was the case, then, if the rider had the smallest sense, he would stop at Hirpletillam.

Tom could continue down the track to the forge and see for himself whether the rider was Hugo Adam. But there would be others at the forge and Tom wanted to beard Adam alone. He had an old score to settle, not concerning Lizzie Lennox now, though she had been the initial cause of that encounter in the Castlegate, but on his own account. Remembering Hugo's mockery when they had come to fetch poor Fanny Wyness from the garden and the morning's sting of that whip across his shoulders, Tom felt anger swell his chest and his heart beat hard and strong. In the garden of Silvercairns he would have throttled Hugo Adam had not the man been surrounded by friends to protect him and, no doubt, hand Tom over to the police for assault. But tonight the horseman was alone and Tom was a free man, bound by no loyalty to his employer, held in check by no fear of dismissal. It was a chance too good to miss. He would confront Hugo Adam man to man, in fair fight, with no bystanders to interfere or summon the law, and he would win.

At the prospect, Tom forgot Alex, Mhairi, his promises, everything. At the forge, Hugo Adam would demand instant attention, but if there was a piece of work already on the anvil even he would have to wait. And so would Tom. He would wait until Hugo Adam rode up the track to Silvercairns. With a slow smile of anticipation, Tom cast around for a suitable place in which to keep his solitary vigil.

'I'm worried,' said Mhairi anxiously when day had given way to twilight and still Tom had not come home. 'Where can he be?'

Alex was worried, too, though he tried not to show it. 'I expect he's finishing off that wall he's always complaining about, at Silvercairns.'

'In the dark?'

'Aye, well . . . But he was going there first. We left him at the gate. I expect he's celebrating his freedom, at Ma Gibbs' or somewhere,' he said lightly.

'Without you?' The simple question went straight to his heart and set it beating hard with sudden fear. They had looked forward with such happy expectation to this evening. He stood up with careful unconcern.

'Likely he met some of the lads on the way home,' he said. 'I'll take a wee look, if you like. Coming, Donal?' With a jerk of the head he summoned his brother from the fireside, where he was engaged in a complicated game of cat's cradle with Annys.

'Reckon we'll come too,' said Lorn and Willy together, but Mhairi put a swift stop to that idea. 'You'll stay here with me, where you belong,' she said, and added, 'Remember Mr Wyness said he might look in, if he'd the time?' Above their heads her anxious eyes met Alex's.

'Don't worry, lass,' he said, reassuringly. 'We'll not be long. And we'll bring that feckless brother of yours back with us, won't we, Donal?' But Tom was not feckless, as they both knew.

Outside in the close it was almost dark, shadowed on all sides by high tenement walls, but once they reached the open street the sky lightened to a twilit paleness in which the first stars shone. There were no clouds and once the moon rose, it would be bright enough. As they passed the doorway of the Lemon Tree Donal plucked his brother's sleeve, but Alex shook his head. He knew the unspoken question, but he also knew that Tom was not inside. He remembered the turmoil of the morning on the road to Silvercairns, Tom's anger and his vows of revenge, though what the cause was Alex did not know. But it was more than the arrogance of young Adam's morning behaviour, he was sure. Remembering Tom's evasive answer when they had parted earlier that evening at the gates of Silvercairns, Alex's anxiety increased. He lengthened his stride and with a jerk of the head and a few quick gestures of the hand, indicated to Donal the road they must take.

They were almost at the smithy when they came upon a pony and trap, in obvious difficulty, for a young woman on foot was leading the horse and the trap lurched drunkenly after, the pale beam of its lantern casting wild and uncoordinated arcs over the twilit hedgerows. She turned her head at the sound of approaching footsteps and they saw that it was Flora Burnett, now Flora Dunn.

'Hello, Donal,' she cried, with obvious pleasure. 'How lovely to see you after all this time. Your brother', she added, turning to Alex with a smile, 'has been most remiss in visiting us. He promised my husband he would call often and we have not seen him for at least a month.'

Donal blushed and looked down at his boots, while Alex made suitable excuses before saying, 'But, Mrs Dunn, you are obviously in trouble. Is it the axle?'

'I don't know for certain, but I fear so. The roads are really so uneven and the dry spell has made them worse, if anything. I suppose it was my fault but we went over a stone and something cracked. I am not sure what, but one of the wheels seems decidedly unsafe. I thought it better to walk after that, especially as the smithy is not far.'

'Let me . . .' began Alex, but Donal had already taken the leading rein from Flora Dunn and soothed the pony with a hand on its neck before urging the animal forward again.

'Donal is so good with horses,' said Flora, 'and not only that. He is a most talented draughtsman. My husband believes he will go far.'

'Aye,' said Alex, pleased. 'He has a rare skill with the pencil.'

'You should see he gets the chance to develop it, Alex – I hope you don't mind me calling you that? – and not spend his life in the stable, good though he is . . . But enough of that. What brings you this way at this time of the evening when you should be at home, round the fire? Surely Mungo Adam has not initiated *night* working?'

'No.' Then, on a rush, he confided, 'We are looking for Tom. He had a wee job to finish at the big house, but he should have been home by now and Mhairi's worried. You have not passed him on the road?'

Flora shook her head. 'No. And I have come all the way from Union Grove. Charity committees are worthy enough, in their way, but so time-consuming. I can't help feeling there is work to do here, at home, before interfering in the tribal customs of remote African tribes who I doubt will appreciate flannel petticoats anyway and will certainly not be able to read bible tracts, but of course it is heresy to say as much, especially if you are a minister's wife, so please don't repeat it.' She smiled with engaging honesty before continuing, 'But about Tom, don't worry. I expect he is enjoying a glass of ale and a slab of fortifying cake in Mrs Gregor's kitchen.'

'Yes,' agreed Alex with relief. He had not thought of that.

'And giving little Lizzie Lennox all the news from home.'

Again Alex agreed, while the taut knot of anxiety loosed inside him and he began to relax. But he could not help wondering at the scope of Mrs Dunn's knowledge. She had the air of knowing everything about everybody, not in any gossiping and malicious way, but with a kindly, maternal interest, as if she cared for their welfare. But of course, they were in her husband's parish, and the manse not five hundred yards away, behind the smithy.

'If it would help,' offered Alex, on an impulse, 'I will wait with the pony and trap till the damage is repaired and bring it home for you. I expect you are anxious to be back at the manse.'

'Would you? I would be so grateful. I am rather late and I would hate Hamish to worry on my account, though on a clear and pleasant night like this there is really no need. And you must both come in and have a cup of tea and a slice of cake.'

Then she was gone, turning once at the corner of the manse lane to wave to them, before disappearing behind the shadowed hedgerow.

Briefly Alex regretted his impulse, but only briefly. He could watch the road from Silvercairns just as well from the smithy and, after all, Mrs Dunn was probably right. Tom often called in the Silvercairns kitchen after work: he said Ma Gregor's scones were as good as Mhairi's and the Silvercairns ale a rare treat after the dry dust of the quarry. Besides, he had suspected for some time that Tom was interested in Lizzie and what more natural than that he should visit her in the Silvercairns kitchen when he had the chance? As he helped the smith unharness the pony and dismantle the trap enough to get at the broken part he forgot his worry in the pleasure of watching a skilled craftsman tackle a challenging task. The metal joint which connected wheel to axle had buckled and the smith decided it would be safest to fashion a new one. Alex was watching him at work, teasing and hammering the molten metal into shape, Donal on sentry watch, with Mrs Dunn's pony, in the yard, when he heard a horseman approaching from the direction of Aberdeen. The smith heard it too, cocked a practised ear, said, 'Cast a shoe and the bastard still riding her. No prizes for guessing who that is,' before resuming his task.

Hugo Adam had had an unspeakably tedious and worthy day, spent, as his father had ordered, at Marischal College. Now he was dyspeptic with Latin phrases and Greek verbs, his head a whirl of jarring gibberish, and his brain tired with the effort of keeping awake. His whole body ached for the solace of the Lemon Tree, for wine and women and laughter and the convivial company of his racing friends. Instead he was under orders to ride home to dine at Silvercairns, under the frowning eye of his cantankerous old father. After the dry dust of scholarship he would have given almost anything for a pint of good claret and a hot mutton pie in the first rowdy hostelry he came to: but he knew his father's spies were everywhere and it was not worth the risk.

Money, he thought moodily, as he turned his horse's head, none too gently, to the west. It all came down to money, and at the moment he had none. Less than none, if you counted all his debts, and whereas he preferred to forget them, others unfortunately didn't. It was no good touching his father, not for a while anyway. Have to give the old goat time to recover and forget. Not that he ever did forget. Last night, for instance, he had dragged up every misdemeanour of Hugo's entire life, including that broken church window when he was a boy of seven and the dead fish he'd nailed under Lettice's dinner table once, for a joke. Trouble with the old man was that he had no sense of humour. Though, to be fair, Hugo had to admit that the Lennox business was something different.

He was sorry about that. She was a spirited baggage, that one, full of fun and energy. He meant her no harm, but she must have known what the risks were and she had been as willing as they come. Forward even. It wasn't his fault if he had no money to give her when she needed it. If he'd been able to he'd have given her fifty guineas and willingly, poor lass. But he owed ten times that and more, with no hope of repaying any of it unless the old man forked out. It wasn't fair, with the quarry earning thousands. The old man could pay off Hugo's debts for him, no bother, and not notice the difference, but instead he hectored and bullied and lectured and kept Hugo on a rein so short it practically strangled him. And now his whole day was planned out for him down to the hour he was to arrive home for dinner. An hour which, he noticed with a twinge of alarm as he drew the hunter from his waistcoat pocket, glanced at it and dropped it back again, was drawing all too close. He dug heels into flanks to urge his horse faster. It would not do to antagonize the old man further, not if he hoped, as he still hoped, to draw his quarterly allowance in two weeks' time.

It was at that morose point in his musings that his horse stumbled and cast a shoe. When Hugo's repertoire of oaths had been exhausted he glanced around him to judge how far he was from home. Too far. The buildings of Aberdeen lay behind him; even the newest houses in the West End, with their neatly laid gardens, were out of sight and all around were fields and hedgerows and here and there a clump of bare trees. It must be half a mile to the smithy and a half mile further after that. There was nothing for it but to press on to Hirpletillam and rouse the blacksmith. At least at this hour the furnace would still be hot.

He rode on, lopsidedly, past the well at Stony town, the nursery gardens, the stepping stones at the Denburn, until at last he saw the low huddle of cottages at Hirpletillam, dark against the evening sky, and the red glow of the forge.

Alex was suddenly watchful, every sense alert. He moved nearer the doorway, though still in the shadows, to where he could see Donal, standing patiently in the yard at the manse pony's side just beyond the path of light cast by the smithy door. Something in Donal's stance warned Alex of trouble: his brother stood straight-backed and still, his feet slightly apart, one hand flat against the warm flank of the pony, but the other . . . Even from where he stood Alex could see the clenched fist. It was the only sign of tension, but it was enough.

The horseman turned into the yard, dismounted, saw Donal, and called, 'Hey, you! Get my horse shod – at the double.'

'Take over, will you, Alex,' said the blacksmith in a low voice, 'and leave this to me.' He stood squarely in the doorway and said, 'You'll have to wait, sir.' He was a big man, red-faced and burly, the smith's hammer swinging loosely in one hand. Behind him, the furnace quivered with heat where Alex was feeding it metal held in a pair of long-handled tongs. The smith spoke civilly enough, but with a dogged obstinacy in his voice which Hugo knew of old. 'I'll not be long, Mr Hugo. Just fixing this piece for Mrs Dunn's trap, then I'll be with you. Can't leave hot metal when I'm working it.'

'Well, see you work fast,' growled Hugo and turned away, striking the glossy leather of his riding boot with an impatient crop.

'Thanks, Alex,' said the smith, taking over the tongs, and

with a jerk of the head towards Hugo Adam, said, 'Take his horse, lad, afore he does it further harm.'

For some minutes Hugo strode to and fro in the yard, muttering impatiently to himself, while Alex hovered watchful in the doorway and Donal continued to stand motionless at the manse pony's side. As if feeling the force of their twin stares, Hugo whirled suddenly and shouted, 'What are you staring at? Keep your eyes to yourself, or . . .' but at that moment the blacksmith emerged with the hissing piece of metal held in a pair of tongs. 'Right,' he said. 'If you'll take this, Alex lad, and fix it for me when it's cooled, I'll see to this gentleman's horse.' He straddled the animal's fetlock and brought the hoof up smartly between his knees, for inspection, then tutted with disapproval. 'Poor beast. Should never have been ridden with a cast shoe, but then some folk have no consideration for dumb animals.' Hugo ignored him, knowing that for the moment the man had the upper hand, and watched in frowning silence as he applied bellows to the furnace and prepared to shape the metal shoe.

Outside in the yard, in the light of a hanging lantern for the twilight had faded almost to night now, Alex and Donal worked together, also in silence, to reassemble the wheel and axle, though Alex kept a wary eye on the forge for Hugo Adam. And another on the road to Silvercairns. He had half feared that Tom had gone in search of Mr Hugo, to settle whatever private grievance he harboured against him. But as long as Hugo Adam was here, that fear at least was allayed.

It took some twenty minutes to fix the wheel to their satisfaction, then they had to position the pony between the shafts and check the harness and finally to lead the animal to and fro to check that the wheels ran smoothly. By the time they had finished, and Alex breathed a satisfied, 'That's it, then,' the blacksmith was hammering the last nail into the Adam horse's shoe.

Hugo Adam swung into the saddle with grudging thanks and no payment. 'Chalk it to the account,' he called over his shoulder as he moved out of the lantern-lit yard and into the darkness beyond. The sharp clop of hoof on cobbles turned to the duller thud of hard-packed earth as horse and rider disappeared westward on the narrow road to Silvercairns.

'Aye, and I'll not see payment this side of Christmas,' grumbled the blacksmith. 'Not like the minister. He may have only a tenth of the Adam wealth, but he settles his bills, no bother. Not like that one. I hope he has the sense to walk that poor animal home. It's a dark and stony path to Silvercairns.'

At the blacksmith's words, a new and awful apprehension gripped Alex and he knew with blinding certainty where Tom was and what he meant to do. The fool. The stupid, reckless fool. Adam was on horseback and what chance had Tom had this morning against him? A man on a horse would always triumph over . . . Then out of nowhere came the memory that had eluded him all day. 'A man on a horse,' Annys had said, all those months ago. And this morning, when Hugo Adam had raised his whip to strike Tom, Donal had flinched as if from long experience . . . He thought of his brother's clenched fist, not half an hour ago, and his unnatural stillness, and knew beyond doubt that he was right. Anger surged inside him till he thought he would split open with the power of it. He turned to his brother, and said with slow intensity, 'Go to the manse. Wait for me there.'

When Donal shook his head in protest, Alex turned him round to face the manse path, put the pony's reins in his hand and pushed him hard between the shoulders. He watched until he was sure Donal would obey, then with a brief nod to the blacksmith, strode out of the smithy yard. The moment he was beyond the lantern's reach, he broke into a run and, fuelled by righteous fury, sped through the night shadows after that unsuspecting horseman.

Tom stood so still in the darkness that a pair of young rabbits grazed, fearless, around his feet. Overhead autumn leaves stirred and whispered against the night sky and every now and then one broke off and drifted silently to join its fellows on the dying grass. Tom's eyes ached with straining into the darkness of the Hirpletillam road, his ears with listening for the thud of hoofs. His neck muscles were tense with waiting, the knuckles of his clenched hands white in the surrounding darkness. Slowly he spread his hands and flexed the fingers to bring feeling back into them. Was that the sound of a horse? One of the rabbits pricked its ears and froze, round eyes swivelling in fear. The other, more cocksure, munched on. Tom could hear the tearing of the dry grass. And beyond it . . . surely . . . hoof-beats? Somewhere in the distance a barn owl mourned into the eerie twilight. Then suddenly, from the direction of Hirpletillam, a dog barked. That would be the collie at the last of the cottages. Possibly barking at nothing? Or at the moon, which had just risen above the trees to cast long shadows over the path? Or at . . .? Yes. He let out his pent breath in a long soft sigh of satisfaction as he heard the muffled thud of hoof on turf and felt the ground quiver under his feet.

The last stretch of the path to the gates of Silvercairns was crowded with shadows from the trees on either side. Black, tangled shadows, thick with treachery, bracken and thorn and bramble hiding a thousand watchful eyes, creatures small and silent, others larger and predatory, night creatures, waiting . . . Hugo Adam, who had ridden the path countless times and on blacker nights than this, though usually so inebriated as to be immune to fear, felt an unwelcome shiver of alarm. It would be Hallowe'en in a couple of days. 'From ghoulies and ghosties and long-leggedy beasties, and things that go bump in the night . . .' The words came unbidden into his mind from some childhood memory just as his horse, high-stepping with reined-in energy, twitched nervous ears, tossed its well-bred head against the restricting halter and rolled a wary, watchful eye.

'Steady, old fellow, steady,' soothed Hugo, leaning forward in the saddle to pat the powerful, muscle-rippling neck.

At that precise moment something moved in the shadows beside the road. The startled horse reared, danced on its back legs, pummelled the air with its front hoofs, plunged, reared again, and had not Hugo Adam been an accomplished horseman he would have been flung from the saddle there and then. As it was he clung on, wrenched the horse's head round, dug in his heels and yelling 'Thieves!' drove the animal at a terrified gallop back the way he had come. Alex, still fired by fury at Hugo Adam's treatment of his brother, saw the horse emerge from the blackness ahead and bear thundering down on him. Fearing to lose his chance of revenge, instead of scrambling out of the way, he shouted, 'Stop, you bastard!' and leapt for the reins. It was hard to say exactly what happened in the next few seconds – except that the horse shied, whinnying with terror, hoofs flaying the air, then plunged again, snorting, before breaking free and thundering down the track towards the forge, leaving one man sailing through the air in a graceful arc, to fall with a sickening thud beyond the hedge, and the other inert and bleeding on the ground.

Donal was bending, weeping, over his brother when Tom ran panting from the darkness. 'Oh, God, what happened?' he gasped. 'I didn't do anything – I just stepped into the road and then . . . Oh, God, God, what will Mhairi say if . . .' But Donal pushed past him with a face of anguished desolation and sped back down the track, past the forge, round the corner, and up the short, hedge-lined path to the manse where he thundered with frenzied ardour at the door until Hamish Dunn himself opened it.

They were lifting Alex tenderly into the newly mended dog-cart when a dishevelled and dirt-streaked figure pushed his unsteady way through the thicket hedge, and lurched, swearing into the road. 'God, my head . . .' he groaned, then he shook like a dog emerging from a river, straightened, looked about him, shook his head once more to clear it, and saw Tom.

'You! I might have known. But I've got you this time, you scum. Attempted robbery with violence on the Queen's highway and murder, near as dammit. I could have been killed. And a valuable horse ruined into the bargain. It's the tolbooth for you, fellow, and if I have my way you'll be lucky to get away with transportation. Hanging is all the likes of you are fit for and for two pins I'd string you up myself from the nearest tree. Now.'

'I think not,' said Hamish Dunn quietly. 'You would be wiser to lie down. You have had a shock and should rest at least until morning. I have sent already for a doctor and would suggest you allow me to convey you to my house to await his arrival. My wife will make you as comfortable as possible.'

'Did you send for a police officer too? No, I thought not,' said Hugo with heavy sarcasm. 'Then allow me to do so for you. You!' He addressed the blacksmith who, with several of the neighbouring villagers had appeared on the scene. 'Fetch the town guard. I want this villain clapped in the tolbooth, tonight! You,' he ordered, turning to another of the bystanders, 'fetch a rope and tie him securely.' Then for the first time he noticed Alex, insensible in the dog-cart. 'A-ha! An accomplice. I'll have him in irons, too, before the night is out. Well, what are you waiting for?' he shouted as the small group of villagers stood silent and unmoving. 'You heard what I said, didn't you? Then jump to it, or I'll personally flay the hides off the lot of you!'

The crowd shifted uneasily, looking from Hugo Adam to their minister, obviously waiting for instruction.

'Stay where you are, all of you,' said the minister quietly. 'We have an injured man here whose life surely takes priority over any imagined injustice.'

'Imagined?' roared Hugo, and clutched his head as a shaft of pain shot through it at the sound. 'I was ambushed, I tell you. Set on by these two villains. That one', he went on, pointing at Tom,' threatened me only this morning, before witnesses, and this blackguard', he sneered, prodding Alex's body with the toe of his riding boot, 'was with him.'

Donal Grant, who had been crouching anxiously over his brother, half rose with a threatening gesture and the minister laid a restraining hand on his shoulder.

'Perhaps, Mr Adam,' he said calmly, 'but that was this morning. It is tonight that concerns me, and the life of this poor young man. You are understandably overwrought, and no doubt still suffering from that bang on the head, and delirium can carry anyone into the realms of fancy and cloud the judgement. Tomorrow will be time enough to . . .'

'Realms of fancy?' roared Hugo. 'Cloud the judgement? How dare you, sir. That villain is a murderer,' he cried, jabbing his riding crop in Tom's direction, 'and his loutish friend's another. I'll see them both on the scaffold if it's the last thing I do.'

'There are laws of slander, Mr Adam,' said Hamish Dunn calmly, 'and I suggest you remember that before destroying a man's name on no evidence and before witnesses. All of us here,' he said with a meaningful glance over the company, 'will take note that you have suffered a blow to the head and are not well.'

'I am perfectly well, sir, and I . . .' but at that moment Flora Dunn came hurrying up the track, a folded blanket in her arms.

'Ah, Flora my dear,' interrupted the minister with relief. 'Is everything ready?'

'Yes, Hamish. And the doctor will be at the manse directly.'

'Then if you will tuck that rug under Alex's head to steady it, we will go. It really would be wise for you to come too, Mr Adam,' he went on, looking gravely at Hugo. 'Head injuries are notoriously deceptive, and you must guard against concussion.'

Before Hugo Adam could begin to answer this infuriating advice, someone appeared on the road from the forge, leading a horse by the reins, a chestnut horse, lathered with sweat and with a white star on the forehead. Hugo Adam strode forward, pushing indiscriminately through the crowd, snatched the reins from the man's hand and swung up into the saddle. 'Keep your advice for your friends, minister. They'll need it. For I promise you I will see those two on a convict ship to Van Diemen's Land if it's the last thing I do.' Then he swung his horse's head westward and rode off into the darkness of the Silvercairns road.

It was the longest evening of Mhairi's life as she waited in her tenement room, knowing in her bones that something was wrong, yet trying with all her brave self-possession to convince her younger brothers and Annys that it was not, to assure them that it was natural for Tom and Alex to stay away when the special meal she had prepared for them lay uneaten on the table, to pretend that the family celebration they had talked of all week was nothing really and could wait. When George Wyness looked in as he had promised, she assured him with almost convincing cheerfulness that Tom and Alex were out in town 'enjoying themselves' and would be back 'oh . . . sometime,' and she had given a bleak, indulgent little laugh. Wyness had been puzzled, then, remembering Alex's confidences about the less-than-welcome baby, had decided there must have been some trivial lovers' tiff and with a brisk, 'I'll be on my way then. Tell them both to look in and see me at the yard tomorrow, early,' had shrugged off unease. They were only lads, after all, and what more natural after seven years' slavery than to celebrate the tossing off of the Adam yoke? Especially as very soon they would be under a different, if less tyrannical, one somewhere else.

But Mhairi knew it was not natural. Today was to have been the happiest of her life, of Tom's and Alex's too, and they had planned to celebrate together. Oh, God, she prayed over and over inside her head, keep them safe, don't let anything dreadful happen, please, please bring them home. But they did not come home. She fed the younger ones, tidied, washed dishes, made up the fire, busied herself with any household jobs she could think of, however small, and when she could find no more, took out her sewing. But the soft, clean material gave her none of her usual pleasure, not even when she put aside the work for the Ladies' Working and took out her own: a tiny garment in fine cotton, made from off-cuts from Miss Roberts' shop. Oh, Ma, she cried, inside her head, what shall I do if Alex does not come back? They were not married yet, and her unborn child three months grown. Soon it would show. At the thought of what her neighbours' comments would be, in particular those of Lizzie's father, up the stair, Mhairi bit her lip with shame. But very soon they would be married. Alex had promised her and now . . . Oh, God, where was he? And where was Tom? If she lost them both . . . The idea almost stopped her heart. How could she keep Lorn and Willy and Annys and her own unborn child on money from the Ladies' Working? The poorhouse loomed huge and threatening in her frenzied imaginings and she bit her lip hard to keep back hysteria. It would be all right. It must be. They were with friends somewhere, drinking. That was all. But *please, please, God, keep them safe.*

It was long after Mhairi, almost distraught with anxiety, had put Annys to bed and persuaded Lorn and Willy reluctantly to follow when Hamish Dunn arrived at her door with the news: Alex was lying injured and unconscious at the manse, and her brother Tom was in the town jail.

Hugo Adam, true to his threat and with his irate father's full backing, had summoned the police and accused Tom Diack and Alex Grant of attempted robbery with violence. He had also brought a charge of causing grievous bodily harm.

Tom denied both charges. He was no robber and the only harm Hugo Adam had suffered had been caused by his own horse. In answer to all questions he said he was walking home late because he had been finishing a job at the big house. Yes, he had his bag of tools with him, yes, it contained a mason's hammer and a sharp-pointed chisel, no, he had not opened it or intended to use either on Mr Adam. Yes, he had been waiting in the trees beside the path. Why shouldn't he be? He had heard the horse coming and was waiting for it to pass. It was a narrow road, especially after dark. No, he had not assaulted Mr Adam, but, he muttered injudiciously, he wished he had. Nor had he lunged at Mr Adam's horse. Something, a rabbit perhaps, had startled the animal and it had bolted. That was all. It had been none of his doing. Nor had he known that Alex was there.

As for Alex, he was in no condition as yet either to answer questions or to go to jail. But when he was, thought Mhairi with bleak dispair, he, like Tom, would be required to do both.

'It is disgraceful,' said Aunt Blackwell complacently, drawing a purple silk embroidery thread through the canvas petal of a pansy. She and Lettice were in the drawing-room after dinner, awaiting the arrival of the menfolk. They had been waiting half an hour already but as Ainslie Sharp was one of the guests and the contract was not yet signed, thought Lettice sourly, they would no doubt be required to wait as long again. Mr Sharp had a long way to go yet before he won his way back into Lettice's favour and she meant to give him no help.

'A man cannot ride home up his own drive these days without fear of armed robbery,' continued Aunt Blackwell. 'I don't know what the country is coming to.'

'Nonsense,' snapped Lettice with the irritation of a tortured conscience. 'They were not armed and there was no robbery that I have heard of.'

'Really!' gasped Aunt Blackwell in affront. 'The impertinence.'

'No, Aunt Blackwell, not impertinence,' cried Lettice, leaping to her feet and pacing the room in exasperation. 'Just the plain truth. I thought that was what was required by the legal system of our country. The truth, the whole truth and nothing but the truth, and it is the plain and screaming truth for anyone with the wits to see it that those two men were unarmed and stole nothing.'

'Really!' said Aunt Blackwell again, fanning herself weakly with an ivory fan. 'To hear you speak, Lettice, anyone would think you were their accomplice.'

'No. Merely someone who values the truth, as too many people hereabouts fail to do.' And Lettice slammed out of the room. Aunt Blackwell could entertain the menfolk, Ainslie Sharp included, if they ever deigned to come to the drawing-room and if her father complained of her absence, then let him. Lettice was going to bed.

In the privacy of her bedroom she stood a long time at the window, looking down the long sweep of the drive into the autumn darkness and arguing over and over in her mind, as she had done ever since this appalling affair began, whether she should speak out or not. Hugo was her brother and she was fond of him but she knew better than anyone that he was no saint, and though he was a firm disciple of expediency, truth was an altogether different matter. He said they attacked him, said they laid in wait in the road for that express purpose. They said they did nothing of the kind. One was working late and the other came to look for him: a perfectly innocent explanation which others would corroborate, certainly on Alex Grant's side. As for Tom . . . Here Lettice hesitated uneasily. Surely someone else must have seen him as well as she?

There was the rub. Out of the most secret corner of her mind where she had firmly suppressed it came the memory of Hamish Dunn's voice on that humiliating occasion saying, 'Beneath that brittle exterior there is an honest, honourable and loving woman,' and urging her to remember before it was too late. And however much she denied it, hated and despised him for saying it, squirmed still with remembered shame, deep in her heart she knew he was right.

She remembered Tom Diack in the garden when he had kissed her. A shocking impertinence, but again, if she was honest, deep in her heart she did not condemn him for it. She had . . . Yes, she told herself bravely with the first small lesson in honesty, she had enjoyed it. He was a simple man, straightforward and open. Not like that smooth-tongued Ainslie Sharp with his disdainful manner and his gloves. She would not trust that one's word if he swore on the bible, whereas she believed Tom Diack.

But suppose no one else did? Suppose no one spoke up for Tom? Suppose he was condemned for lack of such a witness? Then his punishment would be on her conscience, for ever. She reminded herself yet again of his impertinence, of his truculent disrespect, told herself he deserved whatever fate befell him, but it was no good. Remembering his kiss, antagonism fell away and she wanted only to help. She was the last to have seen him before he strode off down the track and she could vouch for the truth of his story that he had been working late. Yet to speak up on his behalf would both incriminate and humiliate her. How could she tell the world that she had flirted with one of her father's masons and had found her comeuppance? 'What were you and Diack doing in the garden?' she imagined the magistrate asking and heard her own voice in the public court say, 'Kissing, my lord.' The court would love it, but she would never be able to hold her head up in society again. So Lettice argued with herself over and over that she had no need to speak out, while her conscience ate deep into her complacency and she grew hollow-eyed with lack of sleep.

Mhairi Diack, too, had dark circles under her eyes, but her troubles were all too real as Alex lay unconscious for almost three days. One of the hoofs had struck his head and though the doctor made reassuring noises, murmuring about Time the Great Healer and 'natural resilience', it was of little comfort to Mhairi. As to Donal, he was distraught with anxiety. He refused to leave his brother's bedside, even when Mhairi was there to take over the vigil, and it was all that Flora Dunn could do to persuade him to eat or drink. As for Mhairi, she thought she would go distracted with worry and anxiety and fear. Flora Dunn was kindness itself, finding room in her house for Mhairi and her sister Annys so that she need not trek to and fro between tenement and manse, while George Wyness took Lorn and Willy into his own home. 'Someone has to see they get to their school on time,' he grumbled in feigned annoyance, 'and they'll put nothing past me, I promise you. As to young Tom, we'd best leave all that to the lawyers.' Headstane Wyness, to Mhairi's eternal gratitude, had undertaken to arrange for Tom's defence, though not before he had visited the lad in the tolbooth and satisfied himself that he deserved defending.

'I'll be straight with you, Tom lad, as I expect you to be straight wi' me,' he said on that first visit to the intimidating cells of the town jail. 'I have a score to settle with the Adam family, but I'll not do it by defending a criminal, whatever my personal inclinations. So you'll tell me the honest truth. Did you assault Hugo Adam?'

'No, Mr Wyness, though . . .' Tom paused, noted the shrewdness of Mr Wyness's gaze, and looked down at his hands which were locked together on the deal top of the small prison table which separated them. He had had many hours of tortured anxiety and guilt since that appalling débâcle on the Silvercairns road. It was his fault that the horse had bolted, his fault that Alex had been injured and if he died it would be his fault that Mhairi had been widowed before she was wed. Tom sat, head bowed, in his cell for hour after hour, weeping inside with remorse and anguish and despair. He had meant to care for his brothers and sisters, meant to do well for them, then, with the firm promise of a better future within his grasp, he had tossed it all away on an impulse of personal revenge. Now he looked up with bleak despair into the older man's face and said, 'I heard the horse approaching and waited. I hoped it would be Hugo Adam. And if it was, I meant to confront him. But the horse was startled by something – a rabbit perhaps? Or my shadow? – and bolted before I could move or speak. I let him get away with it yet again and now . . . Oh, God.' He put his head in his hands and George Wyness saw his shoulders shake with suppressed weeping.

'Yet again?' repeated Wyness quietly. So Tom told him. About Lizzie and Hugo Adam on the occasion of the Queen's birthday, about Tom's suspicions and Hugo Adam's taunts, and finally about Tom's last day at the quarry when Hugo Adam had ridden straight into his father's workmen, scattering them piecemeal and without a thought. 'I thought he'd been with Lizzie, though when I confronted her later she denied it. But I did not know that then and I shouted after him,' admitted Tom, remembering. 'I swore I would kill him. But that night on the path to Silvercairns I did not even touch him, Mr Wyness, and that's the honest truth.'

George Wyness looked at him for a long and thoughtful moment before saying, 'I believe you. Though by the sound of it if you had touched him, it would have been with provocation. But we've no witnesses and it will be your word against his.'

Out of nowhere came the memory of Alex's warning, long ago, 'The likes of him can always touch the likes of us,' and the last shred of hope faded and vanished into the gloom of the tolbooth cell.

'Nay, lad, don't look so downhearted,' blustered Wyness. 'You're not tried yet. And when yon friend of yours regains his wits, he'll likely confirm your story.'

But when Alex recovered consciousness, briefly, some three days after the accident, he could remember nothing. 'I was looking for Tom,' he said, puzzling with the effort of memory. 'Mhairi was worried.'

'Hush, love, hush,' soothed Mhairi, settling him back on his pillows. 'Don't worry about it. Sleep, till you're well and strong again,' and after a few moments, he gave up the struggle to remember and slipped back into unconsciousness.

It was when Mhairi left the sick-room to go in search of Annys that she came upon Fergus Adam, waiting in the hall. 'Oh!' She stopped a moment in blushing confusion before saying quickly, 'You are looking for Mrs Dunn? I will go and find her for you.' But he put out a restraining hand and stopped her.

'No, Miss Diack. It was you I came to see.' As he looked at her, noting her flustered expression, her anxiety, her neat dark clothes and shining hair against the pale walls of the entrance hall and the sweeping stair, he thought how appropriate the setting was for her. He could not imagine her in a poverty-stricken tenement though he knew that such was her home. 'Perhaps there is somewhere we could talk?'

Mhairi led him into the breakfast room, being careful to leave the door open wide behind her. 'I expect Mrs Dunn any minute,' she said hurriedly. 'I believe she is only speaking to Cook about the grocer's order.'

'Of course.' Fergus Adam paused, searching in vain for the speech he had prepared in the sleepless hours of the previous night. 'Miss Diack,' he began and hurried on, 'I came to express my sympathy. To ask after your friend's health. To assure you that if there is anything I can do to help . . .' He stopped, remembering a similar offer he had made her once in the Gallowgate and her scathing reply, 'Haven't you done enough?'

This time she said only, with sadness, 'Thank you, Mr Adam. But there is nothing anyone can do.' In spite of all her mother's teachings, she spoke without hope. As soon as Alex recovered enough to be moved, Hamish Dunn had told her, he must join Tom in the tolbooth to await trial. The minister's word had preserved him so far from such a fate, but could not do so indefinitely, and when the trial date was set, he must attend. But it was Hugo Adam's doing, not his brother's. When Fergus Adam made no comment, she said, with an attempt at cheerfulness, 'Unless of course you can persuade your brother to withdraw his charges?'

'That, Miss Diack, is what I hoped to discuss with you. You will remember the reason for our last meeting?' The question needed no answer and Mhairi gave none. 'I wondered, perhaps, if that had been the cause of the . . . er . . . confrontation?'

'If it had been, it would have been entirely justified,' said Mhairi hotly, 'but it was not. There was no "confrontation" as you call it. My brother was walking home late from his legitimate business at *your* house, Mr Adam, when your brother's horse bolted.'

'And Grant?'

'He went, on my behalf, to look for my brother who was later than expected coming home.'

'Are you suggesting that my brother's account of the business is untrue, Miss Diack?'

'I suggest nothing. I merely tell you what happened. You know better than I do how much credence you can attach to your brother's words.'

There was a moment's silence in which both remembered their previous meeting. But Fergus also remembered the ensuing meeting with Hugo in the library. 'I suppose there are people who could corroborate your friend's story?' he said quietly.

'Mrs Dunn. The blacksmith. They will both tell you Alex asked if Tom had been seen. They will even tell you the time, for Mrs Dunn was late already, and worried.'

'And your brother?'

Mhairi was silent. But Tom's freedom was at stake and possibly his life. 'I believe he called at Silvercairns kitchen,' she admitted with reluctance, 'to see Lizzie Lennox.' That was the part of Tom's tale which worried her, for if Lizzie had given Tom the slightest cause for suspicion, then he would have gone raging after Hugo Adam's blood, as perhaps he had, though unsuccessfully, and once that was known, then no amount of protestation that fate had stepped in first would save Tom from punishment.

'Thank you. No doubt Mrs Gregor can confirm the time.'

'Will it help if she does?'

'It might. I will see what I can do.' He moved towards the door. 'And Miss Diack . . .'

'Yes?' Mhairi looked at him expectantly, her expression a trusting mixture of despair and hope which wrenched his heart. She looked to him at that moment the epitome of womanly beauty and the perfect choice for a wife. *His wife.* Why had he not realized it before? Except that he had realized it, of course, and had deliberately fought against it. She was a penniless nobody, with no background or breeding, and his marital sights had been trained since birth on a different class of prey. For a moment, in the joy of revelation, he forgot everything but the beauty of her face and his own longing.

'Perhaps, when this unhappy business is over,' he began softly, 'you and I might . . .' Suddenly he could not go on. His father's face loomed huge and threatening in his mind's eye, his father's voice boomed disinheritance on any offspring who married beneath them, and Silvercairns quarry danced for one dreadful moment out of his reach. Impatiently he shook his head to clear it, called common sense to his aid and said only, 'I hope we can be friends, you and I.' Then, before she could answer, he had gone.

Mhairi stood looking after him in disbelief and wonder. Friends, he had said and from the expression in his eyes, he had meant more than friends. But that was ridiculous, she told herself briskly as she made her way to the schoolroom where

Annys would be waiting for her. The stuff of dreams. She was handfast to Alex Grant, whom she loved, and she was carrying his child.

But the memory of Fergus Adam's words and the expression on his face when he had spoken them stayed with her to comfort her innermost despair in the silent hours she spent at Alex's bedside. When, as he often did, Donal looked up at her from the other side of the bed with yearning appeal and she reassured him as best she could that his beloved brother would recover, she felt momentary guilt at her heart's disloyalty. She loved Alex and when he was well again, as the doctor promised her he would be, she would marry him. If he was not transported first, on a convict ship to the other side of the world.

Despair was a deadly companion in the days that followed and as Alex's health slowly improved and the trial date drew closer, Mhairi's endurance was stretched to the trembling limits. Then came the day when the minister could protect him no longer and Alex, still frail and bandaged about the head, joined Tom in the town jail. Mhairi moved back to the tenement, collecting her family about her, including Alex's brother Donal, so that she could be near to her menfolk and waited for news from Fergus Adam that Tom's word had been confirmed.

The Adam household had moved back into town a day or two later than arranged because of Mr Hugo's 'accident', but they were now comfortably installed in the Guestrow house for the winter months, though Fergus Adam, as usual, kept on his rooms at Silvercairns. It was in the town house, however, that Fergus Adam sent for the cook and discreetly questioned her. Mrs Gregor had not seen Tom Diack, she said, and as to him visiting Lizzie Lennox, that baggage had been in her kitchen from noon till midnight, she'd swear to it on any bible, making a pig's mess of packing up the family china and chipping as many plates in the process as normal folk would take a lifetime to do and then only if they was trying. If the Diack lad had appeared in the kitchen Mrs Gregor would have known it, for a nicer-spoken, more helpful lad you couldna find and him always seeking her out to offer help, like, with lifting and fetching heavy loads. No, if Tom Diack had been in her kitchen that evening, she finished triumphantly, thinking she was doing him a good turn, then she was the Queen of Sheba.

When Fergus Adam sent for Lizzie Lennox to question her himself, she was nowhere to be found.

'Took the ship to Leith, seemingly,' reported Maggie Henderson gleefully, calling at the Diacks' door to impart the juicy news.

'Aye, and word has it she skipped it, quick, afore she could be pushed,' went on Beth Pirie, her painted face beaming. 'And wi' half that Lettice Adam's jewels.'

'The stupid girl,' cried Mhairi with every semblance of sincerity, for she would do anything to conceal the real reason for Lizzie's flight. 'I warned her over and over, but she always was light-fingered.'

'Aye,' agreed Maggie Henderson. 'Mind that time at the Queen's birthday, when she was wearing that necklace? I reckon that was the Adam girl's, and the gloves.'

'Ma Mackenzie says she had money, too,' said Beth with a knowing wink. 'Wonder how Ma Mackenzie knew?'

At the mention of the midwife Mhairi blanched in spite of herself. Surely Lizzie had not wanted the money for *that*? If Mhairi had known, she would never have agreed to beg for it for her. But Maggie was still talking and as she realized what the girl was saying, her fear and revulsion eased.

'Saw Lizzie on the quay, seemingly, buying her ticket and her with more money than Ma Mackenzie sees in a month of Sundays, so she said. She told Lizzie to keep it out of sight afore it was pinched, and Lizzie said, "After what I had to do to get it, no bastard's going to take it from me. Just let them try." Real belligerent she looked, said Ma Mackenzie. What do you think she meant?' finished Maggie, with a lewd roll of the eyes.

'If she meant what you think she did, then it's a good job she's gone to Leith,' said Beth tartly. 'I'd slit the bitch's throat if she trespassed on my beat.'

'I'll not have talk like that here,' said Mhairi quietly. 'There are children present. So if you've said what you came to say, please go.'

'We know when we're not wanted, Your Highness,' taunted Maggie, and Beth, slipping her arm round her friend's waist, said with exaggerated artlessness, 'Shall we pay a visit to the tolbooth, Maggie dear? I know Lackie Grant, for one, would love to see us, spite of his sore head.'

'Aye, he would that. And Tom. And all those other poor men with no one at all to talk to them. At least we will be appreciated there.'

Then, with a twin shriek of laughter, they scuttled down the tenement stair leaving Mhairi white-faced and trembling with anxiety. Suppose they visited the prison? Suppose they talked to Tom and repeated what they had said here? Then, with the usual sinking of the heart, she remembered. What difference would it make what Tom found out now? He was as good as condemned already, with Alex, the father of her child.

The case was set to come up before the magistrates in the third week in November. Two days before the fatal date, Donal Grant came home from work in some agitation with a sheaf of papers in his hand. At first Mhairi thought it must be some work he had been doing for Mr Wyness and had brought home to finish, for he was now employed in the Wyness yard, designing patterns and inscriptions when he was not helping with more menial tasks. But when he spread the pages on the table, in sequence, she saw that they were some sort of cartoon drawings, little stick men and horses, with trees and a moon. Then, when he pulled her down into a chair at the table, sat beside her, and pointed to the drawings, one by one, she realized that it was a narrative, in pictures, of the events of that dreadful night. Donal, because of his affliction, had been forgotten as a potential witness, and though he could read and write, his vocabulary was limited. Any written account he gave would have been at best stilted and no one had asked him for one. But now, looking at the expressive little pictures, it became clear to Mhairi that Donal, who had hitched the pony and trap to the nearest fence-post as soon as Alex's back was turned and followed his brother, had seen much of what had happened.

In silence Mhairi traced the story, from when Alex and Donal had overtaken Flora Dunn on the Aberdeen road to the moment when the horse struck Alex and he fell. The last picture she found too moving to look at for long. It was of Donal himself, in an attitude of grieving despair, beside Alex's prostrate body.

But it was the pictures immediately before that last one that Mhairi studied the most closely, going over and over in her mind what would be the best thing to do. See Mr Wyness? He was a friend, but could do little more than he had already done. See the lawyer who was to defend Tom and Alex? But it was after office hours and besides, would he attach credence to the testimony of someone who was deaf and dumb? Especially a testimony in little stick-pictures? It must be someone who knew and understood Donal, who knew his pictures told the truth. Remembering her vigil at Alex's sick-bed, she knew, suddenly, who that person was. She turned to Donal with the first smile of many days, a smile of excitement and returning hope. 'Thank you,' she said. 'We will take these to Mr Dunn. He will know best what to do.' Then, warning Lorn and Willy to keep Annys safe until she returned, to see no sparks flew from the fire, to be careful lighting the lamp and with sundry other anxious, housewifely instructions, she put her plaid around her shoulders, took Donal's arm, and set out to walk to the manse.

'You see,' pointed out Mhairi eagerly an hour or so later, when Flora Dunn had welcomed them and insisted on giving them hot tea and scones with home-made raspberry jam before they uttered a word of their errand, 'the horse throws Mr Hugo *before* Alex tries to seize the reins. Donal says Alex was only trying to catch the horse before it bolted. He saw from further down the road.'

'I see . . .' said Hamish Dunn slowly, studying the pictures closely. He opened a drawer, drew out a magnifying glass, and studied them again before silently passing them to his wife. 'I see,' he said again, fingertips together in thought.

'But this is splendid!' cried Flora excitedly. 'Surely this will make everything all right?'

Her husband did not reply, but continued to frown at the table-cloth before at last pushing back his chair and standing up. 'Thank you, Mhairi, for bringing this to me, and you, Donal, for drawing so vividly what you saw. Now I am going to ask you both to come with me, to show the drawings to Mungo Adam himself.'

* * *

They went into Aberdeen on foot, striding three abreast through the darkening streets, past shuttered windows where keyholes in the wood cast needle-shafts of light into the street, past others, unshuttered and bright with lamplight, past darkened alleys and wynds where no light fell, to the turreted eminence of the Adam town house with its massive granite walls and its stout, iron-studded front door. There were lights in many windows and through the nearest Mhairi glimpsed a solid oak table with brass dishes and candlesticks, a gilt-framed picture, polished floor-boards and a brightly patterned rug. Hamish Dunn lifted the heavy knocker and struck it, several times, against the wood. Beside him, as they waited, Mhairi bit her lower lip with tension, Donal stood straight-backed and still, his hands clenched at his sides, and from somewhere in the depths of the house footsteps at last approached.

Mungo Adam had had a frustrating and unsatisfactory day. The quarry production went smoothly enough, though he had the distinct impression that Fergus's mind was not entirely on his work. But that business with Hugo was enough to unsettle anyone. He was a young fool, of course, and no doubt had asked for whatever vengeance those two villains had planned for him, but after all he might have been killed and it was no thanks to them that he was not. One of them, he gathered, was the friend, or was it fiancé, of that kitchenmaid the boy had got into trouble. But whatever the provocation, and after all the baggage had been paid off and handsomely, it was no excuse for violence and Hugo had had a lump on his head the size of a duck's egg, with a temper to match. As for the horse, the animal had been unsettled for days and no wonder. Mungo Adam glowered. They were all unsettled, Hugo, Fergus, himself, that silly Blackwell woman. As for Lettice, she was the worst of the lot, taking to her room without a by-your-leave and deserting their guests before the evening was half-way over.

Not that he entirely blamed her, he thought morosely, remembering Ainslie Sharp's inexplicable behaviour. After that revelation of George Wyness's at the Silvercairns dinner you would have thought the man would have spoken out, if only to retrieve his own good name, but not a bit of it. You would have thought Lettice was not good enough for him the way he carried on with his sneering and his patronizing, and as for that contract, there was not a sniff of it yet and it was days past the closing date for tenders. What the hell was the man playing at? Come to that, what was George Wyness playing at, for he must be up to something. Otherwise he would not have burnt his boats so thoroughly with Mungo Adam. But though both Mungo and Fergus had asked discreetly in appropriate circles, neither had come up with any answer. Mungo Adam was not used to opposition, and the withholding of information which he knew must be there was the worst and most infuriating kind. So when the servant told him that that teetotalling minister of his was at the door he agreed to see him, though it wanted only half an hour to dinner. Ministers sometimes knew what ordinary folk did not and at least he would not have to offer the fellow a drink.

When he heard the firm knock on his study door it was with scant courtesy that he snapped, 'Come in,' and with downright rudeness that he looked Donal Grant up and down, then Mhairi, before saying, 'What do you want? I was told it was the minister calling, not a bunch of rabble. I can tell you now, if you've come for money, you'll not get it.'

'They are here at my invitation,' said Hamish Dunn, courteously enough.

'Oh, they are, are they? And since when have you had permission to invite guests to my house? I don't know what you want and I don't wish to,' he added, losing what little patience he had, 'so get out, the lot of you. I've work to do.'

'Sit down, Mhairi,' said Hamish Dunn, pulling out a chair for her. 'This will not take long, Mr Adam.'

'You are damn right it won't,' roared Adam, striding to the door and holding it open. 'Goodnight!'

Deliberately, Hamish Dunn sat down, indicating to Donal to do the same. 'I think you should listen, Mr Adam,' he said quietly, 'and if I were you I would close the door. Unless, that is, you intend the whole house to hear what I have to say.'

Something in the minister's voice triggered a warning and after a moment's hesitation Adam closed the door and returned to his desk where he sat like a presiding magistrate at the dock. Which, remembered Mhairi with alarm, he sometimes was. Suppose it was his turn when Alex and Tom came up for trial? If so, they would not have the smallest hope.

‘Well?’ glowered Adam. ‘What is it? I haven’t got all night.’

‘This,’ said Hamish Dunn, laying Donal’s drawings on the desk in front of Adam. Briefly he explained, and after one sharp look at Donal, Mungo Adam studied them in silence. Then he pushed them impatiently away.

‘Rubbish,’ he said shortly. ‘Fantasy. The scribblings of a half-wit, nothing more.’ Mhairi flushed crimson and half rose in her chair, but the minister restrained her.

‘On the contrary, Mr Adam, they are a clear and unambiguous statement of what occurred.’

‘What that idiot imagined occurred,’ corrected Adam. ‘Those louts uttered menaces. Where are they in those pathetic pictures of yours? Nowhere, because *he could not hear them*.’ Mungo Adam picked up the papers, looking Hamish Dunn full in the face and deliberately tore them in two. ‘That is what your so-called evidence is worth, Mr Dunn,’ he said, with a mirthless grin. ‘Absolutely nothing. Now, if that was all you came to tell me, I suggest you leave.’

‘It is a pity you did that,’ said Hamish Dunn thoughtfully. He patted Donal in reassurance, leant forward, swept up the torn scraps and slipped them into an inside pocket. ‘But they can be drawn again. And, with a suitable interpreter, Donal can, of course, appear in the witness box. But I hope that will not be necessary. Because if he does,’ and here the minister’s voice changed to one of subtle threat, ‘he will testify to the number of times your son has beaten him, merely for not replying to a question. He will also testify that he met Miss Diack coming out of your son Fergus’s office with the money she had collected from him on her friend’s behalf, to pay for your son’s illegitimate baby. We will call character witnesses for both accused men, of course, but also for your son. Tom and Alex have nothing to fear, but I wonder if you can say the same of Hugo? There will be gambling debts of course, that is nothing these days, then drunkenness and brawling, again nothing where a gentleman is concerned. Whoring the same. But I think beating a deaf and dumb man because he does not answer is not quite as common? It is at best futile, and at worst sadistic cruelty.’

Throughout this speech Mungo Adam had been too astonished to find words. His cheeks puffed purple with rage, his eyes rolled under lowering, bristled brows, while he opened and shut his mouth several times and no words came. Finally, when Hamish Dunn paused for breath, he managed, 'How dare you?'

'I assume that question is rhetorical?' said his minister calmly. 'For I think you know the answer. I dare because it is the truth. But to return to Hugo, there will be the question of his non-attendance at lectures, again you may say understandable, the company he keeps, the unpaid bills the length and breadth of town. Again, sadly, all too common among his kind and even, I fear, a matter of misplaced pride with some.'

'Look here, Dunn, what are you getting at?' interrupted Mungo Adam with something of his old authority. He knew his younger son's character all too well, but none of it was criminal. None of it altered the fact that he had been set upon, in the dark, by thugs.

'Nothing, Mr Adam. Hugo is undisciplined and wayward, but so are many young men. He will grow out of it. I am merely pointing out the line the necessary questioning will take. There will be character witnesses for the defendants, too. In their case, I am happy to say, there will be nothing whatsoever to hide. On the contrary, they will be proved to be loyal, hard-working and honest employees, trusted friends, responsible family men. Even you, Mr Adam, could not find a man in the whole of Aberdeen to testify otherwise.'

'That's as may be,' growled Adam. 'But they still attacked my son.'

'Did they? I suggest you have only your son's word for that and he was – and we will bring medical evidence to prove it – suffering from concussion at the time. Also, it would not be the first time he has been thrown from his horse in the dark. Without the aid of cut-throats, real or imaginary. Am I right?'

'Damn and blast you, man,' roared Mungo, rising to his feet and leaning threateningly forward across the desk, large hands outspread on the tooled leather top. He was a big man, and seemed bigger in rage. 'I don't have to listen to any more of this balderdash. Get out.'

'Very well. If you prefer it. But I would have thought it better to listen to some things in the privacy of your own home, than in open court with the whole world to hear. The matter of the railway company shares, for instance, would be sure to come up, and possibly even that matter of tenders for the northern contract? Only in passing, of course, but in open court.'

'Are you attempting to blackmail me, Mr Dunn, because if you are . . .'

'Certainly not, Mr Adam. The thought never crossed my mind. I merely wanted you to be absolutely sure that you knew what you were doing before you went ahead with this quite unnecessary charge. But I see you are fearless in the pursuit of justice as you see it. What is your own reputation, as a businessman or gentlemen, when a matter of principle is at stake? And it is because I admire such zeal, Mr Adam, that I want you to be absolutely sure that you are in the right. Your son, in his fear, confusion, delirium and no doubt pain, says he was attacked. One of his so-called attackers says he was merely walking home late, in the dark, the other that he had gone in search of him. Both were sober and in their right minds. Do you say they are lying?'

'Show me evidence that they are not.'

'I have already, but you refused to look at it.' Hamish drew a scrap of torn paper briefly from his inside pocket, then replaced it.

At that moment there was the sound of footsteps outside the door. After the briefest of knocks it opened, and Lettice Adam said, 'Papa, Aunt Blackwell says . . . Oh. I did not realize you had someone with you. I apologize.' She made to withdraw, but her father stopped her.

'Wait. I will come with you. These . . . people . . . are just leaving.'

'Ah, Miss Adam,' said Hamish Dunn, rising to his feet and giving her a courteous bow. 'I am glad you have come. I have a question I wish to ask you.'

'Oh?' Lettice looked startled, then, seeing who else was in the room both curious and apprehensive. She looked from her father, on his feet and positively apoplectic with fury, to Hamish Dunn, square-set, pugnacious, and bearing an even closer resemblance to that Highland bull she had once compared him to, then to the white-faced girl in the plaid and the good-looking boy. 'What question, Mr Dunn?' she said uncertainly. When he did not immediately answer, but looked at her steadily with an expression of what she could only call encouragement, she stepped inside the room and closed the door. Her father, surprisingly, did not prevent her.

'Only this,' said Hamish Dunn, fixing her eyes with his and looking deep into them. 'It is a question of corroboration. No one can be found to support poor Tom Diack's story that he was working late at Silvercairns on the night of Hugo's accident. I wondered if perhaps you could help?'

For a long moment there was silence. Even Mungo Adam sensed the tension in the room, before he remembered whose room it was. 'Of course she can't,' he snapped, 'and it's damned impertinent of you to suggest such a thing. What would my daughter know of a stonemason?'

Perhaps it was the sneer in his voice as he pronounced the word, or the piercing intensity of Hamish Dunn's eyes, or merely her own conscience triumphing over pride. Lettice never knew. But, ignoring her father, and speaking only to Hamish Dunn, she said, 'Yes, Mr Dunn, I can. Tom Diack was in the garden with me.'

'Thank you, Miss Adam,' said Hamish with a slow smile that filled her heart. 'And will you stand up in court and testify as much?'

'Yes. If I must. And before you ask, Tom Diack did not molest me. It was I who approached him.' Deliberately, to free her once and for all from her father's thrall, she added, 'I kissed him, and willingly. I will tell the court as much, if they ask me, and be proud to do so.'

'Then it seems to me, Mr Adam,' said the minister quietly, 'that the decision is entirely in your hands.'

'Dammit, boy, I had no choice,' snarled Adam when his tormentors had gone and he had summoned Hugo to tell him the unwelcome news that he had been suffering from concussion and had made a mistake which honour required him to correct. 'Your reputation is nothing, the whole town knows it anyway, and my business would have survived whatever scandal they thought they could dredge up, but when it comes to Lettice, that's a different matter. He threatened to call her as witness, under oath.'

'But Father, it's only . . .'

'Think, man,' interrupted Mungo furiously. 'Use your brains, if you've any left in that addle-pated head of yours. They'd make her admit before the whole gloating town that she'd set her cap at one of my workmen and caught him, in the bushes, after dark. What sort of an offer of marriage do you think I'd get for her after that? Even old Burnett wouldn't have her. I'd be the laughing stock of the town.'

'But surely . . .'

'Surely nothing. And it's all your fault, you good-for-nothing wastrel. I've warned you once too often and now I've had enough. You'll sail for Jamaica on the first available ship. The Burnetts have relations there and Archie will no doubt give you letters of introduction, as a favour to me. After that it will be up to you. Now get out. And tell that Blackwell woman to send my dinner in here on a tray. I've had enough of the lot of you. I'll see no one else tonight.'

He would have to speak to Lettice, of course, but not now. Tomorrow would be soon enough, when he had digested the day's humiliations and decided what must be done. He'd have to find her a husband, of course, and quickly, before she disgraced him beyond recall. If not Ainslie Sharp, then . . . but that, too, could wait till morning.

But the morning brought yet more unpalatable news. Fergus heard it first, but within the hour it was all over town. George Wyness had bought the lease on a Donside quarry, put in old Mackinnon as manager, and taken on Tom Diack and Alex Grant, newly released from the tolbooth, as partners. As if that was not enough to stomach, he had also won the coveted contract for the northern railway works and given it out as his declared intention 'to beat Old Man Adam at his own game'.

Part 4

'I'd like to have seen his face when he heard, lass,' said Wyness, taking another slice of Mhairi's pie. 'Purple as plumcake and steaming, no doubt.'

'Serve him right,' said Tom cheerfully. 'Besides, it's time the Adam quarry had a bit of worthy competition.' He had shed the last traces of his sojourn in the town jail and looked robustly healthy and full of the confident vigour of youth. Mhairi, looking at her brother from across the table, thought how handsome he looked and, as her housewifely gaze ran round the table, checking for any plate or glass that might need replenishing, she noticed that Fanny Wyness thought so too. George Wyness had brought his wife and daughter with him, 'to meet my new partners', and once the initial shyness was over even Annys had consented to talk to the visitors, before climbing on to Donal's knee to inspect the pattern book which Wyness had brought with him. 'Our templates, lad,' he explained. 'You look through them and see what ideas you get, for I'll be wanting you to add to them soon enough.' The tenement room looked cheerfully welcoming, with the fire burning high and the lamps lit, and, after an anxious day's scrubbing and polishing and baking, Mhairi had put out the best linen in Mrs Wyness's honour. Her own mother, Mhairi knew, could not have done better and it gave her a warm feeling, deep in her heart, to think of her mother's approbation. Mackinnon and his wife had been invited too and the occasion was both a celebration of Alex's and Tom's release from the tolbooth and a launching of the new venture on Freedom Hill.

'Are you sure you'll not miss the company, lass?' George Wyness asked Mhairi anxiously. 'There's the smithy, of course, and the farm, but you'll have a mile walk to Woodside village and the school.'

'We'll not be needing a school,' said Lorn and Willy together, and even Mhairi smiled at the pride in their voices. Lorn was to take up his old job in the Wyness yard, with a view to working his way up to something better, though once they moved to Freedom Cottage it would mean an early start for the three-mile journey into town. Willy was to work alongside his brother Tom and Alex in the Freedom Hill quarry and learn the mason's trade from scratch. Donal Grant was in charge of the horses, but only till the quarry was established. 'Then I'll be needing your advice, young fellow, with the pattern book, and in the polishing yard, now that I'm expanding the business.' For as well as leasing the Donside quarry, Wyness had bought a strip of land adjacent to his granite yard and meant to double his trade. 'Wi' my own rock from my own quarry, and that railway contract Old Man Adam would have given his eye teeth, let alone his daughter, to get, I'll be my own master at last, and the likes of Mungo Adam can . . .' But Mhairi's presence stopped him elaborating as he would have done in purely male company and he contented himself with an innocuous 'go chase his tail'.

The quarry on Donside had been worked for some years as part of the Fyfe operations, but as they moved further out towards Kemnay and discovered the rich vein of granite which that area afforded, they had concentrated their money and efforts there and, when the lease on Freedom Hill expired, had been content to hand over to a successor.

But it was a good quarry: granite of a bright blue-grey colour, much like that of Silvercairns, made up of clear quartz, two felspars and black mica mixed. The 'posts' of granite were irregular perhaps, and not very large, though now and then several larger blocks had been found together, and when they were polished, they were as good as anything from Silvercairns. Fine for the headstones, monuments and other polished work of the yard, anyway, and for building work. The smaller stuff was ideal for paving setts and there was an ever-growing market for those from Edinburgh to London. Anything left after that could go for building rubble, so there need be no waste.

George Wyness had seen his chance and, spurred on by what he saw as Mungo Adam's treachery, had consulted Mackinnon in secret, been assured of the quarry's potential, and fulfilled an amibition long cherished. With Mackinnon's expertise (and, incidentally, his savings, freely offered) and the right workforce, he stood to prosper. Not at first, perhaps, while they were getting established, but after a year or so, and with the canal running almost from door to door (and, more importantly, the railway, when it came) they could not fail to make a profit. Thinking of Old Man Adam's face when he heard the news, Wyness grinned in open glee. And smiled with a different pleasure when he saw Mhairi Diack's joyful gratitude and the shining hope and determination on young Alex Grant's face. Momentarily, Wyness frowned. The lad had had a hard time of it, first on his sick-bed, then in the town jail. The worry alone would have aged any man, but with a crippling head wound to cope with as well . . . It was no wonder Alex looked haggard and worn and ten years older than his friend Tom Diack. But he was young and strong: time and a loving wife would soon repair the damage.

As for Tom, freedom (and the news that his enemy was to be 'transported' in his stead to the other side of the world) had washed the cares from his heart overnight and filled him with new enthusiasm and vigour. Wyness had had the greatest difficulty restraining him from striding out to Freedom Hill the moment he heard the news and laying into the rock-face on the spot. He was a good mason, as his father before him had been, and Wyness had no fears where his workforce was concerned.

'We can never thank you enough, Mr Wyness, for your kindness,' said Mhairi now, her blue eyes brimming with gratitude.

'Nay, lass, it's less kindness than sheer good sense,' he blustered, embarrassed. 'I know a good workman when I see one, and when a family's fallen on hard times through no fault of their own, then it's good sense to give them a helping hand back on to the ladder – so they can work all the harder, eh?' and he winked with pretended avarice. But Mhairi was not deceived. Whatever private grudge Wyness was settling by his new venture, he had not needed to employ Alex and her brothers – he had chosen to do so out of the kindness of his heart and she knew it.

'You'll not regret it, Mr Wyness,' said Mhairi proudly, taking Alex's hand. 'A year from now we'll be the best family business in Aberdeen.'

'Let's drink to that,' said Mackinnon, raising his glass. 'To Freedom Hill.' Fanny Wyness, Mhairi noted, went out of her way to touch her glass to Tom's and soon after they were talking and laughing together like old friends. She did not quite catch what they were talking about because of the general hubbub, but it sounded like *weasels*.

It was the end of November before anyone heard anything of Lizzie Lennox. Then a letter arrived at the tenement, for Mhairi. Grubby and ill-written, it said only that Lizzie was well, sent her regards to everyone, and was off to Australia to seek her fortune. She asked Mhairi to pass on messages to her family, said, 'I'll have a family of my own afore I know it,' and added, 'I'll maybe come home and see you all one day, when I'm rich.' She asked after Tom and Alex, hoped Mhairi was well, and signed her name. But there was a postscript, hastily added in cramped, smudged script. 'Guess who I saw on the quay just now? That Ainslie Sharp as was always at the Adam place. He was buying a ticket to Port Philip. I reckon he's upped and hopped it with they railway funds, why else would he pretend he hadna seen me and that he was someone else? So if that Miss Carrot's wanting him, you can tell her where to look.'

Alex and Mhairi were married on a morning in early December. It was a small wedding, with only family present, and afterwards there was no dance. But friends came to celebrate with them in the Mitchell Court tenement and even Alex's morose uncle paid a brief visit, and when he left, pressed a guinea into Mhairi's hand with a grunted, 'Here's good luck, lass. You'll need it.'

Ma Lennox up the stair had promised to keep an eye on Annys and the others for the weekend so that Alex and Mhairi could have at least two nights alone together in their new home before taking up the burden of family responsibility once more, and as Alex tied the last bundle securely on to the dray cart, handed her up on to the wooden seat and took his place beside her, Mhairi's happiness was almost complete. Almost, for she could not help worrying about Alex, whose wound was healed now, even the scar covered by his thick, red-glinting hair, but who still suffered headaches, she was sure, though he never said so. She worried too about their child, now a visible thickening at her waistline, but no longer a reproach. Even Bible Lennox, humbled perhaps by his daughter's flight, had refrained from censorious comment and had even wished her well.

Someone else whose good wishes she valued, but whose gift she prudently concealed, was Fergus Adam. He had sent a fine linen table-cloth, hemmed as that long-ago handkerchief had been, with a dozen napkins and a small, gilt-edged card, printed 'Fergus Adam, Silvercairns'. She had been secretly disappointed, until she turned the card over and read, handwritten in black italic script, the words 'In friendship'. But Alex would not see it as friendship, and nor would Tom. To them the gift would be an insult from the enemy and Mhairi privately decided, should anyone ever ask, that she would say it was a present from the Ladies' Working. They had given her a similar cloth, though smaller and not as fine. The little paste-board card she hid away at the bottom of the clothes kist as a reminder of her childhood dreams.

But as Alex drove the dray cart at a gentle pace along the high road north out of Aberdeen and the town fell away behind them Mhairi forgot even day-dreams in the beauty of the winter countryside and the calm peace of evening. Night fell early in December, but remembering who she would be spending it with, Mhairi was glad. She slipped a hand under Alex's arm and he turned his head briefly to smile at her before concentrating once more on the road ahead. He was a good man and he loved her. What more could any girl ask?

At Elmbank the road briefly skirted the canal and seeing the dark, slow-moving water and the bright outline of a barge, Mhairi remembered other, summer evenings, private evenings on the grass beneath the bridge. At the memory, she blushed with secret excitement and expectation. It was weeks since she and Alex had been alone together and then only briefly. Now they could look forward to two whole uninterrupted days. And nights.

They left Kittybrewster behind them, the spring at Stoneybank, the grand gates of Hilton House, then they were at the edge of Woodside village with the river Don in the valley on their right and all around them fields, some brown with winter ploughing, some meadowland, with low stone dykes and bare trees. Then they left the village behind them and swung left up a long, stony track, till Alex drew the pony to a halt at their own front door.

The house on Freedom Hill was a dream come true. Small, no more than a simple but-and-ben, but with two rooms and a scullery downstairs and two attic rooms above it was paradise compared to the tenement in Mitchell's Court. Known as Freedom Cottage for its proximity to the boundary which marked the freedom lands of Aberdeen, it had a fenced garden at the front, with a gate and a path to the low front door, over the lintel of which were carved the letters A.D. 1749. ('My initials,' Annys was to squeal excitedly on her arrival, 'but I'm not as old as that!') There was a patch of grass at the back for a drying green and from the slope above the house a view of far hills to the west, more hills to the north, with the long, nippled outline of Bennachie, and to the east, the German Sea. While out of sight, beyond Freedom Hill, was Silvercairns.

But those rivalries lay in the future. Tonight was for themselves alone. In the evening stillness, instead of the usual crowded babble of the tenements, there was the distant, rhythmic sough of the sea, a night bird's call, and from a neighbouring field the sound of tearing grass as cattle idly grazed. Her father, thought Mhairi with brief sadness, would have loved it. Suddenly, from high overhead, came the busy mewing and creaking of a skein of geese on the wing. They sat, motionless, in the dray cart, Alex's arm around her shoulders, and watched until the speckled 'V' trailed into the far darkness above Silvercairns and merged with the evening shadows.

'A good omen,' murmured Alex, and kissed her. Then he handed her down from the dray cart, led her up the short pathway to the door of Freedom Cottage and stood holding both her hands in his. 'Well?' he asked softly.

Her eyes were blue as harebells and dark with promise. 'Very.'

With a low laugh, he scooped her up in his arms, pushed open the door with his shoulder and carried her inside.

The last light faded from the winter sky and the ground grew crisp with frost. Night creatures mewed and rustled. A fox barked. And the pony, still in the shafts of the forgotten dray cart, grazed idly among the plants of the tiny front garden.

ABERDEEN
CITY
LIBRARIES